Gray Eagle watched his recaptured Alisha in the dusky light. Quietly, he walked over to where she lay on a blanket by the dying fire. Alisha gave a start when her Indian lover leaned over her, then she relaxed against him. She was finally home!

Gray Eagle enfolded his auburn-haired beauty in his embrace, and nestled his lips in her hair. The cool night breeze kissed them as they held one another for warmth. As Gray Eagle caressed Alisha's waist, she reached out for him. Their breathing quickened and their blood ran hotly through their veins.

The Indian's touch kindled raging fires in the white girl's heart, and her senses reeled with each kiss he traced on her neck. Alisha's senses were feverishly awakened. She knew she could no longer resist his love and surrendered herself to him in utter abandonment . . .

ENTRANCING ROMANCES BY SYLVIE F. SOMMERFIELD

DEANNA'S DESIRE (906, $3.50)

Amidst the storm of the American Revolution, Matt and Deanna meet—and fall in love. In the name of freedom, they discover war's intrigues and horrors. Bound by passion, they risk everything to keep their love alive!

ERIN'S ECSTASY (861, $2.95)

Erin was a beautiful child-woman who needed Gregg's protection. And Gregg desired her more than anything he'd ever wanted before. But when a dangerous voyage calls Gregg away, their love must be put to the test. . . .

TAZIA'S TORMENT (882, $2.95)

When tempestuous Fantasio de Montega danced, men were hypnotized. And this was part of her secret revenge—until cruel fate tricked her into loving the man she'd vowed to kill!

RAPTURE'S ANGEL (750, $2.75)

When Angelique boarded the *Wayfarer*, she felt like a frightened child. Then Devon—with his gentle voice and captivating touch—reminded her that she was a woman, with a heart that longed to be won!

REBEL PRIDE (691, $2.75)

For the good of the plantation, Holly must marry the man chosen by her family. But when she sees the handsome but disreputable Adam Gilcrest, her heart cries out that it's Adam she loves—enough to defy her family!

Available wherever paperbacks are sold, or order direct from the Publisher. Send cover price plus 50¢ per copy for mailing and handling to Zebra Books, 475 Park Avenue South, New York, N.Y. 10016. DO NOT SEND CASH.

DEFIANT ECSTASY

By Janelle Taylor

ZEBRA BOOKS
KENSINGTON PUBLISHING CORP.

*For my mother, Frances, with love
and to the memory of my father A.L.W.*

Acknowledgment to:
Hiram C. Owen of Sisseton, South Dakota for all his
help and understanding with the Sioux language and
facts about the great and inspiring Sioux Nation.

ZEBRA BOOKS

are published by

KENSINGTON PUBLISHING CORP.
475 Park Avenue South
New York, N.Y. 10016

Green-eyed, lovely Alisha Williams paced her darkened room at Fort Pierre. Ill fortune in the new land had taken all she ever loved from the English girl. And when she had finally found happiness in a man's arms, the raging hatred between the white settlers and the red natives had snatched that from her, too.

A raiding party from Fort Pierre had killed many in the Oglala camp of the fierce warrior Gray Eagle. But when the bluecoats discovered the captive white girl in Gray Eagle's teepee, they rescued her and brought her back to her own people at the fort.

In anguish, Alisha threw herself upon her bed and sobbed, they rescued me only to imprison me in their own way! Their hatred of the Indian so blinds them they cannot accept me for having been forced to live with the Oglala.

An outcast amid her own kind, Alisha achingly yearned for her black-eyed, muscular warrior to recapture her. She longed for Gray Eagle's slavery over the white man's freedom . . .

Chapter One

It had been eighteen days since the daring raid upon Gray Eagle's camp. Dawn had awakened the Oglala warriors with her breathtaking majesty, seeming to bestow a special blessing upon the fearless Sioux. They had quickly gotten ready and mounted up, riding to join with the other tribes from the surrounding area. They converged upon Fort Pierre, taking their positions in long and threatening lines before the sealed gates of the only fort left in that vast frontier.

Gray Eagle assumed his place of leadership before the braves. He sat proud and erect upon his mottled Appaloosa, appearing awesome and forbidding. He sat like a pagan god of war ready to swoop down and conquer the entire world.

Only small traces of the roseate color which had invaded the early morning sky now remained. As the sun lifted itself into the heavens, the fingers of pink slowly gave way to the rays of gold, outlining the indomitable warrior against a cobalt skyline. Its tawny hues sent shimmering rays to set the buffalo and bunch grass ablaze with golden light. The wind was nearly motionless, failing to do more than slightly sway the dried grasses. The animals and birds were silent, seeming to be momentarily suspended. It was as if all nature recognized the significance of this day and of this gathering, the day when all white intruders would be driven from Indian lands.

Gray Eagle was dressed as a warrior in sienna-colored fringed leggins, breechcloth, and high-topped moccasins which were all heavily beaded in rich designs of red and yellow. His leather arm and wrist bands were artistically etched with scenes from his many coups. Two small sections of his ebony hair were secured into braids on either side of his mesmerizing face. The rest of his hair flowed over his powerful shoulders and down his back like a sleek mane. The heavy braids were interwoven and bound with yellow thongs. Numerous yellow feathers were in his hair, symbolizing his many deeds of courage. Around his neck was a small rawhide pouch, a medicine bag, suspended from a slender thong. He was the epitome of the greatest warrior; he was the pinnacle of manhood. And when wronged, he was the ultimate enemy.

The Fort Pierre sentry slowly moved his fieldglasses up and down the rows of warriors, but always returned his sights to the one man who sat before the others like a king. Hell! he finally decided, it's got to be him. He sighed and muttered, "We'll have the devil to pay this day, if I'm right . . ."

General Galt called up to him, "How many

would you say are out there? Can you read the markings of the tribes involved? Any sign of their intentions?"

"About two thousand, maybe more or less, Sir," came the sentry's reply. As he scrutinized the warriors once more, he stated, "I'd guess there are five to eight different tribes represented out there. They appear to be waiting for something. Could be for others to join them or . . ." He halted and gaped at the scene before him, for that was when it happened; Gray Eagle had sent his signal with the lance.

He hastily called down, "There it is, Sir! The parley lance; they want to talk. That warrior out front has thrown the pow-wow lance into the ground and is waiting for an answer," he nearly babbled in his anxiety. "My God!" he swore excitedly. "It's him, Sir. The feather is yellow! It's Gray Eagle himself."

The long lines of chiefs and warriors were indeed from many different tribes; many were friends, others only allies for this particular day. Each warrior's face was painted with his own design and color. Most were dressed similarly to Gray Eagle, except for the chiefs; they were attired in full ceremonial dress, wearing their traditional, flowing war bonnets. Their stoical, arrogant faces could instill terror into the heart of the bravest of men. Many of the younger warriors looked fiendishly evil from their chosen designs and colors, which was what they intended; others appeared the epitome of courage and strength. It would be a dauntless, fearsome group of warriors which greeted the inhabitants of Fort Pierre this fateful day.

After Gray Eagle had assumed his position at the head of the tribes, he shifted from side to side upon Chula's broad back to allow his jet-colored eyes to glance up and down the countless lines of Indian allies. His keen eyes detected the presence of several chiefs from other villages. His heart swelled with pride and honor at being chosen their leader and spokesman for this grave meeting. His eyes halted and momentarily lingered on Mahpiya Sapa, chief of the Blackfoot tribe. Strange, uneasy feelings passed through his mind as his eyes met the expressionless ones of Black Cloud, but he quickly dismissed such groundless warnings. It was evident that nearly all of the surrounding tribes had sent warriors to help in this final purging of the white man and bluecoats from their lands. Afterall, they had all received the same vision from Wakantanka during the council meeting of the Warrior Society.

It was then that the warriors had eaten the sacred peyote buttons to instill endurance and courage for this coming battle and to bring about contact with the Great Spirit. They had all chanted and prayed for his guidance and help. He had sent a vision to all of the warriors present, the same vision. It had revealed the will of Wakantanka to them: Alisha was to be returned to Gray Eagle, and the other whites were to be driven from these lands. That mutually shared vision was powerful magic;

no warrior could refuse to aid in the Great Spirit's plans for Gray Eagle and Alisha.

Gray Eagle turned his attention again to the fort, where panic and tension ran rampant. The overwhelming sight of the enormous band of Indians just outside the walls was alarming and intimidating. Terror had broken loose at the implication of the awesome event which might be ready to take place. The soldiers were scurrying about, getting their weapons and preparing to defend their lives and the fort. The few civilians who were present hurried inside their assigned quarters to hide and to shriek in dread. The men began to mill about nervously, anticipating their defeat—or worse, their deaths.

The men who had participated in the raid upon the brave's village a few weeks before quaked in apprehension. All they had done was to recapture the white girl Alisha Williams. But little did the soldiers then know that Alisha had stolen the heart of the fiercest savage in the West! The realization that the raid on Gray Eagle's camp had been a foolish and deadly mistake was all too evident all too late!

When the sentry informed General Galt that Gray Eagle himself was outside the fort, Galt swore at the young soldier's damnable carelessness. How dare the sole sentry of Fort Pierre fall asleep on duty!

Galt nervously wiped the beads of sweat from his upper lip, only to have the moisture instantly reappear. Then he cursed both Gray Eagle and Lieutenant Jeffery Gordon; those two men would be the destruction of his command yet. Neither one of them could be trusted; they were both too proud, too stubborn, and too damn reckless. Both men had been thorns in his side since the first day he had accepted this futile assignment in this godforsaken, savage land. But Gordon threatened his command even more. "Insolent, glory-seeking, young cur!" he fumed just above a whisper. He silently wished that Gray Eagle had been in his village to welcome Jeffery's arrival then. That way, Galt could have been rid of at least one of his aggravations . . .

At that moment, Jeffery seized his full attention as he sneered, "Send that insolent scout Powchutu out to see what they want. With any luck, they'll send his body back rather than a message."

Galt looked up at Jeffery's six-foot frame, and sarcastically replied, "After that stupid raid you pulled on his camp, Lieutenant, it should be obvious what Gray Eagle wants. It'll take some tall talk to get ourselves out of this predicament you've gotten us into. If we do, you had better stay the hell away from his camp, or any camp you lack the orders to attack! That's an order you had better remember."

General Galt called the half-breed scout over to him. He ordered, "Powchutu, it looks as if they want to parley. I best send you out there to see what he wants. Get back in here as soon as you can." His apprehension and fear were apparent to both Powchutu and Jeffery, but

Powchutu did not revel in it as Jeffery did.

"Yes, Sir," he replied. He walked to the gates and waited for the guards to lift the bar and to swing the huge, wooden gates open for him to pass through. He fearlessly walked outside. He absently listened as the gates were pushed shut and re-barred. He gazed out at the sight before him, inwardly wishing he was a part of it, and went straight up to the warrior who sat in the place of the leader. He knew that he had nothing to fear at this talk; the Indian was a man of his word and would not attack under the shadow of the talking-lance. Later, perhaps, but now, never!

He halted before the warrior and spoke slowly and evenly, "I am Powchutu, scout and speaker for the cavalry. The general wants to know why you are here. Why do so many braves and chiefs come dressed and painted for war?"

The imposing warrior answered in a deep, steady tone, "I am Wanmdi Hota, son of Chief Running Wolf of the Oglalas." Gray Eagle alertly noted the effect of his name upon the scout. His face had registered enlightenment, recognition, and respect. But, had it then reflected hatred and anger? As quickly as these emotions had raced across Powchutu's face, they had been suppressed. Gray Eagle could not help but think this mixture of feelings was strange and meaningful.

Powchutu had thought and felt exactly those things and more. His suspicions of this man's identity had just been proven accurate. There

13

should not have been any doubt, for his bearing and courage had shouted his name. Powchutu's heart had been smitten by Alisha as well, and he could not help but be disappointed that Gray Eagle was indeed what his reputation claimed: a man to melt the heart of a woman, a man to strike terror into the heart of an enemy, and a man who obviously stood above all others in many ways. Yet, there was also something else about his physical appearance, something important and intangible which Powchutu failed to discern, something which would have explained Alisha's reactions to him.

Gray Eagle continued in his language, "I have come to demand an apology for the raid on my village. I seek payment for the ruin and dishonor your bluecoats did there. You will hand over the white girl you stole from my camp; this is your payment. I demand your shame. Through her sacrifice, the white man will make amends for the disgrace and suffering brought upon my people. If you value your lives, she will be sent to me. If you refuse, we will attack the fort and destroy it and all inside. If the white girl survives the raid, she would still become my prisoner once more. A battle would cost the lives of many from both sides. It would be futile and foolish. But, your people must be made to suffer as my people have because of the contempt and hatred of the one with yellow hair. I will teach your people humiliation through the girl. They will see and know the foolishness of their actions. They will be made to know shame by giving the girl to me willingly in order to save their own lives. I will force them to reveal the cowards they truly are." He spoke these words with great confidence and boldness as he observed the scout's expression.

Powchutu's eyes had widened in disbelief and shock. He could not comprehend such cruelty as this man vowed to the woman he loved. He would never turn Alisha over to this madman! Powchutu fired at him, "She is innocent of the raid upon your camp! Demand the lives of the men who did this thing, not hers. The fight is between you and the lieutenant. Do not place her in the middle of your battleground. You have caused her enough pain and dishonor. Why should we give her back to you? Why do you not ask for the life of the other white girl you captured from her fortress, the one called Brown?" Too late, Powchutu realized he should have said that Alisha had died from the beating Gray Eagle had given her shortly before her arrival at the fort.

Gray Eagle calmly answered, "The life and sacrifice of a whore means nothing to either of us, but the life and sacrifice of the green-eyed girl would bring much dishonor and anguish from all of you. The men responsible for the raid would be tortured and killed quickly if you turned them over to us; the deed would soon be forgotten by your people. But, living with the truth of what they had been forced to give up to save their own lives would live in their hearts for a very long time. It is far easier to die with honor than to live with shame. Their deaths would be too easy for all of you to accept and to forget, but not hers. Is this not true, scout?" he openly challenged.

Powchutu realized just how smart and cunning he was. Just like the angry, starving wolf, he went for the jugular vein of his enemy. Powchutu's muscles stiffened. His voice was tinged with both sadness and fury as he accused, "So, you have really come back for Alisha! Just as I believed you would one day. Surely even the great Wanmdi Hota realizes her great value. But I will not allow them to send her back to you and to your cruelty. Did you not take enough from her when you killed her people, when you burned her fortress, when you captured her, when you beat her and raped her? Has she not paid enough for being white? Do you not owe her some measure of kindness for saving your life? If she had not gone against her own people that day long ago, they would have killed you. Has she not earned the right to be free and to be happy? Is this too much justice for the great warrior Wanmdi Hota to give?" he sneered in contempt, but his worried expression belied his brave words.

Gray Eagle appeared to ignore all his words. He spoke with an icy, deadly calm, "She will be brought here to me before the sun is straight above my head, or we will attack at that same hour. You will not be able to help her then. I will not be able to spare her life then. If we are forced to attack, no life will be spared."

Powchutu was desperate to keep Alisha for himself and challenged, "What if she will not come to you?"

Gray Eagle's eyes narrowed and darkened noticeably. His jawline tightened. His expression warned Powchutu that he had overstepped his bounds in meddling in this warrior's demands. He glared at Powchutu and stated coldly, "If she will not come willingly, then you will force her to come. Bring the girl to me now."

"I tell you this, Wanmdi Hota, if you harm her again, I will hunt you down and kill you with my bare hands. Powchutu has spoken and so it shall be!" Powchutu's threat was choked. Gray Eagle did not miss the look of anguish which flooded his eyes and tinged his voice as he continued, "You have judged the white-eyes well and true. They will return her to you to save themselves. To them, she is no longer white. But, I tell you this, Wanmdi Hota, her return will be by force. She will never return by your words alone."

Gray Eagle stared at his retreating back, wondering at his many strange words and sincere pleas. How was it possible that a half-breed scout could know her so well in such a short time? Had she dared to befriend an Indian, for that was how Powchutu would be viewed by the white man? Would she not fear and hate him as she did others? Once more, he realized that he had underestimated the green-eyed girl's strength, courage, and gentleness.

Gray Eagle could not help but worry that this scout had been secretly watching his woman. Desire for Alisha had been evident on his face and in his voice. How was it that he knew her so well? Such knowledge of her and her thoughts could have only come from a close relationship, one that Gray Eagle feared. He determined to learn more about this strange friendship. He feared and mistrusted the look of love the scout had innocently revealed to him; he respected the look of hatred and revenge that had also been reflected in the scout's features. Gray Eagle knew that such a combination of emotions within an enemy was dangerous; this scout certainly would require close observation in the future.

Gray Eagle's piercing gaze remained on Powchutu until he had re-entered the fort and the gates had closed. Forbidden thoughts of Alisha's turning to another man out of her loneliness, pain, and fear would not leave him. He could envision the scout at her side, offering her protection and love. Far worse, he could not blame her for reaching out to another for the happiness and acceptance which he himself had denied her. He could not even comprehend the torment that she must have endured. With shame he recognized his own part in all of her sufferings.

He could not deny that he had been responsible for the destruction of her people's fortress, that he had led the raid in which her uncle and her friends had been killed. He could not take back the day when she had witnessed that raid or the night when she had watched some of those same men punished for crimes against the Oglala, crimes which she knew nothing about. He could not erase her agonizing memories of other times when he had made her torments unbearable. He could not justify his brutality to her. He could understand her feelings, but could not have altered his treatment of her to have prevented them. He was the son of the chief, himself the next Oglala chief. He could not have behaved toward his white captive, his enemy, any differently than he had done; his pride and rank would not have allowed it. Alisha could not help being white; he, being Indian. But these facts created problems which he could not change.

He almost wished that he could have explained several things to that angry scout. Yet it was impossible to tell him that he was secretly in love with a white girl, for no one except White Arrow shared that incredible fact. One day Gray Eagle would tell Alisha, and she would then understand the necessity of this day's humiliation. How he hungered to defend the scout's accusation about her beating! But he could not tell him that tribal law had demanded her punishment or he would have lost face before his people. He could not tell this man that he had personally placed the five lashes upon her tender back, that he had done so to prevent her death, that he had suffered terribly to think that she might die from his cruelty, that he had personally taken care of her injuries after that, that he had remained at her side in prayer until the war council had called him away, or that he could not live without her. He could tell no one these facts, for no one would accept the joining of a white girl with the future chief of the Sioux. He could close his eyes and almost hear the mocking laughter at such a match. Who would fear or respect a warrior who captured, fell in love with, and joined with his sworn enemy? But no matter what, he would have Alisha in some way.

Gray Eagle could only hope that the scout had been wrong when he had spoken of Alisha's hatred for him. He could only hope that it was wishful thinking upon the scout's part. He realized that Alisha must fear him greatly, but did she now hate him? "We shall soon see, Little One . . ." he softly murmured to himself. The handsome warrior prayed that he had convinced the soldiers of his motive for revenge. If the scout had suspected more than this, it was apparent that he did not reveal it. In fact, the scout would probably do all in his power to help Alisha. He would certainly be aware of the power of Gray Eagle's words. He would surely convince the white men to hand her over without a fight, if only to spare her life. Alisha's feelings could not be considered at this time. Later, she would be made to understand.

Gray Eagle gazed up at the heavens and he inhaled deeply. He mentally spoke with Alisha. *I fear they would kill you, Little One, if they* guessed the truth. The scout's love for you is strong if he would risk a challenge to me to save you. He dares much in his speech! Bird of my heart, fly to me quickly and safely . . . it has been too long and too lonely without you.

To the Great Spirit he prayed, help me if they reject my bluff and we are forced to attack. Protect her life as you would protect mine.

Powchutu had walked back toward the fort with a heavy heart. He was seething with rage, for he knew what the outcome of this day would cost both him and Alisha. He cursed himself for not taking her away sooner. He had no doubts that the fort would give her up to Gray Eagle. He wondered if she would go back willingly. It would not matter anyway, for they would not give her a choice. He fumed angrily, damning them all.

Powchutu wished that he could read Gray Eagle's thoughts; he wished that he knew if that fierce warrior truly hated her or if he truly desired her. He could not help but ask himself if Gray Eagle would really attack the fort and kill all inside. He already had his answer: Gray Eagle did not make idle threats. There was no doubt in Powchutu's mind that he would attack them—but kill Alisha? Powchutu dared not venture an answer to that terrible question.

The same question kept returning to plague him: did Gray Eagle enjoy the suffering and shame of this tender creature in some sadistic way? Powchutu was aware of Gray Eagle's hatred, though well-deserved, for the white man. But to take it out on an innocent girl . . . This was not the Wanmdi Hota that he knew of and respected. Scattered ideas floated across his mind: did he only wish to make the others suffer through her, and did he only wish to taunt them with their helplessness, and had he lived with her all those months and never truly known her? There were so many critical questions, but no clear answers.

At that very moment, Powchutu vowed to himself that he would find some way to help Alisha, to free her from this brutal warrior, to take her far away from these cruel people. He could only hope and pray that he could find some way to make her his. He wanted with all his heart to give her back some of the happiness, love, and security that they had all long denied her.

Powchutu had slowly approached the wooden gates, stalling the inevitable for as long as possible. He would not permit himself to dwell on Alisha's reaction. First, he had to face General Galt with the brave's ultimatum. The gates had opened to allow him to re-enter. He quickly walked over to the general's office, ignoring the many questions from those around him.

Once in front of the general's desk, Powchutu delivered his report. He repeated the warrior's demands, then lay the leash and thongs down on the desk. The general listened, white-faced and shocked. The other officers glanced from one to the other in surprise and confusion.

Powchutu tried to keep his face and voice void of all the emotions as he related the terms of the truce between the red and white man. He was careful not to mention his personal pleas concerning Alisha. He instinctively knew to make Gray Eagle's demands sound as cold and brutal as possible for Alisha's sake.

When he had finished, the general exclaimed, "He what? That's absurd, Powchutu! Surely you misunderstood him, or this is some kind of joke? Why would he want that girl back so badly? My God, man, he almost beat her to death in his camp only a few weeks ago!" As soon as Galt had said this, he thrust it into the far recesses of his mind, knowing it might color his final decision.

"His pride and honor, you say?" he muttered, almost to himself in deep thought. "Strange that he would demand her return rather than the men who raided his encampment . . . He thinks it'll make us suffer to hand her over to him? Shame us, you say? Make us look like cowards, huh? Either the man's a bloody fool, or there's more to his demand than meets the eye."

Galt's beady eyes glanced around the room as he pondered these perplexing demands. It quickly came to his mind that Gray Eagle had attacked her fortress, killing everyone except her. It had never been rumored that Gray Eagle took white female captives before. He wondered what the most feared and awesome warrior ever born would want with this particular girl. Gray Eagle's feelings for the white man, especially

23

soldiers, were well-known. Was it possible that there was some personal motive behind these ultimatums?

Galt silenced one of the officers who was about to make some comment on this trying situation: he needed more time to sort out his own thoughts. He called to mind every time he had seen Alisha and every word they had spoken between them. He had to admit that she was injured when Jeffery had brought her here, but maybe there was some other explanation for her condition. He told himself that perhaps Gray Eagle was not responsible for her lashing. To him, it certainly did not fit with the image he had of him. No, there was something else going on here, and he was going to damn well find out what it was. So, he wants her back to humiliate us? he sneered. Perhaps she was his woman? . . .

His face brightened with an idea. "You all remember what the Brown girl said? Of course he doesn't want that whore back, but she just might be right about Miss Alisha's being his squaw. If that's the truth, no wonder he's demanding her return. That's all that'll make any sense. Well, well, well . . . this puts a different light on things. I'd venture to say that she's managed to fool all of us. After Lieutenant Gordon brought her here, she didn't have any choice but to claim she was only his prisoner. Why the little tramp! After all the help we gave her, now she's about to get us all killed, is she? The Brown girl claimed Miss Williams saved his life and helped him escape their fortress. It

24

sounds like a good reason for sparing her life to me. Plus, she's a real beauty. Seems he sees that, too. Could be he was enjoying her just a little bit too much to give her up. Wonder how the hell he convinced the other warriors to go along with this farce to get his squaw back?"

Captain Tracy spoke up, "From what I understand, Sir, those Injuns would cut off their right hands for him. Half of 'em love, and respect him, and the other half are scared to death of defying him. You're damn right they would help him do anything! No matter why he wants her back, he'll get her one way or another. You know what shape we're in right now. We don't dare call his bluff. 'Sides, I was one of those with Gordon on that raid. I sure as hell won't go near his camp again." He levelled hardened eyes on Jeffery and stated, "Orders or no orders . . ."

For some unknown reason, Jeffery remained silent for a time. It was Sergeant Percy who spoke up next, "What if it's just a show of power, Sir? Could it be that he's afraid we might hold her hostage against his attack? The whole matter sounds odd to me, too. We might try to call his bluff and see what happens."

"Don't be a bloody fool, Percy!" shouted Captain Tracy. "He wouldn't hesitate to take this fort apart to get her back if that's what he really wants. I should have stopped that raid against his camp."

Percy taunted, "Why didn't you, Tracy? You outrank Lieutenant Gordon."

"I also outrank you, Sergeant Percy, so I suggest you silence your mouth pronto. It's done and over. We just better make certain that we don't go near his camp again."

"Not even to rescue another damsel in distress?" jested Corporal Riley, twinkling eyes challenging Jeffery to speak up. "Whatever would our good Lieutenant do for amusement if we hadna rescued those two young ladies?" Everyone caught the slur on the word "ladies."

"You wouldn't know a lady if she bit you on the nose, Riley," Percy said with laughter filling his barreled chest.

"Would that be a fact now?" Riley challenged. "Could be that I been taking personal lessons from the lieutenant here."

"Gordon give away any of his secrets? I think not. He wouldn't allow anyone to get near Miss Alisha, that is, until she turns him down one more time. Of course he shares his harlot, Miss Brown, with everyone." Bawdy laughter filled the small room. "Have you given up on Miss Alisha yet?"

Jeffery straightened up in his chair as the conversation became too personal for his tastes. His crystal-blue eyes hardened to ice. "Sergeant Percy, Corporal Riley, I suggest that you two men remember your places and your manners. I daresay that I find you both lacking in respect. I do not take kindly to having my personal business bandied about by the likes as you. But just in case you are wondering, I have no claims on either Miss Alisha Williams or Miss Kathy

Brown. I merely offered Miss Williams my protection and friendship, which she chose not to accept. If any of you gentlemen can acquire her friendship, by all means feel free to do so," he sneered, knowing the lift of his orders to leave Alisha alone were coming too late for any of them to take advantage of it. By God, if he couldn't get anywhere with Alisha, he was certainly not going to give any one of these louts the chance to do so. No one had dared to oppose his strict order to leave Alisha to him.

Riley and Percy reluctantly held their tongues; Tracy did not. "Aw, come on, Gordon. Everyone knows you've been after the Williams girl ever since you brought her here, naked and wrapped only in your jacket. Do you plan to send her back to Gray Eagle before you have a chance to win her over? I bet you ain't never had a woman refuse all that charm and wealth before, have you? Kind of sticks in yore craw, don't it?"

"Shut your mouth, Tracy," Jeffery warned through clenched teeth.

"I believe you're forgetting who you're talking to, Lieutenant! If memory serves me, captains don't take orders from lieutenants."

"Some do, Tracy. Could be that you won't be a captain any longer than I remain a lieutenant . . ."

Tracy caught the innuendo concerning Jeffery's social and political power. He shouldn't doubt that Jeffery could get anything he wanted with his family's power. Anything but Miss

27

Alisha Williams in his bed. He grinned as he imagined how that fact must have galled the surly, arrogant lieutenant. He was a man used to getting everything and anything that he desired, until Alisha came along. No doubt she would pay heavily for her public rejection of him.

The general had been nervously pacing the floor as he weighed his options. He had only been half listening to his men argue until they broke into his train of thought. "Silence!" he shouted. "This kind of talk won't get us anywhere. How about if we discuss our situation instead of Lieutenant Gordon's love life?"

Galt had been recalling the first time that he had met and had spoken with Alicia. It had been shortly after her arrival at Fort Pierre. She had come to ask his help in returning to the Colonies, and from there back to England. She had shown good breeding with her excellent manners and poise. She had seemed to be unaware of her low status as an ex-captive. Later, she had unconsciously let her desperation show. She had shown concern for her penniless state, knowing that she had no family or possessions. Then, there was that day when she had forced him to reprimand both Jeffery and Powchutu in public. Had she been so blind or so stupid that she could not see that choosing the scout's company over the lieutenant's was trouble? He had wished that he could have sent her on her way that very day. This girl was nothing but trouble; her beauty and availability would have the men at each other's throats. He had seen it coming, but had been unable to prevent it. Now, here she was at the center of this new and deadly conflict.

The general paced the floor and nervously mopped the perspiration from his brow and upper lip, the stubble of his unshaven face rasping loudly in the silence. His choices were clear: he could either turn her over to Gray Eagle and take the chance that he would stick to his truce, or he could keep the girl as a hostage. He would not even consider the choice of protecting her, even if she were innocent or being vilely used by both of them. No matter his decision, either choice was dangerous and each outcome uncertain.

He muttered aloud, "Without a doubt he can take this fort apart and kill all of us. But does he know this? Why shouldn't he? Hell, it's his scouts that are preventing our supplies and replacements from getting here. His damn braves are responsible for the raids on our hunting parties. Yes, he knows he has us—no food, supplies, or extra men. Damn the red son-of-a-bitch!" he exploded.

"Tracy, do you think we should take the gamble and comply with his demands?"

Jeffery sneered, "He wants to shove our noses into the dirt. I say, shoot the bastard! We can't let him or any savage make cowards of us."

Percy spoke up and reasoned, "Just like you rubbed his nose in the dirt, right in his own encampment? From what I hear, Gray Eagle isn't a man to take such an insult lightly. 'Sides, it's better to be a live coward than a dead brave man."

"One thing for certain, he's much too powerful and important to be our enemy," Tracy concluded. "What does it matter why he wants the girl back. The fact remains that he's determined to have her."

Riley braved the lion when he grinned and added, "Could be that Lieutenant Gordon can't find it in his heart to hand her over to his most envied enemy. Whatcha say about that, Sir?"

"I say that I've warned you before, Riley, to keep your nose out of my affairs. Or else Gray Eagle won't have to rub your nose in the dirt; I will."

"Shut up, the both of you!" Captain Tracy shouted, gaining courage from this trying crisis. "Shame that you sent Major Tully out on that patrol two days ago instead of Lieutenant Gordon, Sir. Could be that Gray Eagle would've captured him and been satisfied with only his punishment. You all know what we're up against out there. There's no way we can defend this fort for very long against that many Indians. Not in the shape we're in. That's one Indian we should make a truce with, and pronto! I say to give him back his squaw. You got us into this, you glory-seeking rich boy! Now shut your mouth and help us get out of it!"

Jeffery's face grew red with rage. He vowed to take care of Captain Tracy later. He settled back into his chair, grinning maliciously at both

Tracy and Riley.

Powchutu had walked over to the front wall near the door and leaned back against it after finishing his report. He had remained silent, listening to the words of the other men, knowing that as long as they continued to carry on this childishly he could stall the inevitable. He had been remembering that first day he had seen Alisha. She had seemed so fragile and beautiful, even though she was so badly injured. He knew that these ruffians had no idea of what kind of treasure she was, no idea of her innocence and pain.

It was clear to Powchutu that what angered them most was the fact that Gray Eagle had taken her first. Jeffery had wanted her from the first moment he had set eyes upon her back in Gray Eagle's teepee. Her only crime against him was the fact that she would not be dazzled by his power and position, that she would not become his mistress. As Jeffery and the others saw it, she had chosen Powchutu's friendship over theirs. She had made the mistake of seeing him as a man, not a half-breed or an enemy. She had not despised him and avoided him as all the others did.

Powchutu had held a tight leash on his anger until Tracy had called Alisha "his squaw." That insult could not go unchallenged. His heart flamed in resentment and hatred at their cowardice. He spoke acidly, "She is not, and never was, his squaw. Not for the reasons you think. She was his slave and prisoner, nothing

31

more. He only seeks to use her to taunt you. He hopes to punish you by forcing you to witness his taking her, to shame you by forcing you to give her up willingly. Dishonor is important to the Indian. He does not care for her as a woman. To love a white woman would bring him loss of face. Gray Eagle cares more for his honor than his own life. I have read his hatred for the white man in his face, and I have heard it in his voice. He does not know how you view her since his capture. He does not know that you scorn and abuse her maliciously. He knows that to force a white man to hand a white woman over to him to be used as his whore would make you suffer worse than to kill you. He believes this act will cut you deeply."

Powchutu watched the effect of his words on the men as he continued, "If you return her to him, it will go worse for her than before. He will be more brutal to her this time out of anger and spite for the raid on his camp. It is possible that he spared her life because she doctored him in her fortress, for the Indian does reward bravery and help. This does not change the fact that he is cruel to her. It is more likely that he is punishing her for helping him. Can you not imagine his anger at having a mere white girl save his life? He holds her responsible for the raid on his camp, for it was done to rescue her. No doubt he feels she is someone special to you. He does not know that you have all been cruel to her, just as cruel as he was. If you do this thing, in time you will come to regret this evil deed. It is wrong to treat her as you have, but far worse to send her back to him. What if it were one of your wives, sisters, or daughters that he was demanding? Would you send her out there to him, even if she had been used by him in the past? Alisha has no one to defend her. Is this why you find it so easy to deny her any help?"

Percy spoke up in embarrassment, "Could it be that you're biased because she's been friendly to you? You'll be just as dead as we are if he attacks us to get her back."

Powchutu quickly shot back, "If she had been as friendly with you, would you still be so willing to give her back to him? We are friends because I do not judge her for her past, and she does not judge me for my color. I have not treated her with scorn and contempt as you all have done. I have only offered her acceptance for herself, which none of you can do. I have not tried to make her my mistress as each of you have done so. She was caught in the middle of this war between the white man and the Indian. She does not understand our hatred and contempt. Because of this, she does not hate what I am, and for this you cannot forgive her. Is she to be blamed for her innocent capture and vile use by Gray Eagle? Is she to be blamed for not wanting to be used by any of you? Is she to be blamed for accepting me as her friend when no one else would do so? Is she to be blamed because her people could not protect her from him, or because you cannot defend her now? I vow that if she were a 'squaw' to any one of you that you would never send her back to him."

Percy flushed a deep red, half in anger and half in guilty embarrassment. He watched the young officer's head turn away. "Do not allow your envy and spite to color your thoughts as they do your views of me. For once this deed is done, there will be no turning back," he warned.

The other officers had been temporarily silenced by Powchutu's words. But Jeffery hastily spoke up, "It is quite obvious to everyone, Scout, that she prefers Injuns to whites. In fact, she told me so herself." Alisha's stinging rejection of him still rankled his pride. He could still envision her lovely face as she had denied him what he wanted. She had talked like it was an insult rather than a solution to her problems. She had treated him like he was some vermin from the gutter instead of the rich, aristocratic heir to a large family fortune and plantation. She had made his offer of joining him in his quarters sound more degrading than her sojourn with that savage! Had she actually said that she might have fallen in love with him if he had treated her differently? Had he then retorted with the words, "No decent white man would marry an ex-Indian whore"? Had he really tried to force his attentions upon her? Had she been about to relent when that damn scout had stopped him? He could still recall her ashen face as he had said, "You think you're something special because you were bedded by the infamous Gray Eagle?" Without a doubt,

34

she would have eventually been forced to come to him. But now . . .

Powchutu was glaring at Jeffery as the scorn and malice dripped like tainted honey from his words. He challenged, "If she were not occupying your quarters as you tried to force her to do, would you still walk out there and turn her over to your most hated enemy, Sir?" Everyone caught the slur that he placed on the "Sir."

Jeffery jumped to his feet, knocking over his chair, and started for the scout. "You sorry . . ."

"Stop it!" the general shouted for order and silence. "We have enough troubles without the two of you going at each other's throats over the girl. There's no place here for her. That's pretty clear by the trouble she's causing. You all know how everyone here feels about her. You saw how they treated her yesterday. Name one person out there who will speak up for her or defend her at the cost of their own life. If she stays, it'll only be more trouble for us and for her. I see no other way but to send her back to him. If all he wants is for us to return her to him with an apology, then we have no choice. How can I justify endangering the whole fort for a missing piece of tail?" The general was speaking crudely, filled with frustration and fear. Gray Eagle had Galt's back to the wall, and they both knew it.

Sergeant Percy spoke up at that point, "It's clear that they've been trying to wipe out every white settlement and fort in this entire area. Powchutu has already reported on the war council's secret meeting not long ago. If they decide to attack here next, we can't hold them off for long. With that large party outside now, we can't hold them off at all."

Captain Tracy sighed heavily. "You're right, Percy. Those men and supplies that we requisitioned haven't gotten here yet, and I seriously doubt they will. What good are guns without ball and powder, or men without food, rest, and replacements? I hope to God those savages don't know how badly we're hurting."

Corporal Riley gave air to their worst fear, "If that Gray Eagle is as smart as we think, you can bet he does know."

General Galt shook his head, then spoke slowly, "Powchutu, you fetch the girl. I guess we'd better hear what she has to say about this matter."

Powchutu left and went directly to the Philseys' quarters next to the infirmary. He rapped loudly on the door. Mrs. Philsey answered it, glaring contemptuously at him. Checking his desire to slap her hateful face, he told her his orders before she could open her unkind mouth. She reluctantly stepped back to allow him to enter her door, recalling how she had ordered him never to enter her home again.

Powchutu knew that he had to talk quickly if he was going to have time to tell Alisha everything before he took her to the general's office. Otherwise, they would tear her to shreds with their venomous words. He wanted her to know the truth of her situation from him. Both the red man and the white man had hurt her enough, and he could only try to prevent them from hurting her more.

He knocked on her closed door and called her name. Mrs. Philsey spoke up from behind him and told him that she had not shown herself since Alisha's public humiliation the day before.

The half-breed scout sent her a malevolent glare which nearly propelled her out of her quarters with its powerful intensity. She scurried away in fear, knowing this man would like nothing better than to slit her throat. Once more he knocked upon Alisha's door and called her name a little louder.

The door slowly opened to a very dim room; the shade was drawn as much against the world outside as it was to hide her own fears and shame. She stepped aside to allow him to enter. What possible difference could it make now for him to openly visit her? Things could not be any worse than they already were. Why should she deny entrance to her only friend?

Powchutu guessed from the looks of things and from Alisha's appearance that she had no idea what was taking place outside her room. The rumpled bed covers told him that she had been lying down. The red, puffy eyes told him that she had been weeping; the dark circles beneath her incredibly green eyes testifed that she had not had very much rest.

Bluntly and simply he stated, "He's here, Alisha. Just as I warned you, he has come."

Soft emerald eyes blankly met obsidian ones.

She noted the concern, anger, and shame revealed there. The last person to come to her mind at that time was Gray Eagle. In confusion she asked, "Who has come, Powchutu? Why are you looking at me that way? Is something wrong?"

His tone was very gentle and soft as he answered, "He has come, Alisha. Gray Eagle is here now. He is waiting outside the fort for you to either come to him willingly or for you to be sent to him. He has demanded his captive back. He is out there now with a large band of warriors. He has demanded that you be returned to him as an apology for the raid on his camp. He has demanded you as a peace offering, or he will attack the fort."

He watched her face blanch, then her green eyes widened in disbelief. Her dry lips parted as if to speak, but nothing came out. It seemed as if a hundred thoughts simultaneously flashed across her mind. The look of terror and shock tore at his heart. He waited for her to absorb this news before speaking again.

Powchutu had been mistaken about her first reaction; only one thought had come to her mind. She had dreamed, even prayed, that Gray Eagle might one day come for her. But not like this. In her dreams he had come to rescue her, to carry her away to safety and to love. Now in reality, he had come to shame her, to punish her, and maybe to kill her. It was not supposed to be like this . . .

Powchutu continued after a short time, "The

general wishes to see you and to talk with you about this." He lifted her trembling chin in his strong hand and forced her to look into his eyes. He then placed his hands upon her shoulders to steady their quivering. "They will ask you questions about your life with him. You must get control of your wits and emotions. Fear does strange things to a person's mind and his judgment," he said.

Alisha realized that she had never been more helpless or frightened in her entire life. She focused her shimmering eyes on him and asked, "What did he say when you spoke with him, Powchutu? After all this time, why does he want me back now? Does he intend to execute me right before their very eyes for revenge? You said that he has demanded my return to him. What else did he say? What did the general have to say about this incredible demand? Will he send me back to him?"

Powchutu knew that it was cold and brutal to tell her the entire truth, but she must know what she would be facing when she walked into that office. Painfully and reluctantly, he repeated his talks with Gray Eagle and the general, word for word. She was already aware of the feelings of everyone concerned; yet, she was still stunned by his story. To hear aloud all her suspicions was almost unbearable. She wavered slightly under the stunning blow of this new cruelty. He caught her arms to steady her. He then wished that he had not been so open and truthful.

"None of this trouble is my fault, and yet they·

blame me for it. They act as if I am guilty of some terrible and shameful crime. It seems as if they wish to see me broken, shamed, and punished for something that I had no control over. They torment me with hundreds of questions; and yet when I answer them, they turn on me for the truth. If I lie to protect myself, they still attack me without mercy. I owe them no excuses, apologies or explanations! They have no right to demand or to expect anything from me. I did not ask them to rescue me."

In her anger and agitation, she jerked away from his gentle grasp. "I wish that I had never left England. This wonderland of new opportunities claimed my parents' lives. If I had refused to come out here with my uncle, we might both still be free and alive. I should never have stopped them from killing Gray Eagle that day. They told me that I would live to regret it. Now they're all dead and I might as well be. I was so blind and so foolish. How was I supposed to know about such things?"

She turned back to face him and continued, "Do you know that this is the same type of prejudice and hatred I faced at our fortress? It's as if they are using my own conscience as a weapon against me. Can I hate and blame all Indians because of what Gray Eagle and his people did to me?"

"For them, Alisha, it is enough reason to hate," Powchutu said softly. "This fight has been going on for a long time. You came into it unprepared for battle, but they did not. They wish to justify their hatred and bitterness because of you. When they realize that they cannot . . ."

"I know. Every day I have come to see more and more how they view ex-captives. I think perhaps the women's treatment of me is the worse, for they should understand what it would be like to change places with me. They should know that a woman cannot resist the strength of a man. Why do they refuse to see the truth? Do they prefer to believe that they would have had the strength and courage, even the honor, to resist it all, at any cost to their sanity and lives? Do they fear facing the knowledge of what they might do if they were ever placed in that same situation?"

"You are a constant reminder of their possible captivity," Powchutu assured her, "of what could just as easily happen to them. They rebel against the truth that they would not resist their captors. They have seen the results of torture. They know inside that they would not rebel against any order. Your condition when you arrived here told them that you had resisted, and yet lived. Their own cowardice and envy blind them to understanding and sympathy."

Powchutu tried to calm Alisha's greatest fears. He spoke of how he would feel and think if he were Gray Eagle. "I believe that he wants you back for himself. He seeks to trick the white man with this farce and to save face with his people. He must also protect your life, for you would be in grave danger if they thought for one minute that they could use you against him. He must treat you this way before all of them. His pride is important to him, Alisha, but I also believe that you are important to him."

Alisha scoffed at this ridiculous idea. Powchutu waited for his words to sink in before he went on, "I do not know how he convinced the other warriors to go along with this deceit. Unless, they must think that it is a fitting humiliation of the cavalry. To force them to not only apologize but to sacrifice you to their dreaded enemy makes for a good trick. He is awed and loved enough that they just might permit it for any reason, even a personal one." He could not tell if she understood any of his reasoning, but he added, "For his and your pride and honor, he must treat you cold and cruel before all of them."

It had been the wrong choice of words, for they struck a raw nerve. "Pride and honor! Face and shame!" she nearly shouted. "I have none of those left. Between my people here and his out there, they have taken everything from me. All except my life. What does my life or freedom matter to any of them? Nothing! I vow that it is all some monstrous trick."

She began to pace around the small room as she reasoned aloud, "Do they really believe that he will be satisfied with my return? I am not that important to him. If I must die, then let it be without more torture and degradation. One day, he will choke on his power and pride. For one day, it will have a price too great to pay or to bear . . ."

Powchutu tried to calm the distraught girl. "Our hands are tied, Alisha. Even if the fort wanted to defend you, they could not do so for very long. I'm not defending them, but a fight would be futile. Who knows, maybe your sacrifice will be, too."

She smiled sadly. "This time the joke will be on him. He doesn't know how very easy it will be for them to do just as he commands. He won't have to use force on them. He won't cost them anything in pride or suffering. He will simply be taking away a very nasty problem for them. Funny, isn't it? He's actually doing them a favor while he thinks he is causing them shame and torment. The hatred and spite will continue after I am gone and forgotten."

Powchutu knew that there was nothing to say, so he remained silent while she worked out her emotions. She walked over to the window and peeped out at the frantic people moving around. She had no doubts that they would comply with Gray Eagle's orders. In a subdued tone she murmured, "He will surely kill me this time. I have been too much trouble for him. He holds me to blame for things I cannot change or control. Why didn't they just leave me in his village? Why did they have to cause more trouble by rescuing me?"

The absurdity of her last words struck her, and she burst out laughing. Powchutu stared at her, soon realizing she was getting hysterical.

43

"Rescued!" She laughed and cried at the same time. "Some joke, isn't it? I stood a better chance of winning his acceptance before than I do now. He knows no mercy. They should have left me in his camp or let me die, then everyone would be happy and satisfied."

Powchutu considered Gray Eagle his enemy because of the severe pain he had inflicted on Alisha. But the half-breed knew Alisha would have no choice in her fate. He swallowed his hatred because of his unselfish love for the green-eyed white girl.

"Alisha, you have forgotten something very important. He did not kill you. He must not have wished your death. He was having you doctored." He hoped his argument would soothe her, but it did not.

"Only so that he could have the pleasure of hurting me again, Powchutu. Such a powerful warrior wouldn't allow death to rescue his most precious captive," she bitterly accused.

"Alisha, he spared your life many times. You kept on taunting him and disobeying him. What else could he do except punish you. He is the chief's son. He cannot show weakness before his people. Think back! You know that he treated you very differently in private. You just kept on pushing him into a corner. You wanted him to treat you as he would an Indian girl. He cannot. Face this truth and obey him in public. I've told you why he attacked your fortress. I've also told you why he killed those other men brought to his camp. Right or wrong, he did have good reasons. Nearly every punishment he gave you was to teach you some vital lesson about him and his ways. Remember this; I beg you for your own sake."

Their eyes focused and spoke without words. All of her old anguish resurfaced to frighten her anew. There had been times when she had allowed herself to forget that they were enemies. There had been times when she had forgiven him of terrible, but understandable, things when he had not asked for or wanted forgiveness. She had found reasons to justify his hatred and cruelty. Worst of all, she had foolishly allowed herself to fall more deeply and strongly in love with him. She had created a beautiful dream world for the two of them, forgetting that it was only an illusion.

But the scene outside was not an illusion; the man waiting for her was all too real and too deadly. Her dream had never called for her sacrifice or her disgrace. She had been ensnared in the trap of blind love and trust, with the hope that his love would be returned to her someday. Her illusions painfully shattered and slashed mercilessly at her tender heart. Tears welled in her eyes, and she bravely fought to control them.

Powchutu pulled her into his embrace to comfort her, knowing their time was running out. She leaned back and looked up into his eyes. She pleaded, "Please don't let him take me back, Powchutu. You are the only one who can help me. You are my only hope."

Her words knifed at his heart, for she was

mistaken. He crushed her to his broad chest and held her tightly and possessively. "I would give anything to save you, my love. If I tried to stop them from sending you away, they would be only too happy to kill me and still send you to him. You would only feel guilt at my useless death. I cannot fight both sides, Alisha. There are too many of them. But, I will promise to find some way to help you. I will get you away from here and away from all of them. Somehow I will help you. Very soon . . ."

Alisha gazed up into his handsome features, knowing that he spoke the truth. Seeing the regret and pain in his face, she whispered, "I'm truly sorry, Powchutu. This is one time that no one can help me, not even you. But your friendship and promise will make it easier for me to get through this day." She smiled bravely into his sad, troubled eyes and kissed him lightly upon his lips.

He tenderly cupped her face between his hands and gazed lovingly into her emerald eyes. He spoke to her without words, but she misread his real meaning. She did not realize that Powchutu was speaking of love, the love of a man for a woman, not the love of a friend for a friend. That first kiss from her had opened up the flood-gates which he had kept secured for a long time. He could not deny himself at least one real kiss from her, one to seal his promise to her. He leaned forward and kissed her full upon the mouth.

Alisha did not pull away or refuse his kiss. It

was a kiss which shared love, promise, and hope. It was gentle and warm in the giving and the taking. Afterwards, he hugged her fiercely once more as he whispered into her ear, "Remember, I will come for you, little heart. Do all he says, and he will not harm you."

She listened to his words "all he says," then trembled. Suddenly, she could not decide what she feared more—the return to his cruelty, or the return to his arms. She prayed Powchutu's promise would give her the courage and strength to endure.

"Come, Alisha, let's go to the general."

Alisha hesitated, then went with Powchutu.

Like wildfire, gossip had spread the news around the fort. The word was out that Gray Eagle had come for his woman and that he would attack if she were not promptly sent out to him. From their point of view, the white settlers could not understand why she was still in the fort, endangering their lives and property.

As Alisha and Powchutu walked toward the general's office, the people gaped at them in open hostility. Here was the girl responsible for their new predicament, along with her Indian buddy. They did not stop to think that here was the girl that they had raided Gray Eagle's camp to rescue; that the soldiers had killed and maimed women, children, and old people in that raid; that the soldiers had burned and

47

destroyed half of his village; that Alisha had been unconscious during her rescue; and that she was new to this land and knew nothing of the mutual hatred between the white man and Indian.

Their cold, hard stares caused her to slightly falter. Powchutu made the innocent mistake of grasping her elbow for support; this physical contact between them increased the crowd's anger. Here was the girl who had publicly chosen a half-breed scout over a dashing, wealthy, white lieutenant. The malice and animosity filled the air, seeming to choke off the oxygen around them. Their stinging words pelted her in the face like a winter rain, and she shivered at their harshness.

Some of the men hurled crude insults and wild threats at her. Soon, others from the crowd joined in on the cruel deriding. "Go back to your Injun lover, slut!" "We don't want no Injun squaws here!" "Tie her up and toss her out on that arse he's so fond of!" "We ain't gonna die for no white whore!" "Harlot! Bloody, red-loving harlot!" The taunting words and vulgar gestures were mercilessly flung at her. Then, there were others who begged her to sacrifice herself for them. They actually pleaded with her to willingly go back to the cruel savage so their consciences would not have to suffer the guilt and shame of forcing her to do so. They made cruel, but earnest, attempts to entreat her to spare them from Gray Eagle's wrath, and appealed to her mercy. Alisha could hardly believe her eyes and ears.

Alisha somehow found the strength to get to the general's office, after what seemed an eternity. Powchutu was blazing in fury at the mob. He could literally have killed every one of them and felt nothing but satisfaction. His muscles and nerves were as taut as a new bowstring. If one of those men had dared to touch her in any way, he would have cut him down right in his tracks.

Cowards! he fumed. I could kill them all . . .

Alisha forced a weak smile to her trembling lips. She softly said, "It doesn't matter anymore, Powchutu. They're only proving to me that this is necessary. I couldn't stay here now, even if they forced me. I'm the only one around that they can vent their fears upon. They don't dare do it to Gray Eagle, so they choose the available target—me. Because of his demand for my return, I symbolize his power. Who knows? Maybe they're right; maybe I will be better off with him, dead or alive. For certain, he is no more cruel than they are . . ."

Her last ray of hope had vanished, for she already knew the outcome of the upcoming meeting. The general's door was opened and they slipped inside. From the looks on the men's faces, they were all aware of the events outside. General Galt tried to avoid the eyes of the girl standing before his desk. He got up and moved about to ease his tension. He was trying to decide how to begin this unpleasant task.

Finding none, he plunged right in, "I

suppose Powchutu has filled you in on our crisis here?''

Knowing the length of time that had elapsed, she knew that it would be foolish to deny his words. She simply nodded yes, but did not speak. He scanned her ashen face with its somber green eyes which were filled with so much pain that even he could recognize it. Damn! he cursed to himself. She was not going to make this any easier for him.

He fought to ignore the guilt and shame of what he was about to do. At least he would not have to balk Jeffery Gordon or Martha Philsey this time; both were certain to go along with his decision. He forced himself to believe that her appearance was colored by her fear of those people outside, not of her return to Gray Eagle. He would not permit himself to ponder the fact that her expression bespoke anything but happiness at the warrior's arrival.

Damn all women with innocent green eyes and angelic faces! the general silently swore. It's too late to change my mind. You made your bed, now lie in it! Willing or not, guilty or innocent, he wants her back, and I haven't got the power to stop him. Within moments, the general had rationalized his decision to force Alisha's return to Gray Eagle.

He pointedly asked her with cold bluntness, ''What do you think we should do about this demand, Miss Williams? You've lived with him. Will he do as he says? Could he want you back so badly that he would attack this fort?'' His words

50

carried double meanings, and she caught both. He wanted her to shoulder the blame for his decision by suggesting the only possible solution. He was also reminding her that she had already been his captive.

She swallowed hard, then spoke softly, "Why do you ask me, Sir? You are in command here. The final decision is yours, and I am not qualified to make any military suggestions. I am positive that you all know him far better than I ever could. As you know, I have only been in this wild country for a short time; and briefly at Fort Pierre. I do not know that much about your people or his. And I cannot venture a guess as to what his plans are. I have only seen and known the one side of him—the brutal, vindictive warrior. He is the man who killed my people and who enslaved me. His honor and truthfulness were not a part of this side of his nature. He never made promises to me, only threats. We did not talk with each other, so I do not know if he keeps his word or not. I am certain that you have been enemies for a very long time. I am also certain that you must be aware of the personality of your worst enemy. So, why do you ask me if he is truthful, or if he is serious in his threat?

"If you offer me your protection, you know what he has threatened to do. Just as you are aware of the outcome if you agree to his demands," she simply stated the facts. "Which is easier to accept, my life and freedom here, or my slavery and death in his camp? As for wanting me back so badly, I cannot imagine why he would want a defiant runaway slave returned to him. I should think it is to spite me and to humiliate you."

She boldly met Galt's stare.

General Galt raged at her brazen words. He spit the tip of his smelly cigar into the cracked bowl on his dusty desk. He inhaled deeply and met her steady gaze. "I have hopes this Gray Eagle won't harm you this time. One thing I know for sure, those people out there won't stand for my giving you sanction here at the cost of their lives. I have no doubts that he will carry out his threat if you remain in here. I'm afraid I have no choice but to turn you over to him."

There, it was said and done! He waited for any of his officers to disagree or to plead her case, but none did. The only officer who would dare to meet her gaze was Jeffery. His bright blue eyes were filled with triumph and spite. Alisha should not have been surprised at his attitude, for he had revealed his true nature to her. If it had not been for Powchutu's interference, he would have ravished her beneath that large shade tree. She could imagine what kind of man could enjoy the suffering of another person; Jeffery was that kind of man. These Colonists were strange and violent people; she was certain that she would never understand them.

Her seeking gaze travelled the room once more. She wanted to make sure that not a single man would come to her defense; none did. The harshness of her dilemma hit Alisha. She tried to force herself to accept the inevitable.

Just above a whisper she stated, "You are all foolish dreamers. You cannot possibly believe for one moment that I will be safe with him. For what you have done to him and his camp, he will not be satisfied with my return. Did his capture of me last time prevent his total destruction of our fortress? No, because it was not Alisha he sought. Today, it is not Alisha that he seeks. He merely wishes to humiliate and taunt you before he comes for the men responsible for his dishonor, just like he did at my fortress. The last time, I did not pay for the crimes of my people against him. This time, I will not pay for your crimes against him."

Alisha alertly noted the reaction her word "crimes" received; still, no one interrupted her. Their fidgeting told her that they wanted this meeting over with as quickly as possible. But she could not leave without speaking the truth.

The men were speechless. They had expected her to be tearful and submissive. They were unnerved and rankled by her comments. What was that old saying about a coward's many deaths? The silence in the office was deafening.

She turned back to face the men in the room. "Are you gentlemen sitting there, waiting for me to offer myself as a martyr for you and this fort? I hope not, for I will never willingly agree to go to him. I have seen and felt his brutality and his hatred for the white man. I still carry the scars to prove it, in case you have forgotten. If you order me to leave, then I will not disobey your command. That would be futile and foolish. I would not give him the pleasure of watching you throw me to the wolves. I will not be a submissive martyr, but neither will I be humiliated by your public show of hatred for me. Never will I volunteer for a mission into Hell. All I can do is to place my safety and life in your 'capable' hands, General Galt."

Hiram Galt nervously cleared his throat and voiced his predetermined conclusion. "I think it is best for all concerned if you're sent back to him. The safety of this fort and its inhabitants depends upon it. I see no other choice. I am truly sorry, Miss Williams."

"Then, you are ordering me to leave?"

The general nodded yes.

"This safety that you speak of does not include mine, does it?" she mockingly queried.

His angry, black scowl answered for him. Galt's face flushed even redder with mounting guilt and fury. He pitifully argued, "If I had more men and supplies, Miss Williams, I would gladly offer you sanctuary here with us. And to Hell with what anyone thought! Please be more understanding of our position." Damn! he fumed. I'll be glad to get this over with . . .

Alisha turned to face Jeffery with a sweet, innocent smile. She asked, "Does this decision also include your approval, Jeffery?"

Lieutenant Jeffery Gordon boldly locked heated gazes with her. He was determined to punish Alisha because she would not become his mistress. He replied, "Go to your brave, Alisha, for that is where you belong now. You have proven that you prefer Indians to whites. There is no place for you here."

Alisha went to stand before him. He stood up to face her. Her eyes searched his handsome, tanned features and piercing blue eyes for the secret to his real character. Speaking very softly she inquired, "If I agree to become your mistress, on your terms, will you still send me out to him?"

He had been observing her close scrutiny of him, mistaking her feelings and reasons. It was only natural for a woman to choose him over a savage. He assumed she was attracted to him.

For a moment, the lieutenant seriously pondered her question. He quickly realized that his answer would have to be no. How could a dead man enjoy her numerous charms? Besides, she was merely accepting him as a last resort, a fact which stung his pride as deeply as her rejection had. After he had risked everything, including his life, to rescue her, she had publicly scorned him more than once. If only he could forget the sight of her nude body beneath that blanket in Gray Eagle's teepee. . . .

Gazing down into her emerald eyes, he was tempted to gladly fight the entire Indian nation to have her as his mistress. Yet, he instantly realized, Alisha's eyes belied her taunt: it was not a real proposition. His face became a mask of livid rage; his body trembled with the force of his anger. He was furious at what she had jokingly offered to him, then contemptuously snatched away before his acceptance or refusal.

At the sight of his blind rage, Alisha leaned very closely to him and whispered for his ears alone, "One thing I know for certain, Jeffery, you are less than half the man he is, in every possible way . . ."

He clenched his hands into tight fists to keep from striking her, and Alisha turned to face Powchutu. "Since I have no personal belongings, I'm ready to leave, Powchutu."

They walked out into the warm sunlight, leaving the room of officers staring after her and at each other in shame. The crowd was instantly aware of the outcome as the white girl and the half-breed made their way through the sullen group toward the front gates.

A hushed, almost reverent, silence settled over the inhabitants of Fort Pierre. There were embarrassed and malevolent stares focused on the stunning girl who was walking to her fate with head held high. Some were thinking that she was heading for a fate worse than death. Others scoffed that it could not be helped. Still others vowed that it was better she than they or theirs. And, some felt that she was getting just what she deserved because she did not share their Indian hatred.

As she and Powchutu walked along, Alisha felt strangely detached from the whole scene. Her thoughts were on what awaited her outside those massive gates, the revenge of Wanmdi Hota. They halted by the gateway to her destiny to allow the guards to open them just enough for them to pass through. Her eyes alit on Kathy Brown's as she stood nearby, smiling triumphantly and cynically.

She studied the embittered, pathetic girl. They had travelled in the same wagon train from Pennsylvania to South Dakota. Yet, during all that time and all those hardships, Kathy had rejected her friendship. She had done everything in her power to cause trouble for Alisha. They were the only two people left alive, not counting their scout who had left long ago, from their fortress. At Gray Eagle's camp, Kathy's jealousy and hatred had grown by leaps and bounds. She had refused to see Alisha's real treatment. All she saw was the fact that Alisha shared the chief's son's teepee, that Gray Eagle had chosen Alisha for his personal captive. Gray Eagle's looks and position had increased Kathy's anger toward Alisha. Kathy had been available to any brave, and yet Alisha belonged only to the handsome and virile Gray Eagle. Kathy was the one who had told Fort Pierre about Alisha's help to Gray Eagle, that she had actually pulled a gun on the men at their fortress in order to halt his beating and death. To make matters worse for Kathy, the Fort Pierre officers had treated her as a whore, but Alisha with respect.

"I hope this vengeance tastes very sweet to you, Kathy. You surely worked hard enough for it. Just remember one thing: while you sleep with every bit of scum in this fort, I will be sleeping with only one man—the brave and handsome Gray Eagle."

For once, Kathy was totally speechless. How dare Alisha pretend she was better than Kathy? . . .

The gates closed behind them. She listened as the huge bar fell heavily back into place. She was being shut out of their lives; and they, from hers. But the inhabitants of the fort did not realize that destiny had just sealed all of their fates. Alisha was free and safe; the fort was helpless. The warriors realized that things were going just as the Great Spirit had shown them in their joint-vision.

They walked a short distance away from the fort, just out of earshot of its traitorous inhabitants. Powchutu tugged at Alisha's elbow and halted her steps. She lifted inquiring eyes to his pain-filled ones. His heart was aching at her obvious anguish and raging at his inability to help her. They both sensed that this might be their last time to talk.

She stood beside him in the bright morning light, wishing that time could be suspended. She lifted her face up to the sun and inhaled deeply several times, trying to calm her racing heart and to bring some small measure of comprehension into her confused brain. The need to show courage and dignity was past.

Powchutu could read the desperation and hopelessness in her eyes. He cursed both the Indians and the white men for what they were doing to her, for never had there been one so beautiful and blameless as she. The abject voice which spoke to him sliced his heart more quickly and expertly than his own hunting knife could have done.

"How is such injustice and hatred possible, Powchutu? Why can't he leave me alone? Why must he continue to torment me this way? He has even turned my own people against me."

He lowered his head, ashamed for his own guiltless part in her sufferings. "How can I explain what I do not understand myself? The Great Spirit will surely punish all of them for this dishonorable deed."

Alisha felt as if her tender heart was being pierced with countless arrows. "My whole life has gone topsy-turvy in only a few short months. I have seen such evil in this land, in these people. I hate the ugliness which surrounds me here. I hate what they have done to me. Worst of all, I hate these feelings of hatred and revenge which they have instilled within me."

He studied the face of the English girl that he had come to love more than life itself. He wondered at the changes that she had brought into his life and heart. He, a half-breed scout, was in love with a white girl, a white girl who was imprisoned in heart and body to the fiercest warrior of all time. She was right; how could such a tragic injustice be possible? Powchutu's thoughts raced back to a day not so very long ago when she had come into his life, broken in spirit and in body. He could not imagine how

Gray Eagle had brought himself to torture such a fragile woman. Now, he had the gall to return to demand her surrender to him.

Powchutu looked longingly into her misty eyes and spoke from his heart, "I will pray to both our gods that he will not harm you this time. He is no fool, Alisha. He knows that you cannot be blamed for the raid upon his camp."

She shook her head sadly, auburn curls swaying at her shoulders. "But he can and will blame me. To him, I am white, his enemy. My innocence or guilt will not matter to him. They never have before. Leave this evil land, Powchutu. There is no place for freedom or happiness here. And no place for dreams either . . ."

He answered softly, "Only when you are free to come with me."

The sun had slowly climbed higher and higher, until it was almost directly over head. The midday air was arid and motionless. She stood halfway between the long rows of painted warriors and the tall, spiked fence of the fort.

Both the warriors and the soldiers watched the strange and tender scene between the beautiful white girl and the half-breed scout. What was causing their delay? Why did the scout not bring the girl who was said to be a gift from Wakantanka to the great warrior Gray Eagle?

The people inside the fort became very nervous and angry as more time passed and Alisha did not make a move to go to the waiting warrior.

The warriors were greatly baffled by the girl's actions. If eyes could be trusted, she and the scout were friends. But why would a white girl trust any Indian, even a half-breed, after what Wanmdi Hota had done to her and to her people? This attitude was indeed strange. Perhaps Wanmdi Hota's torture had sent her mind to dwell in another land . . .

Gray Eagle alertly studied the expressions which came and went on Alisha's and the scout's faces. He did not like the look of tenderness and love which she sent to the scout; those should be for him alone! He inwardly flinched each time that she gazed up into his face with that warm look that he knew so well. From what he could see, she appeared to be pleading with him. But, why? Surely not for help? What chance did he have against all of them? Soon, Gray Eagle became tense. This waiting, after these tormenting weeks of loneliness and separation, was getting to him. Only his many years of training and practice kept it hidden from the eyes of the others.

At last, Alisha looked out toward the warriors. She let her gaze slowly travel the long lines of warriors and colorfully arrayed chiefs. They seemed to spread out endlessly, threateningly, upon the vast blue horizon. They sat so still and erect that they looked like one colorful, gigantic mural hung across the massive skyline.

Gray Eagle once more held her fate within his powerful hands, but were they merciful ones?

Even after all the time she had spent with him, she could not answer. She felt betrayed by her people and by him; she felt betrayed by herself. There would never be another rescue or escape; he would make certain.

She looked at her friend. She knew that she would always love and remember him. Powchutu had done so much for her. If the occasion ever called for it, she would lay down her very life for him. Alisha studied the awesome sight before her, thinking of the people inside the fort. Each one of them had their own selfish reason for her being here now, facing God knows what. Their hatred, jealousy, and fear were once again placing her at Gray Eagle's power and mercy.

"Even during his worst hatred and cruelty, Powchutu, he never hurt me or abused me like my own people have done. The pain and humiliation that I have felt here would not compare with what I knew in his camp. They call themselves the civilized ones! They are far more savage and brutal than he ever was. I must find the courage to do as he commands. I will not give him any more reasons to hurt me or punish me. They demand that I return to him, so I really have no choice but to do so and to hope for a truce between us. Oh, I'm so frightened; my legs refuse to move."

Yes, she was frightened; she feared and dreaded the coming time when she would be tested for her courage and obedience. The problem was that pain had a curious way of dimming with time; yet, love and its memories had the same way of growing greater. The events of danger, pain, and death had gradually receded to a far distance in her mind, just like the shores of England had done many months ago.

She had but to close her eyes to visualize his smile. How long could she have resisted or ignored him when he had forced her to sleep within his heated embrace? When he had forbidden anyone else to harm her? When he had seduced her with such passion and tenderness and completeness? When she was forced to comprehend that he was defying his own conscience and people to hold her captive in his own teepee? There had usually existed a warm and relaxed truce within his teepee. He had been gentle and playful as he had taught her some of his tongue, as they had both worked on their separate chores, and as they had shared meals.

There had been those countless times when he had shown her such a different side of his nature, only to have the warrior image return when in public. There had been that time when he had personally doctored the bloody pricks on her hands from the porcupine quills. There had been that day when a trapper, thinking her an Indian maiden, had tried to ravish her, that day when White Arrow had killed him to save her. But Gray Eagle had been the one to care for her injuries and to comfort her. She could recall the day when she had been caught in a violent thunderstorm while gathering wood. He had searched for her, found her, and protected her with his own body. The memory of their following lovemaking among the tall grasses and fragrant wildflowers during that storm had always remained alive and green within her heart. They had both been relaxed and happy with each other; they had laughed and loved in the rain. If all their days could have been that way . . .

The day had come when she had discovered herself waiting and watching for his returns from hunts and raids, when she had recognized her undeniable desire and love for him, when she had realized the futility and pain of that forbidden love, when she had cried because she was not Oglala, when she had come to hunger for him both physically and emotionally, and when she had dared to escape from his loving torment.

She could not admit that he had always been gentle and forgiving after all of her previous defiances and punishments. Things had always returned to some form of truce between them. Many times she had knowingly or innocently forced him to be cruel toward her. His desire for her had been obvious to even her naive mind. Yet he would not love her or publicly accept her as his woman. It had only made her more understanding and susceptible when Powchutu had told her the truth and the motives behind so many of his decisions and actions. Tragically she could understand and accept him as a man, but he could not ever offer her the same.

Their last night together, before she had foolishly and fearfully fled his camp, before he had punished her at the icapsinte by whipping her unconscious, there had been a strangeness in the atmosphere of his teepee and within both of them. They had joined with flaming passion, with a seemingly total giving and taking. Never had he been so consumed with her, even whispering soft Oglala words into her ear. She had been intoxicated by him. Later, he had returned to being her captor. Watching the warmth leave his handsome face and his stoic expression return, she had finally faced the truth of his treacherous and demanding love, and the betrayal of her own body and heart. Then escape had seemed her only choice.

All her plans had been for naught; she had been no match for the wilderness or his pursuit. She pictured his face that morning when he had caught up with her, that he had arrived in time to save her life. Never had she seen such anger and determination in him. There had been an alien reluctance in his manner on their return to his camp. Even when he had punished her, there had been a strange kind of anger in him; there had been a fleeting look of sadness, hesitation, and bitterness in his last look at her. At that time, she had been too terrified and too hurt to see it. She had lost consciousness during her punishment. For some reason, Gray Eagle and the warriors had left camp that day; Jeffery had raided it during their absence. Six days later she had awakened at the fort and had begun a new existence of contempt and abuse at the hands of its inhabitants.

As if walking to her death, Alisha's life passed before her eyes. She was leaving one hellish existence to enter another. She had changed much in her sojourns, but neither the white nor the red people had. Those in the fort were the same; the Indians were the same. Gray Eagle was still her captor; he was still her enemy. Things would either be the same as before in his camp, or they would be worse.

God help me, she sadly prayed, for I have lost my heart and soul to a brutal savage who will not allow the hatred between us to disappear. Please let there be just a little peace between us . . .

Chapter Two

Powchutu called her from her train of thought, "It is time to go, Alisha." He gently pulled her wrists out before her and bound them with the rawhide thongs. She offered no resistance to her friend. She only stared down at the dusty ground, hoping the day and its events would soon be over. He held out the leash and lifted her long hair to place it around her neck. Her eyes blazed at the sight of the bestial lariat. She grabbed the leash and angrily threw it to the ground in contempt. She had forgotten this humiliating demand. Gray Eagle could take her with her hands bound only, or he could strike her dead here! But she vowed she would not allow that lasso around her neck.

"No! I will not be led by a neck rope like an animal before all these people," she said furiously.

Powchutu tried to reason with her, telling her she must permit him to put the leash on her. "They have demanded you be brought to him bound and led like a prisoner. His pride and power are at stake, Alisha. Do not refuse. I beg you."

"Damn his pride and my non-existent honor! I won't let them do this to me! It is too much to ask or demand of anyone. I might be a sacrificial lamb, but I will not be treated like one! Never!" she shrieked.

Gray Eagle watched the scene in fearful anticipation of her refusal. He thought, for once, Lese, do not defy me and shame me before them. I know and feel your hurt and shame, but it must be this way for both our sakes. Even if you were not in firing range of the fort, I could not come for you. You must come to me!

He watched her argue and plead with the scout. He could see the scout was trying his best to get her to do as she had been commanded. I should have ridden closer and picked her up, he thought. There is much loss of face in what I have ordered her to do. Surely they will all see we are enemies. Her people must hurt and bleed for her shame and mine. It would be far too tempting for one of them to shoot me if I dared to go to her. I would be dead and she would be the captive of another.

Gray Eagle had guessed wrong about the majority of people in the fort. They did not hurt or feel mercy for her. They felt only fear and anger at her refusal to do as she was told.

Powchutu pleaded, "He must force you to cower in fear and humiliation before the warriors. To refuse would be dangerous for you and the fort. Please, Alisha, do not defy him this time."

She lashed out in torment, "Why should I care about the fort or the people inside it? They don't care if he kills me or only punishes me!

They only want to save themselves. I hate them all, Powchutu! One day they'll pay for acts like this!"

Powchutu urged her not to provoke Gray Eagle. "You will be the one to feel his anger, Alisha, not them. Do as he says. It will soon be over. It will prove to them you spoke the truth. It is but a short walk and I will be at your side. Trust me, it is for the best. Does it really matter what they think?"

She met his gaze. She knew he was right and was only thinking of her safety. "It matters what I feel and think, Powchutu. How much more humiliation do I have to endure? Why does he wish to hurt and shame me time and time again?" Tears spilled down her cheeks as she leaned over to retrieve the leash. She pulled it over her head in submission and straightened her hair. She handed the other end to Powchutu and said, "Let's go and get this over with . . ." Both Powchutu and Gray Eagle sighed with relief. The people inside the fort relaxed. The other warriors were aware she displayed courage and wisdom, not fear, with her submission. She was not only beautiful, but intelligent and brave.

Her eyes scanned the horizon and rested on Gray Eagle. He was the pinnacle of masculinity and power. She couldn't help but notice his dignity and noble bearing. Uncontrollably, a look of pride and pleasure at his overpowering magnetism and status briefly crossed her face. It did not go unnoticed by him, even at that distance.

She realized anew he had a way of making everyone and everything around him dim or disappear with his very presence. Their eyes met and locked. His seemed to bore into her very soul. For a minute, that tingling, warm sensation spread throughout her body, until it was smothered by mistrust and anger. He noted the panic she was trying hard to suppress. She gazed at the numerous warriors surrounding him.

"What would he do if I turned and ran back into the fort and refused to let them all use me this way?" She whispered bitterly, "He wouldn't have to do anything. Those people, my people, would only refuse to let me back in. They would laugh. He would be furious, and I would suffer the consequences. It's too late. Let's go . . ."

Powchutu wished with all his aching heart he could whisk her away to safety and freedom, out of all their reach. He walked slowly at her side, careful not to pull on the neck leash.

As they neared Gray Eagle, she whispered to the scout, "We are very much alike, Powchutu. We're both trapped in the middle of a no-man's land, hated by both sides."

He pondered her logic and nodded agreement. As they approached the warrior on his horse, Alisha slightly faltered and slowed her pace, casting her eyes downward. She stopped when Powchutu did, but did not look up at Gray Eagle right away. Her heart raced madly at the thought of looking into those obsidian eyes once more. She could feel the aura of his power and nearness.

Powchutu reluctantly handed him the end of the leash. Malice was clearly written on Powchutu's face. He glared at Gray Eagle with dark, brooding eyes and said in the Oglala tongue, "I lower my pride to beg you not to harm her again. I will gladly sacrifice my life and freedom if you will let her go free. You are a great and powerful warrior. You have the courage to stay your hatred and vengeance from her. She is a gentle spirit who has suffered much at your hands, but even more at the hands of her own people. Do not make her pay for their evil. They have forced her to pay too much already for belonging to you. You did not force them to sacrifice her in shame and torment. The trick is on you."

Powchutu saw his eyes narrow and darken, and the anger flicker across his face before he closed himself from Powchutu's scrutiny. Powchutu was both surprised and shocked when he demanded to know what he meant by his last words. The icy, angry edge in his tone warned Powchutu of more than idle curiosity in the warrior's demand. He wanted to know everything about her and her life at the fort.

Powchutu hoped and prayed it was true concern and interest in Alisha herself which prompted his demands. Would the knowledge of her treatment at the fort soften Gray Eagle's anger and hatred toward her? Powchutu chanced it would. He quickly and thoroughly explained everything to him. Even a man like

Gray Eagle with all his practice and training could not hide the fury which flamed in his black eyes. Powchutu noted the taut muscles in his body and the tightening of his jawline. He was fully aware of the controlled rage and violence the man who towered above him was feeling and suppressing.

Powchutu realized a man would not feel so strongly about the evil treatment of a mere kaskapi. He was pleased and happy at this discovery. He slightly smiled at Gray Eagle.

Gray Eagle ignored his expression and fumed, how dare they take her from me and treat her this way! They will pay greatly for taking their hate for me out on her! He asked Powchutu a few more questions, then stated, "You wish to protect her from me and my treatment, just as you tried to do for her with her own people. But I ask you, scout, which of our people is the greater evil and hurt to her? She has shown great courage and understanding to take you as a koda. You are wise and brave. I shall remember this . . ."

Gray Eagle called to Alisha as he pulled lightly on the leash, "Ku-wa, Lese."

Without regard to anyone's eyes who watched, she turned to the scout and hugged him tightly. She tearfully met his gaze and said to him, "Good-bye, Powchutu. I shall love and miss you always. You have been a true friend, the only person who loves and cares for me. I shall never forget your help and kindness to me. I will never feel shame or regret in having you as my friend. Do not let them hurt and use you as they did me. I had you to protect me, but who will there be to protect you?''

Powchutu returned the hug and sadly replied, ''Nor will I ever forget you, Alisha. Do not fear for my safety. I only wish I could have done more for you. Do as he says, for I do not believe he will harm you if you obey and respect him.''

''What does he know of pain and suffering, Powchutu? He is a warrior and my enemy. His heart is stone. His blood flows with hatred. His mind knows only vengeance. I wish he were not so determined to take me back, for I do not know what he wants from me that he has not already taken. But your words are true and wise. I will try very hard to be a good . . . slave.''

Gray Eagle shifted uneasily at the warm exchange of words and embraces between them. The other warriors looked on in surprise to see a white girl who could show friendship to an Indian of any kind. They realized she was not an Indian hater, perhaps not even an enemy.

For the first time, she looked up into Gray Eagle's face above her. She lifted her bound arms up to him. He leaned over and easily lifted her up to his horse before him. He sat her very close to his body and removed the leash. He threw it to the ground with contempt. He lifted her arms and pulled them over his head and shoulders, bringing them to rest around his waist, forcing her to lean against his broad, hard chest. She settled against him as if it were the

most natural thing in the world to do. Powchutu noted the gentleness in his touch and tone
with her. He was relieved—and jealous.

"I will beg you once more, Wanmdi Hota, do
not hurt her again." Powchutu gambled if she
were special to him he might win her some
kindness and time. Time he would need to work
things out for their escape. "I will tell you this.
She was in love with a dream. She saw you as a
man. She refused to face your hatred. She saw
you as she wished you to be, not as you truly are.
The day of the icapsinte, you forced her to see
and know the real man, the warrior, her enemy,
her tormentor and betrayer. You destroyed the
dream world she lived in. She used it to blot out
the reality of her captivity and your hate and
contempt. That day, she knew the truth about
you and her life. If you care for her, do not let her
see and feel these things again. Perhaps it means
nothing to you for her to love you, but her love
will help her to be more respectful and obedient.
Do not destroy it with your cruelty."

Gray Eagle gazed down at the scout for a
moment, then declared, "Do not return to the
fort, my koda! All there will die this very day!
You will go with the tribe of Grota for your help
and courage. Do not fear for her safety for she
will come to no harm. She was, and is, mine. I
will allow no man, white or Indian, to take her
from me, ever again! I feel no hatred in my heart
for her and never have."

Before Powchutu could speak, he turned and
rode away, leaving him standing open-mouthed

in confusion. *Alisha is wrong!* he realized. *He does care for her. She is more than a slave and enemy to him. He did not say he loved her, but he didn't have to. This is good for now. She will be safe with him until I can take her. I will go with Grota's tribe. I, too, do not care for the ways of the white man. I will return to the forest and the way of life I have hungered for. I will live and wait for the right time, then . . .*

Alisha strained to look past Gray Eagle's arm to watch until her friend was out of sight. She had lost the only other friend she had here, once again because of Gray Eagle. She lay her head upon his strong chest as silent, hot tears ran down her cheeks.

Without warning, Gray Eagle reined in his horse and halted on a small, sandy knoll. They turned to face the fort. She raised herself up in confusion and gazed up into his stoical face. Her face followed his line of vision to the fort far off in the distance behind the band of warriors. Spine-tingling foreboding filled the air. There was a great stillness and silence upon the land. Something was about to happen, but what? she wondered.

She was suddenly startled by loud whoops and yells as the warriors swarmed down on the fort. She inhaled quick and sharp, guessing what this meant. Her eyes widened as she watched the scene before her. *They should not have trusted him this time,* her mind screamed. *She had warned them, but they would not listen. He has not come for only me. He has* come for revenge upon them all. That fort is the last stronghold out here and they are going to destroy it. Its destruction could halt the coming of more white men for a long time. They would not dare to come here without the protection it offers.

They could not possibly hold out for long, not if what Powchutu has told me is true. They wouldn't stand a chance against such a large band of warriors with such power and purpose. He has only tricked them into releasing me first. But why? His joke will be short-lived for such a show of power. They will not have to live with the guilt and pain of my sacrifice as he had said. He planned to attack anyway, so why the farce? He could have taken me prisoner during the raid. It is as if he were rescuing me again, sparing only my life just as before. Why?

Alisha dared not think about this idea.

This time, she watched the battle knowing why his people hated the whites so fiercely and deeply. They are no less savage or uncivilized than we are she mused. We are here to take what is theirs, even if we must kill and rob to do it. They are resisting in the only way left open to them. For today, they will punish them and push them back, at least for a while.

She watched the raging battle without resistance. What could she say or do that would change anything? It is too late for those people down there, and maybe for me, too, she thought. Then she rejected this last thought, for surely he would not have forced them to return her only to kill her later. There had to be more to it . . .

Gray Eagle was keenly aware she made no move to beg or resist him and the battle. He was surprised by this. Terror abruptly crossed her face. She struggled to sit up and look toward the fort. She screamed, "Powchutu! He'll be killed! Please, Wanmdi Hota . . . Powchutu, hiya!"

He studied the panic-stricken face and eyes intently. Her concern and fear were only for the scout. She begged for his life and safety only. Surely they were very cruel to you, Cinstinna, or do you care too much for the one called Powchutu?

She pleaded again, "Wanmdi Hota, Pow-chutu, koda, hiya!" With her hands bound, she could not give the sign for death. Not knowing his words to use, she begged in desperation in her own tongue. "Do not kill him! He has suffered enough because of all of you. Spare his life, I beg you. I will do anything, anything you ask if you will do this for me. Powchutu, koda!"

Tears glistened in her bright, green eyes. He gently took her trembling chin in his hand and turned her face in the direction to the left. "Wayaketo! Kokipi sni. Powchutu koda."

She located her friend sitting next to a chief from one of the other tribes. From a glance, she could tell he was not a captive. Although she did not understand why, she was glad. She sighed in relief and returned her head to his chest. He looked down at the shiny-haired head resting on his chest and he, too, sighed in relief at her being

77

back where she belonged.

The results of the battle a foregone conclusion, he headed Chula for home. The fighting was over for him. He had what he had come for. The others could finish the battle and take what plunder and captives they wanted. He held the only treasure he wanted. The shooting, yelling and cries of battle slowly receded as they rode away.

They rode for a long time at a steady gallop. Alisha was snuggled against his body with his free arm around her waist. She became all too aware of his firm, rippling, iron muscles and the controlled strength in them. She could sense the vitality and sensuous virility in him. The feel of those powerful arms around her and the touch of his muscles in his back began to affect her. His male odor filled her senses and his touch was like fire. She trembled at his closeness and her thoughts. She was confused and alarmed by these intense reactions to him and his nearness. She felt as if she had never left his embrace. All the old hunger and need rekindled.

She realized at that moment how much she had missed him and yearned for his touch. She unconsciously snuggled even closer to him and tightened her hold about his narrow waist. Without knowing, she caressed his chest with her soft cheek.

But Gray Eagle was all too aware of the quiverings of her body. He found himself fighting hard to keep a tight rein and control on his own emotions. He was much too sensitive to her closeness, touch and vulnerability. He struggled with the urge to halt Chula and take her right then and there. He told himself this was not the time or place for their first union after so long.

His decision was quickly made more difficult as he shifted his arm and their eyes met and fused. He had expected to see fear and hate written in hers. Instead, he saw something very different. He was surprised and moved by what his eyes and senses took in. He lifted her chin with his finger to gaze fully into her features. He noted the flushed cheeks, the slightly parted lips, the darkened, alluring, emerald eyes. He read the desire which was clearly evident there. He sensed her plea for his lips to take hers. She caught her breath as he leaned over and did just that.

Their lips and bodies met and locked. The contact was overwhelming, even a little frightening. He kissed her deeply and hungrily, and she responded likewise, clinging to him tightly. She clung to him for more as her bound hands caressed his back and shoulders. His lips left hers and moved across her face and eyes, traveling down her ivory throat and back to her waiting lips once more. His hand was lost in the soft fullness of her silky hair as he pressed her head closer to his. The Appaloosa remained perfectly still and quiet, waiting for his master's command.

Her breath caught in her chest. She felt weak and fiery all over. Her skin tingled and cried with longing. The stirrings of passion called to her from deep within, and she yearned to answer them fully and completely. She was oblivious to her surroundings, as was he. All that truly mattered at that moment was that she was with Wanmdi Hota and of what was taking place between them.

As he continued to spread kisses over her features and mouth, she knew how long she had waited for him to hold her like this. It had been much too long a separation. Her emotions cried out for him to love her, to want and need her, like she did him. She told him without words she was where she belonged and where she wanted to be.

Here in his strong, loving, protective embrace was where she wanted to remain forever and a day. Waves upon waves of heated passion washed over her. She begged for his total possession of her. Hotter and deeper the flames of love and desire leaped in both their minds and bodies.

This is pure madness, she thought. The last time I was this close to him, he almost beat me to death. I should hate and fear him greatly. But her heart cried out how much she loved and wanted him instead. Her mind told her he beat her for running away, not because he was trying to torment her. She had defied and disgraced him before his warriors at every turn. He came for me today, she thought. He is showing me right this minute how much he desires me. She pressed even closer to him and returned his kisses more demandingly.

He painfully and reluctantly pulled away from her. He lifted his face to the sky above and inhaled deeply several times. Flustered and perplexed, she looked up at him and thought she comprehended his withdrawal.

"What is wrong, Wanmdi Hota? Why do you pull away from me?" She was abashed and confused. "Do you still hate me and reject my love? Was it too soon to show you how much I love you and have missed you? You did not wish to see and know what is in my heart for you? Did you only want to taunt and shame me? You only wanted to prove your power over me as you did back at your camp and at the fort!"

He continued to gaze up into the heavens, as if he refused to acknowledge her words or presence. "Don't do this to me, please! I need you, Wanmdi Hota. I need you in many ways. You have the power to save me or destroy me. Help me! Help me before it's too late and Alisha is gone forever. Only you have the power to hurt me, for I love and need only you. This love lives within my heart. If you allow your hatred and cruelty to destroy it, then I am doomed. Please do not reject me again."

Tears of betrayal, hurt and physical frustration filled her emerald eyes and slid down her cheeks. The pain in her heart caused her passion to fade. She lowered her head and let the tears drop unchecked to her lap and his arm.

Gray Eagle had not expected Alisha's unbridled, uncontrolled response to him. It had caught him off guard and unprepared to control the situation. His entire body had blazed with hunger for her. It had taken every ounce of willpower he could muster to pull away from her. Her words had torn at his conscience and her needs at his heart.

He no longer feared her feelings for Powchutu or White Arrow. Even if it is only my touch she craves, he thought, at least it is me and my love she wants and no other's.

He lifted her head with his hand and tenderly wiped the tears from her cheeks with his fingers, watching her eyes and the emotions he read there. Do I dare to believe what I see there? he wondered. Does she deceive me, or does my own heart? She responded to me once before like this, then ran away from me the very next sun! Perhaps she is only trying to win my trust so I will drop my guard again. Could it be she seeks to dismiss any punishment she thinks I may give her when we return home? Is she telling me she yields her all this time, that she will no longer resist or defy my commands? She said at the fort she would do all I asked if I spared the life of her friend. Perhaps she fulfills this promise now . . . only time can answer these questions for me.

I see no hate in her eyes, only . . . no! I see what I want to see and hope is true. After the icapsinte, she must surely hate me.

Gray Eagle's logic and intelligence told him no woman could love and accept a man who had done the things to her that he had done to his beloved Lese. In time, with love and tenderness, perhaps he could win her love and acceptance. For now, he would settle for just having her back with him. *I am sure she only fears I will hurt her again, but I will not. I cannot if I am going to have her completely.*

He smiled at her, his eyes caressing her tenderly. He brushed a light kiss upon her lips and rode away. His arms held her securely in his embrace. *He feared she was only clinging to him for mercy and protection. But one day, Cinstinna, it will be in love. You need not fear the bluecoats or wasichus any longer, for they have paid for their hurt and abuse to you.*

Alisha had felt a glimmer of hope at his tender actions after his withdrawal. The smile on his handsome face, the gentle touch of his finger as he wiped away her tears, and the kiss upon her lips afterwards, told her he had not pulled away in hatred or contempt. She relaxed calm and serene against his chest this time. Her spirits were brightened by his gentleness and concern for her feelings.

How my heart longs to reach out to him completely, she mused, *but I dare not, yet. I must wait to see how he views and treats me this time.* Alisha began to vividly recall their last night of lovemaking before she so foolishly ran away from him. She blushed as she remembered its intensity and her wanton behavior. Things might have been changing between them that night. Had he felt betrayed by her escape as Powchutu had alluded? Did he think she had pretended, lied or tried to trick him that night? Perhaps he did not realize she loved him. Perhaps he thought she behaved like a harlot. Since they were unable to speak with each other, all he could judge her by were her actions—actions of defiance, dishonor, and wanton behavior. No wonder he didn't think she was worthy of his acceptance! She tensed and shifted nervously at these thoughts. Could she somehow change his opinion of her?

She gazed up at him, studying his proud features. He felt her eyes on him and looked down at her with a relaxed expression on his face. She timidly met his gaze and smiled up at him. For a brief moment, his eyes softened as did his features. But as quickly and unexpectedly as it came, it vanished. He closed his emotions to her, not wanting her to see or know too much too soon.

She had seen it and let her eyes linger on him for a time. He hides his feelings well, she thought, but I will try to melt that heart of ice. Once more she smiled sweetly at him, then snuggled back into his arms and embrace.

Do you mock me, Cinstinna? In time, we shall see . . . We shall see. They rode on toward the village, both with little rays of hope and lighter spirits, each secretly sure of a truce to come between them, each planning how to force love from the other.

The day had been long and hard, and the double-back riding slow. Dusk was approaching and they still had a long way to go. They neared a narrow stream and halted to rest and water Chula and themselves. Gray Eagle lifted Alisha's arms over his head and let her feet slide to the ground. He threw his leg over Chula's back and jumped down, agile as a cat. He walked Chula over to the stream to allow him to drink. He dropped the reins to the ground and let him graze about in the lush, green grass which grew at the water's edge. He stretched and flexed his muscles.

He turned to find Alisha standing motionless and silent not far away, silhouetted by the setting sun. The far horizon was ablaze with colors of rose, gold, blue and violet. It looked like a giant fire in the sky. The silvery edges of the nearby clouds spoke a message of peace and beauty without a word.

The pinkish-red ball looked close enough to reach out and touch, sending fire throughout the body. Alisha stared beyond the open plains to the mountains and plateaus which loomed dark and forbidding on the distant skyline. Sparse bushes, yuccas, and cacti dotted the semi-barren landscape. There was such a feeling of oneness with this land, with the universe itself. In this vast openness, she felt like a speck on the face of the earth. A breeze ruffled her hair and filled her nostrils with sweet, fragrant odors from the wildflowers and grasslands.

Gray Eagle observed the scene before him with love and pride. He walked up beside her and gazed down into the peaceful face which reflected the colors of the sunset. "It's beautiful, isn't it, Wanmdi Hota?" She spoke soft and low, ignoring the language barrier, saying his name sweet and loving.

He pulled lightly on her elbow and called, "Ku-wa . . ." The mood-bubble burst and faded, as did the dusky light.

They walked over to the stream where he cut the bonds on her hands, and they knelt to drink. She cupped water in her hands and splashed it on her warm face. She observed her image in the clear stream. She softly laughed at the girl in the water wondering what Gray Eagle would say if he knew he had not captured her today, but in truth rescued her. "I am going home so it doesn't matter now."

She did not see Wanmdi Hota's start at the use of the word "home." He stood up and lazily stretched. He realized it was very late. They would camp here. She looked very tired and had been through a lot this day. He decided he would give her this time for peace and rest before they got back to his village to face her new life there.

He casually strolled over to the trees growing at the water's edge and began to pick up small branches and pieces of wood. She looked up and saw what he was doing. She blinked in astonishment. He, a warrior, was gathering wood for a fire! She quickly arose and went to help him. He saw the look on her face and grinned at her expression. She took the wood from him and soon a warm, cheery fire was going. Its flames reflected a relaxing glow over her weary body.

He called to her, "Ku-wa, iyotanka." She came and sat down where he indicated. She stretched her open palms to the fire, seeing him pick up his bow and quiver of arrows. He headed off into the dim light of early evening.

As the fire began to burn brighter and better, she slowly added more wood. She watched the flames lick at the new wood and give it life. A rainbow of colors flickered from the flames.

Wanmdi Hota shortly returned with a plump rabbit, cleaned and gutted. He skewered it and hung it over the fire on a spit. He sat down beside her. They sat silently watching the fire as it cooked the rabbit. The aroma of the roasting meat began to fill the air.

Alisha rose to her feet, timidly avoiding his gaze. "Wonahbe . . ." She walked toward a small clump of bushes and disappeared behind them.

He smiled to himself, amused at her shyness. Afterwards, she knelt by the stream to wash her hands and face. The water was cool and refreshing. How she longed for a leisurely bath!

He met her gaze as she sat down. She could read nothing in his impassive expression. She returned her attention to the fire, but felt his eyes linger on her for a long time.

When the rabbit was crisp and brown, he cut small chunks off and put them on a long stick with a sharpened point. He handed the stick to her and confused her once more with his kind help. The woman always did the work of this nature, but tonight, he did it for her. Did he sense her fatigue or did he seek to prove some point to her? She thanked him as she took the skewer from his grasp.

She ate the succulent, tender meat with relish. In the past few days, she had eaten hardly anything. The taste of the meat was tempting to her hungry stomach. They ate together, which was unheard of in Indian customs. Her enjoyment of the food and his help pleased her. She seemed totally at ease and relaxed, even happy, in his company tonight. It was as though they had always been together like this.

When they finished eating, they went to the water to wash up and drink. She washed her hands and dried them on the bottom of her dress. She stood up, stretched, and yawned languidly. She filled her lungs with fresh, clean air. She felt like a dove just released from its cage, enjoying freedom and flight.

Gray Eagle yearned to go to her and enfold her in his arms and comfort her, but did not just then. He preferred to watch her possessively at the stream. She must make the first move tonight as she did this afternoon, he decided. He wondered if she would after the way he had pushed her away. Had she not seemed to understand by her later actions that he had not done it coldly?

She lifted her head back and gazed up into the heavens, touched by a feeling of tranquility. She watched the moon shine from behind a small cloud in the star-filled sky. She listened to the music of the many night creatures and insects which she had never noticed before. They sounded all around her as if they joined together in a serenade to them. She hugged her arms around herself as the night breeze settled in on the land. She turned to head back to the campfire for warmth.

The combination of hot food and the long, hot day of riding was quickly taking command over Alisha. She returned to the fire and sat down on the blanket Gray Eagle had spread there. She extended her hands and feet to the heat and rubbed her warmed hands up and down her chilled arms. She stared sleepily into the flames. She let it slowly spread its warmth throughout her body and relaxation creep in. She began to nod her head in fatigue, and to feel her eyelids droop heavily.

Alisha searched around, but did not see Gray Eagle anywhere. She lay down upon the blanket. She curled toward the fire on her left side and recalled the first time she had lain beside a fire in the open night air when she was a frightened, innocent prisoner. That seemed eons ago. She closed her eyes and relaxed her entire body and mind.

Gray Eagle had been watching his recaptured Alisha from the darkness not far away, knowing how tired she was. He was giving her the time to relax and settle down before he came to her. After a time, he came over to the blanket and lay down behind her. He molded his body to hers. He had felt her stiffen slightly at his first contact, but then relax against him. He lay his head on the palm of his left hand and pulled her head to lay close upon his folded arm as he nestled in her hair. Gray Eagle placed his right arm around Alisha's slender waist and tucked his fingers under her, pulling her as close to his body as possible. His warmth spread to her and soon she forgot the cool night air. A coyote howl did not even disturb her for her protector was near.

The brave felt the gentleness of her breathing and her soft lips lightly touching his arm. They remained this way for a short time, each becoming more and more cognizant of the other's nearness. He caressed her skin at her side, then slid his hand up to her breast and gently cupped it. He began to tenderly caress and fondle it through her dress. He shifted his left arm so his hand could touch and stroke her hair.

Alisha waited with baited breath, eager to discover his intentions, knowing this was what she had yearned for all day. His touch kindled flames within her body, intoxicating her senses. Gray Eagle leaned forward and nibbled at her ear, sending tingles of delight over her. Then his lips traveled down her throat and up her cheek. She waited tensely for him to continue. All her nerves and senses were awakened and feverish. And he did continue . . .

Alisha relaxed and let her emotions run free, not wanting to restrain herself one bit. Her mind reeled and she felt a tightening in the pit of her stomach. Her body was now radiating more heat than the flames before her. She craved his touch, his kiss and his love. It was too late to stop the tides of unsated love and desire, even if she had wanted to—and of course, she did not.

Her mind ordered her to lie passively in his embrace, but her body would not be stayed. She pressed closer to him and felt the hard stirrings of his manhood against her buttocks. He put his hand to her shoulder and rolled her to her back. Their eyes met and instantly locked in mutual desire and longing before his lips claimed hers in a passionate, hungry kiss. They kissed and kissed, each kiss becoming hungrier. They touched and caressed with ever-growing, ever-mounting desire.

Soon, Gray Eagle had them both undressed and locked in a fierce embrace. He spread fiery kisses and caresses over her face, neck and breasts. She tossed from side to side in unfulfilled yearning. Alisha moaned in need of him, craving more and more of him. He teased and tantalized her until she felt she would surely go mad with hunger. She was clinging to him breathlessly, begging for him to come to her and possess her.

Gray Eagle entered Alisha and she thrust upward to meet his ardor halfway. Her arms encircled his neck. Her hands moved up and down his sinewy back and shoulders as she pulled him closer to her. She returned each caress, kiss and thrust he gave. She was oblivious to her surroundings. Forgotten were the weeks of pain and hurt, of rejection and betrayal.

His love filled all the recesses of her mind and body. Nothing existed but Gray Eagle and her love for him. She gave herself to him with total abandonment, completely without shame. She surrendered all to him and his touch, withholding no part of herself mentally or physically. All reason had fled. With a great releasing burst, she clung to him, calling his name over and over as she dissolved into the ecstasy of the culmination of love.

For a long time afterwards, they lay quietly entwined until their passion cooled and their ragged breathing slowed to normal. For once, Alisha did not try to defend her response to him. She knew she had given of herself willingly, and completely because she loved and wanted him.

Later, Gray Eagle raised his head and met her steady, softened gaze. She stared into the depths of his ebony eyes and whispered, "I know you cannot understand these words or the reasons behind them, Wanmdi Hota, but I love you. I'm not sure how it happened or why. All I know is I do love you with all my heart and soul. I have loved you since the first day I saw you so long ago. I pray you will someday realize it does not matter to me that we are different. I hope in time you will come to see me as Alisha, not your white slave. We could find happiness and love together, if you would only allow it."

This was the warrior's greatest test of stoical facial expression. He struggled hard to keep his face blank and vacant, to resist letting her know he understood every word she had just said. Something warned him not to speak of his love yet. He wondered, could she be speaking from her passion or loneliness? I dare not give myself away until I am sure of her and her love. How can she love me after what I have done to her?

They replaced their garments and resumed their first position and slept. Alisha did not move all night, except to snuggle closer to him for warmth. Gray Eagle slept better than he had in many weeks, knowing both his emptiness and her terrible ordeal were ended.

Gray Eagle awoke with the first light of dawn. He was lying on his back with Alisha sleeping securely in his protective embrace. Her head rested on his shoulder with her long hair spilling over to the ground. She was sleeping so peacefully he made no moves that might awaken her. She needed this rest to restore her fatigued spirits and body.

Chula's neighing reached her ears and roused her. Alisha's eyelids fluttered and opened dreamily. They made instant contact with Gray Eagle's. He was propped up on one elbow, staring down at her as he waited and watched for her first look. Would she resist him and his touch as she realized she was again a captive? His taut muscles relaxed and his mind rejoiced as she smiled up into his gaze. Her heart and mind were both glad last night was a reality and not a dream.

Gray Eagle got to his feet and flexed his tall,

lithe frame. Alisha devoured his lean body with her eyes, blushing at the way her body responded to the sight of him. She lowered her lids and began to comb her tangled hair with her fingers. She managed to loosely braid it and secured the ends with the ikans Gray Eagle handed her. Then she walked over to the stream and splashed cool water on her face.

Alisha saw a girl in the water and studied her mirrored image. She marveled at the changes she read there. Her eyes and face reflected all that had happened last night and her new happiness. There was a sparkle which had not been there yesterday, and she knew why. Even if she had behaved wantonly, she did not care, knowing she could not help the events which had taken place. When he holds me and kisses me like that, he commands my will and body, she thought. I will always respond to him and his touch. But I must learn to curb these emotions when the time and place are not right to show them. And, until he also feels that way . . .

The face of Gray Eagle appeared in the water beside hers. His reflection was as clear as his reality. His eyes met hers and held hers captive. She glowed with the intensity of desire which she read there. Her breathing quickened and her eyes darkened, answering his with a will of their own.

Gray Eagle leaned over and pulled Alisha to her feet to face him. She met his smoldering, black eyes. She raised her hand to lovingly touch his cheek and to run her finger over his sensuous mouth. Her hand slid around his neck of its own will and pulled his head down to hers. Her lips sealed his in a hungry kiss as she pressed her slender body to his. He willingly came to her and returned the fiery kiss with a heat of his own. Both her arms then encircled his strong back and she clung to him. Gray Eagle cupped her face and he spread hot kisses over her face. His strong arms slid down her back to her tiny waist and pulled her up to his tall frame. His kiss deepened and his ardor blazed. He held her so tightly she could hardly move or breathe.

All thoughts of leaving were quickly forgotten as they sank to the cool grass. He took her with a passion which rivaled the gods', and she returned it with just as much feeling. He fanned the flames of love until they burned out of control . . .

When the fires had been appeased and began to die down, Alisha relaxed in his embrace. Never had she thought love and passion could be like this. They lay there for a time, savoring their love.

He lifted his head and stared curiously into her face, and she into his. His demure Lese had initiated this time of lovemaking! He grinned as he realized she had taken him for a change, for he had been under her spell. She would have ravished him if he had not responded. Never had a woman done this to him, nor made him feel this way. She had wanted him and she had taken him!

Alisha wondered what her brave thought about what she had done. She even asked herself how she could have actually seduced him like that. She thought, I have just as much right to take him when I need him as he has to do the same to me! She saw his knowing grin and guessed its meaning. She, too, grinned back at him.

She laughingly stated, "You are just as much mine now as I am yours. I will fight in any way I can to win not only your passion, but your love as well. I shall melt your heart of snow with the heat of my love and our passion." Alisha would never have dared to say such things if she had known he understood her, even if they were true.

Gray Eagle stood up and pulled his green-eyed beauty to her feet. They were both naked and glistening with the dew of love. He took her small hand in his large one and led her to the water. They bathed and dressed, using his blanket to dry. They walked to his waiting horse. He agilely mounted Chula's tall back easily, then leaned over and lifted Alisha before him. He brushed a light kiss upon her lips. He took her hands and entwined them in Chula's mane, indicating to her to hold on. She grasped the silky mane and they rode off with her leaning back against his broad, smooth chest.

She watched the beautiful scenery slip by as she reminisced on the wonderful change in her life since yesterday. The wind from the west blew blissfully into her face and through her hair, pulling strands from its bindings.

The warm sunlight caressed the lovers from behind. The steady gait of their proud horse gently rocked her into an exhilarating feeling of freedom and happiness. The wind whipped at the bottom of her dress and tore it free from where she had tucked it between her legs. The handsome brave reined in Chula and, lifting Alisha like a feather, pulled her dress under her and retucked it.

She laughed gaily and commented, "I seem to be a constant problem for you, don't I?" Luckily, she did not see Gray Eagle's grin and unconscious nod of agreement.

Her bare feet dangled at Chula's sides. She had discarded the ill-fitting shoes from the fort by the stream. As Chula lengthened his stride, she felt the strength in his sinewy forelegs. The horse matched his master well.

As they rode on, Gray Eagle became more and more conscious of the softness and warmth of Alisha's body. He wondered, how was it possible to crave a woman again so soon after last taking her? He realized it would be all too easy to halt his horse at that minute and make love to her. They had already taken too long to make the return trip to his camp. The others might become worried, he joked lightly to himself. He was at the mercy of a fragile, white enemy! All she had to do was hint at stopping and making love once more, and he would have done so without a second thought to time. He was taking twice as long to return home as he should have, but he had Alisha with him and time did not matter with her so near. He could imagine the celebrating going on at the Oglala camp because of the white men's defeat. Perhaps it was for the best if she missed most of it. Alisha didn't need to be reminded this soon they were still enemies. He inwardly flinched at this thought and its implication, and set his mind on reaching his home quickly.

Shortly before sunset, they approached his village. He slowed Chula to a trot and entered the circles of teepees amidst the stares and curious looks of many. He felt Alisha's body stiffen against his. She pressed closer to him and breathed in quick, short rasps. He felt the quivering in her arms and the tremor run through her body. She was as cold as the snows in the high mountains in the winter.

In a flash, Alisha recalled all that had taken place here, which had been pushed to the back of her mind during her stay at the fort and her reunion with Gray Eagle. She nervously looked around, sudden panic filling her. Had anything really changed for her just because of a day's loving with the brave? What would he do with her here? she fearfully wondered. Would things return to their old pattern? Would he present a different face before his people than he had done to her in secret? Alisha could already note the change in his arrogant carriage. She fearfully realized he was becoming the fierce warrior and leader right before her very eyes. Her lover was gone and her enemy had returned . . .

Terrified of this change she felt in him, she pleaded in a trembling voice, "Please don't turn away from me again, Wanmdi Hota. I could not bear to lose you ever again."

As his answer, he placed a warm, strong hand over her cold, trembling ones and squeezed tightly, then left them there covering hers.

The raiding party had apparently ridden all the way home with few stops. Alisha scanned the village for signs of prisoners, sighing in relief when she saw none. Maybe they were all dead or captives of other tribes. At least, she would not have to witness any tortures or deaths.

She would not know her assumption was correct. The few whites still alive were taken to the Santee and Shosshoni camps.

Chula weaved his way through the teepees and people to the corral near the stream. There were many young Oglala boys taking care of the weary horses. The brave looked around for Jutah to take the horse to be rubbed down, watered and fed.

Jutah came running forward at the sight of his favorite warrior returning home at last. He looked up at the pale, frightened girl clinging so tightly to Gray Eagle and grinned. The chief's son brought her back home where she belonged. Even though he refused to acknowledge her presence, he was pleased to see her back again. She was different from the other ska winyans. She did not deserve to die or be captured by some other tribe. She had offered her friendship many times before, but he had always rebuffed her because of his embarrassment and pride. This time it would be different. What did he care about the taunts from the other boys? She was too good and gentle to be treated badly.

Hero worship and awe shone clearly in the face of the young boy. Gray Eagle laughed, leaned down and tugged Jutah's braids in affectionate teasing. The boy took the reins of the horse while blurting his comments about Gray Eagle's bluff at the fort yesterday.

"Such daring and bravery!" he shouted. "They cowered like rabbits beneath the claws of the great warrior Wanmdi Hota!" He beamed his pride and happiness.

Before they could dismount, White Arrow walked up quietly, glancing over Alisha for any sign of new injuries. He had hoped their delay last night in returning had not meant she had fought him or tried to flee again. He sensed the change in mood of his closest friend and companion. He gazed from Alisha to his friend and back to her. There was a strange aura about them—subtle, but clearly evident. His koda was in high spirits and very relaxed. He noted the way he possessively held his hand over hers and how his eyes held a new light. Her face definitely showed fear, but not of him; not the way she was snuggling so close to his chest. There was anything but hate or sadness in those emerald eyes. He could not quite put his finger on the change, and knew there was a mystery here to be solved.

Alisha looked down. White Arrow met her demure, wary gaze and smiled. She relaxed her grip a little and returned his smile. He reached up and placed his strong hands firmly on her slender waist. She placed her hands on White Arrow's broad shoulders, as he handed her down lightly to the ground before him.

White Arrow was aware of her loveliness and was glad to gaze upon it again. How his eyes had hungered for the sight of her, his ears for the sound of her musical laughter, and his spirit for her companionship! His heart thumped hard at her nearness.

Gray Eagle noted the amity and renewed trust which passed between them. He threw his long, sinewy leg over Chula's back and eased to the ground. Alisha dropped her hands from White Arrow's shoulders and turned to face Gray Eagle.

Jutah led Chula away to care for him. He would rub him down in the cool water of the stream and exercise his heated muscles. Later, he would stake him near Gray Eagle's teepee.

White Arrow was the first to speak and break the silence. He remarked, "You both look very tired, hot and hungry, my kodas." He teased, ". . . or had you forgotten you have not eaten and rested?"

Gray Eagle surprisingly threw back his head and laughed loudly. He retorted with, "Who would think of food or rest with hunwi at your side?"

They both laughed in close comradeship. It touched Alisha's heart to see such total friendship and devotion.

She intently watched the handsome face of Gray Eagle, relaxed in gay merriment, and listened to the deep, rippling laughter of his husky voice. Its rich baritone sent tingles throughout her body. Her eyes saw only him, and her senses were aware only of his nearness. She had not seen him in this strange, wonderful mood and she savored it.

White Arrow observed the way she watched Gray Eagle and commented, "She has had a change of heart since we last saw her, Wanmdi Hota. She sees and hears only you. She caresses and holds you with her eyes."

Gray Eagle shifted his flaming, jet eyes to Alisha. She flushed at the warm sensations which coursed through her body. His hand went out to caress her rosy cheek tenderly, then slid down her shoulder, back and waist. He pulled her to his side as he continued his talk with White Arrow. Alisha lowered her gaze to the ground, her emotions in fiery turmoil at his behavior and close proximity.

He moved his hand back up to her shoulder and subconsciously toyed with a lock of her auburn hair, her ear, and stroked her cheek lightly with his fingertips. He continued his talk on and on as she began to fidget restlessly. What he was doing had a very unsettling, stirring effect on her senses.

White Arrow asked, "Could it be, my koda,

you do not realize the effect you are having on her with your caresses?"

Gray Eagle's chest rumbled with zest and pleasure at his comment. "Yes, my koda, I do. I can feel her trembling and know it is not from fear. She breathes the air of desire and her eyes lower to hide these feelings from us. I have come to know her well these past two days . . .

"Later, I will tell you of the cruelty she faced in the fort at the hands of the wasichus. If they were not dead, I would return and kill each one now." His tone sounded with coldness and violent fury. "The scout Powchutu befriended her and saved her from many hurts. That is why I granted him his life and freedom. Also, he showed great courage in the face of danger. Such a life should not be taken in haste." He did not tell White Arrow that Alisha had begged for the scout's life.

Alisha repeated his name in askance, "Pow-chutu?" He saw the fear and concern in her expression at his words and tones. Again, she asked, looking at him with large, curious eyes, "Powchutu?"

He touched her lips softly with his finger and replied, "Powchutu koda . . ." She searched his face for any hidden meaning, then flashed him a happy smile, hugging him fiercely. She quickly pulled back and blushed at her bold display of feelings for him.

White Arrow gibed him, "She seems much concerned about this scout. I would be careful of such feelings in my woman. If he also feels such things, he might sneak here some dark night and steal her from your teepee!"

Gray Eagle ignored his friend's baited remark and replied, "You will understand her worries when I have told you all. Now, we must go to the . . ."

A harsh, chilling voice cut into his sentence, "I see you have found your ska kaskapi. You dare to bring her back here to our camp and flaunt her before me again! No doubt she serves your many needs well!" Chela's sultry voice caused Alisha to tense and lean closer to Gray Eagle. The rancor and tone of her voice warned Alisha of the girl's fury and hate. She lifted her helpless, panic-filled eyes and ashen face to Gray Eagle, but it was noticed only by White Arrow.

Gray Eagle and Chela's eyes met and locked in furious challenge. His eyes narrowed and glinted dangerously at the girl who dared to confront him in this manner with such a disrespectful tone. Such things were not done in his tribe.

But Chela did not behave as the Indian woman was raised to act. She did not behave subserviently to the male. She would fare well in the wasichu society with that fiery tongue and nature. What she was doing now was unthinkable and disgraceful to both of them. He was a great warrior and future chief, and she was a mere woman! The time was near for her to learn and accept her place, once and for all.

She meant nothing to Gray Eagle, but she was

the winyan he was supposed to join soon. The thought of having this viper in his teepee angered and repulsed him. He preferred the touch and presence of the white girl at his side, even if she was supposed to be his enemy. It rankled him to know he must take this bold, brazen girl to mate. How could he bring himself to touch her, kiss her or even pretend he wanted her? Lese was all he needed in a woman. Why couldn't she have been Oglala? he raged inwardly.

The gleam in his dark, furious eyes should have warned Chela to hush, but she was too full of rage and jealousy to comprehend the full magnitude of it. Alisha felt the muscles in his back stiffen and grow taut. His hand on her shoulder had stilled, then clenched into a hard fist. She watched the muscle in his jawline tighten and quiver in suppressed fury. She cringed at the coldness in his stygian eyes.

Alisha could hardly believe the hate and hardness she read there and the warning tone of his deep voice. If he could behave like this to his future wife, how much more could he do or feel for her, a mere slave and captive, his enemy? Her face paled visibly. Fear and mistrust filled her emerald eyes. White Arrow watched her closely as she stiffened and pushed away from Gray Eagle, gazing in disbelief at her lover's face. Gray Eagle was too full of wrath to note Alisha's withdrawal.

She backed away, studying the two people who were locked in cold combat before her.

Alisha thought, Chela is angry because he has brought me back again. If Powchutu is correct, they will marry soon. How will I ever bear it? How can I let her take him from me, or let him go from our mat to hers? Or will we still be sharing a mat then? Could he have other plans for me this time? If only I knew what they were saying.

He is definitely angry with her, and she with him. He is probably only mad because she speaks and acts so disrespectful to him. Why does he allow her to do this? If that were me, he would flay me to within an inch of my life. Could it be I see wrong? Could he really be in love with her and only seeks to make her jealous or to tame her?

Alisha's eyes filled with anguish and her chin trembled. Tears glittered in her grassy eyes as she concluded, it is Chela he loves and will marry. I am just a tool to vex her with. He wishes to show his power over her and bring down that haughty, bold spirit. He wishes to tame her as he did me . . .

Her eyes left the battle scene and darted about until they met White Arrow's. Their eyes fused and spoke without words. He saw she needed to leave this warring ground. He saw her expression of doubt and fear.

He spoke to Gray Eagle, "I will take her to your teepee while you settle this matter with Chela."

Gray Eagle nodded assent, his eyes never leaving Chela's face. White Arrow did not dare mention Alisha's worry and fear, not for Chela's triumph. He would tell him later of her look of dread.

White Arrow gave Alisha a reassuring smile and gently pulled her by the elbow to lead her away. She cast frightened eyes at Gray Eagle, but he did not even notice her. He was arguing hotly with Chela. He grabbed Chela by her shoulders and shook her fiercely as he spat words of warning out between his clenched teeth. Chela was boldly staring into his ebony eyes and yelling back at him. For once, there was no pleading, sultry tone to her voice, only one filled with rage and rancor.

Alisha looked at White Arrow in confusion, but he motioned for her to come with him. "Hiya, Lese. Kokipi sni. Ku-wa."

She knew the few words he said and the soft tone he spoke them in. Bewilderment crossed her face. He smiled broadly and repeated his words gently.

"Ku-wa. Ya Wanmdi Hota teepee." She realized he was getting her away from the trouble at hand, and she smiled. She followed him down the path toward Gray Eagle's teepee.

About halfway to Gray Eagle's teepee, Matu stepped from behind another teepee and blocked their path. She stared at Alisha for a long time, sending chills down her spine. Matu had not gone to Black Cloud with her news. She waited to see for herself if the girl was unharmed and returned.

At her cold, close scrutiny, Alisha felt a

foreboding of coming evil, danger, or even death. She shuddered involuntarily as if she felt someone walk upon her grave. All color seemed to drain from her face at this chilling, strange premonition. She somehow knew the old woman meant to ensnare her in misfortune. But how and why, she could not guess.

White Arrow tensed at the cold aura surrounding the two women. He asked Matu what she wanted and why she stared at Alisha that way. Matu quickly veiled her eyes and answered innocently. She told him she had taken care of the girl for a long time and she only wished to see if she had been returned unharmed. He knew she lied, but could not fathom why, nor did he understand the look which had passed between them.

Matu thought, I will now go to Mahpiya Sapa. He is camped not far from here. He can be here by morning. In a few moons, I will be returned home with my people. I must thank the Great Spirit for protecting and returning the girl to me. Matu made her plans as she walked away from White Arrow and Alisha. She scoffed to herself, neither you, nor Wanmdi Hota will have her or save her. Matu has big plans for her to buy my way home to my beloved Si-ha Sapa. Wanmdi Hota will join with Chela, as it should be . . .

White Arrow lifted the flap of Gray Eagle's teepee and led Alisha inside. She glanced around the interior of the teepee where she had lost her childish notions about love and had

108

become a woman. Her eyes strayed to the buffalo mat and her face burned with the knowledge of what had happened there.

White Arrow lightly touched her arm and she turned to answer his call. He smiled down into her eyes tenderly and kissed her on the forehead, much to her surprise. He grinned again and spoke one word, "Koda?"

She returned his smile and replied, "Koda . . ." He turned and left.

Alisha aimlessly paced the teepee area, recalling so much of what had taken place there in that short time. This place held many good, but many sad, painful, memories for her. There were things she longed to forget and others she savored the thought of reliving.

Her eyes caught sight of an object hanging on the center pole. She lifted it off the peg and carefully examined it. It was a necklace made of the rattler rings. Between each ring, there were many small white beads. In the center, a delicate, exquisitely-carved, white eagle was suspended from a row of aqua and white beads. She turned it over and over in her hand, fingering the fragile handiwork.

She thought of the beauty of the many forms of jewelry and adornments she had seen the Indians wear. Her father had imported and shown her many gems and stones, but none as beautiful and rare as the desert-barite-rose which Chela wore. It was a stone in the shape and color of a fragile, pink rose.

Alisha felt eyes upon her back and turned to

see Gray Eagle standing just inside the opening. He relaxed his hand and allowed the flap to lower for privacy. He came to her. She remained motionless and tense as she returned his stare. He noted the wariness in her expression and manner. White Arrow had told him of her reaction during the confrontation between him and Chela. She was uneasy in his presence. He knew his friend had sized the situation right.

He came to stand before her and put his hand out for the necklace she held. She passed it to him and he studied it for a moment, pleased with the way it had turned out. To her utter surprise, he placed it over her head and around her neck. He let the little eagle rest slightly above the swell of her breasts. She looked at it in confusion and touched it with her fingers.

In a rich, mellow voice, he said, "Lese wanapin," as he touched the necklace, then her shoulder. There was an umistakably victorious look in his eyes.

She stared at the wanapin and lovingly traced its delicate lines and noted its beauty. She lifted her luminous, sparkling eyes to him and timidly asked, "For me? Is it truly for me?" She smiled at him in stunned silence, then whispered softly as tears of joy filled her eyes, "I shall love and treasure it always. It is the most beautiful and precious gift I've ever received."

Their eyes met and fused with the heat of passion and love. Gone from their hearts was the scene with Chela and the fears and doubts it

110

had stirred. He opened his arms to her and she willingly entered them and clung to him. He enfolded her in his embrace and kissed her hungrily.

He had been pleased by her acceptance of his wanapin and the mood it had generated. He had wanted to tell her it was to replace the one he so foolishly and carelessly destroyed, but let the gift and his behavior speak for him. An old man, gifted in the art of carving, had made the eagle for him and his wife had strung the beads and finished the necklace. It had been completed while he had been gone and had been left in his teepee for him to see when he returned.

Gray Eagle recalled the significance he had placed on the objects he had asked to be placed on the wanapin. The rings of the rattler were thought to ward off evil spirits, but he hoped they would remind her of the futility and danger of escape. He now realized such a reminder would not be necessary for she would never wish to flee from his arms again. There would be no reason to flee and no place to flee to, but many reasons to stay here with him. She had shown him she was totally committed to him and there was no reason now to mistrust her.

The eagle was to denote his ownership of the wanapin. He was pleased by the way she looked at the wanapin and him, but particularly by the way she was responding to him. He confidently thought, all wasichus have been purged from our lands. It is time for peace and love between us, Cinstinna.

A female voice called to him from outside. Gray Eagle answered it and a girl entered, carrying food and water. He had sent an order for Matu to bring them food and water earlier. He asked the girl where she was and why she had not come. The young girl lowered her eyes, flushing at the glare of Wanmdi Hota, and replied the old woman could not come and had sent her to bring it to him. He nodded acceptance of her explanation, but mentally noted he should check on this matter later.

The young girl placed the food by the campfire and left, after stealing another look at the tall, handsome warrior embracing the ska winyan. The look did not go unnoticed by Alisha who glared at the girl's back. As she returned her gaze to his, he was grinning mockingly at her expression of jealousy. She pinkened at first, then pouted prettily at his taunt. She withdrew from his arms and went to sit by the cold campfire.

She caressed the eagle once more, then called for him to come. "Ku-wa, Wanmdi Hota. Mni, woyeta. Iyotanka."

He suppressed a laugh at the pert, wifely tone in her voice, her confidence apparently growing in her place with him. He did just as she said and was served his food. She sat watching him as he began to eat, smiling serenely and toying with the little white eagle. He studied her for a moment, knowing of her great hunger and thirst. She sat as politely and patiently as any Indian winyan would have. He furtively glanced at the closed flap, thinking . . .

He suddenly put his food into her hands, then helped himself to more. She stared incredulously at him with wide eyes. This was never done! His actions on the trail when they had been alone were one thing, but here . . . what if someone came in? What would they say or do? A white winyan eating with a warrior, Wanmdi Hota at that! His behavior bewildered and even scared her.

Slowly she spoke, "Hiya! Lese hiya wota Wanmdi Hota!" She was the perfect picture of shock and confusion. He studied her expression and words with amusement and pleasure, but laughed.

"Wota, Lese." The words and laughter told her he was only relaxing the rules of etiquette this one time because of her hunger and their lack of food today. She had seen him look at the closed flap before, and understood why now. He was not going to make her wait for him to finish.

She smiled sweetly, accepting the food and jested, "Yes, master!"

After he had drank, he handed her the wozuha and she began to drink thirstily. She quickly halted and lowered the skin to look at him in doubt. He saw her confusion and he drank from the skin again to show her it was all right.

"Wanhu mni . . ." She accepted the skin and

113

drank more slowly from it this time. It had a sweet, fruity taste like the bullberries. When they had both had their fill of juice and food, she cleared the remains of the meal and left them by the fireplace.

He pointed to one of her Indian dresses which was hanging on a side peg and said, "Winyan heyake, cehnake . . . Ku-wa. Ihduzazapi . . ."

She promptly gathered the items needed for bathing and dressing and followed him outside. How great this bath would feel after the long, hot, dusty ride! He didn't have to ask her twice about it.

They casually and happily walked along to the stream in the dusky light. It was marvelous to feel so light-hearted and happy. Alisha strolled along behind him. Her eyes adjusted to the fading light and she studied him as he walked ahead of her. He did not seem so cold, forbidding or intimidating now. She hopefully wondered if he had finally accepted her being there. Was he even coming to like her a little?

His behavior to me is anything but cold and brutal! she mused. I hope things between us will be different. Perhaps he will not hurt me again. When the time comes, I will somehow deal with Chela's prior claim on him. Until then, things could not be working out better.

When they reached the bank of the stream, she plopped down on the ground to dangle her tired, hot feet in the cool water. She heard a loud splash and looked to see her brave glide into the water in the pool. She sat still for a time, savoring the quiet and peace here. Later, she undressed and slipped gracefully into the murmuring water.

It felt exhilarating to her dusty body. She scrubbed her skin until it glowed and warmed in the night air. She washed her hair and dipped up and down rinsing it. She had never had a more refreshing, reviving bath.

Gray Eagle slipped up behind her as she turned to place her soap and cloth on the bank. The amber moonlight bathed her scarred and scabbed back in its light. The marks of his lashing slapped him hard in the face. He sharply inhaled. How could I have done this to you, Cinstinna? he chastised himself.

Hearing his gasp, she quickly turned to ask what was amiss. The fury in his face and eyes terrified her. She panicked at this sudden reversal in moods as fear flooded her features. What had she done? Why did he look at her that way?

Coming to himself, he noted her expression and reached out a hand toward her, saying, "Ku-wa!" just a little too harshly. He tried to pull her to him, but she backed away from his touch. He was disturbed to see how much she still mistrusted and feared him. He called softly to her, "Ku-wa, Lese. Kokipa ikopa."

Hearing his softened tone, she wavered in doubt. She recalled in grim detail the last time he had called to her like this and held out his hand to her. She remained rigid in the waist-high water, watching him and his eyes for a clue to his intentions.

He tenderly stretched out his hand and called to her once more. She gazed at the outstretched hand like it was a snake, then met his eyes. He realized from the look on her face what she was thinking about. He moved closer to her, taking the first step. "Ku-wa, Cinstinna . . ." he whispered in a husky, rich tone.

Knowing the meaning of "Cinstinna" and the tone he said it in, she extended her small, trembling hand to him. He took it firmly in his grasp and pulled her into his arms. He held her tightly for a long time, then began to cover her face and mouth with searing kisses. He whispered her name over and over between his kisses. She accepted his embrace and hot kisses and returned them with an ardor of her own. Alisha clung to him now, comprehending he meant her no harm.

"Wanmdi Hota, I am so confused. I do not know what to think or believe anymore. It is so frightening not to know where I stand with you. Your changing moods bring terror and alarm to my heart. Hold me . . . never let me go ever again . . ."

At these words, he picked her up and lay her down upon the grassy bank on her back. He lay half on her, kissing and caressing her until she thought she would scream if he did not come to her and take her immediately.

116

They were soon completely absorbed in their lovemaking, fused together like white hot iron in the forge. Colored lights and music filled her eyes and ears as she climbed the ladder of passion. Then, everything inside her seemed to explode and she claimed all his love with a wild, fierce emotion. He held her for a time afterwards and never wanted to free her from his arms. But when he felt her shiver from the night air, he got to his feet and returned to the stream to rinse off. She sat up, regaining her senses, then joined him. They dried off on the blanket and dressed. They retrieved their belongings and went back to camp.

Later in his teepee, Alisha sat by a warm fire, alone, drying her hair. After she brushed her hair with the porcupine brush Gray Eagle had given her long ago, she braided it. She finished her grooming, put her things away, and lay down.

Her warrior returned just as she reclined. He had gone to a meeting in the ceremonial lodge for a short time to hear the report of all that had happened after he left the fort. He came to lie beside her, pulling her possessively into his arms. She snuggled there, laying her head upon his shoulder. She placed her arm across his chest and pressed closer to his side and slept.

He lay quietly, but unable to sleep just yet. He noted Alisha's steady, even breathing which told him she was asleep. He kissed her forehead and thought, sleep peaceful, Cinstinna, for you are back where you belong. He lay thinking of all which had taken place in his life since he had first seen her. He recalled the events in vivid detail which had passed between them. After so much hurt and shame, here she was at his side, willing and happy. He reflected upon her words and actions of the past two days and rejoiced at them and their meaning. How very much his heart had changed with the flight of this white bird of love and joy into his lonely existence!

He had not even known he was lonely and in need of a love like hers until he had almost lost her. Tonight, she lay with him protected under his wing just as the little bird in his vision. All had happened as the Great Spirit had shown him. The eagle had rescued the little white bird and she had flown safely home to live with him forever in happiness. They had easily destroyed the bluebirds of the cavalry.

But the Great Spirit had not shown him the greater bird of prey who would come to take his white bird, leaving him powerless, sad and alone. Was it not written somewhere, "Clouds rain on birds, even the mighty eagles"? Is it not also true the fierce, daring, brave bear can destroy the eagle's nest, even kill the eagle if he can capture him with his powerful limbs armed with razor-sharp claws?

"Great Spirit!" cried Hunwi, "why do you not warn him?"

The Great Spirit smiled and replied, "It will be for Wanmdi Hota's own good if the little bird is taken from his life."

Hunwi sadly asked, "But can he live without

the light of her love?"

Wakantanka spoke again, "We shall soon see who is the mightier—the little white bird, or the great eagle."

Alisha would recall this dream for a long time and wonder at its meaning . . .

Chapter Three

Gray Eagle's hunter instincts were dulled that night by his happiness and his belief that all was well now. His keen ears had not heard the quiet intrusion of an enemy, nor had his sixth sense warned him of the approaching danger. His usually alert mind had other thoughts in it tonight. Had his watchful eyes not opened in sleeplessness, he would be mourning the loss of his one true love.

A flash of light had caught his eye and he lunged upward to stop the hand of Chela before it drove the knife into Alisha's back. He gave a loud cry of rage, threw her roughly to the ground and pinned her down. She struggled with him, fighting, scratching, biting and cursing her thwarted attempt to kill her rival.

The abrupt movement of his body and the loud noises of scuffling and shouting awakened Alisha from her deep slumber. In the dim moonlight, she could see Gray Eagle straddling Chela, who was fighting him like a tiger and screaming in Oglala like a madwoman.

He seized Chela's wrists and locked them together with one of his hands above her head. With his other hand, he grabbed her head and forced her to look at him as he issued threats to her. Alisha touched his bare shoulder and frantically asked what was happening. He ignored her in his wrath. He allowed his full weight to crush Chela's chest and stomach. She gasped to breathe and struggled to free herself.

Without warning, the torchlight suddenly flooded their teepee as White Arrow and Little Beaver came running in. They immediately understood what had happened. They spoke with Gray Eagle rapidly. They informed him they had heard the commotion and thought an enemy had sneaked into camp and was attacking him in his sleep. They had been astounded to see who the culprit was.

Alisha had been just as shocked to see Chela in their teepee at night. She was far more disturbed when the torchlight revealed the whole story. Her eyes widened in alarm as they viewed the long knife that had been clutched tightly in Chela's grip. Understanding filled Alisha's brain as she took in the scene and read the intense hatred in the girl's face. Her mind reeled at the impact of this discovery. Someone here hated her enough to want to see her dead! Chela was holding her responsible for Gray Eagle's desire of a white girl.

Alisha gazed past Gray Eagle to the girl and asked, "You hate me this much, Chela? Do the others? Do they wish me dead rather than see me as his kaskapi?" But of course, Chela did not understand her questions. She only knew the white girl was talking to her.

Alisha turned her back on the scene as her

tormentor screamed, "Kaskapi! Wayakayuha! Ista ska! Sunka ska! Witkowin! Ska witkowin!"

Alisha pressed her hands tightly to her ears to shut out the curses and insults Chela threw at her. She feared things would never work out for her here. How could she ever fit in or belong in the Oglala camp with Gray Eagle, even if she did love him? Sometimes love and desire were not enough to block out the hatred and pain. They were from two separate worlds with a gap too wide to be spanned with only love and passion. There had to be more to life and love! Alisha knew she would never be accepted here. She had been foolish to believe things could change so drastically in only a few weeks.

She cried out in anguish, but no one heard her for they had already left the teepee. She had not realized she was now alone until she opened her tightly closed eyes to find herself in total darkness.

She quickly ran outside and looked about. Her gaze found them dragging the screaming, fighting girl to the stake in the center of camp. The chaos alerted many others who left their teepees to come forward to see what was going on.

Gray Eagle bound Chela to the post as White Arrow was giving the details to the others who had gathered around them. He informed them of how she had tried to kill him and his white captive while they slept. She had dared to interfere in the life and way of a warrior and leader, and had dared to enter his teepee and strike out at him in revenge, hate and jealousy.

Chela shrieked at the group, "Hiya, Wanmdi Hota! Never you! Only the ska wincinyanna who has bewitched you and turned your heart from me, your chosen mate. You have let a ska kaskapi, a witkowin, take my place in your teepee! She is the enemy! She must die to free you of this evil spell she has cast over you! Do you not see how she tricks and defies you? She is an evil spirit, Wanmdi Hota. Kill her, or you will one day regret it!"

Gray Eagle cast murderous glances at Chela as he spoke coldly, "She has not cast any spell over me. She has not taken your place in my heart, for you never had one! Do you think my eyes cannot see she is white? You act more like my enemy than she does! She has helped me, but you try to kill me! I see no tricks in her, for I have taught her I am the warrior and she is but a woman. My regret lies in the fact I have too long allowed you to dishonor me with your words and actions. No more! You were told the Great Spirit sent her to me as a gift. He showed us in the warrior lodge how to free her and kill the bluecoats. I was told to bring her here and protect her under my wing. The others also shared this vision from the Great Spirit. You must be punished for your evil deeds and thoughts. If you do this again, He will punish you. She is smiled on by Him, for He has sought to protect her life many times. He will not permit her death!"

Gray Eagle took the whip in his hand and

cracked it on the ground. Alisha had stood mesmerized by the deadly episode before her. She heard and recognized many of the words Chela had said and knew they discussed her. She knew Wanmdi Hota was about to beat the defiant Chela, and Alisha's heart went out to her enemy. Alisha recalled all too well the agony of the whip. She still carried the scars from her whipping. She could understand the girl's feelings, although she loathed her actions.

Alisha ran forward through the small crowd and grabbed Gray Eagle's taut arm which held the wicked whip. "Hiya, Wanmdi Hota! Please don't do this because of me! Your people hate me too much as it is. What will they feel if I cause the punishment of the Shaman's daughter? I understand and forgive her. She loves you and is to marry you. Don't you understand, she cannot accept my place in your life and teepee, not even as a kaskapi? I would feel the same in her place if she were between us, but I would not try to kill her. Please, let her go . . ."

Her eyes darted around wildly. "How can I make you understand? Don't beat her for wishing my death. The whip is much too cruel for a woman. It gives agony and pain beyond belief! I know! Please, hiya."

Feeling guilt at her reminder of what he had done to her and the fresh reality of her near death caused Gray Eagle to close his ears to her pleas. So soon after her submission to him and his will, here she was openly defying his judgment again! He knew the crime and punishment and she could do or say nothing to change them. If he backed down now, they would believe Chela's words about an evil spell over him. She was backing him into that deadly corner again and he would have to once again fight his way out at her expense.

Why, Lese? he agonized. Why do you force me to hurt you this way? There is more at stake here than her attempt to kill you. There is my leadership and honor! I could kill her with my bare hands for what she tried to do to you, but she must take her punishment as is our way—two lashes of the apa.

Gray Eagle had heard the loud gasp of astonishment as Alisha had grabbed his arm. His thoughts of the crowd's reactions were, a ska kaskapi had dared to touch a warrior in anger, to argue with him, and to interfere with his judgments. But, he was mistaken . . .

They were shocked and amazed to see the white girl beg for the life of the one who had tried to kill her, her enemy. Could one be so forgiving and kind of heart? More and more, Gray Eagle's people had come to accept this rare and special girl who was their captive.

He roughly yanked his arm from Alisha's grasp and shoved her backwards to White Arrow. His black scowl told her to be still and silent. Alisha broke free and ran to the post, placing herself between him and Chela's back. She pleaded again, "Hiya! Hiya, Wanmdi Hota."

The air was charged with the intensity of

violent emotions. He came forward with the catlike grace and ease of the puma, a cryptic expression upon his face. He forcefully pulled her away from Chela and spoke to his koda.

"Take her to my teepee and hold her there, even if you must bind her. Do this before our truce is cruelly ended and Chela has her revenge . . . but in a much different way. See to it, my koda, that she does not force me to . . . to do something I might regret to my dying day."

White Arrow seized her in his strong, iron vise and pulled her away. She called back to Gray Eagle over his shoulder, "Hiya, hiya, Wanmdi Hota . . ." He willed his ears to close against her pleas, for he could not change his responsibilities.

Chela comprehended Alisha's actions and many of her words. She was astounded and confused. She begs for me after what I tried to do to her? Why? I have tried to hurt her many times and tonight, I would have killed her. Could it be the Great Spirit has given her the heart of an Indian and the body of a wasichu? Could it be she is not an evil spirit? But why! Why should she try to help me?

Chela realized, she knows why I tried to slay her. She understands my hatred. She sees I love Wanmdi Hota and knows he is mine. She knows he has put her in my place in his teepee. I have been blinded by hate and jealousy! She cannot control Wanmdi Hota's actions anymore than I can. She is at his mercy more so than I. If he truly loved her or was under some spell of hers, he would not hurt or use her as he does. He taunts us both for loving and wanting him! I have placed the blame on the wrong one. It is Wanmdi Hota who should feel my hatred and anger, not the white girl. She can no more help being born wasichu than I can help being Oglala. I can also see she is truly different from other wasichus. Wanmdi Hota will be sorry, for the Great Spirit will punish him for his cruelty to one He has chosen to honor and protect. He will pay for his dishonor and abuse to me also! It would serve him right for the Great Spirit to take away his little white bird . . .

Truth has its way of shining through in the darkest hour, as it did for Chela just then. Chela knew there was no way Wanmdi Hota would ever love or want her, but as the law of their tribe demanded, they would join. He would never belong to her. What will he do with the white girl when we are joined? she thought. Will he trade or kill her, or will he keep her? Perhaps the Great Spirit has sent this white girl to soften the hard, cold heart of Wanmdi Hota. She is protected from everyone but him. I do not understand this, for she is wasichu. She has suffered much. I hope if he trades her, it will be to someone kind like Wanhinkpe Ska. I must think and pray on these matters later . . .

Belatedly, Alisha had recognized the warrior's icy stare and chilling voice and knew their meaning. Powchutu's warnings about open defiance and disrespect returned to haunt her. She could still see the smoldering, raging eyes and hear the deadly tone in Gray Eagle's voice.

I do not care if he does punish me this time, she fumed defensively. I had to try to stop the beating. He does not understand the heart and mind of a woman in love. At least this time, the punishment will have a just reason! I will know I did what I had to do. Now, he will do what he has to do. Can we be any less than we are? Could I live with myself if I had not tried to prevent the beating?

Alisha sadly realized they all had their roles in this drama and they had no choice but to play. If I must suffer for what I did, then so be it, Alisha concluded. It will not be the first time.

Alisha tried to summon her courage to defend her actions, but knew she had made a grave mistake in judgment. She thought, which is more important—me, Chela, or Wanmdi Hota's leadership and honor? All the pleading in the world would not have changed things tonight. How could I have been so stupid as to think he would listen to me?

Alisha realized then she was lucky she had not taken Chela's place at the stake. If he beats me again while the old lashes are still unhealed, she thought, I would surely die. The next time, I will never be able to remain silent. I will never know how I did so before. She cringed as she heard the loud snap of the whip. An agonizing scream rent the night air, and she heard Chela cry out for mercy and forgiveness. Another lash, an anguished scream, then silence . . .

Two lashes? Alisha thought. He only gives her two lashes? Perhaps it is because she is Indian and I am white, or because of who she is to him and the tribe. Still, even two lashes are agony.

Alisha had not heard White Arrow leave or Gray Eagle enter. She was startled when he stepped before her line of vision. She inhaled nervously and tugged at her lowered lip with her teeth. He studied her face for a long time as he fought to control his anger and disappointment in her behavior. She gazed deep into his unfathomable, jet eyes. Her own eyes were begging for understanding and love.

Her alert senses made her aware of the tight rein he held on his emotions. For once, his face revealed these things to her. He was thinking of how much depended upon his next words and actions. In just a few minutes of cruelty and coldness, he could wipe out all the love and tenderness they had so recently shared. He was torn between wanting to reach out and pull her into his embrace and tell her he loved her and understood what she had done, and wanting to punish her brutally for shaming and defying him so soon. Why could she not bend all her will to him? Why could she not love and trust him enough to obey him without question?

Gray Eagle believed if he gave into his first desire, she would sense his leniency and weakness toward her. Would she take advantage of it? Would it only bring out more defiance and dishonor at another time? If only so much did not ride on this decision . . .

He saw and heard how his people were amazed at her attempt to help Chela. They had learned of Alisha's friendship with Powchutu from the braves who had been at the fort. They were all aware of the Great Spirit's vision concerning her. They knew Alisha felt no hatred for the Indians. She had befriended one in need, even at the risk of harm to herself. They knew how she had done this very thing for Gray Eagle when he was the captive of the white people. Had she not proven she was a friend to the Oglala and would accept them if they would allow it? Had she not shown she could, and did, love one of them? It was as if she were Indian in heart and soul. Was this what the Great Spirit saw in her which made her special to Him and deserving of His protection?

An eternity seemed to pass as they faced each other in the quiet stillness. Alisha stared at him, wondering what was going on inside him. Her heart hammered in her chest as she handed him the same knife which Chela had tried to kill her with earlier. She had seen it lying on the ground by the mat and picked it up without White Arrow's notice.

He glared at the knife she held out to him, but did not move to take it from her. She reached for his hand and placed the knife in it with the blade pointing toward her. She lifted his hand, allowing the blade tip to rest at her heart. Her hands on his were cold and trembling. She raised her eyes to his in sadness. Tears glimmered there. Her expression tore at his heart.

Gray Eagle was shocked. Was she asking if he wished her death, or if death was the punishment for her deed tonight? Surely she was not begging him to kill her! Had his actions wounded her this deeply? Did she feel there was no hope for his love and acceptance? Did she want to die rather than live here with him? Why did she not speak and let him know what she was telling him with her behavior? Why did she just stand there looking so tormented and vulnerable? Did she think he might whip her again and was pleading for a quick death from the knife?

How could she believe he could ever plunge a knife into the one whose heart he loved? The past two days have not wiped out the fear and mistrust from her heart, he realized. This is the second time this day she has shown this to me. If I punish her now, I will only prove this to her.

The warrior pulled the knife away from Alisha's heart and turned to leave. She sighed in relief and closed her eyes as the tears began to flow down her ashen cheeks. The flap dropped back into place and he was gone.

Alisha walked over to the mat and sat down, trying to make some sense of the drama between them just now. At least he did not kill me or beat me, she mused. But what does this mean? What does he want from me? Could it be possible he does not wish to hurt me? Could it be he has feelings for me after all?

131

Perhaps he only wants to think of a better torture this time. He will never let this go unpunished. Pride and honor! Shame and face!

Those four words burned into her brain, just as they had done at the fort. They had cost her everything but her life.

I have ruined everything with my actions tonight, she agonized. I have helped Chela to win him! I have handed her victory on a silver platter. No doubt, he is out there now trying to come up with some dreadful torture, or perhaps taking care of his beloved intended . . .

Alisha began to cry at her own folly and for the loss of her short, blissful reprieve. Having seen and felt Gray Eagle's desire and tenderness would only make his hate and rejection more painful. Oh, Wanmdi Hota, she cried in anguish, what have I done? For a short time I chipped away at your heart of stone. My love heated it and caused its coldness to melt a little. But there was not enough time for more. It isn't fair! It isn't fair . . . I have not had you long enough to lose you again . . .

A cold chill ran down her spine. She trembled with the certainty that this time she had lost him for good. Her dream of the night before flashed vividly in her mind. Had it been a premonition? A little white bird was not greater than an eagle. A power stronger than his would take her from him. Was that power hate, revenge or death?

Alisha mourned her mistake as she rocked herself near the mat she and her brave had shared. Softly sobbing, she fell into a deep, dark sleep.

From his seat by the center campfire, White Arrow had seen Gray Eagle leave his teepee and walk into the edge of the forest, alone. From the look on his face and the slump of his proud shoulders, he knew his koda needed to talk to someone who loved and understood him.

He joined him as he leaned against a large tree trunk and asked, "Do you wish to talk, koda?"

Gray Eagle nodded yes. He talked for a very long time, telling White Arrow things which had been bottled up inside him for many weeks. He poured out his heart to his best friend. He told him of Alisha's stay at the fort and of all that had taken place there. He spoke of her many heartaches and abuses at the hands of the whites. He told him about her troubles with Mrs. Philsey and the Lieutenant. He spoke of her conflict with General Galt and the other men at the fort. He spoke of the hard and painful time given her by the Brown girl and the other women. He talked about her life and abuse at his own hands. He explained her friendship with the scout Powchutu and of his help to her those many times.

White Arrow's face and eyes flashed anger and pain many times during these revelations. He smiled and happily nodded as he heard of what had taken place between his two kodas on their way home. Gray Eagle spoke of everything which had taken place since he had first met and captured Alisha. He talked on and on, purging his mind and heart of all hate, bitterness and revenge he had ever felt toward her. His speaking cleared many of his own doubts and fears. His thoughts and emotions became clearer to him as he talked about her and of how she had changed his life, and he, hers. He spoke of happy times, sad and lonely times, cruel and bitter times—all the times which had passed between them.

"She did not resist the taking of the fort. She accepted its necessity. But most of all, koda, she did not resist me until tonight. She came to me in love and desire. I tell you, Wanhinkpe Ska, she was totally mine, of her own free will. My people watch my courage and wisdom. I do not know how to deal with her actions and words of this night. I feel as if the ground is sliding from beneath my feet. There is danger nearby for I can feel it breathe upon my neck. I smell a storm in the air, and I am helpless to prevent its coming. I have nearly lost her twice before. I cannot do so again. She is my heart and spirit. Life without her is dark and lonely. What I do this night will be between us forever."

White Arrow listened to all his koda said and replied, "She knows you are very angry with her and greatly fears your reaction. But I feel she fears your turning from her far more. I saw this in her eyes when you argued with Chela. I saw her shame and sorrow at her actions tonight. She knows she did wrong. I would forget what she did and go on as yesterday and today. If you return to your coldness and torture, you will surely lose her forever. She waits for you to come to her in love and with forgiveness and acceptance. If you do not, she will close a part of her heart to you forever, and you will never feel or know her complete love and trust. She will not view forgiveness and tenderness as weakness on your part, nor will our people. She knows what a great warrior you are. Our people know what she did tonight and understand. Mercy is also a part of a great leader and chief. As I have said to you before, her life and destiny are in your hands. Do not let her slip as water through your fingers as you nearly did before. Her people made her suffer, and you have made her suffer. She has not known or felt happiness and peace for a long time, but for the past moon. Let her have this happiness and peace now, Wanmdi Hota. Allow her what she has earned. Forget she is wasichu. See her as Alisha, the woman you love and desire above all others. I pray you will not lose her again by your actions this night."

Gray Eagle knew White Arrow spoke aloud what he alone wanted to say. "You are right again. You speak wisely, Wanhinkpe Ska, my koda. All you say is what I feel and believe with my heart and mind. I will go to her now and act as if this night has never passed between us. Soon it will grow dim and disappear from both our thoughts. There must be only love and trust between us. It is time to tell her of all that is in my heart for her. I must teach her the ways and laws of our people, and she will learn, understand and accept." He embraced his friend and thanked him for his understanding.

Lighthearted, he returned to his teepee to find Alisha asleep on his mat. There were salty trails of tears still damp on her cheeks and lashes. So, he thought sadly, she has cried herself to sleep. He stared at the pale, innocent face which had experienced so much pain and suffering in such a short time. He wished he could return to the first day he had met her and begin anew, without the mistakes he had made.

"Istinma, Cinstinna. Tomorrow will be soon enough to heal the hurts and tears of many moons. Let the pain of tonight fade with the coming sun. Then, I will tell you of my love for you. I will forever protect and love you. I will hold you close to my heart and with my spirit."

He spread the other buffalo skin close to hers and lay down to sleep. Alisha was so very tired and needed this undisturbed sleep. She was too hurt and fatigued to deal with the important things Gray Eagle had to tell her. Tomorrow will be the day for truth, love and a new beginning.

As he lay there with open eyes staring at the stars through the small vent, he recalled White Arrow's last words to him, "She has endured enough punishment and hate. Do not turn your heart away from her now. She is in great need of your love and help. Go to her in love and tenderness and you will never regret it." He was aware of her restless tossing and turning for much of the night, but finally, he also slept.

Early the next morning, Alisha was rudely awakened by loud voices outside the teepee. She sat up and rubbed her eyes which were swollen and red from her crying in her restless night. The flap opened and Gray Eagle entered, followed by two other Indians. She stared at them in confusion.

A deadly chill warning touched her senses and fear knotted her stomach. She struggled to breathe the close air. Something had to be vastly wrong for Gray Eagle to bring strangers to their teepee like this. Her eyes watched them in fear and suspicion. She studied the men carefully, trying to determine their purpose.

The stony hardness in Gray Eagle's face and voice warned her of a coming maelstrom. The three men spoke acidly to each other, as if they disagreed over some important matter. The older man was unmistakenly a chief from some other tribe. This was evident to her from his headdress, attire and jewelry. His age was undeterminable because of his heavily lined, leathery, tanned face and flashing, obsidian eyes.

The old chief appeared very upset and excited over some matter they discussed. He continued to point and nod at Alisha many times as he spoke in a deep, rich voice. Gray Eagle argued back at him and shook his head no several times. What did they have to say that concerned her?

The other brave only spoke occasionally as he

stood proud and alert at the chief's side. He was dressed and had the bearing of a great warrior. He was ruggedly handsome with strong, chiseled features. Strength, pride and courage surrounded him like an aura. He emulated maleness and animal magnetism, and yet there was a gentleness in his manner. The hard muscles flexed in his arms, chest and shoulders each time he shifted or moved. Around his neck he wore a medallion in the shape of a bear's head. She stared at it and paled visibly, recalling in the dream, "Bears can destroy the eagle's nest and can kill them if they can catch them . . ."

He was wearing long, deerskin breeches and low-cut moccasins. In his hair, he had three red and gray feathers attached to a beaded headband. His keen eyes took in Alisha's delicate beauty and fear. She had the look and body of a woman, but her eyes spoke of childlike purity. He mused, So this is the white girl who held off an attack on the fort until she could be rescued. She is the one they say is protected by Napi.

Could it be the Great Spirit has protected her because of who she is? Could Matu be right? I have heard many stories about this girl who is the captive of Wanmdi Hota. I see they did not lie. If she is who Matu says, then she will soon be mine! Wanmdi Hota was indeed lucky to have found such a rare, beautiful flower among the wasichu. Whether she is wasichu or Indian, she is a prize worth taking. It is easy to see why he so fiercely resists Mahpiya Sapa's demands. He does not wish to lose her again, and so very soon. But, she will be mine! He will indeed have to fight a challenge to keep her if she is Shalee. I will slay the great warrior before I will allow him to keep what rightly belongs to me and Mahpiya Sapa. It might be the Great Spirit has sent her here for me and has protected her until I could find her and come for her.

Alisha watched the possessive look which was rapidly growing in the eyes of the younger warrior and wondered at it. His look was one of bold scrutiny.

Brave Bear noted the fear and suffering in Alisha's large, green eyes fringed with thick, dark lashes. Her skin looked as soft and white as the clouds. He wanted to reach out and touch and caress it. He watched her intently as he listened to the words between the other two men. He read the terror and panic in her eyes, but also something else. Was it a suspicion or instinctive knowing of who they were and why they had come here? Had she guessed who she was? Had the Great Spirit told her He would send them to find and rescue her? There had been such a strange expression in her eyes when she had looked at his wanapin. It was as if she knew who he was and had been expecting him to come. No, she could not know anything for certain. He saw her tense at his scrutiny. He flashed her a secretive half-smile. She pinkened shyly and lowered her gaze and he broadened his smile.

Black Cloud had related his story outside to Gray Eagle and they had argued bitterly. Gray

Eagle insisted that Alisha had been through enough lately and he refused to subject her to more. He had tried every reason and argument he knew, but Black Cloud would not be dissuaded. The standoff ended when he demanded proof that Wanmdi Hota did not speak with a double tongue. Gray Eagle's back was to that treacherous wall again and he had no choice but to prove his word and honor.

How could he put her through this new shame? Today was the day for all things to be out in the open. How could he explain what he was about to do to her? Later, when they were gone, he would make her understand. Once more, their talk must wait until later . . .

Black Cloud had told him many, many winters ago he had taken a white squaw himself and he had loved her dearly. She had long, dark hair which glowed in the sun like fire. She had eyes the color of grass and skin the color of snow. She had lived with him as his woman for three winters and had given him a daughter who resembled her.

When the child had been two winters old, she had been kidnapped in a raid on his camp and taken away. His woman had been killed in that same raid and he had never seen or heard of his daughter again. He related how Matu had come to him the day before and spoken of the white girl who was the captive of Wanmdi Hota. She told him of the beating the white girl had received many moons ago and of how she had been left to tend the girl while Wanmdi Hota came to the war council. She said she saw the akito of Mahpiya Sapa on her buttock while she was tending her injuries.

She had spoken of the girl's fiery hair and green eyes, of who the girl looked like. Gray Eagle's blood chilled at these words. He knew now Matu had lied before. She had not come to warn him that day, but to see Black Cloud about Lese. The raid and Lese's capture had prevented her from speaking to him that day. This was the meaning of her strange actions yesterday which White Arrow had related to him. This was why she did not bring the food and water to him. He vowed she would pay for her lies.

Black Cloud was holding up his right hand for Gray Eagle to view. He was saying Matu had told him the white girl had one to match it on her left buttock. It was well-known in these parts that the Si-ha Sapa used tattooing for family member recognition. Each man had his own symbol. All members of his family carried that same mark for identification in times of raids and accidents.

Gray Eagle looked at the akito, a half moon with one star high on the left and another star low on the right. He studied the pattern and said the white girl had no such akito on her body.

But Mahpiya Sapa insisted on seeing for himself she did not bear his akito, especially after seeing her appearance and likeness to Jenny. Gray Eagle had told him Alisha had come here only a few moons ago from a strange land far, far away, but Black Cloud still would

141

not be deterred. He said she could have been sent there to live with the wasichu after her capture long ago. Once more, he demanded to see the akito for himself!

Gray Eagle coldly stated, "She is not the cunwintke of Mahpiya Sapa! She is mine! She was sent to me by the Great Spirit. You know of the vision He sent to us about her. She will be shamed and hurt by this. I do not like being forced to make her endure this. Wanmdi Hota is a man of truth and honor. If she carried the akito, I would have seen it before. I also doctored her that day. Matu lies!"

Black Cloud calmly retorted, "Maybe the Great Spirit placed her in your safekeeping until I could learn of her return and come for her. The vision told you to rescue her and bring her here for protection and to kill the bluecoats. I say He told you nothing more, did He?" He saw the look confirming his words cross Gray Eagle's face before the brave could hide it. He continued, "She will soon forget the hurt and shame of this day if she is truly my daughter. I, too, do not like to force Wanmdi Hota to do this. You are the son of my koda. But you make this necessary. Perhaps Wanmdi Hota's heart has blinded his eyes to the akito of Mahpiya Sapa on his winyan! I hear and see your actions do not speak of love or concern for this girl. Your resistance is only false pride. Matu has told us of her treatment at your hands. If you have gone to such bold lengths to take and keep her, then why do you treat her as such?

"Does Wanmdi Hota fear the voices and taunts of other warriors? Did it take this much cruelty to save face? Could you not teach her obedience and respect with a little kindness? Hatred is a two-sided knife, Wanmdi Hota. It cuts the one who holds and uses it, as well as the one it touches."

Black Cloud did not realize his vision and thoughts were colored by the girl who sat before him, the very image of his beloved Jenny. He should have recalled things were different when he captured Jenny. The hating and killing had just begun and they had not had many years to fester and grow. Only the women had resisted his taking a white squaw. Jenny's treatment had been very unlike Alisha's. The times and emotions back then were different. Then, too, no one dared to question the deeds or words of the great chief Mahpiya Sapa of the Blackfoot tribe.

Gray Eagle reasoned, if by some quirk of fate Mahpiya Sapa believes Lese is his daughter, then I will accept her as such and join with her. With Lese as his mate, no one would dare to argue his claim on her ever again. I will never give her up! But when he spoke his offer to Black Cloud, he flatly refused.

"I have no sons and have chosen Mato Waditaka as my successor. If she is my daughter, she will be joined to him and live with her people. I will not allow her to be joined with another, one who has abused her so brutally! She will leave with us today. My heart is closed to your pleas. It is settled."

Gray Eagle angrily exclaimed, "Hiya! She is mine! I have captured her two times. She has lived with me as my winyan and she will remain so! I have taken her many times and will allow no other man to take her as mate. I would accept her as your daughter, but she will remain mine!"

Alisha watched wide-eyed, listening for any words she knew or understood. Gray Eagle's muscles were taut in fury. His voice was low and threatening. His eyes burned like two, hot coals. They flashed in warning, but why?

The other warrior stiffened at his words and his eyes also narrowed in rage. Alisha could not figure out what was going on. Were these men friends or enemies? Surely not enemies, for they carried weapons and were in here alone with him.

Brave Bear stepped forward and spoke to Gray Eagle. "We cannot change what you have done to her, but if she is Shalee, I will take her! She is not to blame for your actions and abuses. Matu has told us of her great strength and courage. She has told us of her kindness and friendship to the Indians. She has told us everything about her!"

Brave Bear went and knelt before her on one knee. He placed his finger under her chin and raised her head to face him. Her eyes met his and she gazed into the depths of them. It was as if he sought to view her very soul. His eyes roamed her features, then returned to meet her steady, curious gaze. A look of desire was clearly evident upon his face and in his eyes, but there was something else there. Was it tenderness or gentleness? No matter, his look and closeness made her uneasy. She flushed pink at his continued, bold scrutiny. She quickly lowered her eyes to his wanapin.

Pleased with what he saw in her eyes, he stood up and said to the others, "She is very beautiful. Even if you have taken her first, she is more than acceptable to me. She still retains an air of innocence and purity. I would still wish to trade for her, Shalee or not. The things I read in her eyes make your cruelty even harder to understand. If all I see and hear are true, she is a prize to treasure and protect. We will look for the akito!"

Brave Bear leaned over, took Alisha by her forearms, and pulled her to her feet. His strong hands slid down her arms to her wrists and gently, but firmly, gripped them in a steel vise. Alisha stared at his hold on her wrists, and a look of panic flashed across her face. Her eyes frantically went up to his to read his intentions, but she could discern nothing. The easy, half-smile was playing on his lips once more.

Suddenly terrified, she tried to yank free, but Brave Bear did not give an inch. She cried out in fear, "Wanmdi Hota! What do they want? Why are they here? Who are they? I do not understand what's going on."

No answers came. She observed Gray Eagle and the chief move behind her. She tried to turn around to see them and what was happening, but the brave's hold on her made any movement of her body impossible.

A feeling of impending doom chilled her to the bone and she shuddered. She paled, dread filling her bright eyes.

Alisha strained to peer over her shoulder, to see the chief lift her dress-tail, to watch and feel him touch her *derrière*. Her face burned in humiliation. She struggled to fight the panic which rose in her chest and battered her heart. She squeezed her eyes tightly shut as if to block out her shame. Her lips and chin began to tremble and she clenched them together to still them. She could hear the old man speaking to Gray Eagle. Their voices carried a different tone, but she could not tell what this meant. This is an outrage! she fumed. It is too much! How dare he do this to me! Anger began to surge and grow in her at this wicked insult.

She struggled furiously against Brave Bear's hold. She cried out, "Let me go! Stop this instantly! Release me, I tell you!"

Her resistance had absolutely no effect on the Indian's grip at all. His strength was even greater than Jeffery's had been. She was completely under his control and power until he chose to free her. Alarmed, she pleaded, "Please, Wanmdi Hota! Hiya, hiya . . ."

She saw he made no attempt to stop them and what they did. He did not try to help her or prevent their actions. His full attention was on the old chief as he spoke with him. There was

146

something new and strange in his voice and expression which frightened her immensely: a deadly calm.

He dropped to one knee behind her and looked at her *derrière* as the chief had done. She pleaded again, "Hiya, hiya . . ." Now she could make no sense of the Indians' strange actions and expressions.

Why wouldn't he listen to her and help her? Why did he permit these men to treat and touch her in this manner? They acted as if they were examining a piece of merchandise to buy . . . no! Surely not that! Alisha blanched and shook violently at this idea. Was he going to sell or trade her to these men? Hadn't Powchutu said they either killed or traded slaves when they no longer wanted them? He had not killed her last night. Was this the new torture he had decided on? Was this to be her punishment for her defiance last night? She wept silently, Does he wish to be rid of me and marry Chela? Perhaps he had planned this all along!

Her broken heart cried out, betrayal . . . deceit . . . lies, all of it was only lies . . .

Powchutu had warned her before she left the fort not to openly defy and show disrespect for Gray Eagle again. Would he go this far to be certain she would never shame or resist him ever again? Were these past two days a cruel joke on her? Did he want to prove his contempt and hate for her by selling her like some animal? Had he sensed her love for him and mocked her with his tender response? He had wanted to show her his power over her body and life. Could he be that brutal and heartless, to play with her emotions so cruelly? Could he? There was no other answer or explanation for what was going on.

Brave Bear was acutely aware of Alisha's ever-growing terror, but he was also reading anguish and betrayal in her eyes. Why? he wondered. She fought him again to break free. She leaned forward and bit his hand. When she heard deep, rumbling laughter coming from his chest, she stopped and looked up at him. He was laughing at her feeble attempt to hurt him! Tears began to flow down her rosy cheeks from her lucid, grassy eyes. Her chin and lips quivered as more tears flooded down her flaming cheeks. She lowered her forehead to their locked hands and wept. She knew it was futile to resist them.

Brave Bear retained his grip on her wrists, but he lifted their hands to pull her face to rest on his bare chest. She did not resist, but instead lay her face against him and relaxed her body limply against his. He released his hold on her and put his arms around her. His embrace was imprisoning, but gentle.

"Why, Wanmdi Hota? Why?" she whispered sadly.

Gray Eagle burned with jealousy and rage at the sight before him. Why did it always have to be someone else who comforted her in her pain and suffering? First it was Wanhinkpe Ska, then Powchutu, and now Mato Waditaka! It is my turn to comfort and protect her. I am the one she loves and needs, not them!

Alisha sank deeper and deeper into her thoughts, trying to block out the scene surrounding her. This was what the warning had been about. Powchutu had been correct. Gray Eagle is tired of me and wishes to sell me. Why couldn't he trade me to Powchutu or Wanhinkpe Ska? No, that would be too kind! Could the council have demanded he send me away and marry Chela? Do they blame me for what happened last night? Do they want me out of the teepee and life of their beloved warrior? If this were true, would he say no to their demands? He is to be their next chief and would surely possess this power. No, he would not refuse their command even if he wanted to.

Perhaps he would change his mind if she begged, promised to be good, and told him she would never defy him again. She spoke to him, "Please, Wanmdi Hota, I'll never, never defy you again. I promise. Please don't sell me to them. I'll be your slave, and I'll do anything you command. Please don't send me away. Let me stay here with you. I love you. Hiya! Don't do this. I beg you. Anything, anything but this . . . ."

Alisha's pleas seemed to fall on deaf ears and a cold, hardened heart. But in truth, they cut and ripped at the warrior's heart. Little did Alisha know of the pain which tore at Gray Eagle's heart, of the anger which flooded him at his lack of power to help her.

Alisha grasped the reality that Gray Eagle

was not going to help her. He would not heed her pleas or promises. They were all too busy bargaining for her. She silently prayed this new warrior and chief would not want her. This warrior appeared to be kind and gentle, and he certainly was attractive. And, at times there seemed to be a kindness written in the old man's face. But Alisha feared to go to another village, to be without her Wanmdi Hota.

Alisha mournfully reflected, yesterday was he only teasing me? Was he trying to trick me? He's probably laughing at the way I behaved to him, thinking I am a slut. To think I even seduced him! It was all a joke, a cruel joke . . .

I should have known him by now. How many times did I have to be shown the truth before I accepted it? I am his enemy! I should look at him and see him for what he is, not for the illusive lover I dreamed up. He is a demon, a killer . . .

If this is how it must be, I shall not beg or plead with him. I shall not give him the pleasure of my tears. As before, I must find the courage to remain silent and dry-eyed. If I could do this during a flogging, then surely I can do this while he sells me!

Brave Bear felt the stiffening of Alisha's body and pulled back to peer into her face and eyes. She no longer cried or pleaded with Wanmdi Hota. She had a look of fierce determination and pride on her lovely face. The empty, sad expression in her emerald eyes tugged at his heart. They screamed anguish, betrayal and sadness, but also acceptance of this situation. He noted her inner strength and courage and secretly beamed with pride at this girl who would soon be his.

Gray Eagle had stared in utter disbelief at the matching akito. How could this be? Lese was not this missing daughter of Mahpiya Sapa's. How did the akito get there? Did Cinstinna know of its presence? Did Powchutu? Was this some kind of trick to free her from him? Was it some new deceit on her part? Had she merely fooled him for the past two days, giving Mahpiya Sapa time to get a message? Had she been toying with his emotions, teasing him with her body and love? Did the wasichus do this to protect her when I took her back? Is this the true reason they gave her up so easily? Does she mock me? Wanhinkpe Ska told me of the strange looks which passed between Matu and Lese yesterday. What trickery do they seek to pull on me?

Gray Eagle's mind was in chaos until he suddenly realized, Matu said she had seen the akito while she tended her after the icapsinte. That was before Alisha went to the fort. The wasichu could not have placed it there, nor had they guessed the meaning and importance of it.

This information was even more confusing. I am not even sure it was not there when I captured her. How could I have not seen it?

This thing is a mystery and I do not know

151

who lies or why. If Lese is innocent, she could suffer death. If guilty, she could still suffer torture and death. How can I speak out against the akito or her without the truth? What can I do to help us now?

Black Cloud was telling Brave Bear the akito was there as Matu had claimed. "She is truly my cunwintke. She will go home with us this very day. She will be joined with you on the next full moon. We will first give her the time to learn her new home and accept it and her true people."

Gray Eagle knew his hands were tied for now. There was nothing he could do without risking Alisha's life. Even if she were guilty of some trickery, he knew he still wanted her and did not want to see her killed. He had surely given her enough cause to hate him, to want to be free of him and to do anything to escape him. He wished he had the power and courage to take advantage of the akito. It was impossible to stop a chief from claiming his own daughter, whether Alisha was truly Black Cloud's child or not. Gray Eagle had to let her go or see her dead. He had no choice. At least with her alive, he stood a chance of finding a way to get her back. That is, if he could find that way in five days. He had to!

Just as Gray Eagle swore his resolution, Alisha looked over at him and said, "Sell me or even give me away if this is what you wish. I don't care anymore. I hate you! I will be happy to never see your face ever again. It will be a great relief to never have to feel your touch again. You can never hurt me or use me again. I shall cut you out of my heart with your knife of cruelty. To me, you are dead!''

Gray Eagle felt fear leap in his heart as he watched the bitter coldness growing in Alisha's features. She went on, "The past two days have been your most brutal torture of all. To let me think you . . . we . . . how you must laugh at me and my stupidity! I was a fool not to realize your full hatred and contempt for me when you tried to beat me to death. I was right when I told Powchutu you only wanted me back because I had cheated you out of torturing me more! I foolishly believed his naive explanation. I have been so stupid and naive! No more! My one assurance is the knowledge there is no man alive you could sell me to who could ever be half as cruel as you! Surely you are the Devil himself and I have lived in Hell!''

How could I have done this to you, Lese? Gray Eagle inwardly wept. Do you really believe what you are saying? Why shouldn't you, after how I mistreated you. What can I do or say to you that would make any difference now? To speak out would surely bring your death. If I didn't mention the akito, you would never believe I could love and want you and then send you away with them. If I told you the truth, what good would that do? You would only resist them and try to convince them you are not Shalee. They would kill you. I can do nothing

153

for now. Love me and trust me, Lese, Gray Eagle's heart cried out.

Alisha became aware of the warrior before her unlacing the bodice of her dress. She glared at him, then closed her eyes tightly, forcing a tear to squeeze out and slide down her cheek. She stood as rigid as a marble statue as he lifted the garment over her head and removed it. So he wishes to see all of what he bargains for, she thought bitterly.

She inhaled deeply, her chest rising and falling gently. The pinkness from her cheeks spread down her neck and graced her chest. Still, she did not plead, cry or resist. Gray Eagle watched her, concerned by her distant mood. Had she given up? Was she conceding defeat to them? Did it no longer matter to whom she belonged? He angrily realized she did not fight another man's undressing her or looking at her naked. He recalled her reaction to the Teepee Sa as he closely observed her mood and reaction to Brave Bear's actions. This was something new and different in her—total surrender to whatever he chose to do to her. He inwardly raged at his inability to stop this.

Alisha was thinking much the same as Gray Eagle. What good did it do to try to shield herself from the warrior's touch? If he wanted to see all of her, he had the strength to do so. Hadn't she learned the futility of defiance from Gray Eagle? It would only make things worse for her if she resisted him. What did it matter?

Alisha hadn't realized that as she struggled with Brave Bear, she had torn the scabs loose on her back. Her dress was soaked in red, sticky blood. Black Cloud had ordered her dress removed to tend the wounds before they left. When the dress was off, he wanted to be told once more why this terrible thing had been done to his daughter. Gray Eagle bitterly related the story of what had taken place. Black Cloud asked for salve made from the mountain herbs he brought to rub upon her back and seal the welts to stop the bleeding.

Alisha was unaware of the pain in her back, for the pain in her heart was much greater. It was as if Gray Eagle had shot white-hot arrows into it. She retreated into her inner self to avoid facing her predicament. She forced herself to think of other times and places. She did not feel the salve rubbed onto her back. She did not notice the look of admiration for her beauty on Brave Bear's face, nor the look of desire for her in his eyes. She did not feel the tremors in his body as he pulled her nude body to his chest to peer over her shoulder to view her back. The warmth and softness of her breasts against him stirred feelings of intense passion and protectiveness for her. His face went livid with rage at the marks on her soft, white flesh. He glared at Gray Eagle in fierce hatred, who returned his look at the way he held Lese's body so close and intimately. He fought the urge to draw his knife and strike him dead and the desire to blurt out the entire truth to Alisha. His logic and wisdom warned him to do neither. Brave Bear ignored the threat written in Gray Eagle's eyes.

Gray Eagle was recalling the hunger he had endured for Alisha between the day he first saw her in the wasichu fortress and the day he captured and possessed her. He remembered his greater suffering during her stay at the fort. That time, he could not even wait to get her back to his teepee to take her. Thoughts of Alisha together with Brave Bear infuriated Gray Eagle. He raged, I will surely kill him if he touches her . . .

Brave Bear pulled a clean dress over Alisha's head and laced it up. He tilted her chin up to look at him as he gently touched her cheek and smiled. The look he gave her told her it was now done: she belonged to him. She realized he had redressed her in a clean, fresh dress and was grateful; at least she wouldn't be led away naked.

Alisha had thought nothing could hurt more than the incidents at the fort, but now she knew better. She knew she loved Gray Eagle and would be forever pushed from his life and embrace. How could she possibly endure losing him forever? How could she face life as another Indian's slave, even one so handsome and seemingly kind as this one?

Anguish flooded her heart, as she thought, Why does fate deal these cruel blows? Why did I allow Cupid to pierce my heart with love's cruel arrows? Instead, why could they not soften his heart toward me? It is not fair to allow me to feel and taste his love and then brutally snatch it away from me so soon.

Powchutu! Where are you? Why are you not here to help me and protect me from this treacherous evil?

Gray Eagle had painfully observed as she submitted to this outrage, knowing he was unable to stop any of it. It was beyond his power and must be left in the hands of the Great Spirit. To openly defy would call for a challenge. He must try something else first. A challenge would cause too much enmity between the two tribes, probably even war. He must bide his time until he could come up with a peaceful solution.

Black Cloud refused to hear of leaving Alisha until the joining day. Brave Bear refused to give up his claim on her. They both refused to hear of his joining with Shalee, their name for Alisha.

Never before had Gray Eagle felt so helpless and worried. Never had his patience worn so thin, nor his anger flamed so bright. Only his many years of careful training hid these intense emotions from them. His temper and rage had shown itself more today than ever. His rigid self-control had taken a beating. The indomitable warrior of the region was as helpless as a newborn babe!

Black Cloud announced they would leave immediately for his camp. He would send his other two braves who were waiting outside on ahead to order preparations for their coming. He would also send Matu with them to care for his daughter after their return. Gray Eagle allowed Matu to leave with them. He needed her alive until this mystery was settled, then . . .

Brave Bear took Alisha's arm and gently pulled her forward. She opened her eyes, but kept them downcast as she followed him outside. She bitterly wondered, Where is the leash for the purchased beast this time? The deal has been made and I must go with him. She was certain now it was not a trick, or a scheme to frighten her. He was really going to trade her and send her away. She had hoped at the last minute he would . . . but she knew he would not change his mind.

The horses were brought to the front of the teepee. They asked if she knew how to ride alone. Gray Eagle nodded yes, telling them of her expertise on the horse. Black Cloud mounted a black and white pinto, sitting tall and erect upon its back. Brave Bear placed his strong hands on her tiny waist and lifted her easily to the back of a chestnut roan. He mounted his own horse which was as white as a ghost.

Alisha lifted her eyes to stare at the distant horizon as she heard Brave Bear's deep voice addressing the Oglala people. She didn't even try to listen and figure out what he was saying to them. Why should she? It was of no interest to her.

Brave Bear told the proud, dauntless Oglala the Great Spirit had placed the life of the cunwintke of Chief Mahpiya Sapa into their care for a short time. They would be blessed and rewarded for sparing her life and protecting her. He had given them a vision which told them to rescue her and bring her here until they could come for her.

"She is not wasichu! She is Si-ha Sapa! She is the child of Chief Mahpiya Sapa! She bears his akito. She will return to her people. On the full moon, she will join with me. We will send many gifts to show our gratitude for your protection."

The Oglalas stared in astonishment. This was the reason for her protection from the Great Spirit and the meaning of His vision to them. This was why Alisha had touched a special feeling in the heart of their great warrior. They saw the look on the face of Wanmdi Hota. They could tell he did not want to give her up, and most of them knew the real reason why. He had been the first one to see and know this girl was rare and special.

They felt shame at their treatment of her, but how could they have known she was one of them? The Great Spirit had chosen his own time to reveal the truth to everyone. Still, they should have guessed how important she was and treated her better, as a koda. She was going back to her people and would soon join with the chief's son.

Alisha thought the cheer which rose from the

crowd was happiness and relief at her impending departure from their camp and the life of their beloved warrior. Chela breathed a prayer of gratitude that she had not killed her, and for the fact she would finally be out of the life of Wanmdi Hota before their joining. The look on his face told Chela that Alisha would be out of his life, but not out of his heart.

White Arrow stared in total disbelief. Alisha was Shalee! She is leaving here forever! She is lost to him for good, and to me . . .

Brave Bear took no chance Alisha might be tempted to flee in fear. He took the reins of her horse, forcing her to cling to the horse's mane.

Gray Eagle could not let her go without some small sign from him. He could not bear that lost, sad look in those same eyes which had sparkled with life and love for him just yesterday. He touched her slim leg and softly spoke her name, "Lese . . ."

She would not acknowledge his word or presence. She slowly lifted the beautiful wanapin from her neck and dropped it to the ground. She wound her fingers into the horse's mane as she had done many times before in a time and place far, far away.

She spoke her last words to him, or in truth, to herself, "Give the wanapin to your next kaskapi and witkowin. Betrayer!" Almost inaudibly she whispered, "For as long as I live and breathe, I shall hate you with all my heart and curse the day I first met you . . ."

She kneed her horse and moved up beside

Brave Bear. She mockingly addressed him, "It appears I am now yours. So be it." The pain in her voice and the meaning of her words cut Gray Eagle's heart like a razor.

Brave Bear gave the command for them to leave.

Chapter Four

Gray Eagle and White Arrow watched as the three rode away. They remained rooted to that spot until the last bit of dust had resettled and Alisha was lost from sight. He held the wanapin tightly in his grip for a long time, then placed it around his neck.

He called to Little Beaver and Running Elk to join him. They went to his teepee to talk and plan. They decided to send Little Beaver and Running Elk to the Paha Sapa to tell his father of all that had happened and to bring him to the camp of Mahpiya Sapa as quickly as possible. The two chiefs had been close friends and allies for many winters. If anyone could help Gray Eagle change the old chief's mind, it was his father. Gray Eagle and White Arrow were to ride to the camp of Grota to find Powchutu to speak to Alisha for him. The two groups of warriors prepared themselves and rode out swiftly in separate directions on different missions. There was a full moon due in only five days . . .

Little Beaver and Running Elk were two of the warriors who had witnessed the vision with him and believed Alisha belonged here with their koda. They rode with very few stops for resting and eating. Their great leader and friend needed their help and they would try not to disappoint him. If necessary, they would battle to get the girl returned to him!

Gray Eagle and White Arrow rode for two grueling days to get to Grota's camp. only to find Powchutu gone on a hunting trip. They nervously paced around waiting for his return. At dusk, he arrived and was very surprised to find them here. Why had the great Wanmdi Hota come to see him, a half-breed? Had something happened to Alisha? He suspiciously approached the two Oglala warriors.

Gray Eagle related parts of what had happened omitting the entire truth. He asked for Powchutu's help.

"So, she is the daughter of Black Cloud and a white woman. It is good! But why do you come to tell me of this?" His delight at this news was clearly evident on his face. Was there a sneer below it? Gray Eagle's neck prickled in warning.

He stated simply, "I come because I need your help. You can speak the Oglala, wasichu and Si-ha Sapa tongues. You must talk to her and the Si-ha Sapa for me."

Powchutu scoffed and answered, "I have never known the great warrior Wanmdi Hota to need anyone's help. Why do I need to speak for you?"

"You must come with us to the camp of Mahpiya Sapa and convince them to let her join with me and not Mato Waditaka."

"Join with you!" Powchutu nearly shouted.

"After all you have done to her, do you think that I, her koda, would ask them to let her marry you? I do not think Mahpiya Sapa would wish you to marry his daughter. Your cruelty to her is no secret, Wanmdi Hota. No! I will not go!"

Gray Eagle firmly stated, "I think she will be happiest with me, Powchutu. I believe she loves me, even though she tries to hide this from herself and others. She was happy before they came to take her away. This could someday cost her life," he mysteriously added, but Powchutu did not comprehend Gray Eagle's last statement.

Instead, Powchutu asked harshly, "Why do you call her Lese? Why would you think she feels anything but hatred and fear for you?"

He answered, "Lese is the name her family called her and she calls herself when she tries to speak with me. I know many of the wasichu words and know she once told me she loved me. Also, I have seen this in her eyes and felt it in her touch." He did not tell Powchutu he spoke the wasichu tongue fluently.

But Powchutu sensed there was more to this situation than he told. He asked uneasily, "When she spoke these words of love to you, did she know that you heard and understood? Did you also hear and know when she begged for mercy from you? Did you try to calm her fears and tell her of your feelings?"

Gray Eagle winced and nodded no. He scowled and replied, "No! She did not know. I heard her cries for mercy, but could not change what happened. It would have hurt her more to know I understood and did not help her. I needed time to show her these things first and time for her to learn obedience and trust." He was angry at having to explain his innermost secrets and motives to this man. Still, he knew he must have his help. Lese trusted him and would listen to him.

Powchutu flamed at Gray Eagle's deceit. "I cannot help you, Wanmdi Hota. You are wrong for her. She has suffered much because of you. I will not speak for you. Leave her in peace."

As he turned to walk away, Gray Eagle asked, "I ask you to think on it until morning before you decide, Powchutu. Once she is joined with Mato Waditaka, we can do nothing to help her."

Powchutu focused his ice-hard eyes on the Oglala warrior and replied, "If I asked for her hand in joining, it would not be to you. It would be to me! I would love her more than you could ever hope to. I do not carry the hatred in my heart for her color as you do. She has never been my enemy, nor I hers. When I look at her, I only see Alisha. You do not and never will!"

Angered by his revelation, Gray Eagle shouted at him, "You must be aware she could never marry a hanke-wa . . ." He halted.

Powchutu finished for him, ". . . Wasichun. She does not care if I am! It has made no difference between us before. She will be better off with Mato Waditaka than either of us. He is also a great warrior. He will love and protect

165

her. She will never feel hatred and cruelty again with him and his people. Leave her alone this time. Let her find love and happiness with him." He walked away with mixed emotions of joy and jealousy at this sudden and unexpected turn of events in Alisha's life.

White Arrow said to his friend, "I will go after him and speak with him. He may listen to me. I have done her no harm and she was my koda. If he knows this, he will listen."

Gray Eagle sat down by the campfire and waited as White Arrow went after Powchutu, calling for him to wait up just a bit more. "Powchutu, I must talk with you. It is clear you love her also, but I am sure she loves Wanmdi Hota. I have seen how she looks at him, especially since she has returned from the fort. She may have told you about him while she was there. Many things have changed since their last unhappy parting, for she now belongs with him."

Powchutu recalled all too well the things Alisha had said about Gray Eagle. He could still imagine the look on her face and hear the tone of her voice when she spoke of him. Many of the changes White Arrow spoke of in her were due to what he had told her, he bitterly realized. Were hate and jealousy the reasons he did not want to help Wanmdi Hota?

He pondered, she can never be mine, but can she be happy with him? They are both right about one thing, she does love him—or did. But Mato Waditaka has more to offer her. Might she learn to love and accept him and be happy in the Si-ha Sapa village? Could I trust Wanmdi Hota not to hurt her again and to make her happy? That was the haunting question. There was something illusive about Gray Eagle and his words. I do not know when or if he speaks the truth. In the future, which would be the easier task for me: to rescue Lese as the wife of Mato Waditaka or as the wife of Wanmdi Hota . . .

White Arrow began again, "She is more deeply hurt now than ever. She does not know why she was sent away from our camp. She believes Wanmdi Hota sold her as a slave. She is confused and suffering. Wanmdi Hota had no choice but to let Mahpiya Sapa take her with him when he saw the akito. It was right where Matu said it would be. Theirs matched perfectly. She was forced to submit to this and to undress before them to tend her wounds. She was greatly shamed and hurt. She does not know what all this means. All I ask is that you come with us and tell her these things. There is no one else who can tell her. If you love her, then come with us and help her."

Powchutu listened and pondered what to do and say. Knowing he would once again get to see her, he finally agreed to go to tell her why she had been taken away and who she truly was. But he would not agree to talk for Wanmdi Hota. They rejoined Gray Eagle and told him of Powchutu's decisions. They thought it best to get a good night's sleep and head out first light in the morning.

In the meantime, Little Beaver and Running Elk had arrived at the Pa-ha Sapa camp where their people came for the winters. In the spring, summer and fall, they lived on the plains and in the open country near the great forest for hunting game and buffalo. They always made one big, permanent camp near the water and forest. During hunting trips, they would take small teepees to camp in. When the hunters and winyans who went along killed and smoked enough meat, they returned to the village with their meat, hides and skins.

At the end of each summer and during the early fall, they would prepare food, clothing and shelter for the coming winter. Then as the winter began to show its face upon the land, they would dismantle the teepees and camp and move to the Pa-ha Sapa. There they would camp for the winter in the mountain-protected ravines and canyons. This location provided protection from the weather and grass for the horses. Here they could worship the Thunderbirds and collect mountain herbs and plants for medicines and spices.

Running Wolf had been here recuperating from his wounds and had almost healed and regained his strength. The two braves had ridden like the wind and had arrived in only one and a half days. They realized the urgency of speed in Gray Eagle's request. He could not be certain Brave Bear would wait for the full moon, due in only a few days, for Alisha would be a constant temptation before the brave night and day. The old chief would have been ready to return to his camp in a few more days. He had only remained away from his people this long because he knew a chief had to be at his best physical condition to lead his tribe. Besides, there was his son Wanmdi Hota to fill his place bravely and wisely.

Little Beaver and Running Elk hastily told the chief all that had taken place in their camp since his last message before the raid on the fort. They also told all about what had taken place in the life of his son, beginning with his capture at the wasichu fortress. Gray Eagle had not wanted to send any personal message by his warriors concerning him and his white captive. He had wanted to wait until his father's return to tell him everything and to let him judge Lese for himself. The old chief was surprised at the things he learned about his son and the white girl, who it seemed was Si-ha Sapa.

Now, Running Wolf understood his dream of a few moons ago. He had seen Chela standing before the ceremonial chief to be joined, but the warrior at her side had not been Wanmdi Hota. His face had been in partial darkness and he could not see who it was. Wanmdi Hota had stood watching the ceremony with a small, white bird sitting on his powerful shoulder. The Great Spirit has spoken and this is how it should be. The old chief decided, I will not argue for the joining of Chela and Wanmdi Hota.

Running Wolf told the braves to prepare to

break camp and move out early the next morning. As it was now, it would take three days to travel to Mahpiya Sapa's camp, the very day of the next full moon. Would he be able to help his son? Would he get there in time? It remained to be seen who is the braver and smarter, the bear or the eagle. What will my son feel if he must watch the girl he loves be joined with another? This is why he has never found a winyan before. His heart and spirit searched and waited for this special girl. Now to lose her . . .

Alisha had no idea how much time or distance had passed since they had departed the camp of the Oglala when they reined in the horses for water and rest. She was gently helped down by the rugged warrior. She walked about aimlessly, flexing her back and shoulder muscles. The many days of long riding had made her stiff and sore. How she had longed many times for those daily rides she had taken with her father!

The younger warrior came to her and offered her food and water. She accepted the water, but refused the food for she had no appetite. The water felt good to her dry lips. She avoided all contact with the brave nor did he press her for attention. He returned to the old brave to offer him food and water.

Both men sat down to relax and eat as the horses drank and rested by the water hole. They talked and laughed together as she watched them. They made no attempts to bind her, nor did either of them make any move to violate her. She closely studied the two men, confused and bewildered. They seemed so different from the Oglala and from Wanmdi Hota. There was a relaxed aura surrounding them. She did not feel the hate, contempt or coldness toward her which she had felt and seen in the Oglala camp. For some strange reason, she did not feel threatened by them. Why? Their behavior was so different it frightened her even more.

She did not know what to expect from these men or their people. What was going on here? She thought of the coming night and what it would bring. Was this what they waited for? What kind of men would they become when darkness touched the land? Would they convert into brutal, cold-blooded savages and ravish her? She shuddered. Why had Wanmdi Hota sent her away to the mercy of other men? Her mind reeled in turmoil, for she could not imagine these two laughing men harming her. Could it be because she had not resisted or defied them yet? Would they turn on her if she did resist, as Wanmdi Hota had many times? Could she do anything they wanted or commanded without fighting? Anything . . . could she?

If this was a new start for her, then she must try very hard to be silent and willing. This time, she must not constantly remind them she is their enemy, as Powchutu said she had done with the Oglala. She must endure and accept them and all their ways . . . all of them! She must be friendly and work hard to please them. Could she persuade one of them to like her enough to take her as his own as Wanmdi Hota had done? She must find a way to belong to only one man and never be sent to the teepee sa. She could endure anything but that! Never!

She knew the younger brave already desired her, but did he have the power to claim her for his very own?

She sat down beside a large rock and leaned back against it to rest. The sun soon lulled her tired body and spirit to sleep. Brave Bear gazed over at her and saw her sleeping. His eyes engulfed the lovely, delicate creature who looked so small and helpless sitting there. His loins flamed with desire for her, but also, his heart warmed with feelings for her even then. He touched the chief's arm and nodded in her direction. The old chief looked intently and sadly into the face which reminded him so much of his Jenny. She, too, had looked that innocent and fragile when he had captured her so many winters ago.

He spoke quietly to Brave Bear, "In time she will come to love me as her mother did. She will be the happiness to light an old man's heart." He had never forgotten his lovely white squaw, nor would he ever now with his daughter, her very image, there as a constant reminder.

He had loved Jenny deeply and completely and missed her still. He recalled the heavy vengeance he had wreaked at her death and his daughter's disappearance. Now, the Great Spirit had seen it in His way to restore her life to him and his tribe. He was saddened by her treatment by his kind. She must hate and fear the Indians very much. Wanmdi Hota is a fool if he truly believed I could ever leave her with him after what he has done to her! She will return to her people and join with Mato Waditaka. She will soon forget the shame and hurt Wanmdi Hota has shown her. She will be free and happy with my son and her people. The scars in her heart and on her body will soon heal and fade.

He observed the brave as he went to Alisha and eased her weary head to his broad chest. He watched the gentle way Brave Bear handled her and the tender way he looked at her. He will be good for my daughter, he decided. Surely she will accept such a kind and handsome warrior as her mate and protector. He saw Brave Bear close his eyes and fall asleep. He smiled, pleased with the sight before him. He closed his eyes and also slept.

Brave Bear was awakened by Alisha's movements. She stirred sleepily and sat up. She gazed around, looking confused for a time by her surroundings and the two warriors near her. Reality dawned on her. She moved away from the younger warrior, realizing she had slept in his embrace. He pulled her back into his arms and studied her delicate, lovely features. She tried to pull away, but was locked in his grip of iron.

She met his steady gaze with fear in her eyes,

as if she waited for death. He could feel the quivering in her body and saw how she fought to control her rising alarm. He comprehended what she must think and feel, and understood her panic. He relaxed his hold on her, but did not release her just yet. She must see and learn I am not like Wanmdi Hota and that I will not harm her! he vowed. She must accept my touch and closeness without fear or pulling away. She must realize she now belongs to me.

He spoke to the old chief, "She is much afraid of us. She must think we have traded for her as a slave and captive. She does not know how we will treat her. She looks as if she expects us to abuse her in some terrible way. She does not even suspect you are her father and I am to be her mate. Wanmdi Hota has instilled great fear in her. I must free her of it quickly. She will soon see and know I am not like him, nor her people like his. She must learn she is free and safe with us."

Black Cloud nodded in agreement as he watched Alisha and her expression. She had the look of a cornered animal in her eyes. He said, "We must be very careful not to frighten her while she learns who she is and why she is with us. She will soon see and know we will do her no harm."

Her eyes went from one man to the other as they spoke in a low, calm tone. They finally came to rest on the younger warrior, who was gazing at her with a sensuous half-smile on his lips and laughter touching his ebony eyes. She stared at the kind smile on his lips, knowing it was not a sneer or smirk, then met the bright, glittering eyes. She looked like she had never seen a smile or glowing eyes before. He grinned more broadly as he stood up and helped her to her feet.

He assisted her with mounting her horse. This time, he handed her the reins, showing her he trusted her not to try to escape. She instantly knew she would never betray an Indian's trust in her again! The last time had been much too painful. Brave Bear and Black Cloud placed their horses on either side of hers and rode away. She rode between them until nightfall.

As the sun sank in the western sky, she began to feel panic at the coming night and what it might bring. Brave Bear noted her rising alarm once more as they made camp. She quickly went to fetch wood like a good slave and built a warm, cheery fire.

When she had the fire going, she pointed to some nearby boulders and rocks and timidly said, "Wonahbe . . .", hoping he understood. She walked toward the rocks, occasionally looking back at him, but he remained where he was. She finished and returned to sit beside the fire, not really knowing what was expected of her. He had placed a blanket by the fire, and she sat down.

Brave Bear handed the chief food from a pouch and they ate. When they had both finished, the brave came to sit beside Alisha and offered her food from the same pouch. A slim, quivering hand reached into the pouch to take some wasna. The look in her eyes told him she fully expected him to withdraw the pouch the moment her hand touched it. He was acutely aware of the fear and mistrust she had in them. He placed the pouch in her lap and handed her a mni bag, telling her she could have all she wanted of either.

She ate and drank slowly, trying to stall what she felt was sure to come later. He watched her closely. His watchfulness and gaze made her nervous. She began to fidget restlessly and attempt to keep her eyes averted from his.

When she could delay no longer, she pondered, how will I ever endure it? How could you have done this to me, Wanmdi Hota? For a moment, we touched and loved. I'm sure of it. But you cast me out of your life and heart. Would it have been so tragic to love a white girl? Did you send me away to avoid the temptation to love and keep me?

She was deep in thought when Brave Bear touched her arm. She flinched in alarm and shrank away from him. She quickly glanced toward the old man and found he was asleep. Brave Bear pulled her stiffened body down next to his on the blanket.

She lay on her back, rigid and trembling. He propped up on one elbow and gazed down into her face and eyes. She could not help but meet his look and was confused by the gentleness and lack of coldness she read there. He reached down to caress her cheek and gently stroke her soft hair. He watched her fear grow larger in her eyes with each new touch. She began to breathe fast and hard as she stared, mesmerized by those jet eyes.

He brushed a light kiss upon her lips and lay down, pulling her into his strong embrace. He lay on his left side with her head nestled near his throat. She lay very still and quiet . . .

Time passed on and on and nothing happened. She watched his hard, smooth chest rise and fall gently in a rhythmic pattern. She furtively peered up into his face. He was asleep! He was actually asleep! Now, she was totally befuddled by this entire situation.

Why didn't he take me? Why is he being so gentle and kind? What do they want from me? Questions, questions, with no answers or explanations. They stormed her mind, until she finally slipped into a restive slumber.

When morning came, they ate and rode on. As she rode between these two perplexing men, curiosity began to gnaw at her mind. She would study them secretly from beneath lowered lashes. Where were they going? What was she being saved for? Why would a chief come in person to buy a slave? Why were they treating her so well? She wondered if the younger warrior were the son of the older man. She could not understand why he had slept with her and not touched her. Maybe she was not for him. Perhaps she was a gift for an older son. She silently prayed if that were true, that he be as kind, gentle and handsome as this son. She

177

bitterly scoffed, I bet he's mean as a snake and as ugly as sin! That's the kind of torture and humiliation Wanmdi Hota would want, not the kind this warrior shows.

She glanced over at the younger warrior and studied his appearance. He was indeed a marvelous speciman of manhood. He turned in time to catch the way she was looking at him and grinned. Before she realized what she was doing, her eyes automatically softened and she returned his smile. The way he responded to her beauty and smile alerted her to her behavior. She blushed and looked away.

So, he mused, she does respond to kindness, but does not know how to accept this from an Indian as yet. He was encouraged. It is good . . .

Shortly before nightfall, they arrived at the Si-ha Sapa encampment. The people stared at them and the girl as they entered the camp. She unconsciously edged her horse closer to the younger warrior's. Her eyes begged mercy and reassurance from his. The smile he flashed her told her not to fear. She began to notice the people around them showed her no open hostility. In fact, they seemed to stare at her in awe and friendliness. She had no way of knowing the tribe had been told all about her. The older women recognized Jenny in her, but the younger ones looked on her beauty in envy.

Many of the young winyans sighed, to have once belonged to the famous Oglala warrior Wanmdi Hota and now to the handsome warrior Mato Waditaka! How lucky could one girl be? Alisha would have cried with laughter if she had read their envy and the reasons for it. She would hardly consider what she had gone through as lucky!

She was glad no one taunted or mocked her. This would make it easier for her to try to make friends with these new people. They approached the largest teepee and dismounted. They went inside as the horses were led away by a young brave.

There was a very large campfire in the center of the teepee and puffs of pearly gray smoke swirled and rose to escape from the vent. She stared at the campfire where the old woman from the Oglala village was sitting and preparing food.

She paled as she recalled their last meeting and her chilling sense of foreboding. What did the old woman have to do with all of this and why was she sent here too? Mato Waditaka observed the fear and apprehension in Alisha's face as she looked at the old woman. Was she afraid of Matu? he wondered. If so, why? Had there been trouble between them? Perhaps Matu had been cruel to her, or taunted her, or been the reason for some abuse, before she learned who Shalee was. No matter now, Matu would never harm her again, not in any way . . .

Alisha wondered if the old woman had anything to do with her being sold, or had she, too, been sold to these people? Even so, she still had that chilling, uneasy feeling when she looked at Matu or was near her. She could not guess what part this old woman was playing in her fate. She looked away from Matu to study the rest of the large teepee.

She took in her new home and surroundings. She noted how one side of this teepee was used as a living area and the other side for storage. Clothes and weapons hung from pegs jutting out of the brace poles and on a handmade, wooden rack, constructed of willow poles lashed together. There were extra buffalo skins and blankets; many weapons, new and used; and clothing. There were many bags, pouches and parfleches that were stored there also.

Black Cloud and Brave Bear sat down on a buffalo skin and were served by the old woman. Alisha did not know what to do or what was expected of her, so she simply remained by the fireplace. Soon, the younger warrior came over to her and led her over to his buffalo skin and placed her at his side. The old woman came to her and served her food also, secretly grinning as she did so. Alisha ate the food given her as she watched Matu move about working and cleaning up after the two men. By now, she was completely confused and she could make no rhyme or reason from what was going on. Until they chose to tell her, she had no choice but to do as they bid.

When the two men finished their smoking and talking, the warrior stroked her hair gently as they rose to leave. His moods and actions were completely perplexing by now and she only stared after him. When she had finished, she got up and walked to the flap. She slowly lifted it and peered outside. She found the two braves sitting with many other men by a large campfire, talking, laughing and smoking pipes. He looked up and caught her eyes watching him and smiled. She stared blankly and guiltily for a moment, then lowered the flap. She went back to the mat and sat down. Time passed monotonously.

When her head began to nod and her lids drooped sleepily, she lay down and was quickly asleep. It seemed as if she had only been asleep for a short time when movements at her side aroused her from her light slumber. She cried out in alarm and would have screamed instinctively if the younger warrior had not covered her mouth with his hand. He tenderly shushed her. She stared at him wide-eyed until she realized he meant her no danger and had only meant to calm her down. Her rigid body relaxed and her bewildered eyes met his. He removed his hand from her mouth and lay down beside her. She waited . . .

Nothing . . . was he actually going to sleep again tonight without . . . I do not understand him or what is going on. Do I belong to him or not? She gazed warily at him from the corner of her eye, but he made no move to touch her. This waiting and not knowing is torture in itself, she thought. When is he going to take me? What is he waiting for? Will he be cruel or brutal? I remember the first time Wanmdi . . . But this man is so different from him. I cannot even

181

compare the two. Powchutu told me nothing which would explain this situation. Why this standoff and how long will it last?

I wish he would go ahead and take me and get it over with! At least that way I would have some idea what I am up against. I've seen the way he looks at me and I'm sure he wants me that way. Why does he hesitate? Does he wait for me to accept him? He has been so tender and kind. But why should he care how his slave feels or what she thinks? Still, it would be like him to care from his previous actions. The axe will soon fall, but which way will my head roll?

She assumed from his steady breathing and stillness he was asleep. She propped up on her elbow and stared down into his sleeping face. Her body trembled and her pulse raced to think she had been sold to this handsome warrior. Perhaps Wanmdi Hota had done her a great favor without realizing it! For certain, he was almost as handsome and virile as Wanmdi Hota. But this man possessed winning qualities which Wanmdi Hota did not. It was like comparing black to white, or good to evil . . .

Alisha recalled how easily Brave Bear smiled, revealing white, even teeth. His features softened and life was added to his obsidian eyes. She could still picture his smile and glowing eyes. His touch was always gentle, even when firm. His voice was rich, deep and vibrant.

Her eyes traced his facial features—the strong, chiseled jawline; the aquiline nose which was just right for his face; the proud, arrogant chin;

and the sensuous mouth which curved in a slight smile even in sleep. His hair was sooty black and silky and she was tempted to reach out her hand and touch his braids. She could tell from the small, thin lines at his eyes and mouth that he smiled much.

Her eyes drifted down the thick, muscular neck to the hard, smooth chest. She admired the network of brawny muscles there. His skin was almost flawless and bronze, with only two diagonal scars to mar its perfection and beauty. He had also submitted to the obedience and daring of the Sun Dance, proving his courage and stamina. She noted the power and strength of his shoulders and arms. Yes, he was a proven warrior.

Her eyes slid still lower to his hard, flat belly, the slender hips and sinewy, strong legs. She pinkened and hastily passed over the bulge in his breechcloth. Her eyes slowly and pleasantly traveled back up the full length of his body to find his jet eyes grinning at her inquisitive boldness.

Her face, neck and upper chest flamed as red as blood. She quickly lay back down, not wishing to provoke him. She waited for his reaction to her daring study.

He turned on his other side away from her, savoring the thoughts of the way she had been looking at him. Didn't she know hunters and warriors had a keen, alert sixth sense which warned them when they were being watched, even in their sleep?

He dared not touch her or even look at her right now, not after her reaction to him moments ago. He was much too moved by it and her and this was why he had to turn away. His condition would have been very obvious to her also in a few more moments! She was not ready to deal with him in that way yet, nor was her father! He had no doubts he could have easily seduced her that very minute and she would have willingly come to him. He was even afraid to kiss or touch her, knowing neither of them would stop there. He was confident Wanmdi Hota's memory would give him no trouble.

I must not take her until after we are joined, even though she has known a man before. I must not teach her to hate or fear me as she does Wanmdi Hota! As it had been with Gray Eagle, he had been caught unprepared to deal with what he had read in her eyes—desire and passion. Let these things come and grow in her, then I will possess her, not before. It must be her idea to come to me first. I must not take her forcefully or before she is ready. I am sure she wonders why I do not take her. She will come to think I wish to give her time to accept me and come to me of her own free choice. She is ashamed I caught her watching me. I should have feigned sleep, but I could not resist seeing the look of desire for me in her eyes. Perhaps it is best for her to see even if I do want her, I will not rape her. Her fear will be replaced by gratitude.

She is greatly aware of me as a man. I thank Napi for the looks and strength of body he has given to me. When it is time, she will come to me in desire and willingness. Later, maybe in love also . . . I feel her heart softening toward me even now. I will be very careful not to cause her any hate or fear toward me.

Alisha's pounding heart finally slowed and her erratic breathing came more easily and slowly. It was so humiliating to have him catch her staring at him that way. What must he think of the way I was observing him? He smiled as if he were pleased! He must realize what I was thinking and feeling. It was probably written all over my face and in my eyes. Mama warned me . . . I should've spent that time before my mirror like she said. Sometimes openness and honesty can be a woman's downfall.

Suddenly, she wondered why she had been looking at him like that. Why had he made her feel so trembly and fiery inside? His smile and eyes had touched her like a physical caress and made her warm all over.

If he had tried to take me, would I have resisted him? she thought. Would I have wanted to? I think not, for I truly wanted him as a man. I wanted him to hold me, to kiss me; even worse, I wanted him to make love to me, passionate, consuming love as Wanmdi Hota has done many times. What has come over me? We are strangers and I love another! Is it possible that once a woman knows love with a man, she craves and hungers for it, like the women back home I used to spy on? Perhaps it doesn't even matter who the man is at that point! Is that why they behaved so brazenly? Am I becoming like them, or like Kathy?

She shuddered to think she might be turning into an unbridled, wanton hussy. Will all virile, attractive men affect me this way? I suppose not, for neither Jeffery nor Powchutu did this to me and they are both handsome and sensuous. Why this man? Is it because he is so kind and gentle when I feel so desperate and vulnerable?

Perhaps I am only reaching out to him in spite and revenge against Wanmdi Hota and myself! Am I trying to use this brave to wipe all thoughts of Wanmdi Hota from my heart and mind? Can another man's touch do this? Could I forget him in this man's arms? I will, if it is possible . . .

I might not even belong to this man. He has not taken me. Could it be he doesn't even desire me, that I have misread the look in his eyes and touch? It would not be the first time I have made this mistake. If I do belong to him and he does want me, then why did he withdraw just now? This is maddening!

Perhaps his only attraction to me is physical. What if he is brutal with his lovemaking as I have heard some men are? I wonder what he would do if I pulled his shoulder down and went into his arms and kissed him? What would he do and think if I seduced him as I did Wanmdi Hota? Would he take me and be pleased, or would he be angry and push me away?

She mocked herself, my how you have

changed Alisha! A few months ago, you would never have been having this kind of talk with yourself! In fact, you wouldn't even be having these kinds of thoughts and feelings about a man! Do not act the harlot! Wait for him to make the first move. When he wishes you, he must come to you and you will not turn him away.

Dreams, thoughts and illusions coalesced one with the other until sleep came to both of them. Sometime during the long, cool night, he pulled her into his arms. She naturally embraced him.

They awoke at the same time the following morning, locked in a loving embrace. Their eyes instantly fused. He caressed her with his warm gaze and she flushed in answer. He placed a light kiss upon her lips and stood up, flexing and stretching like a cat. Her gaze followed him as he moved about the teepee before he left.

The knowledge she had been at his mercy for two days and he had not harmed her in any way was foremost in her mind this morning. She laughed at the thought of being a virgin sacrifice to some god of his. I am sure I will learn soon enough what his plans are for me.

Alisha yawned and stretched lazily as she waited for his return. She asked herself what this new day would bring. More secrets and questions, no doubt. Without warning, Gray Eagle's face visualized before her and thoughts of him tugged at the edges of her mind. She realized her mind now betrayed her as her body had. I must force all memories of him from my mind, she sharply warned herself, then sadly added, and banish my love for him from my heart. I live here now and belong to another. I must accept what Gray Eagle has done. If only it did not hurt so much . . .

The flap of the teepee lifted and the young brave ducked and strolled in, apparently in a good mood. Her eyes followed him and his movements as he gathered some items from the storage area. He had his back to her so she could not see what he was holding. He motioned for her to come.

"Piintwike, Shalee."

Her face betrayed her confusion and mistrust. He came to her. Taking her by the hand, he pulled her to her feet. He led her to the flap and outside into the warm sunlight. They walked along the river bank to a place where the hills formed a high cliff like a wall at the edge of the rocks. She gazed at the beautiful waterfall which cascaded over the cliff into the river.

Brave Bear guided her along the bank to the edge of the falls, then pulled her under the spray to a protected path beneath it. A light mist touched her face and arms. The sunlight danced in bright colors on her and the rock wall beside her. He led her to a cave-like opening, then inside to a natural, three-foot round pool which nature had cut into the floor of the cave. Water trickled down the side of the wall and into the pool which evidently ran out simultaneously from somewhere near the bottom. The filtered sunlight gave the cave an irridescent glow and a mystical, enchanting aura.

Brave Bear lay the bundle which he carried down on a flat rock by the pool. When he unfolded it, she saw it contained a small cloth, blanket, and a bar of yellow soap—no doubt booty from some raid.

He pointed to her, the items and then the water, saying, "Menuah."

She knew he indicated for her to bathe. He turned and left. She stared at his departing frame in relief and astonishment. She assumed she was to bathe or be bathed; so she hastily undressed and slipped into the cool, refreshing water. At first, she scrubbed hurriedly, wanting to finish before he returned, but began to dawdle at the relaxing and delightful feel of the water and the smell of the yellow soap. The soap had a creamy texture and wildflower scent. A real bath, with real soap!

In spite of her former intention to hurry, she found herself relaxing in the pool and leisurely bathing. She shampooed her dusty hair several times, until it was squeaky clean. When she finally forced herself to get out, the scent of jasmine filled the air and clung to her skin and hair. She dried off with the blanket and turned to reach for her clothes.

They were gone! He had come and gone unnoticed and silent while she had been bathing. Her face paled, then reddened at the thoughts of him secretly watching her. She wrapped the blanket around her slender frame and knelt to squeeze the water from her dripping hair.

Moccasins loomed before her vision. She lifted her eyes to his face. He held a garment over his arm. As she raised herself up, he held it up for her view. It was a fawn color and laced up the back for some reason. It was soft and lovely. It had a deep band of exquisite beadwork on the neckline. The midarm sleeves and hem were fringed.

She stared at the dress in disbelief and asked, "For me?"

His hand reached out, released the blanket, and let it fall to the floor at her feet. The brave gasped sharply at Alisha's naked beauty. He averted his eyes, for he knew he must wait until their wedding to consummate the passion he felt for her. As he went to place the dress over her head, Alisha lifted her arms to aid him. The garment fell into place and fit perfectly. But then it should have, for it was Matu who had made it for him and she knew Alisha's size well.

Brave Bear gazed at her in admiration as she childishly twirled around for him. He caught her shoulders and stilled her long enough to lace the back. She lightly fingered the softened skin and delicate design of beadwork. He smiled his approval.

She quickly returned his smile and beamed, "It's beautiful!"

He handed her a porcupine-tail brush, some beaded ikans and a winyan cehnake. He left once more to allow her to do these things in private. She donned the breechcloth, then combed and braided her hair.

When she had finished and was waiting for him to come back, she hummed a lively waltz. She began to pirouette gracefully around the cave. As she twirled and whirled with dreamy, half-closed eyes, she landed right in his arms!

Brave Bear cupped Alisha's flushed face between his hands and pressed a light kiss on her mouth. She panted breathlessly, but did not pull away. He was glad to see her so light-hearted and relaxed. He called to her and motioned for her to come.

They walked along the path and back through the village. Her rising spirits soared even higher at the friendly smiles and nods she received from the people they passed along the way. Not a single person gave her a sneer or taunt. Instead, they seemed to be studying her closely. A feeling of acceptance of her was felt in the air. She warily looked around in utter confusion.

He regarded her troubled face. Taking her hand in his, he smiled and walked on. I do not understand this, she thought, but I'll accept it and be grateful.

Soon, they arrived at another teepee and went inside. A brave who was sitting by the fire spoke to him and motioned for them to come and be seated with him. They came forward and he said to her, "Lalematahpi," and sat down. She sat down very close to him. He pointed to the brave and said, "Kola," meaning friend. She nodded understanding.

She watched them as they smoked and talked for a short time. There was a young winyan preparing to serve the men food. She came forward and served them. When they had eaten their fill, they returned to their talking. The girl then served herself and Alisha.

She smiled shyly at Alisha as she handed her the dish containing a soup of meat and berries. Alisha returned the smile and said, "Thank you . . ."

The soup was very good and filling. For some reason, Alisha felt totally at ease here and now. It was like the gathering of good friends for luncheon, except she could not join in on the conversation. The girl took her dish when she had finished and they exchanged smiles again.

Seeing Alisha had finished eating, Brave Bear rose and called to her. She came forward, but halted at the flap and turned to the girl. She smiled and thanked her. They all grasped her meaning and smiled. She beamed at their politeness and kindness.

Brave Bear and Alisha walked out into the warm sunlight and returned to their teepee. He walked to the buffalo mats and told her to sit down. She did, but eyed him carefully as he went to get something from the storage area again. He came back to where she sat with a pair of "mihkissons" which were beaded and quilled. She took them from him and put them on. He had measured her foot while she had slept and let Matu make them for him.

He had wanted to surprise her with this gift. Alisha smiled happily and her green eyes danced as she pulled the rawhide strip snug and tied it securely. He then tied a beaded, leather headband around her forehead. There was one red and gray queque attached to the back. He held up a mirror, also taken with plunder, and let her view herself.

She carefully examined the girl in the mirror, the clothing, the features, the dark hair, the slightly tanned complexion, and feathered headband. She realized, except for her green eyes, she could easily pass for one of them. She gazed at her reflection in bewilderment. Why was he doing this? Why did he try to make her look like an Indian? Why was he giving her such lovely things to wear and have? Why were the others treating her more like a respected, honored guest than a slave and enemy? It was very clear Brave Bear was her owner and was pleased with what he saw.

No matter his reasons for her pardon, she would accept and enjoy it, until it was taken away. She was too timid to try to further reason or understand this change in her treatment. If her situation remained like this, her new captor and captivity would be most bearable. If Wanmdi Hota had even suspected she would have been treated like this, he would never have sold her.

Still, her mind could not help but think and warn her, this is only the lull before the storm—and she was too scared to think about what the storm might bring. Not knowing what else to do, she just stood there. She watched him for a clue to this puzzle.

He sat down on a straw mat near the fire and began to work on making new arrows. He took the sharply honed arrowhead and secured it to the slender shaft. Then, he placed the tapered feathers in a slit cut into the other end. He was very careful to get the balance and weight just right to insure true aim and flight. He secured the arrowhead to the shaft when all was set and ready.

While he worked, she strolled over to a rack-like shelf which held bows, arrows, tomahawks, and other weapons for hunting and warfare. Some of these were new, and others were in need of repair. She picked up an item here and there and examined its lines and artistry. She was amazed at the red man's ingenuity and intelligence that overcame such crude working conditions and supplies. He did not seem to mind her inquisitiveness or her handling of the weapons. She mused, how very trusting . . .

She picked up a long, slender shaft resembling a spear with red and gray feathers on one end and a very large head on the other. Evidently red and gray were Brave Bear's personal colors. She touched the feather in her headband and guessed it was to denote his ownership of her. She happily thought, I am his!

There were pottery jars on the ground which were filled with similar feathers. There were many pouches which she did not open. She left the storage area and just walked around.

He had been secretly watching her and was pleased she did not try to conceal any of the weapons or try to use one on him. She looked perfectly at ease and happy with her new home. He relaxed and returned his full attention to his work as she came to sit beside him.

She watched the deft workings of his strong, masculine hands and the object he worked on. He handed her the one he had just finished. She smiled and took it. She twisted it over in her delicate hands admiring his workmanship.

She put it down on the stack of others and leaned forward to watch him as he began another one. She became so engrossed in her observations that she did not realize she was leaning so close to him. Her breast lightly touched his bare arm and her hand came to rest upon his leg.

As time progressed, this had a very unsettling effect on Brave Bear and his work. Her fresh, sweet smell, her warm nearness, her beauty, gentleness and serenity made him want to crush her to him and possess her this very moment. He knew he could not until she was his in three more moons.

He turned his gaze to her. The stillness of his hands and the quiet of the teepee caused her to look up at him. Seeing that he was staring at her with an open look of desire and tenderness in his eyes, she flushed. He put the half-finished arrow down and pulled her face to his and kissed her softly.

In spite of herself, she stiffened in fear and sought to pull away. He felt the trembling in her and saw the pleading look in those large, brilliant eyes. She did not understand that the cold, dangerous glint in his angry eyes was against Gray Eagle and the things he had done to her to make her feel this way.

She stared at him as his lips grew taut in fury and he gritted his teeth. Her face slowly lost all color and fear leaped into her face. She gazed at him without moving, mesmerized like a cobra before the flutist. She could not seem to look away or move. She could only whisper, "I'm sorry . . ."

Her words broke into his thoughts and fury. He saw her ashen face and the green eyes so full of panic watching him in anticipation of punishment. His jaw and eyes quickly softened as he reached out to caress her cheek with the back of his hand. He returned to his work.

She stared at him in utter confusion. Why had he acted like that? She could not comprehend the gentle kiss, the sudden violent anger, then the tenderness when he saw her fear and panic. He was not going to press her or punish her? What kind of a man was he? He was far more unpredictable than Wanmdi Hota!

Why had he been so forgiving of her withdrawal? He could have easily overpowered her with his massive strength and done anything he wished to her. She could not figure out what he was saving her for. Is he trying to make me fall in love with him? she thought. But why would he want her to love him? Did he think she might compare him to Wanmdi Hota? If only I knew what he wanted from me, Alisha fretted. His actions seem to ask for more than a submissive slave.

She tried to recall what Powchutu had told her about all tribes being different in laws, customs and ways. The tribes out here were only alike in one way—their fierce hatred and contempt of the white man and his coming. She had come to see and know one thing for certain and that was how greatly her own people had underestimated the intelligence, physical strength, skills and courage of the Indians. Her people had been correct in one assumption: that they were aggressive, restless hunters and warriors, and very powerful enemies. But they were so much more. Alisha sighed. The two peoples could have learned and shared a lot together if they had not insisted on being enemies.

She was lightly shaken from her deep thoughts by Brave Bear's hand on her shoulder. She looked up in askance. She had been unaware of his departure, but surely he had gone for his garments were clean and fresh and his braids still wet. She must have been lost in her thoughts for a good while.

He stood tall and lean above her. He was wearing what Alisha called a weskit and leggings of matching deerskin, which were fringed and quilled. He placed a grizzly bear claw necklace around his neck. She knew from the stories Powchutu had told her that he had bare-handedly killed a fearless grizzly bear. Only a brave who had slain the fierce animal was allowed to wear its claws. A deed like that would certainly take a great deal of courage and daring. Powchutu had also told her the Indian tried to never kill a bear because it was believed to carry great spirits and magic, just like their brothers the buffalo. When it became necessary to do so, the animal's death was mourned as a fallen forest warrior.

She gazed up and down Brave Bear's lithe frame, thinking how much he reminded her of a story about a fierce Viking conqueror. He was so warlike and brave, but yet, gentle. His stance was one of self-confidence and boldness. Her face betrayed her awareness of his good looks and prowess. He was pleased by her expression and smiled knowingly.

Alisha hastily tore her gaze from his and pinkened. How she wished she could overcome this disconcerting habit of always blushing! Why did she feel so guilty at the way he made her react to him?

He pulled her to her feet by both of her arms to face him. He scanned the curious eyes and colorful face very slowly.

Alisha's gaze settled on his wanapin. She could not resist the urge to reach out and touch the long, sharp, deadly claws at his neck. She had heard the grizzly could open a horse's side or man's abdomen with one swipe and empty their insides to the ground. She lightly fingered them, then looked up at him with pride and respect glowing in her eyes.

She softly said, "You must be very brave and strong."

Her tone was very soft and gentle. He knew from the sound of it and the look on her face she had said something pleasant and nice to him or about him. How he wished she knew the words in his tongue to tell him what she meant.

He smiled and called, "Piintwike . . ."

It was nearly dusk. There was a huge campfire not far away which dispelled the chill and dark of the coming night. She hesitated and drew back in sudden panic. He cupped her face in between his hands and gazed into her eyes with reassurance. His mood and expression conveyed protection and peace to her. She followed him.

They sat before the campfire on a buffalo skin along with the old chief. The people appeared to be very happy and excited about something about to take place. A feeling of expectance and joy was felt all around her.

She involuntarily jumped as a low whoop abruptly sounded in the still, quiet night. Brave Bear's hand covered hers and held it securely. She watched as an Indian man danced around the fire, chanting some unintelligible song. He wore part of the head of a buffalo over his own with the skin falling down his back like a cape. She knew she was observing some type of ceremony, but could not fathom its meaning.

She studied the faces of the people around her. They held no malice toward her so she was not the center of attraction for what was about to take place. But if she were not involved in some way, then why was she, a captive, allowed to join them? Perhaps she was wrong! Maybe she would be the star attraction later . . .

After the buffalo dancer completed his part, other braves danced and chanted for a time. Later, they were joined by some young maidens who began to sing and dance with them. Soon, they appeared to pair off, but never touched. They would dance toward each other, giving what Alisha called romantic gazes, then dance away once more. Over and over they would repeat these actions.

The drumming suddenly stopped and five blankets were brought forward and given to the five girls. Each in turn walked to her partner and stopped before him, placing the blanket around her shoulders. She then embraced him, drawing him into the blanket with her.

Loud whoops of joy and excitement filled the area as the couples each ran laughing toward separate teepees. A thought hit her, a multiple wedding!

The chanting and dancing started again and she turned to watch what would happen next. Feeling for sure she was not expected to do anything, she began to relax and become absorbed in what was going on around her. Brave Bear was closely scrutinizing her and her behavior. He noted the disappearance of her apprehension and the smile upon her lips. She was thinking of how beautiful all weddings were.

Someone stepped before her vision and handed her a fork, spoon and cup which had been carved from the horns of a buffalo, along with a clay-type plate. She was then given food and water. She looked at the menu before her, buffalo roast, wild vegetables, corn cakes, and berries. At this feast, she was being allowed to eat at the same time as the men. She ate as she watched the merriment before her.

Several men came forward and seated themselves by the fire and began to play a variety of musical instruments. One beat on a kettle drum, one clicked sticks of different lengths together for a variety of sounds, several blew on eagle-bone whistles and others shook gourd rattlers of varying sizes and shapes. The music was very enjoyable. Alisha found herself nodding her head to the beat of the music.

When the eating was finished and the music stopped, she watched as two braves came forward to the fire, each carrying a small baby. She tensed in anticipation. Surely they did not practice pagan sacrifices of babies? The ritual was the same in both cases. First the father and then the child was tattooed. The tattoo was made by first scratching the desired akito on the skin with a sharp bone. Then, the ceremonial chief rubbed cold, black ash from the fire into the etchings. The marks were identical for the man and his child. The man's was on the back of his right hand and the "papoos" was on its left buttock. The child's placement was to avoid confusion when he became an adult and had an akito of his own.

Observing the ritual held no special meaning for Alisha. She did not even recall what area of her body the old chief had examined and touched. The thought she carried an akito on her left buttock to match the one on the old chief's hand never entered her mind.

She looked over to find both men watching her very intently as if they waited for her to do or say something. She stared bewildered, wondering why they stared at her like that. She did not comprehend the ritual's importance in her life, nor the curious looks from the two men. She nervously forced her attention back to the events before her.

The feasting and celebrating went on and on. She realized the young warrior beside her was appropriately dressed for this occasion and began to wonder at her own dress and appearance. She could easily pass for an Indian and his mate from her looks and his behavior toward her. She felt like the missing piece to a puzzle, where everyone but she knew where it fit!

I feel like a lady being presented at court by the king himself, Alisha thought. How could he possibly feel anything for me when we have just met? I shall surely go mad if I do not guess this riddle soon. He treats me like his prized mate. No, not even that, for he doesn't even touch me at night. For the hundredth time, her mind screamed, what does he want from me? Why do these people look at me and treat me like I belong here, like this is a natural, normal situation? But I wish it could be like this forever . . .

Alisha began to get very tired and sleepy. Her head began to nod sleepily. Brave Bear realized her fatigue and took her back to their teepee. She trustingly followed him like a child and lay down to go to sleep. He stayed there for a time watching her sleep. He thought, soon you will be mine, Shalee, and then I shall not have to leave your side at night.

He left the teepee to return to the feast and the others. He would sleep later. He did not need to be so close to her right now. Her beauty had outshone itself tonight. She would be far too tempting lying there so close and warm. He beamed with pride at the comments from some of the other men.

Morning dawned with a bright burst of sunlight and music from eager songbirds, ready to begin their new day. Alisha lazily stretched on the buffalo skins as she attuned herself to her surroundings. It still seemed strange to wake up here, knowing she now belonged to another man. But what a man he was turning out to be! If he was trying to settle her down and get under her skin, he was doing a very good and quick job of it!

She suddenly thought, I bet I'm the only white person anywhere near here. I wonder how long it will be before more whites and cavalry come and the bloodbath begins all over again. Why can't they just leave the Indians to their lands and in peace? Could anything be worth so many lives and so much suffering?

The flap was lifted and Matu came in, bringing food. She shocked Alisha with her new-found kindness and friendliness. Alisha felt alarm creep up her back and neck at the old woman's behavior and attention toward her. Alisha had caught her watching her many times with that secretive, knowing smile.

Seeing Alisha's expression of wariness and suspicion, Matu lovingly patted her hand and spoke rapidly to her. She could only grasp a few of the words, for Matu had slipped back into the use of her own tongue.

"Shalee . . . hiya . . . iksisakuyi . . . Mahpiya Sapa . . . Mato Waditaka . . . Shalee . . . hiya Wanmdi Hota . . . lalematahpi . . . Shalee . . ."

The young girl stared at her in confusion. Was Matu trying to say Alisha when she kept saying Shalee so many times? She had never called Lese anything before, so she assumed she could not say her name correctly. Why Matu was brought here was a mystery to Alisha.

Why is she waiting on me like a servant rather than me doing the work of a slave? Alisha thought, for she knew she had not been forced to do any work since she had been brought here. Why?

So many questions filled her mind, but still no answers. At least none which made any sense to her. Perhaps she would never understand this strange situation. If only one of them could speak English, or she could learn their tongue. She could tell it was a different dialect from the Oglala, so the few words she had learned in the Oglala village were of no use to her here. If this brave and his people were willing, she would learn his tongue and be able to communicate with them. He certainly did not view and treat her as Wanmdi Hota had done. Would he care if I tried to learn his tongue and talked with him? she wondered. I cannot help but believe he likes and accepts me, white or not! I only hope I am correct. She silently prayed, please let me find peace and acceptance here.

She decided to find out what he would think about her attempts to communicate with him. Powchutu had told her each tribe had its own dialect, but could communicate with each other with a sort of sign language. Powchutu had spoken some of the different dialects for her to show her how they differed. Some of them sounded guttural, some nasal, some harsh, and some mellifluous. Powchutu was very quick and talented at picking up a new dialect. I wish he were here now to help me learn just this one, she sighed deeply.

As she was eating, she was wondering where Brave Bear was this morning. She decided she was restless in the confines of his teepee. What would his people do if she walked outside? She looked out the opening in the flap and gazed all around. There did not appear to be anyone guarding her, so she stepped out into the warm sunlight. Still, no guard pounced upon her to force her back inside.

Everyone seemed absorbed in his daily chores and duties. Some of the women were sitting in a group making pemmican, while others bagged it for storage. She came near to where they worked and stopped to watch them. She observed how they pounded the dried meat into a fine powder, mixed it with a type of melted fat, and added crushed, dried berries. They pressed it into rolls and packed it into leather bags to store for use later. It would last for months after this preparation.

Although the Indian women seemed to do most of the work and chores, they were highly respected. The women were allowed to join the men for certain feasts and ceremonies, but most of the talks, meetings and rituals were for the warriors and men only. Powchutu had told her the winyan owned all the family's property, except for the horses and weapons. Indian women were indeed different in many ways from white women.

Alisha moved on to where other women were cooking meat on a large spit. Others sat talking as they sewed on new garments and moccasins. There were many others, alone or in small groups, doing various chores. As she walked among them or stopped to observe what they did, Alisha was surprised that they would look up and nod or smile to her! She could not believe her eyes, but would nod and smile sweetly in return. Then, she would move on to view others.

She strolled through the edge of the village toward the river. Near the last row of teepees, she saw women scraping meat and fat from animal skins. They would stretch them out and attach them to wooden frames to tan and cure with the juices of the sumac and other bushes. She noticed many skins and hides from buffalos, deer, elk, wolf, and other animals. Like most of the plains Indians, they also survived mainly on the buffalo and larger game. She saw one hide which was particularly soft and beautiful. It was from the wapiti and was known for its tender meat and beautiful skins.

She pondered if these Indians were what Powchutu had called nomadic, those who only stayed in one location as long as the hunting was good. Then they would pack up and move on as the game would become scarce. The camp looked permanent to her, but what did she know about such things?

She noted evidence of sun worship here, too. She had studied the pictures drawn on the teepees with great detail and skill. She saw the sun etchings on armbands and shields. She had seen the morning salutes and chants to the rising sun and heard him called Naki. Did the scalp-hair decorations on the teepee poles and weapons mean they also practiced scalping? Alisha wondered.

Powchutu had told her scalping was not done to kill or torture a person, but to show bravery and daring. The warrior was to touch his enemy by taking a scalp lock of his hair, but not kill or injure him. In the process, he was to avoid death, injury and touch from his enemy. The daring was not in the killing of an enemy, but in the touching him at great risk to oneself. This was a very great coup for any warrior or hunter.

Some braves believed that by taking a man's scalp, he could be endowed with that man's power and courage. For that reason, warriors always tried to scalp brave and powerful men. Alisha had a hard time understanding this concept when Powchutu had spoken of it to her.

She recalled the many long talks she and Powchutu had back at the fort about the Sun Dance and its meaning in the life of the Indians. It would soon be time for it. Alisha was excited that she could learn first-hand of its importance and meaning.

Each dance and ceremony had its own chants, songs and dances. Many appeared to be beliefs about the elements the Indians worshipped, like the sun, wind, rain and fire. Others were about battles, animals and events in the tribe's life. She remembered Powchutu had said they believed all things, whether living or inanimate, had good or bad spirits which dwelled within them. When Alisha learned Brave Bear's tongue, she swore, she would learn more about these beliefs and customs.

She determined to watch and learn all she could so she might someday be wholly accepted. I shall always be grateful to my friend Powchutu for all he has taught me, she thought. He was right when he advised me to learn all I could about them, and quickly.

Do all Indians worship the cottonwood trees, the buffalo, the sun, eagle and snake, as Wanmdi Hota's tribe does? she wondered. I must learn of these similarities and differences. Those things are painted on nearly everything, but is it for decoration or for some purpose?

She realized, if the eagle had to do with the symbol of Wanmdi Hota's name, this warrior here must have bear in his name. He not only wore the bear claws to the ceremony, but usually wore a bear's head wanapin. Perhaps I will soon know, for I shall find some way to ask him.

Englanders would call this kind of life and existence primitive, but these people were well-suited to this wild, untamed wilderness, and it to them and their way of life. They were free and happy people.

Alisha strolled on a little further. She saw children playing games in a meadow across the river, while older children gathered wild vegetables and berries. The older boys and girls worked in a small garden near the river on this side. It looked as if it had corn, wild greens, and a type of tobacco growing there. Evidently these Indians had been at this campsite for a long time.

The river bank was busy with women doing their washing or fetching mni. She had noted the Indians did not seem to care for fish, or maybe, they considered it too time-consuming for the small amount of meat one got. They went after the larger game which had more meat and skins. The buffalo, besides supplying food, clothing and shelter, gave sinews for thread, paunches and bladders for water and storage bags, bones and horns for cups and utensils, and hooves for tools and glues. Nothing was wasted from an animal. All parts had some use. They did not kill for sport or only for select cuts as the white man did. This was a great wrong in the red man's eyes.

Alisha looked up at the sounds of loud thundering of horses' hooves and Indian shouts. At the far end of the village, older boys were practicing horsemanship, wrestling, weaponry, warfare and hunting. Some of the older warriors and younger braves were instructing them. Alisha remained there to watch for a while.

She observed boys target-practicing with bow and arrows, knife throwing, and lance fighting and tossing. They used padded tomahawks and war clubs. She noticed the circles in which many boys were practicing wrestling and fighting in groups of twos. All things which had to be mastered by the young braves were being taught and learned on that dusty, hot field.

Her green eyes wide with interest, Alisha watched others as they raced and exercised to build their muscles and develop agility and self-confidence. These and other qualities were essential for a warrior and hunter to insure his safety and success. They appeared to be serious and alert in their studies, but they also appeared to be having fun.

She longed to go for a ride on one of those swift ponies which the Indian boys practiced mounting and riding. How she missed her riding! How she yearned to run over there and hop upon one of the horses' backs and speed away with the sun and wind in her face! There was nothing else like that wild, carefree feeling of freedom—the wind whipping her hair and clothes, tingling her skin and caressing her hair with an untamed, unbridled spirit.

Perhaps she could persuade the warrior to take her for a ride some day soon. She immediately mocked herself, Lese, you foolish girl, women don't do that sort of thing out here!

She recalled the lesson Powchutu gave her on the Indian and his horse. The Indians had only had horses for about twenty-five or thirty years. They had been brought to the New World by the early Spanish. Before the horse had come to them, they had hunted and fought on foot and had used dogs for burden bearing along with a travois.

Powchutu had told her hunting and warfare had increased with the coming of the horse. The Indians had quickly become very skilled in horsemanship. They had even learned a few tricks of their own, such as the master's knee command and whistle. They now rode with the ease and skill of experts. She had laughed as she recalled Powchutu saying they had called horses the "big dog." She could easily imagine the burden the horse had lifted from the backs and shoulders of the women.

She walked along the river bank for a time, then sat down. She took off her moccasins and dangled her feet in the cool water. How peaceful and quiet it was here. Who would have guessed only a few days ago a terrible bloodbath had occurred near here? Time seemed so remote here, so unimportant, so out of place . . .

She contemplated her new surroundings and life. Her life and treatment here were so unlike what she had experienced in the Oglala village. She liked and respected these people here already. She could easily accept them for who and what they were and could pass no judgments on them or their ways.

The warm summer sun beat down on her, the fragrant flowers and wild grasses across the river in the meadow filled her nostrils, and the cool water licked at her feet. She sank to the ground on her back, staring up at the billowy, white clouds moving across a periwinkle sky. She was thinking about the warrior who now held her prisoner. She knew in her mind she would go to him and accept him in any way he wished her.

Alisha mused, I must show him this very day I accept him and my new life here. Perhaps that is what he is waiting to see. I will look for the peace and happiness I was denied in Wanmdi Hota's camp. This day, I will belong to him in every way if he but says the word. It is time to lay the past to rest and try for a new beginning here with him.

Her eyes closed and she was soon fast asleep.

212

After what seemed but minutes, she yawned and stretched like a feline, slowly awakening. A shadow fell across her face and she hastily turned to see the person who cast it. The brave was sitting beside her cross-legged, gazing off toward the hills at the edge of the meadow.

She quickly sat up and flushed hotly at her lax behavior. He gave her a few minutes to straighten her clothes, compose herself and put on her moccasins.

"Piintwike, Shalee. Matu tipi."

They walked back to the village. He did not appear to be upset or angry with her for leaving his teepee or for wandering off alone like that. They walked to a teepee, ducked, and entered. Matu was sitting on a buffalo skin sewing on a garment.

She looked up and spoke with the brave. She held up the garment for his inspection. Alisha noted its delicate beauty and feminine design. The skin was a creamy white, but she did not know if it had come from some unknown animal or an albino. It looked to be about her size. The old woman was working on a design of beadwork around the neckline with small gold beads.

He took the dress from her and held it up before Alisha. He was pleased with the beautiful sight she would make in it on their joining day. She was astounded. Is it for me? she wondered, but knew it was. It is exquisite and very special. Why would he have such a lovely dress made for me? What could it be for? She shyly and carefully touched its softness and the fragile beadword. He saw her look of pleasure at the dress. He smiled and she returned it.

He handed the dress back to Matu and they spoke again. He turned and spoke to Alisha. Pointing to Matu, he said, "Matu." She looked confused. He thought for a minute, then spoke again, "Mato Waditaka," pointing to himself. Pointing to the old woman again, he said, "Matu." He touched Alisha's face and called her Shalee.

Her eyes quickly went to the old woman, realizing this was what she had called her. She shook her head and said, "Alisha," pointing to herself.

He realized she did not understand he was telling her the name her father had given to her at birth. Recalling what Wanmdi Hota had called her at his camp, then what she had just called herself, he began again.

He spoke clearly and distinctly. "Hiya Lese . . . hiya Alisha." He touched her face and softly said, "Shalee."

For a short time, she looked perplexed, then her face brightened. He was giving her an Indian name! She beamed her understanding. Pointing to herself, she replied, "Shalee." Pointing to the old woman, she said, "Matu." Then she lay a small hand upon his chest and said, "Mato Waditaka."

He smiled broadly and replied, "Sha."

He spoke again with Matu for a few minutes.

214

He called to her to come. She smiled at him and followed him outside. She was overjoyed with the events of moments ago.

He was accepting her as an Indian! He wanted her to look, act and live like one, and had even named her like one. Matu had smiled at her and treated her with respect and friendliness, as had all the others today. Could this really be happening to her? Matu had returned to her work as they were leaving, but had handed him a small bundle first.

They had walked along happily until they reached his teepee and entered. A different girl served them food this night, but she was too excited to notice what she even ate.

When the meal was over, Brave Bear and another man sat talking and smoking by the campfire while she sat on the buffalo skins watching them. Brave Bear called her to come to lie down to sleep. She quickly and unhesitantly did so this time. She was soon asleep, but it took him quite some time to relax and sleep.

He had to fight the desire to hold her and love her. There will be time for loving and touching in two moons, he reassured himself. I must be patient until I have won her to my heart. I saw the look in her eyes this day. She has accepted me and her life here. I am pleased by the softness I see growing in her. She no longer fears me or my people. She would come to me in willingness this very night if I but asked her and this inflames my blood and body. If I but kissed her or touched her, I would take her, so I dare not.

Once again, he felt the hatred and rage for Wanmdi Hota and his abuse to her. How could he have crushed this lovely flower? Gray Eagle had not realized what he had, but by now he surely realized what he had given up.

He smiled and went to sleep.

Chapter Five

When Alisha awoke the next morning, she was surprised to find Brave Bear still there. He was sitting near the fire, sharpening his knife, then restringing his bow. She lay quietly for a short time, feigning sleep as she watched him. She saw the powerful muscles in his arms and shoulders harden and bulge at the strain of bending the bow taut to attach the new string. Possessing the hunter's sixth sense, he knew she was secretly watching him. He glanced over at the mat and called to her to come. She sat up and stretched as if she had just awakened. He smiled to himself in amusement.

Matu came with their food. When both of them had finished eating, Brave Bear handed Alisha the bundle he had carried from Matu's teepee the day before. Alisha excitedly opened it to find two more garments equally as lovely as the first one. To her mild disappointment, the white one was not among them. She recalled Matu was not finished with it yet.

She held one of the dresses up and twirled around like a child at Christmas time. She squealed with unsuppressed delight at the new pair of moccasins which were prettier than the other pair.

217

"Oh, Mato Waditaka! You're wonderful! How can I ever thank you for all of these gifts and your kindness?"

She ran to him and hugged him tightly. Throwing her arms around his neck, she impulsively kissed him. He did not have time to return the kiss, for she danced away holding her new possession like valued treasures. She recalled all too well her time at the fort when she had no possessions of her own at all. Brave Bear was much too good to be true!

He could not withhold his laughter as he watched her gaiety and happiness. She was scurrying around like an excited chipmunk collecting a windfall of cone nuggets. He began to gather the items needed for bathing and called to her.

"Shalee, piintwike. Menuah."

She quickly selected the prettiest dress and new moccasins and followed his lead. She walked closely behind him through the village in happiness. She smiled and nodded to everyone she met and they returned her greetings. He shook his head and laughed at her openly.

She had been through so much heartache and suffering lately that she hungered for this kindness and attention he was offering her. She accepted his treatment without reserve or caution. For so very long, she had lived under constant fear, uncertainty, and intimidation that it was totally intoxicating and exhilarating to be freed, accepted and treated so very specially. His tender behavior, along with his gentle smiles, dissolved her fear and doubts about him and her life here.

When the time came, she would go to him even if she had to force herself to submit to anything with him! But somehow, she imagined he could use his prowess and charm to easily seduce her.

She vowed, I will make him replace Wanmdi Hota in my heart. I should thank my guardian angel it was Mato Waditaka who found and took me. If I had searched a lifetime, I could not have found another warrior such as he. I must learn to love him. Surely it cannot be so difficult, for my body leaps with desire for him even now when he is near. If I can want him that way, then surely I can love him in time . . .

He gazed over at her as they walked along the river bank, studying the relaxed, happy face and sparkling, green eyes. She is happy here, he thought. She is truly mine as she could never be Wanmdi Hota's. In spite of his jealousy, Brave Bear was glad he had not found and taken her as wasichu, but had only known her as Shalee. The few remaining feelings she has for him will soon dim and fade in the light of my love and our happiness together. I wonder if he even knows what he has lost. Perhaps this is why he fought to keep her so fiercely. Blinded by his own growing love for Alisha, Mato Waditaka thought, nothing could explain Gray Eagle's cruelty to her. If he dares to harm her again in any way, I will kill him!

To Alisha's mortification, this time he sat

down to wait for her to bathe! She stood rooted to the floor, watching him with an uncertain gaze. If it must be, then so be it, she thought. She came forward very slowly and began to unlace her dress. Her face flamed in embarrassment. He noted her shame and hesitation and stood up. She looked up at him in suppressed modesty and shyness. He smiled knowingly and left.

She sighed in deep relief, undressed, and quickly bathed. She dressed and was very careful with her grooming to look her best for him. She wanted to show him she accepted him and was glad he accepted her.

These feelings he aroused in her were new and frightening to her. She knew what it was to want a man in love, but in lust? That was a very different situation altogether. Was this why she always pulled back? Did her inner self know something about her that she did not? Would she be unable to make love to him when it really came to the actual act? Would she pull away at the very last moment and resist? If she did, what would he do or say? Would he accept such a stinging rejection the same way Jeffery had? Fear prickled in her.

I must find out if I can respond to him. I must not ever pull away from him. How long can I expect him to be so understanding and patient with my fear? I have already decided to try to love him, or at least, accept him completely. So do it, Alisha! No more withdrawals! No more freezing up! No more pulling away, no more withholding anything from him!

Mato Waditaka is waiting out there for you, Lese, Alisha scolded herself. Forget Wanmdi Hota and all he ever was to you. Go to Mato Waditaka with open arms and an open heart. Love him, for he is worthy of your love. Belong to him in every way and in every part of your mind and body. Let him see and know this very day that you are Shalee and you are his . . .

She walked to the cave entrance and found him standing there propped against the rock wall. He stepped up to meet her. To his great astonishment, she placed her arms around his neck to pull his head down to hers, and kissed him fully on the mouth. That kiss held some surprises for both of them.

He felt the tremors in her body and the warmth of her closeness. Her sweet smell filled his senses as she pressed her slender body to his. For a moment, he was taken off guard by her unexpected actions and heated responses to him.

He moaned huskily and pulled her into his full embrace. He returned the kiss with growing passion and longing. She pressed even closer to him and tightened her hold around his neck. Her kiss became more intense and demanding. He had to stop this before . . . he gently pushed her away and gazed into her passion-glazed eyes. He saw what he had waited and longed to see since the first day he had looked into those depths of green.

She was telling him she wanted him as a man; she no longer feared him or his taking her; she wanted to belong to him completely; and she desired him to take her right here and now!

It took every bit of willpower he possessed not to do as she begged with those tempting eyes of hers. To pull away from her was the hardest thing he had ever had to do in his entire life—and he would soon regret he had.

Only one more moon, my love. Then I shall take you with a love and passion you have never known or felt before. Tomorrow night we will be joined and you will be mine forever.

He smiled into her eyes and gently kissed her on her nose, forehead and cheek, then lightly brushed her lips. She had seen and felt how much he wanted her, but was telling her this was not the time and place for lovemaking. The glow in his black eyes and the smile on his sensuous lips told her he knew and understood what she had just told him without words. He knows what I mean. He received the message and will answer it in the best time and place. Until then, he knows . . .

This time, they did not return immediately to the village. Instead, they walked along the rocky, protected path to the other side of the falls and out into the flower-filled meadow on the opposite bank. A light breeze played through the tall grasses and wildflowers, sending fragrant smells into the wind and their nostrils. Delicate, colorful butterflies and humming bees darted to and from the flowers gathering nectar. Alisha watched their flights with delight and wonder, while Mato Waditaka watched her.

The sky had never looked bluer or clearer, with white clouds like drifts of snow. Alisha stooped to pluck a flower here and there as they strolled along. The meadow was an array of color and beauty filled with purple and yellow violets, black-eyed susans, goldenrods, bluebells, primroses, and pasqueflowers. He soon stopped and pulled her down to sit beside him amidst the grasses and flowers.

She watched his troubled, thoughtful looks from beneath lowered lashes, wondering what he fretted about. He seemed engrossed in some deep and perplexing matter. She was right.

Mato Waditaka was trying to decide how to tell Alisha who she was and what was going to take place tomorrow, for it was time she knew. How could he explain his feelings for her and ask for her love in return? How could he tell her to forget Wanmdi Hota and all he did to her? If only there was not this language barrier, he thought in exasperation. He must teach her his tongue as soon as possible. Evidently from the few words of Oglala she knew, Wanmdi Hota had not tried to teach her his tongue for she had been with him long enough to know more. She was quick and smart. He could tell this from how quickly she had picked up the few words and names he had told her. Why had Wanmdi Hota tried to keep her in silence? Did he think she was unworthy of speaking with him and his people? He has missed much in not working for her friendship. Brave Bear had learned already how warm and good it was to be with her.

Alisha lightly touched his arm and asked in a concerned tone, "Mato Waditaka, is something wrong? Are you displeased with me for what I did?" She gazed into his warm eyes and knew she could not make him understand.

Her concern and worry for his mood touched him and he wondered how he would ever be able to wait until tomorrow night to have her. Tomorrow seemed like winters away! She was surprised when he caught her shoulders and pushed her to the ground upon her back. He lay half on her body and half off. He propped up on his elbows, one on either side of her head and stared down into her face. His look was intent, but tender. He smiled. She revealed no fear or doubt in her lucid, green eyes.

He did note the confusion and curiosity in her expression at his steady gaze. Here was what he had waited for all his life. Here was that special prize a man finds only once in his entire lifetime. He smiled into the depths of those green pools of magic and whispered, "Une hunwi . . ."

He slowly leaned down until his lips made fiery contact with hers and kissed her hungrily. She made no move to pull away or resist, but held back emotionally. She did not want to become heated with desire and passion, for she did not know how to suppress it when it was not satisfied. Surely he did not mean to take her here and now out in the open. If she allowed herself to become engrossed in his kiss, she would be consumed with passion, then he would pull away to return to the village, leaving her hanging with her feelings unsated. She willingly accepted the kiss, but did not openly respond to it.

A dark shadow loomed over them like a black, ominous storm cloud. Alisha looked up into the stony, cold face of Wanmdi Hota . . .

Their eyes met and locked, his in fury, hers in sheer terror. Her face went ashen and her eyes widened in disbelief. Her body froze and chilled even in the heat of the afternoon. Her nails unknowingly dug into the skin of Brave Bear's back.

Seeing the change in her mood and action, he lifted his head to gaze into her petrified face and panicked eyes which looked beyond him. His sixth sense of danger had been overpowered in the heat of the moment. But her fear had instantly brought it back. He knew the man was there before he looked. He bolted up and turned to face his enemy, his knife quickly in his grip.

Alisha stared into the face whose only expression was the unconcealed fury which blazed in his coal eyes and the taut muscles in his jawline. His entire body strained in violence and anger. Alisha blanched even more and began to shake uncontrollably. Gray Eagle was not sure which alarmed him the most, her situation with Brave Bear, or the look on her ashen face.

Brave Bear had been so consumed with passion and desire which had swept through his body like a fire out of control, he had made the worst error a warrior could ever make: he had dropped his guard. If this had been a true enemy, he would be lying dead in the meadow and she would have been taken as another's captive. Gray Eagle was also very much aware of the effect his Lese was having on Brave Bear.

Brave Bear was furious with himself for this brief lapse of training in alertness, for the timing of Gray Eagle's arrival, and for the look on Alisha's face. His eyes narrowed and his jaw grew taut as he glared at Gray Eagle. This was the man who had first taken what was to be his own. Gray Eagle had first known her and now he dared to come here and frighten her like this!

Just yesterday Alisha had begun to relax and accept him and her new home. Her fears, hurts and suspicions were turning into acceptance and friendship. Would she think he had anything to do with Wanmdi Hota's being here? He had seen how his gentleness and kindness had relieved and relaxed her. He had seen her reaching out to him as a man, of how she had hungered and thirsted for love, a smile, some tenderness and acceptance. He had given her these things and she had devoured them as a starving person would food and water.

Today, she had radiated with new life and happiness. Now it was all shattered with Wanmdi Hota's coming. He had reminded her of all the hate, cruelty and suffering she had been forced to endure at the hands of the Indian.

They faced each other as foes, teeth clenched,

eyes blazing fury and fire, bodies tight and tense for action, and their faces cold, gray masks of hatred. They were so intent on watching each other's moves, they failed to notice Alisha's head begin to nod from side to side in refusal of the meaning of his appearance here, nor did they see the quickened breathing from the parted, dry lips.

She bolted up and slowly began to back away from the two angry braves. Her voice, almost inaudible, touched their ears as she muttered, "No ... no ... no ... It can't be! Not again ..."

Sheer terror gripped her heart and mind and she turned to flee. She ran as fast as she could toward the forest at the edge of the meadow. She did not hear the voices call to her, nor the feel of the grasses and wildflowers as they brushed against her legs. Her mind screamed, run, run, Alisha ... you must get away! You must hide where he can never find you! Don't look back. Just keep running and running ...

Her heart pounded in her chest calling out, why is he here? Was this all some new game, a cruel taunt to disarm me? Is this why Mato Waditaka hasn't touched me? Do I still belong to Wanmdi Hota? Is this my punishment, to see what it would be like to be accepted, to be loved completely? Was it only a cruel jest? Has he come to take me back with him ... to Hell? I won't go! I won't go! I hate him, I hate him ... please, Mato Waditaka, do not let this happen! Let me belong to you!

Her chest heaved. Her lungs burned and ached. Her throat was dry. Her legs began to cramp and stiffen as she realized it was hopeless to try and flee. With their power and stamina, they would easily overtake her anytime. What's the use? But, she knew she must keep on running and trying. Make the axe come to you, Alisha! Don't go to it willingly and foolishly.

A strong arm snaked out and seized her, stopping her. Her first thought was, it is Wanmdi Hota. She spun around and began to fight blindly like a cornered wildcat, kicking, biting, and scratching. Two, powerful hands grabbed her forearms in a vise of steel and commanded her to stop.

"Shalee!"

Her face jerked up to see Brave Bear. She was breathless, staring up into his concerned, worried eyes. His expression touched her. She flung herself into his strong, tender embrace and cried hysterically. She clung to him like a drowning person to a lifebuoy.

She begged, "Don't let him take me, Mato Waditaka. No! Please . . . Shalee hiya ya! Shalee ku-wa Mato Waditaka . . ." He caught and understood the desperate words she struggled to get out. He tightened his embrace on her.

Her labored breathing slowed slightly, but the tears flowed unchecked down her flushed cheeks. She continued her pleading. "Please, Mato Waditaka, he'll hurt me. Maybe he'll kill me. I'll do anything you ask if you'll let me stay here. Please don't send me away . . ." She took his strong hands in her small, cold ones and squeezed them tightly. "What if he sells me to someone else who is cold and cruel like he is? Don't trade me back to him. I am happy here."

Brave Bear comprehended many of her words and meanings. He knew she feared returning with Wanmdi Hota and pleaded with him to keep her here with him. She chooses me over him! he beamed with pride and confidence. She shows who her choice is, surely he can see this also. She wishes to remain here forever with me and our people, and it shall be!

She was begging from him and not Wanmdi Hota. She believed him to be the better man. The effect Wanmdi Hota had on her pleased him greatly. She could not possibly love or want a man she feared so much.

He pulled her into his fierce embrace and held her lovingly. "Sh . . . sh . . . Shalee Mato Wadi-taka's." He gently shushed her with his finger to her quivering lips. She understood his tone and meaning but not his exact words, spoken like a soft caress. "I will not let him or anyone harm you ever again, Shalee, my love and heart." She felt protection and love in the circle of his powerful arms and snuggled there to draw comfort from it.

That was, until the voice of Gray Eagle touched her ears . . . she inhaled sharply as she buried her forehead into Brave Bear's chest and tightened her hold around his waist. I cannot look at him, she wildly thought. Mato Wadi-taka won't send me back to him. Brave Bear wants me. I am safe here with him. Why has Wanmdi Hota come here today? Does he wish to scare me or torment me? Does he wish to remind me of his hatred? Will he forever seek some way to torture and hurt me? He would only kill me, or sell me, or abuse me again. Has he heard how gentle and loving Mato Waditaka is and wishes to find me a cruel and harsh master instead? I must stay here with Mato Waditaka at all cost . . . he must keep me. He must!

The two warriors glared at each other. Brave Bear was the first one to speak, "What do you want here? Why have you come?"

The answer was brief and coldly stated, "I have come for Lese. She belongs to me."

Hearing the words "come" and "Lese," Alisha guessed what he said . . . she must come back to him. She looked horrified. She snuggled even closer to Brave Bear, clinging to him frantically. There was silent pleading for mercy in her bright, terrified eyes.

She said to Gray Eagle, "I hate you! I will never go back with you! I will die first! Never! You sold me to Mato Waditaka and I now belong to him. You have no claim on my life!"

She felt his gaze pierce her very soul to dig into her most secret thoughts of her brain and feelings of her heart. She trembled. In despair, she cried out to him, "Free me, Wanmdi Hota! Leave me in peace. I beg you, do not take me back. Haven't I suffered enough at your hands? What do you want from me? Why must you continue to torment me at every turn? You must free me from your evil grip of hatred and cruelty. Let our spirits separate and go their own ways. Take Chela and leave me here with Mato Waditaka. Is that so very much to ask for?"

Gray Eagle spoke with Brave Bear, but kept his eyes on Alisha. "She is mine, Mato Waditaka. Soon you and all the others will see and know this also. I will not leave here without her!"

Brave Bear tightened his hold on Alisha. She wrongfully assumed Gray Eagle had threatened her in some way. Brave Bear answered him, "You will never take her from me." Then, he scoffed, taunting him, "Do you not see how she hates and fears you? Do you not see she clings to me? She has made her choice. It is me, not you. She rejects you and accepts me. So it shall remain. I would be mad to let you take her from here for any reason. Leave us!"

Gray Eagle spoke low and ominously, "Lese de mitawa!" He held out his hand to her and called, "Ku-wa, Cinstinna . . ."

She glared at his opened, extended hand in contempt and fear. She shouted, "Never! Never will I accept your hand again." She turned her face away, fearing her tears would show the hurt she felt at his calling her "Little One" as he had done on many other occasions. But he had seen her tears before she turned away.

Brave Bear laughed in his face at her cold rejection. He retorted mockingly, "You are a fool, Wanmdi Hota. You held the moon and stars in your arms, but only hatred and cruelty

231

in your heart and mind. She is loved here. She is happy here. Why can you not leave her in peace? We will be joined in one moon. Then, she will forever be mine. I will not give her up, now or ever. She was happy until you came. She will never belong to you. Accept this and the loss of her.''

He took Alisha by the hand and led her back toward the camp. She mutely followed, not daring to look at either man.

Gray Eagle remained where he was, watching them walk away together. Only then did his face and eyes reveal the pain and doubts he felt within. How will I ever convince them to let her return with me when she so clearly shows her choice for Mato Waditaka and his camp? Anguish tore at his heart like a vulture at its prey.

He had seen them walking in the meadow, hand in hand. He could discern her relaxed, happy face from where he had stood observing them. Mato Waditaka is right about one thing, he thought. She is happier here. But why shouldn't she be? She is looked on as the daughter of the chief and accepted as such. The people here see her as Si-ha Sapa, not wasichu like it was in my camp. She can only accept what she sees with her eyes and feels with her senses. Wouldn't she choose the love and acceptance they have shown her over the fear, rejection and hatred of my camp? She sees only love and tenderness from him, but recalls cruelty and hatred from me. If only you knew the whole truth, my love . . .

He realized his wish that she were an Indian had become a reality, but now, she was not his. She is so frightened of my coming and of any claim I might still have on her. I can imagine what fears and doubts came to her mind when she first saw me towering above her. Lese . . . Lese . . . he begged, do not force a love for him and a hate for me. I saw him hold and kiss you, but I did not see you return it. Jealousy, he mentally added, nor did you fight or resist him. Then he chided himself, why should she? Have I not taught her myself the pain and futility of resistance? Did I not prove to her many times she must yield to power and strength or be broken?

I must know of what has passed between them. Why did she say she now belonged to him? Does she only cling to him in friendship and for protection as she did with Powchutu and Wanhinkpe Ska? How far has their friendship really gone? A dark, brooding scowl crossed his face. Does she seek to strike out at me in revenge? Does she hope to let him drive me from her heart, or has he already done so? Their touch was nearly intimate . . . this, I do not like. Has he not waited until the joining day to know and love her? Has she found all the things I gave and taught her in him, or more? I greatly fear this tenderness he has shown to her, for it will be hard to fight.

I fear she thinks I have only come to harm her. What will she believe when Powchutu tells her

233

the truth? When she learns I did not sell or trade her and had no choice but to free her, what will this knowledge mean to her? Perhaps it will make no difference to her at all. What if she still wishes to remain here with him? Could she truly have fallen in love with him this quickly? I have hurt her deeply and perhaps she will never forgive me or trust me again. She might seek forgetfulness and healing in his arms.

She was far too relaxed at his touch. Could she desire him more than me? Could his touch and love give her more than mine did? I will kill him if he has touched her! She says she hates me, but she did not show this to me back at my camp. But so much could have happened and changed in these past four moons that I do not know about. He could still see her face the morning he had sent her away with them. He shuddered.

Will the truth matter to you, Lese? Will it take away some of the pain and hurt? You had forgiven and accepted all the past hurts and shames, but now, you have this new pain to hold against me in your heart. What will you say when Powchutu erases it, or my part in it? Still, you have known love and happiness here. Does your love possess the strength and courage to choose me over what you have found and known here? Will you trade your new life here for my love? He winced at what his answer was . . .

There is so much she must learn this day, but even more to accept and understand. Can you,

Lese? Will you? Has there been too much pain, hurt and suffering for the truth to wipe out? Was there too much to forgive from him? Can she not see I love her and need her? No, for I have not allowed her to see or know. What if I lose her for good this day? What then?

He could not imagine his life without her in it. He had gone through great suffering while she was at the fort, knowing he would soon have her back again. But to think of losing her forever, and to another man, this he could not bear.

He raised his arms in supplication to the Great Spirit and vowed, "You can return the love of my life to me. I ask you for this as I have never asked for anything else. Hear me, oh Great Spirit. I must have her."

He shook his fist at the sun and declared, "Before you cross the sky once more, Wi, she will be mine, or my spirit will walk the Mahpiya Ocanku with Cantoohpi!" He turned and slowly walked back toward camp with a heavy, sad heart, but filled with determination to regain the woman he loved.

He was not too far behind them now, for they had stopped by the river to allow her to wash her face and calm down before they returned to camp. He had watched Mato Waditaka take a cloth from his waist and gently wipe her face with the cool water and remove the tears streaked there. Doubt and alarm rose in him at the loving exchange between them by the water.

I should be the one showing her love and

kindness, not him. It is I who needs you, Lese, not he. He ached to go to her and take her in his arms and tell her all the feelings he carried in his heart for her. But they had to wait until she was his once more, or remain unspoken forever.

As they re-entered the camp, she glanced about wondering what all the commotion was about. People were standing around talking, whispering, and . . . Powchutu!

Her eyes widened in surprise and joy. She pulled her hand free from Brave Bear's and ran, shouting and calling loudly to Powchutu. Brave Bear stared at the confusing scene before him. The scout turned at the sound of her voice and opened his arms to gather her into his embrace. She clung to him, crying and saying his name over and over. He held her very possessively, boldly, and tenderly as everyone looked on in astonishment.

He whispered words of love and comfort into her ears. She laughed and cried all at the same time. They were both oblivious to everyone and everything but each other for a time. Soon, the initial shock and excitement wore off. She leaned back and gazed up into his face, taking in every line and expression. The looks which passed between them were understood only by Gray Eagle and White Arrow.

Brave Bear's eyes narrowed in suspicion and alarm. Who was this man brought here by Wanmdi Hota, and for what reason? It took a few moments for the change in Powchutu's appearance to register and spark recognition in his mind and eyes. The scout from the wasichu fort! Why was he here?

She stormed him with questions, but did not allow him the time to answer one before she had the next one out. "How did you get here, Powchutu? When? Why are you here? How have you been? What are you doing now? Where are you living? Are they kind to you? Do you like living with them? Have you been well?"

Sensing hesitation and something akin to mystery in his face and eyes, she slowly and fearfully asked, "Did you come with Wanmdi Hota?" She paled as he nodded yes.

"Why is he here, Powchutu? Why did he come back into my life again? What does he want from me this time? Why did you come here with him? It has been terrible since the fort. I have been so frightened. He sold me, Powchutu . . ." Her face filled with anguish and her eyes glistened with unshed tears. To hear it said aloud made the hurt cut deeper.

She asked just above a whisper, "Did he tell you he sold me to Mato Waditaka?" Then, to cover her hurt, she added, "But I am glad, for he has been very good and kind to me, and his people have, too. He treats me as if I matter, as if I am one of them, not some camp slave and wh . . . he is not like Wanmdi Hota at all. He is kind and gentle. Please tell me he has not come to force him to send me back. He can't make him give me up if he does not wish to, can he? I could not endure his hate and brutality again, Powchutu. You must beg Mato Waditaka not to return me to him."

This was her only chance to retain what she had found here and she seized her only hope of communication with him.

"Tell Mato Waditaka I beg him to let me stay here. Tell him you will explain what he expects of me and I will do whatever he asks. I will do anything to remain here! Tell him this, will you, Powchutu? I have been happy here with these people and him and do not wish to leave ever. Tell him of Wanmdi Hota's hatred and cruelty to me. In his kindness, he would not send me back there. I'm sure of it. Powchutu, I think he likes me, maybe even loves me. And I know he wants me, but he hasn't harmed me in any way since I've been here." She pinkened at these words and their apparent meaning.

"You must make him understand that I long to stay with him. You must convince him not to re-sell me to Wanmdi Hota. I would prefer death instead! I told you once, I hoped and prayed I would find the courage and willpower to say no to him and his love. Here with Mato Waditaka, I have found that courage and willpower. Mato Waditaka has taken his place in my life and heart."

Powchutu gazed deep into those green eyes and wondered how much of what she said was really true, and how much she only wished was true. For once, he could not read it in her tormented eyes. Still, he would do as she asked. Until . . .

Gray Eagle felt the knife plunged into his

heart and cruelly twisted at her words. He wondered if he should just forget it all and mount up and ride away, out of her life forever. Had he finally succeeded in destroying their fragile love? Could any love survive what he had put theirs through? Do I love her enough to leave her here and let her find happiness with him? He turned away to gaze out across the meadow, visualizing her running through it with Mato Waditaka, laughing, singing, talking and gathering wildflowers. Could he spend the rest of his life without her? Could he endure the pain and emptiness of never seeing her face again, or hearing her musical laughter, or feeling her body and lips pressed to his in desire, passion and love, or forget she might even be carrying his child at this time? Could he ever give her up forever, even if this was what she wanted? He resolved, hate or no hate, love or no love, she is mine and I must have her!

Her words reached his ears again and he listened. "He lied to me and betrayed me, Powchutu! He showed me the most painful torture of all, what it would be like to love him and to have him love me. How could he be so cruel? I hate him! I'll never go back to him . . . never!"

Her tone of voice had shifted from anger, to hurt, to hate, and back again. Powchutu had never seen her like this before and he was deeply concerned. Wanhinkpe Ska had been right when he had said she was hurt more now than ever. He could feel her heart bleeding. Anger flared in him against Wanmdi Hota. He was to blame for all her hurt, shame, torment and suffering. If he had only shown her love and kindness from the beginning, none of this would have happened. He did not know Wanmdi Hota also realized this truth and cursed himself daily for what he could never change . . .

Powchutu looked at Alisha sadly and hopelessly and replied, "I am here to speak with you about things you do not know and must be told. Wanmdi Hota asked me to come with him and tell you of these things. I have learned many surprising things since I last saw you and you must learn these things, too." He sounded mysterious. She gazed at him in uncertainty.

Perplexed at his tone and words, she asked, "Why?"

He answered calmly, "There is much you do not know or understand. Wanmdi Hota said you are confused and frightened by what has happened to you. He asked me to explain it to you."

She softly retorted, "What is there to explain? I already know what has happened to me and what he has done!" She bitterly added, "Why should he care how I feel or what I think? He merely wishes you to tell me in my own tongue what he has done to me and why. He hopes it will be crueler. Well I do not need to hear the words to know of his hatred and contempt for me. His actions speak far louder than your words could. I will listen to no more, not even from you."

She jerked her arms free and turned to walk away, but he caught her arm and said, "Alisha, I must speak with you! There are things you must know! I will not speak of him or what has passed between you if this is what you wish."

A warning chill passed over her. She wondered what Wanmdi Hota wanted him to tell her if it did not concern him. She turned to glare suspiciously at Gray Eagle. The look he sent her surprised her. What was that strange gleam in his eyes? She could not understand it, for she had never seen it before. The look she could not read and he had not completely suppressed was the hurt and fear her words had given him.

He lowered his head, concealing his expression from her sight and that of the others. She boldly studied the lowered head. He had never looked away from her before. His eyes usually bored into hers. What did this mean? Why could he not look at her, or not want to? What did he know about her that could make him look and act this way? She trembled . . .

Brave Bear had demanded to be told why the scout was here as he was talking with Alisha. Gray Eagle told him. He reminded him of Alisha's and Powchutu's friendship and trust in each other. He reminded him it was this man who had befriended her at the fort and was the one who brought her out to Gray Eagle that day. He said he had granted Powchutu's life and freedom for his courage and help. He said she must be told all the things she did not know or understand. She would trust only Powchutu to tell her the truth.

Brave Bear vividly recalled the scene between Shalee and Powchutu at the fort, the looks and embraces which had passed between them. He cautiously asked, "What will he tell her about you?" He feared what the whole truth would do to his relationship with Shalee and to any remaining feelings for Wanmdi Hota.

Gray Eagle calmly and quietly replied, "He will not speak to her about me or us. He believes as you do that she belongs here. He wishes her to join with you, not me."

These words pleased Brave Bear, but he doubted if the scout would keep his word, or if Wanmdi Hota spoke the truth. He asked, "How will I know he speaks the truth? I do not know the wasichu tongue."

Gray Eagle retorted coldly, "By the look on her face! She thinks you bought her for a slave, that I sold her to you. She is much afraid and confused. He will tell her what took place in my camp that day and why. Do you not wish her to know who she is, who you are and why she is here? If so, then he can do this for you. Also, he can tell her of the other things you wish her to hear and know, of the joining . . ."

The old chief had listened to the exchange between the two warriors. He smiled and said he wished his daughter to hear and know these things. Her heart would be free and happy to learn she was at a home where she was loved.

Brave Bear was still reluctant, but could not

change the old chief's mind. Black Cloud called to Powchutu and Alisha. They came to him. He asked the scout many questions and told him many things. Powchutu listened with great respect and interest.

"We are friends, Mahpiya Sapa. I will tell her the truth. She is confused and afraid. I will not hurt her with lies or tricks. She needs to know these things about you, herself, and her people."

Satisfied with the honesty, pride and love for his daughter in the scout's eyes, he agreed. He led them to his teepee.

Alisha gazed around her in total mystery. Powchutu had said they would speak in the chief's teepee. She saw Brave Bear, Gray Eagle and Wanhinkpe Ska sit down together by the campfire, while the chief was leading them to his teepee.

She had seen the smile of reassurance on Brave Bear's face. She had been unable to read anything in Gray Eagle's. For a brief instant, there had been a flicker of something there, but it had gone before she could read it. What she did not know was his flicker was brought on by the flash of light in her eyes when she had looked at him. He had seen and recognized it, and relief had touched his eyes.

Powchutu began his talk with caution. "Alisha, what I will tell you will be confusing and hard to believe. But you must hear me out before you question my words to you. I will answer all the fears and doubts which plague you now. Do you understand me?"

She tensed at his warning. Will I know at last what is going on here? Why does he look so hesitant? Could his words be this hard to hear and accept? What is it they all want from me? Am I ready to hear this truth and know everything as he says? Suddenly, she wanted to run and hide, to cover her ears, to get away from all of them. But did none of those things. She looked up into his face and waited for him to begin . . .

He opened with, "I'm not really sure where to start. So much has taken place since I last saw you. You recall, I told you at the fort that one of the reasons you were rejected and hated so much was because of who had been your captor. I have already told you Wanmdi Hota is one of the most feared and respected warriors of the Sioux nation. Because you had been his woman, they took their hatred and revenge for him out on you. I told you of the seven tribes who are members of the 'Dakota Ocenti Sakawin.' As you know, Wanmdi Hota is a member of the Oglala tribe. These men here are members of the Si-ha Sapa tribe. There are five other members, but these two are the largest and most powerful. They are considered invincible and are widely respected and feared."

Alisha would nod understanding to his words every so often and he would continue. She waited and listened to see what all of this had to do with her, a ska kaskapi.

"You can see and understand why the whites and the cavalry feared and hated Wanmdi Hota so greatly after what he did at your fortress and at the fort. I have also told you Wanmdi Hota is the chief's son and the next Oglala chief. Chief Mahpiya Sapa has no true sons, so he has chosen Mato Waditaka as his son and heir. Both of these warriors are respected and honored by their own and other tribes. Mato Waditaka will be the next chief of the Si-ha Sapa."

Alisha thought in self-mockery, from one chief's son to another! At least a ska wincin-yanna is fit for royalty! But at least here, there was no Chela to compete with.

Powchutu began to speak more slowly and distinctly. "Mahpiya Sapa had only one child, a daughter. Many winters ago, he captured a white girl with flaming hair and grass green eyes. He kept her as his squaw. Her name was Jenny Pilcher. He says you look just like she did, with the same hair, skin, and eyes."

Alisha quickly interrupted him here, "Surely he cannot want me to take her place! Or does he wish to give his son a gift of a woman like he had?" She stared at him in horror of the old chief possessing her sexually, and maybe his son as well. Powchutu was rapidly shaking his head no. "Then what does all this have to do with me, Powchutu?"

Powchutu shook her gently and said, "Wait until I have finished and you will understand and know all. He does not want you for his squaw." She sighed in deep relief, but instantly realized he had only excluded the old chief, not his son. Was that her purpose here?

Powchutu was asking the chief some questions to clear up his own understanding. He turned back to Alisha and told her the whole story, about Jenny, her life among the Indians, her death, the love and child she had shared with the chief. He spoke of how Jenny had been killed in a raid on his camp and of how the small child had been captured and taken away, never to be seen or heard of again. He spoke of Matu and her banishment to the camp of the Oglalas for her lack of protection for Jenny and his child.

Alisha realized at this point, no wonder she hated me and looked at me with such contempt. If I look exactly like this Jenny who caused her such grief, such sadness and even banishment from her people and perhaps the old chief's life, I understand . . .

Powchutu waited until he had her full attention again to continue. "After the cavalry took the child, Mahpiya Sapa could not locate where they had sent her. The child bears a mark called an akito on her left buttock to match that of her father's for identification." He spoke to the chief.

Black Cloud came to her and held out his right hand for her to view and study the tattoo. She noted the half moon and two stars, but it meant nothing more than to remind her of the ceremony she had viewed here and the very strange way the two men had watched her. They had tattooed the father's right hand and the baby's left buttock . . .

Without warning, the fuzzy events of that morning at Gray Eagle's camp and this man's behavior cleared and flooded her mind. Cold, soul-shaking, unexplainable fear gripped at her heart as she vividly recalled what area of her body this old chief and Gray Eagle had viewed. Humiliation filled her just remembering it and she pinkened like the sunset. The way the chief and Powchutu were looking at her now, warned her of his next words. Her heart screamed, don't listen, but her brain retorted, you must!

With quavering in her voice, she softly asked, "Powchutu, what is it you are trying to tell me? I suddenly feel I am overshadowed with danger. There is a cold warning in the air around me. Say it!"

He gazed deep into her somber eyes and stated, "You are Shalee . . . you are Black Cloud's daughter. You bear this same akito on your body which Mahpiya Sapa bears on his hand. The old woman saw the akito when she doctored you after the icapsinte. She immediately knew who you are and why you looked so much like Jenny. She left to come to Mahpiya Sapa to tell him this news, but the raid on Wanmdi Hota's camp and your rescue that same day stopped her. She did not dare come to him and tell him she had found you, only to lose you again. She waited until you had been safely returned to the Oglala camp to come to him."

She recalled Matu's look at her that day she had returned. She had guessed right, for Matu had held her fate in her hands. Was this what she had felt in the air that day? Was this why she was here now? Is this why they were "friends" now?

I am Shalee? An Indian? My parents are not my parents? I am from this savage land . . . that old chief is my real father? Jenny, a woman I have never seen or known, my mother? His daughter . . . my people . . . that mark . . . Mato Waditaka, my brother? No, my . . . what?

Alisha's mind reeled and fought the turmoil of knowing all she had ever loved and known had been trickery and deceit. To be told she was not even herself, that she was in truth this Shalee . . . no! no! no! her brain and heart screamed in unison.

She looked at Powchutu and shouted so loudly the men outside could hear her voice, but only one of them knew her words. "Liar! Why do you, who calls himself my friend, come here with that man and betray me like this? What did he give you to make you turn on me this way? Why, Powchutu? Why? Are you now Indian and my enemy also? Don't touch me! Don't speak your hateful lies to me again! It isn't true. Lies, all of it, lies!"

With that, she began to cry bitterly, releasing all the pent-up hate, fury, hurt and betrayal which had filled her heart for so long. He let her cry for a long time. She had paled and trembled so, he had thought at first she was going to faint at this news.

He knew how difficult it must be to hear your whole life was nothing but lies and illusions.

To hear nothing was true, or was as it was believed to be, or no one was who they should be. He had just shattered all her beliefs about herself and those she had loved all her life. Her words and accusations about him hurt and cut him deeply, but he knew she would soon know he was her true friend and spoke only the truth to her.

As her sobbing slowed and his words sank in and took hold in her mind, she said, "I am not his daughter. I am not his Shalee. I was not born here. My parents did not lie to me or deceive me. You are wrong. All of you are very wrong. I will not be used this way. I will not take the place of someone else. I am Alisha! Alisha, do you hear?"

She challenged him with her words to prove his. She tried to ignore the hurt and pain in Powchutu's face. He deserves it for trying to hurt and use me this way, she raged.

Powchutu said very slowly, "I am truly sorry if my words have hurt you, Alisha. I only know what they have told me. They say the mark is there. He says he is your father. I will show you the mark and let you judge the truth of their words."

She studied his face, so full of hurt, and weakened. "They are wrong, Powchutu. They have lied to you. It is only a trick. They are trying to use me in some cruel game. Help me, Powchutu. Help me! I have no one if you turn from me," she cried in anguish.

He pulled her into his arms and let her cry

again. He spoke encouraging words to her to calm her. "Alisha, take the looking glass and see if the mark is there for yourself. Then, if it is, we will decide what to do."

She looked up at him and nodded agreement to his logical suggestion. He asked the chief for a mirror, then handed it to her. She hesitantly accepted it with a trembling hand, suddenly afraid of what she might find. Why would they try to bluff her with something she could easily disprove?

The two men turned away as she lifted the hem of her dress and put the mirror near her left buttock. What she saw could change her entire life. Did she dare look? Did she want to find the truth? Her eyes went to the reflection in the small, oval mirror, freezing there . . .

Her vision blurred before her and her thoughts crashed upon her mind like storm-driven waves upon a sandy beach. It cannot be . . . it's impossible. . . . She lightly touched the little half moon, then the two, smaller stars etched there for all time. She tore her eyes from the mark as full comprehension filled her. All he said was true . . . me, Shalee? Me, an Indian? All the events and actions of the past few days fell into place, finishing the puzzle. The akito had been the missing piece to make all the others fit to complete the picture.

This is why I am here! This is why they have treated me like this. This is why Mato Waditaka has not taken me and used me as his slave and whore. Other realities settled in, too. This is why I had to leave Wanmdi Hota's camp! Now, I understand why he was so angry, he lost his trophy of war! They forced him to give up the chief's daughter so they could bring her home! But, Mato Waditaka's treatment to her had been anything but brotherly!

"Powchutu was saying at that moment, Wanmdi Hota did not sell or trade you to them, Alisha. He was forced to return you to your father. He was shown the proof of the akitos. You are free here, Shalee. No one will ever hurt you again. This was what I came to tell you. You will be accepted and loved here. You will be happy. These are your people, not your enemies. This is your father, Chief Black Cloud."

Black Cloud. . . . She remembered her dream when clouds rained on mighty eagles. . . . Would she really be free? Accepted? Happy? Her people and her father? Each bit of knowledge fought to be first to fill her mind, to be understood, to be accepted. Still, it all seemed crazy and wild. She stared off into space and spoke mostly to herself to clear her thoughts, "I have lived a lie all my life? They were not my real parents? This Jenny Pilcher and Mahpiya Sapa are? I wonder if Uncle Thad knew the truth. If he did, then why did he bring me back here? Was he trying to return me to my people? Did he think I would be safe from them? Did he die before he had a chance to tell me who I am? This is too much to grasp and understand so suddenly. The chief, my father. . . . How this truth could have changed my whole life here,

Powchutu, if only we had known sooner . . ."

She questioned Powchutu, "Is this why I have been treated so kindly here and accepted by these people? You say I am free, an Indian, not a slave or captive. This is so much to absorb out of the blue, Powchutu. That day they came for me was terrible. I have never felt such hurt and shame. Why didn't they tell me at the tattooing ceremony, or show me the marks then?"

He related her questions to the chief, then his answer back to her. "He says you were in great fear and did not trust them. They wished to give you a few more days to see and learn you were safe and accepted here."

"But, if all you say is true, then I am also a hanke-wa wasichun like you. Why do they not hate me as they do others like us?"

He retored hotly, "No! You are the daughter of a chief. It matters not if you are of mixed blood as I am."

Alisha did not feel this should make a difference in her treatment and his, but did not say so. Alisha stared at Powchutu and asked her most feared question, "Why is he here? Why didn't he just send you? Why did he come with you? Why should he care whether I know the truth or not? Does he wish to get on the good side of the chief's daughter now? Does he come to beg forgiveness for his cruelty to me? I hope not, for I shall not give it, ever! Or maybe, he comes to beg forgiveness from my father for the abuse of his only daughter. Who cares now?"

Powchutu did not wish to answer her last few

questions. He looked away as he continued, "You are to join with Mato Waditaka on the full moon tomorrow night."

"Join?" she queried innocently in confusion, then remembered the meaning of that word from another talk long ago at the fort. "You mean marry him?" she asked incredulously. Powchutu nodded yes. She asked again, "But why is Wanmdi Hota here?"

Powchutu stated flatly, "He demands that you are joined with him, thus joining the two tribes. He is very angry at their taking you from him by force!"

She flared in disbelief, "He demands what! Never! He only wishes to marry me to prevent my joining with Mato Waditaka and finding happiness here. He does not want me to be happy or free. He wants to keep me as his slave and under his thumb of cruelty."

She recalled the expression on his face and in his eyes in the meadow this morning when he discovered her kissing Mato Waditaka. "He thinks he still owns me, but he does not and never will again!" For the first time in months, she felt anger and resentment instead of fear, and the freedom to express it. "What do they say about his bold and daring demand?"

"Mahpiya Sapa has said no. He said it was decided that you join with his chosen son Mato Waditaka and live here with your people. He would not hear his words or demands. He is greatly angered and ashamed of the cruelty he inflicted upon you. Wanmdi Hota has no claim

253

on you any longer, but he does not see or think this way. He says you belonged to him first, and still do. He says he will not be forced to give you up. The chief is happy to have found you again. He says it was the will of Napi to return you to him in his winter years. He says he wants you to know peace and happiness here with him."

She looked at the kindly, old chief and tried to think of him as her father. He had been gentle with her. He had accepted her without question of her white upbringing and appearance. How can I possibly turn my back and heart on him if he is truly my father? How can I hurt him like that? If he believes I am his daughter and I have been divinely returned to him, how can I break his old heart and spirit by refusing to accept it? The akito is there. I cannot deny its presence. Whether it is true or not, they all accept and believe it. If I also accept it, then I can live in peace. But the question is, can I accept it and believe it? My heart says yes, but my mind says no, that it is only a lie and illusion. What if this new illusion were suddenly shattered?

I could live here as his beloved daughter and wife to Mato Waditaka. Dare I go along with it? Dare I not to? Common sense told her it would be foolish not to take advantage of this quirk of fate. She had been given the opportunity to become one of them and no longer a captive. Could she say no to the chance of her lifetime? Could she give up the chance of becoming Mato Waditaka's wife instead of Gray Eagle's slave and whore? No, no, no, came the answer from her heart and mind.

She fought to ignore his words about her marrying Gray Eagle. That would be impossible for more than one reason. She said to Powchutu, "Accepted . . . I still cannot seem to stop thinking about that. It was so strange, always waiting for the storm to follow the lull, to wake up and find it had all been some cruel joke. This explains Mato Waditaka's treatment to me. Is he really going to marry me after all Wanmdi Hota has done? I was certain he desired me, but could not understand why he did not take me. He waits to join with me? But is it me or Shalee that he wants? How will I ever know or be sure? Who can I really believe, Powchutu?" She covered her face with her hands.

Powchutu pulled her hands away and looked into her lucid eye and replied, "Me, Shalee. You can trust and believe in me. I will always be here for you when you need me. I believe you can find your happiness, maybe even love, here with your people and with Mato Waditaka. Accept what I have told you and free your life and heart of Wanmdi Hota once and for all." Powchutu knew he must also accept this news which would alter all his plans and dreams. How could he ever hope to escape with a chief's daughter? If he must give her up, then it would be to Mato Waditaka, not Wanmdi Hota . . .

She smiled and said, "For once, the mighty eagle was powerless and helpless. I wonder how he felt to be caught on the wrong side of power for a change. How it must have infuriated him to be forced to give up his property to another! No wonder he was so furious this morning. It is a matter of his damnable pride and honor again. Besides, he still has Chela. I don't see why he would want me, his old slave and witkowin, not to mention being a hanke-wa wasichun. He hates me and always has. Does my being half Indian suddenly reverse his feelings for me? I think not! This time, I will be free of him and his hold on me. I have allowed him to hurt me for the last time, Powchutu. He would never accept me fully. In fact, he would probably make things worse for me after this humiliation I have caused him.''

They talked on and on for a long time until all her fear, doubts and questions were fully explained. When she was sure she knew everything there was to know about her situation, she asked Powchutu, "What now?"

"Will you accept all you have been told as truth? Will you accept your life here as Shalee?"

She thought on his words carefully before answering him. She asked herself what harm it would do to become this Shalee everyone wished her to be. Somehow from the deep, hidden recesses of her brain the warning came, it is a farce, Alisha, but you must go along with it. Gnawing doubts would not allow her to accept what she had been told and shown. Why, she did not know.

If I must live here in this savage land, then it will be as Shalee, beloved daughter and wife, not as Alisha, hated wasichun and slave. She trembled at the reality of giving up herself to become another girl, possibly a dead girl.

Her decision made, she answered him, "Tell Mahpiya Sapa I will accept my place and life here as Shalee and him as my father."

She silently prayed, forgive me, father, but I must do this thing for my welfare in this land. You taught me to do what was best in a situation. This one demands for Lese to be put to rest with you and mama, and for Shalee to return from the past. But in my heart, you will always be my true father.

Powchutu had given the chief her answers. He came to her and embraced her. He smiled and called her, "Cunwintku."

She returned his friendly, loving smile and replied, "Father . . . A'ta . . ."

She asked Powchutu to give her new father another message, "Tell him I was raised by the wasichu and do not hate them as they do. Tell him I will neither watch nor accept the torture of captives. Tell him I do not hate the Si-ha Sapa or the other Indians and never have. I only dislike those peoples from both sides who have tried to hurt and use me. Not all whites or Indians are alike. There are good and bad men on both sides. Tell him I feel no dishonor for either of my parents or their different bloods. Tell him I am Shalee, daughter of Mahpiya Sapa and Jenny Pilcher, and I will be proud of this."

Powchutu translated her words to him and he stared at her in astonishment and pride. "Tell my daughter she is indeed wise for one so young. Tell her, her words please me and it shall be as she says. It is good, my daughter."

Powchutu told Alisha all the chief had said and she smiled and replied, "It is good, my father."

With everything settled, Powchutu and the chief sighed with relief. "We will go and tell the others of our decisions."

Alisha tried to forget the implications of this whole thing about her possible relationship with Gray Eagle. This news changed her thoughts and feelings about what she had believed he had done to her that day in his camp. She could not suppress the memories of how things were going between them before Chela had tried to kill her. She knew he had not punished her that night. He had left to deal with his anger. Would he have punished her that next day if they had not come for her? She would never know now, for she could not risk losing what she had found here.

She knew he had had nothing to do with this change in her life. He had not sold her or betrayed her. Would things have gone on in truce between them if it hadn't been for Chela and her father? Would he have forgiven her violent outburst? Would he have continued to treat her with passion and desire, perhaps more? Did she even dare to think of such ideas now? No, for she now truly belonged to Mato Waditaka and would marry him tomorrow night.

I know how he will treat me as his wife, but I do not know what would happen between Wanmdi Hota and me. Would my love be enough for our happiness? Would it be enough to wipe out all the hate and hurt between us? I fear the love of one person is not strong enough to withstand such evil forces. I shall marry Mato Waditaka as I have been told, but it will be Wanmdi Hota that I shall always love.

As they lifted the flap to go outside, Gray Eagle involuntarily flinched at her last statement to Powchutu. In somber mockery, she said, "Long live Shalee, and may Alisha rest in peace. . . ." She gazed up at Powchutu and finished, "If this is what they want and demand for my peace and happiness, then so be it. As you said, Powchutu, I really have no choice, do I? Besides, Alisha died many days ago when a little, white bird left her heart."

Powchutu looked confused at her statement, but did not ask her to explain for the pain in her eyes stopped him. But Gray Eagle heard and knew the meaning of her words. He was alarmed at her defeated attitude.

Powchutu curiously watched Gray Eagle's expression as Black Cloud told them she had accepted him as her father and the Si-ha Sapa as her people. He then said she willingly agreed to accept his son Mato Waditaka in joining, who eagerly stepped forward and smiled down at her. He placed his arm around her waist possessively. His victorious face met Gray Eagle's, which was a mask of livid rage and fury.

Gray Eagle stepped before her for one last chance to win her back without bloodshed. Taking her chin firmly in his hand, he forced her to look at him. She had seen his great anger and rage many times, but never like this! There was something else there, too, but she could not understand it. He compelled her eyes to his by the sheer force of his will. His burned like two black coals in a fire, making her blood burn in her veins. His eyes flashed defiance and revenge . . .

He spoke through clenched teeth as the muscles in his jawline tightened and twitched. Confused by his fierce reaction, she asked Powchutu, "What did they say to make him so angry?"

He knew what had done it and hastily replied, "That you would willingly marry Mato Waditaka, that you chose him."

Her trembling chin was still imprisoned by his hand, only her eyes could move. They quickly riveted to the scout in surprise. "But that is not what I said! I only agreed because my father told me I must join Mato Waditaka and live here with him and my people. My father said no to Wanmdi Hota's demands and would not listen to them. You said so! I was not given a choice between them. Does he think I was? Why is he looking at me with such anger and spite? I am still a captive and I have no say in any of these matters."

Knowing Wanmdi Hota might understand some of her words, if not all of them, and hoping she would repeat her rejection of his love once and for all, he tested Wanmdi Hota's truth and challenged her, "If you could choose between them, Shalee, which warrior would you take?"

She stared into the cold, hard eyes of Gray Eagle and quietly replied, "Neither! Mato Waditaka is very kind and gentle, but I do not love him and fear I never will. If I must marry him, then I will do so and try to be a good wife for him. But in my heart, I believe he wishes to marry Shalee, not Lese. He is in love with the illusion of Shalee, not the reality of Lese. I do not wish to marry him because of what I shared with Wanmdi Hota. Neither can I marry Wanmdi Hota for he hates me too much and my father has forbidden it. He is cruel and unforgiving of my wasichu blood and upbringing. I would live in constant fear of his turning on me at any moment. I would never know love and happiness with him for he would not allow it. He will always see me as Alisha. His hate and vengeance will always be there between us. I could not make him a good wife for he would not permit it. The love of one person is not enough for a happy life together, Powchutu. My only hope for any kind of life is here. The best solution would be for me to marry you, my friend. We could love and accept each other for who and what we are." Her last two statements were spoken in lighthearted jest, but Powchutu took them to heart.

So, I was right! Powchutu thought as he

watched the glint in Gray Eagle's eyes at her words. He understands what she is saying. He lied to me and deceived her. She did not exactly say she loved him, nor did she say she hated him, only that he hated her and their joining would be impossible. I will not tell her he hears and knows her words for this would hurt her deeply. It would shame her to know he heard her pain and did nothing to stop it. She would know he heard her pleas and turned a deaf ear. I cannot hurt her this way, even to bring hatred in her heart for him. Soon he will be gone from her life and the need for knowing will also.

Powchutu did not know what his silence would cost her and would live to regret this deadly mistake.

Gray Eagle's rich, deep voice broke the silence like thunder, "Ask Shalee if she will accept me to join?"

Brave Bear pushed his hand off her chin and shouted at him, "No! It is decided! She will join with me. She fears and hates you. She has chosen me."

Gray Eagle's gaze softened. His eyes glowed and a half-smile played across his sensuous mouth. "She fears me for I have hurt her deeply, but she does not hate me and never has. If you did not blind your eyes, you would see the truth. It is me she loves and wants, but is afraid to say so," he finished confidently.

His softened expression and deep voice had a strange, warming effect on her. It recalled the heat and memory of their passionate nights.

This was his mood the day before all the trouble began. Helpless, she gazed into the handsome face and lost herself in the bottomless pits of his night-black eyes.

Her hand longed to reach out and touch him, her lips to kiss his, to be engulfed in his strong embrace, and to once again know the delights of his love. Her face flamed at these thoughts and feelings as she realized how she was staring at him. She quickly lowered her head, but he had seen the look of love and passion written there, as had Powchutu. Gray Eagle's confidence was increased twofold. He knew what he must do now . . .

He nodded to White Arrow who came forward carrying a lance. There were two feathers attached to one end, one yellow and the other, gray and red. He faced her and spoke directly into her eyes. "Shalee was mine first. By the right of law and custom, I call challenge to Mato Waditaka for her return. I call the right of her return or my death. I will not leave here without her at my side. The Great Spirit sent her to me, and I will not give her up without a fight. She has known only my touch and will know no other while I live and breathe. I say she is mine! Who says differently?" He forcefully jammed the lance into the ground before her. "Ki-ci-e-conape!"

The silence was deafening . . . she stared at the lance in the ground between him and her. Did he pass a death sentence on her or cast some evil spell?

Brave Bear quickly snatched the lance from the ground and broke it over his knee. With a look of anticipation and arrogance on his face, he glared into the face of Wanmdi Hota, accepting his challenge for Alisha. Whispering and expectation filled the air.

Black Cloud glared at the lance in shock and surprise. Wanmdi Hota wanted her this badly? Had he misjudged his feelings for his daughter? He could lose both his daughter and his son this very day. Was it pride or love ruling Wanmdi Hota's actions? He spoke rapidly to both men as they faced each other in open antagonism. He gave them both the one and only chance to withdraw the challenge or refuse it. Neither man gave ground.

"Powchutu, what is happening? Does he threaten me in some way? What does the lance mean?".

"The lance is a challenge for you. Wanmdi Hota says you were his first and he claims the right to join with you. He says he will not leave here alive without you. He says the Great Spirit gave you to him and he will not let you go without a fight. He says that as long as he lives and breathes you will belong to only him. He says you are his and he will die before he gives you up. Then he asked who disputes his claim that you are his and he will join you. Mato Waditaka answered the challenge when he withdrew the lance from the ground and broke it over his knee. The chief gave them the one chance to withdraw the challenge and acceptance. They both kept silent. It will be a fight to the death of one of them, the winner will claim and join with you. It is the custom of their tribes when two great warriors desire the same woman. They are also both chief's sons and you are a chief's daughter. Maybe they will both die, then I will claim you!"

She hardly heard his last words. "To the death of one of them?" she asked in distress and alarm.

He lightly replied, "To the death . . ."

Chapter Six

Perceiving the full meaning of this challenge, she grabbed up the two ends of the lance and screamed at both of them, "No! I will have no deaths on my hands, not even yours, Wanmdi Hota. Powchutu, tell my father I will not be a part of this. I will not be a trophy in a game of death."

Powchutu related her message to the chief. The chief looked at the frightened, distressed face of his daughter and replied, "Tell Shalee this is the law of our people. She is Si-ha Sapa and must obey our laws and ways. He is a chief's son and has taken her first. He has the right of ki-ci-e-conape. She must join with the winner. I have spoken!"

Her eyes flashed rebellion and anger at him as she said, "I will not be sold again! When the time comes, I will choose! I will not allow either of them to die. I cannot!"

The Token-pi-i-ceyapi Itancan came forward to announce the challenge would take place in one hour. They were to go to separate teepees to prepare. Hearing his words, both men nodded and turned to go to their appointed teepees, to meet in one hour in a death struggle to possess her. She stared on helplessly. Was there nothing she could do? Was she a pawn in the hands of fate once more? Whose time had come to die? It angered her to know she was to be the weapon to take away a man's life. Will I never have any say in my own life and fate? Will others always choose my paths for me?

Crying bitterly, she turned and ran to a tree near the river bank. Such pain filled her heart and mind. Why did this revenge not taste sweet? Why did Wanmdi Hota's possible death not make her feel happy and free? If he died today, would she always feel this emptiness and longing for him deep inside? How would she feel if she never saw him again, if she never touched him again, if she never kissed him again, and never belonged to him again? She thought she had come to terms with all these "nevers," but she realized now she had not. For somewhere deep inside, she had felt she would one day be his again. She had not given up the hope or dream he would come to love her as she loved him. But if he died . . . his forbidden love would haunt her forever.

She would never be able to marry Mato Waditaka and love him if he killed Wanmdi Hota, no matter what they demanded she do. But if by some chance of fate Wanmdi Hota won, could she ever forgive the death of Mato Waditaka in order to win her back? Why was life so harsh and cruel out here? Why did it demand so much from her?

She gazed out along the horizon into the sky of endless blue. Would she ever adjust to the people and land out here? She gazed at the dry, vast land in the distance and longed to see the rolling, green hills and dales of England. To feel the rainy mist instead of this arid climate for just one day would be pure bliss. To feel the fog and mist touching her skin lightly in the early spring morning, to smell the sweet fragrance of the grasses and flowers, to smell the hot-crossed buns sold by the street vendor, to ride through the park and stop for a picnic, to hear the cooing of the doves and pigeons, to hear music and laughter, these were the things she missed out here in this vast wilderness, alone . . .

Was it only yesterday at this time that her life had seemed to settle down? Was it only a few days since her suffering at the fort? Was it only a few months ago she had been an innocent girl searching for happiness and a new life with her uncle at their fortress? Such devastating and drastic changes had taken place in her life. Was it really done in such a short time? All these events seemed like only yesterday, and yet, they also seemed like eons ago. Her mind reeled with so many new and conflicting discoveries.

Powchutu knew she needed to be alone to sort out some of these things in her mind. Too much had happened too quickly for her—captivity, rescue, recapture, and now this. How could one so young and innocent deal with all of this at once? I see and know why she thinks she cannot trust or believe anyone, he thought. The pain is great for her now, but in time . . . ha! he scoffed. How many times had he thought time lessens pain? But did it? No! The pain was still fresh and bleeding in him from many years of suffering. No, time does not heal and bring happiness and forgetfulness. If she lived for a hundred more winters, she would never forget Wanmdi Hota or what he has done to her.

Unless . . . if she were far away from here and him, then maybe she could forget. If she were to return to the land far across the giant waters she spoke of, then she could begin a new life without this hurt and pain. I must think on this further . . .

He walked down to the trees where she was standing, looking dreamily off into the far distance. How could she bear the sorrow which he read in her eyes? If only there was some way to help her or to lessen her torment.

"Shalee?" he called softly to her.

She turned to look at him. "Let the others call me that, Powchutu, but you, please call me Alisha. For you and you alone does she live and exist. I cannot bear to let her slip away, as if she had never lived. Alisha's life has been filled with lies and deceit. Will Shalee's life be any better for me? I cannot become this Shalee just because they say I am she. I do not feel or think as she would have. You are the only one here who knows or sees the real me. I am Alisha!" she cried in desperation. With these words, she trembled and wept.

"Powchutu, yesterday I thought it was finally over, this Hell I have lived in for so long. I believed I was about to begin a new life here in this village. Why did he have to come back to tear my heart out again? Why can't he leave me in peace? Now, one of them must die, and I cannot stand the thoughts of it being either one of them. I cannot think of what will come after that death." He reached out to caress her cheek and wipe away a falling teardrop.

"If only he had not beaten me, then Matu would never have seen that mark. If only he did not hate me so much, then this would not be happening. If only I had never agreed to come to this godforsaken land. If only I had not tried to help him at our fortress, maybe he would have killed me by now. If only my people had not hated him and treated him so cruelly, maybe he would not have destroyed our fortress and killed them. If only I had never seen or known him, then my heart would not be breaking now. If, if, if!" she cried out. "My thoughts and heart are filled with all these 'ifs.' But the most painful if of all, Powchutu, is if only I did not love him . . ." She began to weep at the agony of this reality. "What shall I do, Powchutu? There is no way out for me anymore. Help me!"

His words and expressions at the challenge today haunted her and she could not decide what she believed anymore. She vividly recalled in detail everything that had happened and had been said between them since that morning bluff at the fort. She had been so wrong about many things. All the misgivings and suspicions cried to be released for they were untrue . . .

Her heart was a bloody battlefield between

common sense and love. They fought bitterly and fiercely to overrule each other and dictate her actions and emotions. Desperate emotions surged throughout her ravaged heart until it cried out in surrender. She would have to accept what it commanded, for his love had invaded her heart and body and would not be conquered or pushed aside.

Her heart skipped a beat when the sound of the can cega reached her ears. Its slow, rhythmic beat told her the time was nearing. She was consumed by this feeling of total panic and helplessness. Had the time come already? I must go to them at once. I must find a way to stop this farce. She ran toward the village and to the teepee where Brave Bear had gone. She did not call out for permission to enter. She threw back the flap and ran inside. He was sitting by a small fire, praying and chanting.

She went to him and knelt before him as tears coursed down her cheeks. He stopped and gazed into the face of fear and beauty before him and touched her tears with his fingers.

"Please don't do this, Mato Waditaka," she pleaded. "I cannot bear the thought of your death. You have been so kind to me. You have brought light and happiness into my life for the past few days. I will tell my father I demand to join with you and he will end this farce."

Powchutu had been right behind her and he now translated her words to him. He smiled into her luminous eyes and spoke, "It cannot be stopped now, Shalee. The challenge was given

271

and accepted. We must do this thing and end this war among the three of us. This must be settled before our joining day. His claim on you must be torn away for all time."

She cried out, "But that claim can only be torn away with the death of one of you! I will join with him, then he will have no reason to kill you. I will tell my father to join me with him and save the life of his son."

When Powchutu related this to him, he shouted, "Never! You are mine. I will not give you up to him. I will kill him and you and I will be joined this very day!" he said angrily. Then softly added, "It pleases me that you would sacrifice yourself to him to save my life."

But Alisha knew it was to save both their lives. How could he expect her to celebrate their joining while others mourned the death of her true love? But of course, he did not know of her feelings for Wanmdi Hota. On the other hand, how could she go to Wanmdi Hota, if he should win, with the blood of this man on his hands? Such a deadly quandary . . .

Still, she persisted, "You cannot kill another man because of me. I am not to be traded about from one man to another like some animal who has no feelings or guilt. It is wrong."

Hearing the meaning of her words, he calmly replied, "I would be dishonored if I refused to fight for what is mine. He has challenged me and he must die or kill me. I will not allow you to go to him while I live. You must learn the ways and laws of your people and accept them as I do.''

Powchutu translated his words. She screamed in anger, "Dishonored! What is dishonor to death? I have been shamed and dishonored and yet I live and accept it. I have known great humiliation but I do not beg for death. Can you do no less for me?''

He studied her anguished face for a time then said, "You are not a man and a warrior. You do not yet feel and think as a Si-ha Sapa, Shalee. A warrior cannot live in shame and disgrace. His people would not follow a coward, a man who broke his word and retracted his challenge. This, I cannot do for you or myself. Do not ask this of me. I would not be a man if I did not fight for you. If I refused, you would be sent to him and I would be less than a woman in the eyes of my people and the other warriors. This is the only way to save both of us.''

She saw that nothing she could say would change his decision. His laws and customs were too deeply ingrained in him. He viewed this as something he must do and he would never turn back now. Her pleading only brought hurt to him for he could not listen or hear it. She could not expect him to do otherwise. He was Mato Waditaka, Si-ha Sapa, warrior and future chief.

Seeing she was powerless to do more, she reached out and tenderly touched his cheek and whispered, "I do not fully understand what you say, but I will accept the fact this is something you must do for yourself and your people. I will pray to the gods to protect you and spare your life, for you are truly a man above others and your death would be a terrible loss."

As Powchutu related her words to him, happiness flickered in his eyes and he smiled at her. He removed his wanapin and placed it around her neck. He kissed her lightly on her lips and said, "Always remember, Shalee, there is honor even in death."

Comprehending the meaning of his words, she gazed into those proud, dauntless features and smiled. She stood up and departed without looking back. She stood outside his teepee for a time, thinking on his last words. She listened to the low chanting as it began inside once more and grieved for what might come. Powchutu told her they must leave him to prepare for what was to be. They slowly walked away.

Powchutu asked, "Shalee, will you also go to Wanmdi Hota? If he is the one to die this day, then he will be forever spared your last words to him." He saw the anxiety flash across her face and the doubt settle in her eyes.

She quietly replied, "He would not listen either, Powchutu. He issued this challenge, therefore he is also willing to die for this honor they speak of. How he must hate me if he wants me back under his power at the cost of a life, possibly his own. Why must it be this way, my friend? Is there no other way this matter can be settled without bloodshed?"

She did not know they were standing before Gray Eagle's teepee while they spoke and that he heard her words. Powchutu knew he was giving her the opportunity to do what she really wanted but feared to do. He was also hoping she would refuse and Gray Eagle would hear her.

She finally looked up at him and answered, "Yes, I will go to him, but not to beg for the life of Mato Waditaka. I will not give him the satisfaction of knowing how deeply his death would hurt me. I must see him once more, perhaps for the last time alive . . ."

He turned and lifted the flap of the teepee directly behind them and pulled her inside. Gray Eagle turned and she called his name. Their eyes met and locked.

"Wanmdi Hota . . ." she faltered and stopped. Turning to Powchutu, she said, "No, Powchutu, it was a mistake to come here. There is too much hatred and mistrust between us. He would not believe I do not wish his death, nor Mato Waditaka's. One of them must die this day for this honor I do not understand. The pain it will bring will live on in my heart and life forever. If you had known and told me of his intentions, I would have begged my father to allow me to marry him before things went this far. What could he possibly do to me that he has not already done many times before? How he must hate me to do this terrible thing. It has passed the time for words between us now. They would change nothing. He does not fear death for it is a part of his daily life." She turned to leave, but was halted by White Arrow's hold on her.

She looked up into his face and returned his

smile. "We have not been able to speak the words in our hearts before, Powchutu. Will you thank him for all the help and kindness he has shown to me in the past? Many times I have felt his understanding and attempts to help me. Tell him I am grateful and happy to have known him as a friend."

Powchutu related her words to him and he beamed at her. "Tell Shalee it is I who am happy and thankful at knowing her. Tell her I have never wanted to hurt her in any way She will always be my koda."

She gave him a brilliant smile, knowing he referred to the teepee sa incident. "Thank him for telling me this. It lessens the pain and hurt I felt at his actions. Tell him I did not think he would hurt me even if he was commanded to do so. We shared many happy times and sad times." Gray Eagle flinched at her stinging words. She continued, "Forever kodas, Wanhinkpe Ska," and kissed him on his cheek.

Once more she turned to depart, but this time, Gray Eagle blocked her path. She tried to go around him, but found herself locked in a grip of iron, secure, but painless.

She gazed up at him in helplessness. Her breathing quickened and she trembled at his smell and closeness. She placed her open palms against his hard, muscular chest and tried to push away from him.

She frantically spoke, "Let me pass, Wanmdi Hota. There is nothing I can say to you. You would only laugh at my pleas as you always did.

I can do nothing to melt that heart of ice, so I will not even try."

He continued to study her closely as if he sought to memorize her face for a last time—and perhaps he did! She hesitantly asked Powchutu, "Will you ask him one thing for me, Powchutu? Will you ask him why he hates me so much and why he has never allowed himself to . . ." She abruptly halted and changed her mind. "No, for I could not bear to know. The 'why' does not really matter. If only he would have let himself love me just a little. If only he had not hated me so much it would have been enough for me. Ask him nothing and tell him nothing, for in his heart he knows and sees all things, even though he chooses to reject and hate me."

She looked deep into his jet eyes and softly whispered, "I pray you do not die this day, for then I would never be free of you. For illusions of what might have been would haunt me forever. With you alive, I will be reminded every day that I have loved you in vain. I could not bear to see you lying dead in your blood and know you are lost to me forever. Why, Wanmdi Hota? Why couldn't you love me just one bit? I could have loved enough for both of us if your hatred had not hardened your heart to me and locked your mind against ever accepting me. I would give anything, even my life, if I had first met and known you as Shalee."

Tears blurred her vision as she struggled to break free and leave this place of torment and him. She pleaded, "Shalee ya. Wanmdi

Hota! Please . . ."

The anguish in her eyes and voice ripped at his own heart, but his face and eyes remained blank and void of the intense emotions churning inside him. "Don't you see, it does not matter now?" She cried out at him, "It has gone forever, as yesterday. There is no time or place for our love. I see this now. I will never torture my heart with the hope that someday you might come to love and accept me. It is time I accept the fact you never have and never will love me. Had I but realized this the very first day I met you! My one remaining joy is the knowledge you did not sell me. I shall have that along with the bittersweet memories of other days. Powchutu, please make him let me go! I must get out of here! I can take no more today . . ."

Gray Eagle's eyes stopped him cold in his tracks. His eyes fell to the wanapin of Brave Bear around her neck. He told Powchutu, "Tell her what it means to wear his wanapin during the challenge."

He carefully observed the effect of the explanation on her. "Alisha, to wear Mato Waditaka's wanapin to the challenge shows you choose him to be the winner. This is the way you tell everyone present you love and choose him and hope he wins. This is also supposed to discourage the man you do not want and give encouragement to your love. It is believed this show of preference instills more daring and bravery in your lover's heart, and hesitation and doubt in the heart of his challenger."

She lifted the wanapin and lightly fingered it, pondering her indecision. How could she hurt and discourage Brave Bear by removing it? It would surely embarrass him before his people and might cause a slight loss of concentration which would cost his life. She must do this in payment for the past few days of happiness and freedom. She owed him this much. It would make no difference in the emotions and bravery of Gray Eagle if she removed it, so she did not.

Perhaps it might aggravate and spite Wanmdi Hota for all the anguish he had put her through, but it could not possibly harm or discourage him. If Mato Waditaka dies, then he will die thinking I chose him. If he lives, then it will be best if he thinks I prefer him. It would be foolish to reveal her love for Wanmdi Hota to the others.

Her hesitation alarmed Gray Eagle. She settled the bear's head against her heart as she told Powchutu why she would not remove it. As Powchutu translated, he seethed inside. How it galled him to be used against her by Gray Eagle. He would pay dearly . . .

Gray Eagle released the grip of one of his hands and removed his white eagle. He held it out to her in askance. She glared at the wanapin in torment and asked, "Does he demand for me to show my choice of him instead? Surely he doesn't ask me to let everyone think I love and choose him? No, he only seeks to antagonize and anger Mato Waditaka, or inflame him against me. Wanmdi Hota needs no encouragement from his ex-slave to aid his bravery and daring, for there is no man braver or more daring than he."

This had been a gift to her the day they had returned from the fort to his camp. She recalled the happiness the gift had brought to her and her two days of love with him. She recalled her reasons for removing it and leaving it behind that day. She called to mind the vivid details of where the rattler rings had come from and what had followed that incident. It had not been a gift of love, but a symbol to denote his ownership of her and to warn her against the futility of escape.

Pain filled her heart and eyes at the memories the white eagle brought to mind. Tears filled her eyes and ran down her cheeks despite all her efforts to control them.

"I . . . I cannot take it! It meant too much, and yet, nothing. I gave too much of my heart and self those two days. I cannot take it, even to prevent his rage later."

Again, she tried to pull free and get out of this torture chamber. She begged Powchutu to help her. White Arrow placed his knife to Powchutu's stomach and said in warning, "This is between them. Let it be. He will not harm her."

Powchutu retorted, "His words and closeness cut deeper and crueler than any knife could. He does harm her. Let her go, Wanmdi Hota. It is over!"

Gray Eagle glared at the scout. "Tell her I will never hurt her again. She will forever belong to me and love only me. The eagle is hers, and she is mine." He placed the wanapin around her neck as before, covering the bear's head.

She struggled and cried out to him, "Please do not force me to wear it!"

He took her left hand in his and raised it before her vision as he told Powchutu what to say. "Tell her she is mine and has been since the day I put these marks on her hand. This akito holds more power than the other one, for she willingly accepted it. I will allow no man to take her from me, not the soldiers, or kodas, or Mato Waditaka, not while I live and breathe."

She stared at him in disbelief and confusion as her friend related Gray Eagle's words to her. How Powchutu wished to lie, to tell her Gray Eagle despised her—but Powchutu was a man of honor.

"He does not know how truthfully he speaks, Powchutu. For I have loved him and belonged to him since that first day, no, from the first moment, I saw him. I loved him even when he did terrible things to me. But I always deluded myself by believing his hatred would one day vanish. But it did not. He is wrong, for he may have no choice in losing me or his life, for he might do both this very day."

She gazed deep into his smoky eyes which told her nothing and whispered, "My heart will forever belong to only you. I am a fool, Wanmdi Hota, for I love you more than my own life. If you have not guessed this already, you will never know or feel it again. For as long as I live and breathe, I shall try in every way to kill it."

This statement pleased Powchutu and he struck out for more. "What will you do, Alisha, if he dies this day?" he asked, hoping to remind him she would join Mato Waditaka and go to his mats this very night.

Alisha lowered anguish-filled eyes and missed the cold, dark anger which leaped into Gray Eagle's at Powchutu's words.

"I cannot bear the thought of his death. How could I go to Mato Waditaka with Wanmdi Hota's blood upon his hands? And yet, I would have no choice. I cannot hold Mato Waditaka responsible for what will happen. Doesn't he realize if he kills Wanmdi Hota his ghost would forever be between us and I could never love or forgive him? I thought for a time I could forget my love in another's arms and life, but I did not and cannot. I know this now. I cannot think upon what I will do if he dies. I'm not even sure of what I will do or feel if he wins and takes me back with him. Only time can answer these questions for me."

Everything was crashing in on Alisha at one time—her past, her cloudy future, her love for Gray Eagle, and her confusion at his present words. Everything coalesced and nothing made sense. She was suspended in a vacuum, tensely awaiting the outcome of this day which ruled her entire future. God give me the strength and courage to accept and face what this day will bring, she prayed.

Gray Eagle lifted her trembling chin with his hand, forcing her to meet his gaze. He held it firmly in a secure grip as he lowered his head and kissed her passionately, but tenderly. Unable to free herself, she was soon lost to the heat and temptation of his kiss and embrace. Her mind struggled for resistance, but soon admitted defeat to his lips and her hunger.

Her arms went up to encircle his neck and she pressed closer to him. She returned his kiss with a fiery response. The kiss became more demanding and passionate and she had no will or desire to pull away.

Powchutu shifted restlessly at the scene before him. Jealousy and anger flickered and grew in his eyes and heart. He would kill Gray Eagle someday for this! How dare he use her love for him as a weapon against her! Soon, he raged, he will have no power over her for I shall kill him if Mato Waditaka does not. You are wrong, Wanmdi Hota, for she will be mine . . .

Alisha hungered for each kiss he gave her, knowing it could be the last one forever. But her body yearned for more than his kiss. There was an ache growing in her which she desperately wanted to satisfy. What if this was the last time he would ever hold and kiss her? Terrified at this thought, she clung even tighter to him.

He knew she begged for more than just his touch. All doubts about her total love and desire for him alone vanished. This was what he had to know for sure before he took the life of Mato Waditaka or gave up his own. He, too, wished there had been some other way to get her back. He did not like having to take the life of one such as he.

The beat of the kettle drum changed, telling all the time was near. He removed his lips from hers, silently cursing the lack of time. He held her tightly in his arms to allow both their passions to cool and her trembling to stop. He could not seem to bear to let her go, perhaps forever. He wanted to pick her up and run to his horse and flee with her, but it was not that simple. If he ran he would never be able to return to his people. He desperately thought, I know of no other way to have you back at my side, my love, my Cinstinna. I hope you will someday know and understand this no matter what happens this day.

How he had missed her these past days. It felt good just to hold and kiss her again, to see her face, to feel her response to him, and to know she still loved only him. If the Great Spirit is willing and my life is spared, you will soon know the truth, from me. He leaned back and drank in her features one last time.

She felt he was scanning her every thought. She silently mouthed the words, "I love you . . ." He wondered if this would be his last chance to tell her he also loved her and always had. Would this be his last chance to beg her forgiveness and understanding for his treatment to her? Would this be his last chance to tell her everything within his heart and mind? Would he die this day and leave her here as another's winyan?

Would he die without her ever knowing how much he loved her and why he was doing this? Would he never see the look on her face when he said those words of love to her? Agony cut a savage path throughout his body, leaving nothing in its way untouched.

I love you too much to tell you these things now, Cinstinna, he thought. If I am killed this day, the pain of forgetting me will be far greater. It will be easier to forget your enemy than your love. She would not have the time to know if I spoke the truth and would be in torment for a long time. She would think it to be a last, cruel taunt. It would be far too cruel for her to know of my love just before my death. I will remain silent until you are mine. If it is to be, I will carry your love to my death.

She spoke one last time, "May your god and mine watch over you, my love, and keep you safe."

Powchutu looked on in pain and fury. White Arrow returned his knife to its sheath and nodded for them to leave. Powchutu took her arm and led her outside, her eyes remaining locked to Gray Eagle's until the last moment.

Outside, she asked Powchutu in anguish, "Is there nothing we can do?"

He shook his head and answered, "It is too late. They are both committed. You love him greatly, do you not? I had thought at the fort I read this in your eyes even before you spoke of him. Come, we will wait in your father's teepee until it is time."

In her father's teepee, Alisha entreated, she begged, she pleaded, she cried, she threatened, and she argued for Black Cloud to stop this challenge. He would not listen to any of her words.

"As Shalee, I beg you to intervene. They are both great warriors. They are deeply loved and needed by their tribes. A death of either one would be a tragic waste. Could you not settle this with some contest or fight?"

He looked at her, studying her reasons and answered, "You are Si-ha Sapa. You must accept our laws and ways. It cannot be changed or stopped. They know and accept this, as you must, my daughter."

"But," she cried, "must one of them die for this honor?"

He sorrowfully shook his head. "It must be. Unless, at the point of victory the winner grants life." He grieved at the thought of the death of his son or the death of the son of his koda. He missed the light which sparkled in his daughter's eyes at his last words.

There was a way to prevent a death! But would either of them do this? Was their hatred and anger to each other more important than sparing the life of a rival? If she could intervene at the right moment and plead with the winner, would he show mercy? Would the right moment even be granted to her? She prayed, I must hope it will, for no one must die . . . no one . . .

She paced around the teepee nervously until the drumming stopped. Once more the silence was deafening to her panicked heart. Expectation filled the air outside. The area was charged with excitement.

They walked outside and over to the large campfire. She was placed between her father and Powchutu as the two warriors left their appointed teepees and came forward.

Such fierce pride and arrogance, she thought as she watched them come forward. Each of the two men was a pinnacle of virility and handsomeness. If her heart did not already belong to Gray Eagle, it would have been impossible to choose between them. They approached each other fearlessly and proud, eyes locked in nonverbal combat. They faced each other and took a spread-legged stance. If either man felt the slightest iota of fear, doubt or misgiving, it did not show.

They were dressed in breechcloths and low-cut moccasins, nothing more. They both had three stripes painted across their noses, cheeks, foreheads and chests. Gray Eagle's was in yellow and Brave Bear's in red. There was a narrow, rawhide thong tied about the upper arm of each man.

To Alisha, they looked like two fierce war gods, come to do battle for the world itself. Their bodies spoke of valor, strength, courage, agility, power and self-confidence. It was evident to all they were evenly matched and either man could win. It would only depend on who made the first mistake.

They both possessed the strength and skill to

be the winner. There was no fear in either man's eyes. They looked as if they dared death to strike them down. Their eyes challenged one another to prove who was the better man. Was either of them capable of showing mercy to the other? She was afraid to answer after seeing the looks which passed between them. Then, too, she knew Gray Eagle and his love of vengeance.

The incessant drumming began anew. She felt her pulse catch and keep time with it. The two warriors were joined by their two closest friends. Wanhinkpe Ska went to Wanmdi Hota and the brave they had eaten with the other day went to Mato Waditaka. In turn, the friend called the coups of his friend and gave a prayer for his guidance and protection.

When this was done, the two warriors came forward to the chief. Both men stared openly and boldly at her. Their desire for her flickered in both their eyes. She reddened at their heated, lustful stares. Brave Bear's gaze lowered to her neck and flared in anger for a moment. Then, he smiled in amusement. He thinks to trick me and put me off my guard with his wanapin. She does not know the meaning of his token, or she would not have accepted it. Very cunning, my foe, he thought knowingly.

He smiled at her and she instantly returned it. She shifted her gaze to Gray Eagle as Brave Bear was speaking to his father and embracing him. As usual, he wore a blank, unreadable stare. There was nothing there to remind her of the scene they had so recently shared.

Unable to stop herself, she asked in pain, "It meant nothing to you, did it? Nothing . . ." Torment and humiliation filled her face and eyes.

He relaxed his hard, cool stare and spoke softly for her ears alone, "Lese, Cinstinna . . ." The husky tone of his voice and his tender expression bewildered her. His gaze lowered to his eagle which was still covering the bear's head. He raised his gaze to hers once more and gave her a possessive, desirous look which told her she was his and he wanted her, love or no love. Her blood flamed within her body and her eyes automatically answered his. He smiled and nodded understanding.

Her eyes were glued to his beguiling half-smile and gleaming, devilish eyes. God, how she loved and wanted him, even now after everything. Suddenly aware of what was taking place between them there in the open, she flamed deeper and meekly lowered her head.

She was only faintly aware of the chief's voice as he spoke with the two men of the coming challenge and its deadly consequences. Her senses rocked at Wanmdi Hota's proximity and magnetism. Her emotions were tossed about in a tempest of conflicting thoughts and feelings. She unconsciously touched the eagle wanapin near her heart.

Each of the men nodded agreement to the rules of the challenge and turned to walk away. She looked on in fear and anxiety. She must not allow her attention to stray for a single moment.

She must be on constant alert for that one split-second between victory and death . . . God, help me, her mind screamed.

Each of the men prepared himself mentally by blocking out all thoughts but this battle to the death. Gray Eagle was handed a bow and three arrows. Brave Bear was led to a line about twenty feet away. He immediately dropped to a crouching, loose position with feet and legs apart, arms swinging free and nimble at his sides, nerves and muscles alert and tense. He locked his eyes on Gray Eagle's and nodded he was ready.

Quicker than the flash of lightning, Gray Eagle fired the three arrows directly at him. He moved like a flame in the fire, leaping from side to side, agilely dodging all three. Alisha sighed relief when she saw him stand up straight, signaling his first victory. He was then handed a bow and three arrows. She stiffened, knowing it was Gray Eagle's turn to be a live target. She watched wide-eyed as he easily and nimbly evaded the arrows. She exhaled painfully, not realizing she had been holding her breath.

The two men remained in their places as three lances were brought forward and handed to each man. Powchutu leaned over and whispered to her, "It will only take the slightest nick, for the points of the heads are dipped in a strong, speedy poison." Alisha blanched white and swayed against him, not daring to ask how much time he would have if he were nicked.

They simultaneously threw and dodged the

290

three lances. Again, each man was unscathed and had eluded death. Alisha's nerves were as tight as a bowstring. Which man would die? How much longer could her nerves withstand this pressure? The challenge would go on until one or the other of them won. In time, one would tire or make an error in timing, and that deadly mistake would cost his life—and her fate.

Tension mounted and filled the air as they all watched and waited to see which man would make that first and fatal mistake. She could no longer pray. She could only look on in fear and terror. How could she pray and ask for one to die and one to live? Must it be so? She twisted her hands over and over as she watched the battle go on and on . . .

The ceremonial chief came forward and drew a large circle on the ground. The two men were then handed knives and they stepped inside the large circle. The leader chanted a few words and the two nodded readiness to each other, continuing the death ritual.

The signal was given and they both dropped to stooped positions, feet apart, arms and hands hanging loose, and knees bent and flexed. They moved around each other sizing up the foe for weaknesses and strengths. Each knew that a split-second delay in his reactions could cost him his life. He must be on constant alert. Their eyes met and never left the eyes of the other man. Their faces were expressionless and taut. The knife blades glittered brightly in the sunlight.

With a loud yell, they each lunged at each

other and the fight began. They slashed at each other as they slowly circled around in half-crouching positions. They shoved with their arms and kicked out with nimble, hard feet. Alisha felt as though she were viewing an athletic display, but for the knives which sliced at each other, bringing red, warm blood. They flirted with death, enticing the other to drop his guard. Their bodies glistened with intermingled sweat and blood. Dust rose about their legs from the quick, rapid movements they made.

Alisha could not suppress a scream as Brave Bear tripped Gray Eagle and raised his knife high in the air for a plunge. But Gray Eagle easily blocked his arm and rolled free at the last moment. Alisha licked her dry lips and bit into her lower one.

"Someone must stop this, Powchutu! They'll kill each other! Enough! Stop them!" she cried out in panic.

Mahpiya Sapa curiously observed his daughter's strange outburst and concern for her enemy. Powchutu seized her and held her tightly, not allowing her to interfere. The two warriors had heard her outburst, but could not afford to drop their attention for an instant.

Time passed on and on as the two men began to show signs of fatigue and strain. They breathed and panted heavily in the arid air, their chests heaving rapidly. Sweat poured from their faces and chests. Their muscles were cramped and tight. Soon, one would miss a step in retreat or fail to deflect a blow, and it would swiftly be over. Only the muffled sounds of scuffling feet, labored breathing and grunts of exertion, the swishing of knives, and that incessant, steady drumming in her heart and chest. She would surely go mad if this lasted much longer. Her nerves were frayed and on edge. Her heart pounded wildly as her chest heaved in labored, quick rasps.

Each hit scored brought fresh, sticky blood and a cry of alarm from her lips. Each miss brought a sigh of relief. Increasing fatigue was overcoming both men. Each was acutely aware of his own waning strength and that of his opponent. He did not dare make an error in judgment and timing or all would be lost.

Each man gained strength and daring from the thought of the prize of this battle. Each deeply respected his opponent's skills, abilities and power. Each knew the other to be a man of honor and truth. Each was well aware of the other's courage and daring. It was too bad they both wanted the same woman. Not only would defeat bring the loss of her, but it would also bring his death.

As they cautiously circled each other closely, Gray Eagle's words were Brave Bear's undoing. He spoke low and deep, only to him. His eyes blazed in truth and pride as he whispered, "She is mine. I will die before I allow any man to take or possess the woman I love."

A look of startled disbelief and surprise lit Brave Bear's face and eyes. He gave that slight hesitation and dropping of full alert. Like a flash, he was thrown to the ground hard, his free hand pinned securely beneath his body by the full weight of Gray Eagle's body on his.

Gray Eagle gripped his other wrist in a vise of steel and brutally twisted until Brave Bear was forced to drop his knife into the dust and dirt. Gray Eagle's knees pressed hard into his chest allowing for no movement. His legs twisted back in a sort of fashion to imprison the movement of Brave Bear's.

His glare bore into the dark eyes of his defeated opponent. Gray Eagle's eyes and face were alive with the glow of victory and Brave Bear's glinted with the anticipation and acceptance of his coming death . . .

Gray Eagle raised his knife high, but before he could plunge it into the heart of his opponent, Alisha broke free from Powchutu's grasp and dashed to the warriors. She grabbed Gray Eagle's wrist and cried out, "Hiya! Wanmdi Hota. Do not kill him! Spare his life. I beg you. His people need him for his father is old and getting weak. You are the victor. Do what you will with me, but I pray you to spare his life."

He stared into the ashen face with large, misty, imploring eyes and thought, this I will do for you, Cinstinna, to show my love and because I, too, do not wish to take the life of Mato Waditaka. Gray Eagle was secretly grateful she was giving him an honorable way out of this challenge.

While Gray Eagle studied her eyes, Alisha

quickly removed the bear wanapin from around her neck and returned it to the neck of Brave Bear. Desperately thinking of how to show her capitulation to Gray Eagle, she hastily untied her headband with the red and gray queque and secured it around Gray Eagle's arm for all to see and know she yielded to him.

"Free him, I beg you," she pleaded once more. She had done all she could. Would he listen this one time? Would he grant her just this much? He had what he had come for and there was no need for the death of Mato Waditaka.

He looked down at Brave Bear for a moment. He took his knife and slid the blade under the ikan on his arm and cut it free. He said to him, "The match is made and won. Your life is in my hands and I grant it back to you. She begs for this and I will grant it for her and myself. I have no desire to claim the life of Mato Waditaka. I only wish to claim what is mine for I love and want her above my own life. Do you accept truce and defeat with honor?"

Brave Bear had seen the look which had passed between them just now. He had also seen the look and words between them before the challenge, but had ignored them as a trick of light. It is him she loves. She wishes to spare my life but not share it. She has chosen him in challenge and in heart. There is no need for my death, he conceded to himself. He nodded agreement.

Gray Eagle threw his knife into the ground above Brave Bear's head and, holding the ikan high for all to see, he spoke. "I do not wish the death of Mato Waditaka. I only wish the life of my woman. I grant him his life with honor and I will take my woman, the daughter of Mahpiya Sapa, to join on the full moon."

There was loud shouting and joy at his words. The Si-ha Sapa shouted both their names in respect and happiness. They chanted this latest coup of Wanmdi Hota's with great relief and joy. Generosity was one of the highest coups a warrior could earn. What could be more generous than sparing the life of their future chief? Gray Eagle had proven himself once more to be a great and daring warrior. The battle had been fought with honor. Both Alisha's and Gray Eagle's actions had freed Brave Bear from any shame at his defeat. It was their way to grant life whenever possible or the best for both men.

Would Mato Waditaka have done the same if he had been the victor? they all wondered, hoping he would have. Would Alisha have begged for the life of Wanmdi Hota if he had been the loser? Would Wanmdi Hota have spared his life if she had not begged for it? These are things they would never know, but in the hearts of the two warriors, they knew all the answers were yes.

Gray Eagle stood up and pulled Alisha to her feet. He extended his hand to Brave Bear in a gesture of truce and friendship. Brave Bear met his steady look and accepted it. They all three walked to the waiting chief. He handed him the severed armband, greatly relieved it was not the body of his dead son.

They spoke for a few minutes, then Gray Eagle said to them, "We can twice join our two tribes in friendship and truce if your son will accept the Shaman's daughter Chela to join."

Brave Bear turned to him with a look of surprise and puzzlement. He asked incredulously, "You will give me the one promised to you to join? You do not wish to make her your second wife? I have heard she is also very beautiful. Would she accept me in your place? Why do you wish to favor me with this great honor?"

Gray Eagle looked at him steadily and answered, "I have no need of a second wife. Shalee is the only woman I need. Chela is indeed very beautiful, but also fiery and stubborn. She will need taming by a very strong-willed, forceful man." He grinned broadly and jokingly asked, "Do you think you can handle this she-cat of an Oglala, my koda? She will accept you, for my father will order it. You are a great and honored warrior. This will seal the truce and join our tribes in great friendship. I do this also because of your kindness to Shalee while she was here with you."

Once more Gray Eagle laughed and joked, "Besides, Shalee was raised as wasichu and they take only one mate. I do not think she would be happy if I shared her place with others. Life would be hard and sad with the two of them, for they are still enemies. It is for the best if Chela comes here. Then too, she is very demanding of my time and love." They all laughed and knowingly shook their heads.

Unfortunately, Powchutu and Alisha had left the group unnoticed and did not hear the conversation among the men. She would not know of these events and Gray Eagle's feelings until too late. This talk could have prevented a lot of pain and fear on her part. It could also have prevented hatred and spite on Powchutu's part. These few words could have changed what was shortly to take place . . .

Black Cloud exclaimed to Gray Eagle, "You are indeed a great and noble warrior. You speak with much wisdom and kindness. You bring pride and honor to your father, yourself and your people. I do not fear for Shalee to go with you now. You have proven your love and worthiness to have her. I will miss the light of my daughter in my life. I will accept the hand of Chela for my son for joining. Our tribes will be forever joined in peace and friendship."

Brave Bear spoke up, "Shalee does not know of your love, does she? I can see that she fears and doubts you. When will you tell her of these things?" Brave Bear realized even if he had won her to join, Wanmdi Hota had already won her heart and love. Did she even realize herself how much she loved him? I will take the beautiful and fiery-spirited Chela to join. It will prove another challenge in itself to tame her! Maybe in time, she will take the place of Shalee in my heart. It is best not to have one whose heart belongs to another.

Gray Eagle met his look and replied, "She will soon learn of these things. She will learn trust, then love will bloom and grow in her heart for me once more."

Brave Bear commented, "Her love for you already shows in her eyes. She might not be aware of these feelings for you. If she is, then she tries to hide them from everyone, including herself." Gray Eagle nodded affirmatively.

The ceremonial chief came forward and led the two warriors to the pezuta teepee where the Shaman would treat their wounds and injuries. They talked and laughed like two kodas as he worked on the cuts and scrapes.

"I am happy I did not have to take the life of Mato Waditaka. I could not give Alisha up to any man and I saw no other way but the challenge. She is and has been mine for many, many moons, since the day of my capture by the wasichu."

"Why have you not shown her or told her of your love? If you loved and wanted her this much, why did you treat her as you did?"

Gray Eagle related the reasons for her treatment. He explained the things she had done, how she had behaved, the reactions of his people, her defiance, her rebellion, her interference, her betrayal of his trust, escape, and her attempts to strike him physically. He told him how he treated her when they were alone. "She refused to be subdued. She defied me many times, bringing shame and dishonor to me as a man and warrior." He told him why he had treated her the way he had at the fort that day when he had reclaimed her.

"I met and knew her as wasichu and our enemy. How could I have shown weakness in treating her less than a kaskapi? I tried to show her in my teepee how I felt in my heart, but she was too hurt and afraid to see this. I could not lose face before my warriors and people by showing love and kindness to a ska wincin-yanna. You did not have this problem, my koda. You have only seen and known her as Shalee, a Si-ha Sapa and your chief's daughter. I saw and knew her as Alisha, a white girl and prisoner. You had no honor to lose as I did.

"I did not tell her of my love that morning you took her away for I felt it a cruel taunt for her to learn of it and then be forced to leave me to marry another. I had tried to teach her love and trust the two days before you came and I was to tell her all that very day. Your coming wiped out her trust in me. She felt betrayed and would not have listened or believed me. I also thought it cruel for her to know of my love and then join with you. I did not tell her this morning because I believed if I died this day it would be easier for her to forget me as her enemy, rather than her lost love. It would not have been good for me to have forced her to reveal her love for me to you, her promised one.

"So many things seem so pointless and cruel now, but at the time, they seemed to be important and unbending. I see where I have

300

made many mistakes with her. I was much too harsh on her even as my enemy. I have not known the love of a winyan before, and I have treated her very badly. She will have much to understand and forgive. There are many things I wish I could undo, but I cannot. Things would have been very different if I had shown her my love long ago. I should have been kinder and gentler with her. There were many things I, too, had to learn to trust and accept in her.

"With Shalee as Si-ha Sapa, I could have told her of my love for her. I could have told her all the things I have longed to tell her for a long time."

Brave Bear had listened to all his words very carefully. Then he said, "I see your reasons now. I understand and agree. Her father also felt the taunts of others about his Jenny, but not like it was with Alisha. I can see why you had to be cold and unfeeling toward her. I hated your treatment to Shalee, but now I see this treatment was to a ska kaskapi named Alisha. I can see why you wanted her and captured her. I can see why you kept her even at such a risk to your honor. I, too, believe now she was sent to you by Napi. She will be where she belongs. Yes, this is good."

The two men talked on and on about many things. A strong bond of respect and friendship was budding and growing. It would take time for Brave Bear to get over the loss of Shalee, but Gray Eagle had made it possible in honor. They spoke of other events in both their lives. Each man had a rich understanding of the other's feelings, drives and thoughts. This made acceptance of each other easier and quicker.

Later, they walked along talking as they returned to Black Cloud's teepee. Only Powchutu and the chief were present. Gray Eagle glanced around anxious to see Alisha and the look upon her face. He yearned to gaze into those lucid, green eyes and the lovely face of the girl he loved and had just won. He asked Powchutu where she was, recalling their leaving the challenge together while he spoke with the chief and Brave Bear.

"Where is Ali . . . Shalee?"

Powchutu shifted uneasily causing Gray Eagle to become slightly alarmed. Surely she would not try to hide from him or escape again! He demandingly repeated his query, "Where is she?"

Powchutu glared at him icily and replied, "She went for a walk near the falls. She is not ready for this confrontation with you yet. Let her be for a while. Give her the time she needs to accept this and come to you."

Brave Bear quickly and alertly sensed the hatred, tension and jealousy between these two men and answered Gray Eagle's question himself. "There is a hidden cave under the falls where she goes to bathe. Perhaps she went there if she wishes to be alone."

Gray Eagle cast Powchutu a warning look, nodded to Brave Bear and left to look for her. As he walked along, his face darkened in worry.

Will she still resist me and my love? I am weary of this coldness and bitterness. I will accept no resistance from her! She is mine and I will take her! She has been too long from my life. She will join to me willingly or by force. I will tolerate no interference from anyone, not even her.

After the battle had been won and while the men talked, Alisha and Powchutu had quietly slipped away from the crowd. Powchutu had observed her face, the emotions written there. He knew she was not ready to deal with Gray Eagle yet. She needed time alone to think things out and come to grips with them.

She had looked up at him and said, "I am glad no one had to die today, Powchutu. But how will I live with his hatred and cruelty again? I can see he desires me as a woman, but not as Alisha, not as a person. Even if we join, I will still be like his slave and prisoner. Things have not changed that much between us. Only my name and position have changed, not me. I must have time to think. Do not tell him where I am. I will go to the cave and be alone for a while."

She left him standing there as she walked toward the falls. Soon, she disappeared beneath the cascade of water. He watched her until she was out of sight. How he longed to go with her and hold her in his arms and comfort her. But it was too late for that now. Or was it? . . .

He spoke softly into the wind, "You must face this thing alone, my love." He returned to the chief's teepee to wait for Gray Eagle and the others to forestall the scene which was sure to come between them. She must have this time to think.

Alisha sat down on the large rock beside the pool in the fading dusky light. She pulled her knees up to her chest and encircled them with her arms, clasping her fingers tightly together. She rested her chin on her knees and stared at the water trickling down the back wall. She watched the moonlight touch and sparkle on it like hundreds of tiny diamonds. She listened to the sounds of the night creatures and insects as they came to life. She noted the singing of the cicadas and katydids. She listened to the hooting of an owl not far away. She caught the calling of a nightingale to its mate. She listened to the silence in the cave around her . . .

Her mind was tired of trying to fight the inevitable. Her heart was weary of trying to suppress her love and desire for Wanmdi Hota. Her body was tense at trying to fight and control its hunger for him. Even if he did hate her, she was his, bought and paid for with his challenge today. I can live without his love, she mused, but can I live with his hate? My mind and body both turn traitorous when he holds me and touches me. All thoughts of hatred and cruelty are washed away in the flood of emotions he starts within me.

Will it be any different now that he thinks I am an Indian like he is? Is this too much to hope for? Surely he would not torture me physically again, but what will he do to my heart and soul?

Will he try to find other ways to hurt and taunt me? He could use my own love and weakness against me. Would he whip me again if I rebelled? He did Chela and she is Indian. I was at his mercy as his slave, and I shall be just as much at his mercy as his wife. What shall I do? How should I act now? I do not know what to expect of him, nor do I know what he expects of me. Suddenly, I don't know what to think or believe. I don't know what to say or how to act. He is such a mystery to me. Will I ever know or understand him?

The events of this afternoon in his teepee flickered before her mind. She shuddered to recall the overwhelming passion which had engulfed her and forced her to lose sight of all things except him and his touch. His kisses had been burned into her memory and his remembered touch caused her skin to flush and tingle.

She lowered her forehead to her knees and spoke in torment, "Wanmdi Hota, why must it forever be like this between us? Why do you wish to hurt me like this? Please try to love me this time, if only a little. Do not close your heart to me forever." She sat in silence for a few minutes, then sensed someone's presence. She slowly turned . . .

His tall frame was outlined by the moonlight, but she could not see his face which was hidden in the dark shadows. She stared at him for what seemed an eternity. It will be different this time, her mind told her. It must! I will be his wife . . . or will I? What if he doesn't have to marry me now? What if he only keeps me as his . . . and marries Chela?

Her thoughts quickly scanned the events of the past few months. Her whole life had been torn asunder by certain events, but at the center of all of them was Wanmdi Hota, her nemesis.

Darkness descended and the moon grew brighter. They both remained where they were staring at the other, she in uncertainty and anticipation, he in relief and satisfaction.

He could see her features and expression clearly, but she could see none of his, for his face had still remained in total darkness. She was held transfixed by the sight of his outline.

Gray Eagle moved toward her and held out his hand to her. He called, "Ku-wa, Lese." He saw a flicker of confusion and sadness at his calling for Lese instead of Shalee.

A chill passed down her spine and over her body. Was he telling her he would not accept her as Shalee, that she would forever remain Lese in his mind? Did he already close his heart against her so soon? Perhaps the slip really meant nothing at all. Soon, she would know . . .

Her lips and mouth were suddenly very dry and she wet them with her tongue. Her heart pounded madly within her chest and the pulse raced like a wind within her veins. He saw her look of indecision and panic. He noted the flushed cheeks and luminous eyes filling with tears. Come to me willingly, he prayed fervently.

Again, he spoke softly, but firmly, "Ku-wa!"

She rose and came hesitantly to him, stopping a few feet before him. She extended a small, quavering hand out to him with pleading in her emerald eyes.

He remained where he was and folded his arms across his hard chest. "Ku-wa, Lese," he commanded, a little more sharply than he intended.

Dismay and sadness crossed her features. She whispered in a small, quiet voice, "So, it's to be a power play again. Will you never take the first step to me, Wanmdi Hota? Must I always bend and yield to you first? Can't you show me one small measure of giving and tenderness? Must you forever remain above me, unreachable and cold? Would it be so very hard to melt a little, to show I mean something . . . anything, to you? Will I forever be your enemy?" Tears sparkled brightly in her eyes as she stepped forward.

He lowered his arms, ready to take her into his embrace. She placed a small, cold hand on his chest near his heart and said, "I yield to your power and ownership, Sir Lucifer. I am once more in your circle of life, with no beginning or end to your hate." At her last words, the tears gathered in her eyes and began to roll down her cheeks. She lowered her head in defeat.

One of his strong hands went around her slender waist and the other one went to her trembling chin to lift it to face him. Her eyelids remained lowered, staring at his chest and refusing to meet his gaze. His hand slid behind her head, burying itself into her soft hair, and pulled her to him. His lips came down on hers in a gentle kiss. He continued to spread light kisses over her eyes, face, ears, and mouth.

Very quickly, fires leaped and burned within her body. A tingling warmth spread throughout her. It flamed and grew in leaps and bounds, growing hotter and bolder with each new kiss or caress. She panicked and tried to pull away. I'll not submit like chattel this time, she vowed. This time, I'll not allow his hold and control on my mind and body. I must withhold my heart. But her mind argued a losing battle with her passionate body. His kisses seared across her mouth and throat as passion coursed in her blood. There was a hunger for him which was starving within her and screamed to be fed.

His lips claimed hers over and over in bruising, fiery kisses. He pressed close to her body, his smell and heat filling her senses. This heat from his body fused with hers to ignite the flames of desire higher and brighter. Her mind whirled in suspense and her body quivered with waiting.

She became aware of the heavy fast pounding of his heart beneath her small hand resting there. She felt the heat radiating from him and the intense hunger of his mouth on hers. She listened to the husky tone of his deep, rich voice as he whispered her name softly into her ear.

"Lese . . . Lese, Cinstinna . . ."

Could there possibly be more than just passion and desire in his kisses and embraces? This was how he had been those last two days before she had been taken from him. Was he telling her this was the way he wanted things between them? Was he trying to let her know he. . . . Don't reach for the moon, Lese, she warned herself. Her brain had lost its capacity to reason in the constant onslaught of his actions on her senses and emotions.

As his mouth took hers once more, she could no longer control or hope to prevent the love and passion which coursed within her body like molten lava. Her arms encircled his neck and she clung tightly to him in hungry need. She pulled his head closer to hers, her kiss and response becoming more demanding. She could not have left him if her very life had depended upon it.

She caressed his back ardently with her hands. She kneaded and fondled his hard network of muscles and smooth skin. She could feel the firmness of his body and the hardness of his manhood against her. For her, the only thing that mattered now was he was here, holding her, kissing her, wanting her. She would deal with any other problems later, much later. She had no willpower to resist him or to remain impassive in his embrace. Her breathing quickened to quick short rasps.

She wanted him with such intensity her body shook violently and quivered with unrepressed desire. She thirsted for his kisses as one thirsts for water in the desert. She craved his love as one craves food when starving.

"Wanmdi Hota . . . love me . . . love me

now . . ." she cried out to him in an emotional fever. Caution was thrown to the wind. She wanted him too deeply to think of anything or anyone, except herself and her passion.

A voice called out from the falls, "Wanmdi Hota, did you find her?"

Startled, he jerked his mouth from hers and answered White Arrow in a strained voice, "Sha, Wanhinkpe Ska."

White Arrow called out, "They are all waiting for you both at the village. It will soon be time for the feast. Is there some trouble?"

Silently he cursed himself for letting things go this far. This was not the time or place to make love to her. When she had responded so feverishly to him, he had lost all sight and thought of the others and the time. He had been about to take her right then and there. He had only meant to hold her, to kiss her, and to let her know he wanted her back the way it had been before. He had not meant to incite her, or himself, to such heights of passion.

He called back to White Arrow, "We will be there soon. Leave us for a time."

Understanding what was going on by the tone of his koda's voice, he smiled and returned to the village to tell the others all was well and they would shortly return.

Gray Eagle's loins ached painfully with unfulfilled lust and desire for her. He struggled with himself to gain control and quench these fires which ran rampant throughout his entire body. He fought to gain control of his heavy, labored breathing and unleashed emotions. Curses, how he wanted and needed her! Why could he not take her here and now? She was his! She was willing and hungry for him! But it would be too swift for her to enjoy it and this was not the way to take her for the first time again.

I must find the strength to quell this hunger for her until later. He drew from every source of willpower, energy and strength he possessed to help him. I had forgotten for a time what her touch and kiss does to me. When I hold her, only our love is real. How does she have such power over me and not be aware of it? She has a way of making all things dim in her presence. If you only knew how much I love you, Cinstinna, would you use it against me?

He held her possessively in his embrace, allowing each of them the time to bring these feelings under control. He had finally managed to do so, but she did not want to dispel her desire for him. She breathed raggedly and trembled with unsated desire. There was an aching emptiness in the heart of her womanhood.

She desperately wondered, how do I bring these feelings under control? If he can do it, then why can't I? Surely there is some way to quell hunger when it is impossible to fulfill it, but how?

To go to the point of losing all control over her body, then to be pushed away, was more than she could bear to accept. She felt pain, hunger, anger and frustration. She fought and struggled with this weakness his kisses and caresses had unleashed inside her. How could she when he was so close, when the warmth of his breath touched her, when she remained within his arms, and when his smell filled her senses?

She cried out to him, "Help me, Wanmdi Hota! I do not know how to stop these things I feel. Teach me to resist this hunger for you! Teach me how to stop this pain inside! I want and need you, now! Please love me . . . I don't care about the others . . . just love me and hold me!"

Her desperate pleas both stirred and pained him. He had to halt her pleading or all would be lost, for already his body threatened to revolt against his rigid control. He knew the only way he could help her was to brutally change her emotions of this moment. He must do what was necessary!

He roughly pushed her away and coldly said, "Hiya, Shalee. Ku-wa!" His roughness and tone destroyed her feelings of desire instantly. They dwindled quickly and died with the coldness and cruelty of his anger and manner. He pulled her by the arm toward the cave entrance.

She tried to yank her arm free from his iron grasp, but could not. He pulled her struggling body out of the cave and along the rocky, wet pathway. The emotions of anger and humiliation flooded her. All her thoughts and feelings of passion fled.

She flung the stinging words at him, "I hate you! I'll never belong to you! Never!"

She was hurt and bewildered by his sudden change of mood. Would she ever come to understand this man she loved and wanted so desperately? Her emotions were in an upheaval as they walked back toward the camp.

He impatiently thought, I helped you in the only way open to me, Cinstinna. This is not the time or place for the renewal of our love. Surely you can see and know this!

He walked slowly to give her the time to bring her rage and embarrassment under some kind of control. In time, you will know I only did what I had to do for you, he thought defensively, but futilely.

As they reached the edge of the camp, he allowed her to break free and flee to her father's teepee. Thankfully it was empty. She threw herself upon the buffalo mat and wept.

When all the tears and emotions were spent, she sat up. She asked herself if this would be the new way of things between them now. Was this some new way of tormenting and punishing her? Did he hold her responsible for the challenge? Was he showing her the power he still held over her? Could he have been trying to find out if he did still have this power over her after her encounter with Mato Waditaka, especially after what he saw this morning in the meadow?

Would he now use this power over her to force her to do as he commanded? Would she be at his vengeful mercy now? Would he kiss and caress her until she burned with desire for him, then cruelly push her away, leaving her with this empty, hollow feeling in her body and heart? I could not bear for him to use this as a weapon to master me, she cried. He knows he commands my will. I am his prisoner of love as well as his prisoner in life. What shall I do?

I do not possess the knowledge to resist and reject him. How he must enjoy having this control over my very life and existence. He taunts me with his love, always just out of my reach. Just like Tantalus was forever taunted by the food and drink eternally just out of his reach. I must be free of him and this hold he has over me . . .

As his wife, I would be subjected to his every whim of cruelty. He would never allow me to be happy. I must flee this place and him. But how? Powchutu! I could not escape last time, but with his help, this time I could! Would he dare to help me? Could I risk his life in a deadly plot against Wanmdi Hota? No . . . I must stay and face this thing alone. Besides, how much worse could things be than before? Fearfully, she knew . . .

She arose from the mat and gathered her things to go for a bath in the cave. It had been a long, hot day and she felt the need to freshen herself. She furtively peered out and noticed no one nearby. She quietly made her way out of camp and to the cave with her belongings. The men had retired to another teepee to

314

prepare for the feast and to give her privacy to prepare herself.

She quickly undressed and slipped into the cool water. She held the wet cloth to her eyes, hoping to take away some of the traces of her tears. She would not give him the satisfaction of seeing her weakness toward him. She must pull herself together. She scrubbed and lathered her body with the jasmine soap several times. She would appear fresh and alive, smelling like sweet wildflowers at the party tonight. Thank goodness her hair was clean, for there was no time to wash and dry it now. In fact, she would have to hurry. She finished and redressed in a fawn-colored dress with the bodice unadorned. She gathered her things and quickly returned to her teepee.

She laced the flap shut from the inside to finish her grooming. She shook her braids loose and brushed her long, chestnut masses until they were soft, shiny, and silky. She let her hair hang free and loose down her back. She took her headband from the peg where Gray Eagle had placed it earlier and secured it around her forehead. She fluffed the little feather and smiled mysteriously and coyly to herself.

She hung Gray Eagle's wanapin on the peg from which she had taken her headband. She went to the storage area and searched through the parfleche which held some jewelry. She selected a necklace of small, cream-colored claws and brown wooden beads and placed it at her throat. She put on two wristlets of rawhide which were delicately etched with colorful wildflowers. She took the mirror and surveyed her appearance with close, critical scrutiny. She placed the intricately quilled moccasins on her small feet. Checking every detail of her grooming with great care, she was finally pleased with her new look. Yes, she would make a fine-looking chief's daughter tonight.

She would show him a thing or two! She would show him he meant absolutely nothing to her, that he held not the slightest interest to her. She would ignore him all night! She would smile and laugh and talk with the others and pretend he wasn't even there. Talk! she laughed. I can't even speak my own tongue! Maybe she couldn't make him jealous, but she could surely aggravate and irritate him! I will show him our little interlude did not phase me at all. He will have to assume I had only been upset at my loss of Mato Waditaka.

I will remain near Powchutu, Mato Waditaka and Wanhinkpe Ska. I will show him his threats mean nothing to me. I am Shalee now and why should I ever fear him again? I will not let him see how deeply he has hurt me. Tonight I will show he can't hurt me.

As revenge and spite flickered in her mind, she said to herself, I will never yield like that to him again! He will be sorry for tonight! I will make him pay for what he did to me! She considered her actions, then mused, damn the consequences!

She pinched her pale cheeks to give them

some color. She walked to the flap when she heard the drums start, announcing the beginning of the feast.

It was time . . . she inhaled deeply several times, stiffened her back and held her chin high. Shalee unlaced the flap and stepped outside.

Chapter Seven

Alisha looked about, her eyes and ears taking in the sights and sounds of merriment and celebration. They dared to celebrate her new capitulation to that man! The savages! Those barbarians! They dared to be happy about her return to his hellish *demesne!* She would show him!

Her eyes roamed the sea of faces until they met and locked triumphantly with his. Her own eyes blazed with defiance, spite and rebellion at him. She let her eyes sweep over him in mocking inspection, taking in his entire body and dress in slow calculation and deliberation. Then, she sneered contemptuously and turned away, dismissing him entirely.

She searched until she found Mato Waditaka. She flashed him a dazzling, sensual smile, eyes glowing and softening. The heat from her eyes could have melted the snows on the mountaintops.

She let her gaze continue its journey until it settled on Powchutu and Wanhinkpe Ska. Once more, she smiled and began to walk their way. Before she could reach where they sat talking, her arm was seized by Gray Eagle in a harsh, forceful grip of iron. He whirled her around to face him, his eyes flaming in rage at her open and icy display of rejection for him. His eyes narrowed and hardened as they encountered her expression. The fire in his eyes flashed warnings to Alisha, but she bravely chose to ignore them.

She glared back at him and remarked, "I am not your wife yet! Let me go or I shall call out to my father and tell him you are hurting me. Brutally forcing the chief's daughter in public might tarnish that golden image of yours. Tonight you will taste how it feels to be the one spurned and rejected! You might have won my body, but you shall never have my heart! You will not touch me again until I am your wife." The word "wife" was spoken with disgust and contempt. What did it matter since he did not understand her words? But just saying them made her feel better. She wrenched her arm free and stormed off to join Mato Waditaka and Powchutu.

She went to where Powchutu was and sat down beside him. He had seen the heated exchange at a distance and was confused by it.

She said tartly, "He does not own me yet! I will not tolerate his treating me like some . . ." She caught herself in time and then continued, "How dare he tease and taunt me like that! I will not yield to him this time, or ever, Powchutu. He is cruel and I hate him! I hate him!"

Powchutu spoke in astonishment and surprise, "What has happened, Shalee? Why are you not pleased with the way things have gone?

No one was killed. You are free and safe and you are back with the man you love. So what is wrong? Wanmdi Hota is the man you love and want, isn't he?''

She met his gaze and sadly replied, "But he doesn't love or want me, Powchutu. Things have not changed between us at all. It makes no difference to him if I am Alisha or Shalee, Indian or white. He still wishes to hurt and shame me. When he came to me, I offered to yield to him willingly, to try for a new beginning for us. He just teased and taunted me, then pushed me away in anger and hate as usual. Why, Powchutu? What have I done to cause him to despise me so? When I went to him, nothing happened. He only tried to prove his power and hold over me. He feigns desire and tenderness until I am overcome with passion. But as soon as I yield, he just shoves me away as if I repulse him. I do not understand the things he does to me or the way he makes me feel. Once he lights a fire within me and turns away, then I do not know how to stop it or put it out.''

She asked Powchutu with innocent honesty, "Teach me how to resist him and his love, Powchutu. Teach me not to yield to him and his touch. I cannot and must not love him anymore, for it will one day bring death to my heart. There are all kinds of deaths and this is only death of another kind . . .''

Powchutu studied the anguished face and eyes before him and replied, "He would have no effect on you if you did not love him, Alisha. If you could learn to hate him, then the passion would die also. It is impossible to stop these kinds of feelings for one you love when he is so near."

Alisha looked at him with terrified eyes and exclaimed in panic, "Then I am surely doomed . . ."

She stared into the flames of the fire before her in a trance-like state, unaware of the people or feasting around her. Neither Alisha nor Powchutu had observed Gray Eagle standing behind them in a group of men. He alertly listened and watched all that had taken place between them.

Powchutu stared at the beautiful profile beside him, frantically thinking of how he could help her. She had cried out to him in helplessness and pain one time before and he had been unable to help her that fateful day. But this time, he would not rest until he found some way to free her from him, even if he had to kill him to do so.

He angrily thought, love that hurts and destroys is not good. I will find some way to help you this time, my love. How can my life be happy when you are suffering so? I can bear the pain in your eyes and heart no more.

Alisha and Powchutu had not hesitated to speak openly, for who could know their words? But the man not far behind them did. He had heard Alisha's anguished words and pleas to her friend, but had been mildly surprised by Powchutu's replies to her. But, why do I feel he spoke of himself and not us, Cinstinna? he questioned himself suspiciously. I fear he spoke of his love for you and this is not good. He still desires to protect you and I cannot allow his interference. I must watch him closely to be certain his love and protectiveness do not get out of hand. I fear you would never forgive me if I were forced to kill him.

I see now I did not handle the meeting between us in the cave right. I should have found some way to conquer your feelings rather than try to quench them so coldly. But I see your game tonight. You wish to make me angry and ashamed. You seek to punish me. But secretly, you hope to make me jealous. You try to pretend my actions did not hurt you. Ah, Cinstinna, your love speaks loudly! You only wish to lash out at me in anger and confusion, but it will soon be over and there will be peace between us. This, I promise you. We will leave after the joining, for we must be alone for this talk which has been too long in coming.

He came to stand before her, looking down at her. Her vision shadowed with a body before it. She lifted her eyes to meet his gaze. He extended his hand down to her, but she only glared at it and refused to take it.

Powchutu quickly spoke up, "Go with him, Alisha. This is not the time or place to defy him. Others are watching. Do you not recall my warning at the fort about defiance and honor? We will speak later. For now, go! Do not anger him further tonight."

She glanced over at her friend's look of worry

and concern for her safety and smiled. She knew he spoke wisely for he always thought of her first. She held up her hand to Gray Eagle who took it securely in his large, strong grasp. He easily pulled her to her feet and placed his arm around her slim waist.

Together, they walked toward the large campfire near the center of camp. He seated her next to him on a buffalo skin to watch the dancing and to listen to the singing and chanting. He moved very close to her, too close for her comfort. Alisha concentrated on the dances and music, trying to ignore his nearness and magnetism. She had to rage a fierce battle with her eyes to keep them from straying to his face, and with her brain to keep it from thoughts of him.

Gray Eagle grinned in amusement at the warring emotions and fierce determination which continually surfaced in her face and eyes. She turned once in time to see what she assumed to be a mocking sneer and fumed. He could not help but smile more broadly at the angry look on her face.

She retorted hotly, "Do not mock me, Wanmdi Hota! I have endured enough from you for one day. Perhaps one day our positions will be reversed. I could become the tormentor and you, the sufferer. I might even become the hater and you, the lover. That would really be something to watch, wouldn't it? I can see it now, the handsome, fierce warrior groveling at the feet of a mere half-breed girl, begging for her love. And of course, she would turn up her nose in contempt and coldly reject all his attentions and pleas.''

Watching a devilish light flickering in his smoldering eyes, she angrily added, ''Why do I even bother to talk to you? You cannot understand my words.'' A smug, naughty gleam lit her eyes and a wicked, beguiling smile touched her lips as she answered her own query, ''I do it because it makes me feel better and braver. But if you could only speak my tongue, I would tell you what a cad you are! I wouldn't even care how angry it made you or what you did to punish such disrespect and rebellion. It would be worth it just to see the look on your face.''

His eyes continued to look into hers seriously, causing her to become uneasy and tense. She flared at him, ''Don't stare at me like that! You look as if you can see into my very heart and soul. Who knows? Perhaps you can with those devil eyes of yours. If you could, then you would know that I . . .''

The heat from his stare conquered her temper. The smile and anger left her face and honesty replaced them as she finished her statement with the truth, ''. . . love you. How I wish with all my heart I could learn to hate and despise you, as you do me.'' She turned her back to him.

As the evening progressed, she became enthralled with the festivities before her. The steady, rhythmic beat of the can cega, the shaking of the gourds, the tapping of the sticks and the haunting whistling of the eagle-bone whistles, lulled her into a state of relaxation. She began to hum a tune which matched the beat of the music, and to sway gently to and fro to its tempo.

She nibbled on small, berry-filled pones of aguyapi and pieces of dried wild fruits. She took the juice Gray Eagle offered and drank it slowly, without hesitation or thought, at least for the first few swallows.

He observed her as the juice from the wanhu berries took effect and she began to relax more and more. Her cheeks began to look flushed and her eyes flashed brilliantly. For some sudden, unknown reason, she felt deliriously happy and gay. Her head twirled as did the music and dancers. The world was enchanting and wonderful here under the stars and the moon. The air was fresh and crisp and she was in love.

Why shouldn't she be happy? Wasn't she going to be married to the man she loved and wanted tomorrow night? Wasn't he the bravest, most handsome and virile man alive? She looked over at him, smiling and laughing gaily. Yes, life was wonderful . . . he was wonderful . . . everything was wondeful . . .

Gray Eagle pulled her closer into his embrace. Unable to know or think why she should refuse, she willingly and happily went, snuggling up to his strong, bare chest. He smiled down into her eyes and she smiled back at him, love shining clearly in both their faces.

Alisha's eyes were soft and alluring, her lips parted and tempting. He fought the urge to bend over and place a kiss upon them. She flirted, teased and tempted him with her eyes, lips and smiles.

Damn! he swore to himself, knowing he would be sleeping alone tonight. Didn't she know or care what she was doing to him? How much longer could he sit still and take this torture of not having her?

She gazed deep into his eyes and murmured, "Isn't it wonderful, Wanmdi Hota? Wouldn't it be sublime to stay like this forever? Just think, tomorrow we will be joined and I will have you for my very own. Dreams do come true, don't they? Do you know how very much I love you? I wish I knew the words in your tongue, for I would say them to you a hundred times and more. Your wife . . ."

He knew it was the nectar of the juice which had loosened her tongue, but it was the truth she spoke to him. She would have known by his smiles and nods that he understood her if the wine had not dimmed her wits and clouded her vision.

She impishly chatted, "Mrs. Wanmdi Hota . . . Mrs. Wanmdi . . . Or do you have another name too? Alisha Wanmdi . . . No, Shalee Wanmdi . . ."

She giggled at her jesting and he could not suppress his laughter at her game and mood. He knew of the wasichu's custom of the wife taking her husband's last name after joining. She joined in his laughter as she lay her weary head upon his shoulder. He soon knew by her slow, regular breathing she was asleep. Unaccustomed to wine and the strong power of the wanhu juice, it had only taken a small amount to affect her this way.

He gathered her into his arms and lifted her light, relaxed body and carried her to her teepee. He placed her upon the mat and stared down into the sleeping, peaceful face. "E-cana . . ." he whispered, placing a kiss upon her lips and left to rejoin the celebration.

Powchutu still waited outside the teepee. He had intercepted Gray Eagle heading there with Alisha's unconscious form. He had gone for a long walk after his words with Alisha and had not observed Gray Eagle giving her the sleeping potion. He had rushed forward at the sight and exclaimed excitedly, "What has happened?" Then, he had threatened, "What have you done to her now? I'll kill you if you ever harm her again! I'll . . ."

Before he could finish his statement, Gray Eagle had warned him ominously, "I told you before, Powchutu, do not interfere! Do not forget whose winyan she is. She is mine and I will do with her as I choose. I gave her the juice of the wanhu to relax and help her sleep tonight. Do not go against me again." Then he had entered the teepee with her.

Powchutu did recall his earlier warnings or threats to him. Neither mattered to Powchutu, for her protection from Gray Eagle was all he cared about now. He angrily thought, he lied to me and tricked me into helping him, just as he has tricked and used her. If he loved her as he had said, he would never have rejected her and pushed her away tonight as she had told me. Powchutu silently spoke to Alisha, I cannot understand any man turning from you when you show your love and willingness to him so openly. You are right, my love. I have been fooled by him once more. You would know if he loved you, for he would be unable to hide it from you. I will not allow him to be cruel to you again.

If Wanmdi Hota had spoken the truth to me about loving you, then he would have told you of his love in the cave tonight. Yet, he remains silent and taunting. He would not have hurt you that way. How dare he push you away after he has forced your submission with his kisses! I have seen how he works on your weakness for him. He has betrayed us both, Alisha. He has used me to get at you. I should not have come and helped him. You were better off not knowing who you are and why you are here. He would have been helpless without my tongue. He used my love and concern for you against us both. I will see that he pays for this . . .

Gray Eagle was not one to underestimate the power of love or hate, or the cunning and vengeance of an enemy. Powchutu was under the influence of both powers, and had chosen to be his enemy. After the joining day, he must learn of the truth also. There must be truce between us, for I could never trust his thoughts and actions as an enemy . . .

Gray Eagle rejoined White Arrow and Brave Bear at the fire to talk and smoke. The feasting went on and on as it would for many hours to come, far into the night.

Alisha began to toss and turn, fighting off specters in her fuzzy, groggy brain. She fought to pull herself out of the grips of the drugged sleep. Her thoughts were hazy and incoherent and the sounds of the feast were muffled and far away. She felt clammy and sticky, her mouth and throat dry and thick. Her body felt heavy and limp, but her senses light and floating. She was confused and frightened by these weird sensations.

She struggled to force herself to sit up, to try and clear her foggy mind of the cobwebs. At first, she swayed and reeled as she tried to still her blurred vision into clearer focus. What was wrong with her? Why did she feel so strange? she asked in panic and fear.

She finally managed to stagger over to the campfire inside her teepee and sit down. She took the mni bag and splashed water over her face and neck and drank from it several times to quench her parched lips and mouth. She cupped water in her palm and rubbed it over her clammy arms and legs. What had caused this weakened condition? Had she had some terrible nightmare but could not recall it? Was she taking ill? Maybe her body and mind had been forced to endure too much for one day and were fighting back. At least she was beginning to feel better now. Her head was clearing and the tremors in her body were fading. Soon, she would be fine.

She forced her mind to think. *The last thing I remember was being at the feast with Wanmdi Hota. We were watching the dancing and listening to the singing and chanting. I recall eating and drinking . . . Drinking! That's it. There must have been something in the drink or food, for right after that I can't remember a thing. Thank goodness I didn't like it and poured most of it under the buffalo skin! I wonder what was in the juice. Was it a sleeping potion or poison? Did he want to put me to sleep for one night, or forever? Could I have angered him that much tonight with my actions? Why didn't he just send me off to bed if he wished to be rid of me for the remainder of the evening?*

Why would he want to drug me? Did he think perhaps I might try to escape during the night? That would be an excellent plan—to escape on the eve of our joining! His loss of face would be immense if his winyan had chosen to flee rather than join with him. What a blow to that arrogant ego of his! She sneered, so, he doesn't wish to be parted with his trophy again so soon!

That is, if it was only a sleeping potion. . . . It was a good thing I poured it into the dirt under the mat when he wasn't looking or I could be dead now.

No, Lese. You've got to be wrong. . . . He

330

would do a lot of evil things to you, but kill you? Surely not. Besides, you'd get off much too easy that way! He doesn't want your death, he wants your total submission.

How tragic Alisha could not recall the looks, smiles and words of the previous hours, for they could have altered her future suffering. If only she could have noted his nods and expressions of understanding at her words and jokes, or his laughter at her giggling and teasing. If she had seen and recalled these things, she would know the deep, dark secret he had hidden so well from her.

She was confounded by the flashing warning signals in her mind which made no sense to her. She felt there was something urgent she should recall, something from long ago and far away. It would hover near her mind, then fade like the mist at sunrise, just as she was about to seize it and understand it. For a brief moment, she would almost see the bright warning clearly, then it would shimmer and vanish just as quickly and mysteriously as it had appeared.

She mentally struggled to grasp this omen, but it was as illusive as fog. It blew across her mind softly, hovered, then disappeared. Knowing a person cannot chase or capture the fog, she dismissed it from her thoughts for a time.

She wondered just how long she had slept. She could hear the festivities still going on outside from the sounds which reached her ears. It must be late, for the moon had already passed its arc overhead. She was fully awake and clear-headed now.

She began to recall the events of this fateful day for some clue of his intentions of tonight. So much had taken place in the small span of a day. She began to try to put these events into proper light and perspective, but it all seemed so illusive. Just as she would begin to accept the rapid changes in her existence, there would be more changes, even harder to understand and accept. Each new change would be more confusing and frightening than the one before it.

It was evident her little ruse tonight hadn't worked, for after his initial anger, it hadn't phased him at all. Maybe he saw through it all along and was only taunting her by pretending rage. Perhaps he had been enraged that she would dare to behave that way to him in public. Curse his honor and damn his face! What did it matter except she had lost another battle with him. One day, Sir Nemesis, I will be the victor!

The more she tried to reason things out in her own mind, the more confusing it all became. How can I hate him for selling and betraying me, when he did not? I recall the last times we were together before Chela . . .

Chela! I had forgotten about her. So, she did not win him after all. He came after me. What will he do about her now? Will he marry both of us as I have heard they do? That would surely make a happy teepee—me, Wanmdi Hota and Chela! How could she share her husband and home, such as it was, with another woman, especially one who is an avowed enemy? How could she live like that?

She was amazed she not only felt repulsion and anger at such an arrangement, but also jealousy and hurt. How could she feel this way if she did not still love and want him? It would never work . . .

If I only knew his thoughts concerning me, Alisha fretted. If only he would let himself know me as a person. Am I not Indian like he is? That ominous chill swept over her body again! She shivered and let it pass.

She decided all she could do was wait and see how he chose to treat her this time. She would deal with any trouble later . . .

Alisha trembled just thinking about what she had felt in the cave with Gray Eagle tonight. For a short time there, she had believed he was actually reaching out to her, but she must have been mistaken. How sad! she thought. We could have loved with a love to rival Helen and Paris!

Alisha could not forget her moments in the cave with Wanmdi Hota, she dreamed, how he held me and kissed me and touched me as one who loves. Things were going so well between us until Wanhinkpe Ska came . . . Could it be he was angry for being disturbed and he took that anger out on me? Did that interruption give him the sense to realize it was not the time or place for us to make love? Did he sense my problem and use anger to dispel my mood and the passion between us? How else could he have so quickly and effectively brought my unbridled, wanton emotions under control?

You're a fool and dreamer! Lese. To hope for his love would be like hoping to reach into the heavens and gather a handful of stars. Don't wish for what can never be. Accept what you have. You can never have his heart. The sooner you accept this, the sooner you can regain some peace. She shifted and paced restlessly and nervously.

If only that infernal drumming would stop! It beat within her head, her chest and her veins, crying, run . . . run . . . run . . . run . . . She clamped her hands over her ears tightly to shut out the sounds. Her tension and agitation mounted with each passing minute. I've got to get out of here. Fresh air and a long walk, that's what I need.

She jumped to her feet and went to the flap. She looked out. No one seemed to sense her presence. She slipped around the side of her teepee and walked off between the tents. She walked until she came to Matu's teepee and halted, staring at it . . .

Something way back in her mind urged her to go inside Matu's teepee that night. Here was the cause of her being here. Here was the reason for her fragile, new beginning with Wanmdi Hota being destroyed. Here, somewhere, was the key to her fate and destiny. How or why, she did not know. But she knew without a shadow of doubt her life was somehow held in Matu's grip.

Matu is the cause of all that has happened to me lately, Alisha realized. If she had not come to

Mahpiya Sapa and told him about that akito, then things would be as they were for those two unforgettable days. Why do I still sense danger and foreboding each time I see her? If she has fulfilled her role in my destiny, then why do I still have these mystic touches when she is near or in my thoughts? Why do my secret thoughts still warn me about her? What is there to remember that keeps tugging at the edges of my mind? I seem to hear a voice from long ago and far away trying to tell me something very important, but I can't seem to quite make out its message. But I know I must grasp its meaning, for my fate rides with it. Perhaps there is something here which will help me to hear and know the truth. Perhaps there was a missing clue hidden here, just like the akito had been the missing piece to the other puzzle.

Alisha did not know where Matu was and it did not really matter to her. She must find what had pulled her here tonight. A small glow from the fireplace lit the teepee with an eerie light and aura. She strolled around, not really knowing what she searched for. She could see or feel nothing which appeared important or urgent to her future. Perplexed, she sat down on the mat by the little fire and began to unknowingly finger through Matu's work wozuha.

She suddenly froze and shook violently as cold, unearthly chills ran over her entire body and mind. She knew before she dared to look what her hand held. Horrified, she stared at the objects in her small, cold, trembling hand. She could not seem to move or replace the small bag of ash and the tattooing bone. She nodded her head in disbelief and understanding.

Matu had been the one to find the akito and tell of its existence. Matu had been the one who had been banished from here because of Shalee's loss. Had Matu found a way to return home to her people and Mahpiya Sapa? Had she found a way to lighten the pain in the heart of an old chief at his two losses long ago? Was Alisha a pawn for Matu's revenge, for her return to Mahpiya Sapa's life? The results of either game could be deadly for Alisha.

Alarm filled her mind and raced through her body like wildfire. Wildfire! Reality flooded her mind like a storm of water through a broken dam. Wildfire . . . that was the key! Her favorite pony as a child . . . he had been bitten by a rabid fox and had thrown her. She vividly recalled the incident as if it had happened only yesterday—the cuts and bruises. One particular injury came to mind with terrifying perception.

She could still see the long tear in her green, velvet riding habit on her left buttock. It had happened when she had struck a sharp, protruding rock when she had fallen. Her mother's words and voice resounded in her ears and head, "It will be all right, Lese. Don't cry. I can mend the habit for you. Besides, the scar looks like a little half-moon. We can always laugh and say the Goddess Diana touched you there one night. Then, too, no one will ever see it there, save your husband one day . . ."

Alisha's head pounded painfully as she tried to stop and suppress these memories from ripping through her mind, shattering these new illusions about who she was. Stop it . . . stop it! she screamed to her mind, but it would not be stopped. The floodgates were opened wide and all the truth came rushing forth.

From the deep, hidden recesses of her mind came the voices of two other people. She covered her ears trying to close out their words, but she could not halt them, for they came from within her own mind. A man's voice answered, "It appears to be some kind of brand or mark of ownership. Can't tell for sure." A woman's voice asked, "I wonder who put it there of all places and why?" He replied, "I guess those Injuns did it to tell who she belongs to. Could be 'his' mark. Hasn't been there long though. See, the scratches are still red and irritated. You get a wet cloth and see if you can wash some of that ash out before it gets infected."

Those two voices . . . the Philseys! When she had been unconscious. . . . Somehow their words had creeped beneath the wall of blackness and reached her inner mind and lodged there.

Was this the mist she had been trying to grope through? Was this what her mind had thought so urgent to reveal? Were these the memories which had been fighting to surface and warn her? But of what? Of whom?

She had been right the first time. It was a trick. But whose? She was not Shalee. She was not Mahpiya Sapa's lost daughter. She was still

Alisha, the wasichu and the enemy . . .

She could not marry Wanmdi Hota tomorrow night. And if he knew, he would not marry her! Why had Matu done this to her? Did Wanmdi Hota know? Was he a party to this deadly scheme? Would he possibly do this to trick her into marrying him, only to betray her as a fraud at the last minute as his final, cruel revenge against her? Were the others in on this plot—Mato Waditaka, Wanhinkpe Ska, Mahpiya Sapa or Powchutu? No, she told herself, not Powchutu! He would never be a part of a thing like this. Perhaps this had been the price for his life and freedom that day of the fort's massacre! No, he would never betray me like this, even at the cost of his life.

Her mind reeled with the terrible implications of this trick. Surely Matu was the only one involved in this. All clues pointed to her. But why had she done it? Would she keep it a secret? Would she really allow a ska wincinyanna to marry an Oglala warrior? Was her only motive to be freed and sent home, or was there more to it?

Does she seek some twisted revenge against this Jenny through my torture and death? Alisha worried. But, she would surely be punished, too! Perhaps she thought she could plead innocent to any knowledge of how the akito got there, and be believed. Or worse, maybe she thinks it will be worth her death to have this insane revenge for her hatred of Jenny . . .

If only I knew her tongue and could speak with her. I must know why she did this to me. I know what the warnings were for now, for she does hold my life in her hands. God help me if she sees me as Jenny! What can I do now? Who can I turn to for help?

I dare not go to Wanmdi Hota with the truth. Alisha trembled violently just imagining the look in those obsidian eyes when he learned the truth. He would kill me for sure. The knowledge he fought a challenge which could have cost his life and the reality he would have unknowingly married a wasichu will bring a rage such as I've never known in him. But if I keep silent and allow him to marry me knowing what I do, and if he ever learned the truth about me, I would never be able to convince him I did not know. Or, that I had done it because I loved him and wanted him. Once more I am trapped between Scylla and Charybdis . . .

Powchutu is the only one I can trust. I must find him and talk with him. He will know what to do. He can speak with Matu and learn the whole truth. Then, I will decide what is to be done. If Wanmdi Hota or the others should learn of this before I have had a chance to work things out, I shall never know the truth about myself. I shudder to think what Mahpiya Sapa and Mato Waditaka would think and feel if they learned I was not their precious Shalee. I dare not think what will happen if Wanmdi Hota finds out I am truly only Lese.

For now, I must remain Shalee, for that is my

only protection and chance for freedom. But how can I be happy and at peace when I must live in constant fear of their learning this deadly truth? I know what will happen when they find out—I will be horribly tortured and killed . . .

Alisha ran a light finger over the akito through the skin of her dress, then pressed harder. Yes, one side of the little moon was different from the other. One was firm and deep, and the other only surface etching. Why had Mahpiya Sapa not noticed this that other day? Had he been blinded by hopes of finding his lost daughter? Had they not all said I look just like this girl Jenny? She dropped her face into her hands and wept. What now? What now, for all was lost?

Dread washed over her. Matu had been the one to alter her scar to form the magic akito, but it would be she who would have to pay for this deception with her life. Could Gray Eagle possibly be in on this farce, this trick, this deceit? No, for he would not use the other warrior and chief that way. Or did he hate her so much he would stoop to such vile trickery for revenge? Was he only waiting until the joining or the last minute before the ceremony to reveal her true identity and wreak vengeance on her? Did his hatred go that far? If only she knew the truth, or if only he cared enough about her to protect her.

There had been too many coincidences. I should have known and fought them harder, Alisha wept. I should have refused to accept this, then they could not have blamed me for it. I should not have allowed myself to be put in this precarious position. Why did I fall for this rose-colored illusion?

Do I dare reveal these things to anyone, even my friend? Is he my friend first, or Indian first? What will he do if I tell him everything? How could he help me anyway? Besides, his knowing about this could endanger his life as well as mine. But I must know the truth, tonight! I must decide what to do. If there is some trickery being practiced here for revenge, then I cannot wait until after the ceremony to find out. This night, I will know what path my fate will take . . . it has been in the hands of others for too long.

She slipped from Matu's teepee and made her way to the first row of teepees, concealing most of her face and body in the shadows. Most of the men were near the center campfire talking and smoking, except for Powchutu and a few younger braves who sat around a smaller campfire close by.

She softly called his name and he glanced her way in surprise. She placed her finger to her lips, signaling for silence and secrecy, then motioned for him to come to her.

The other men thought it a bit strange, but did not question their chief's daughter speaking with her friend and looked away unconcerned. Powchutu looked around and seeing no one watching him, he stood up and walked her way. She reached out and took him by the hand and

341

pulled him into the darkness with her.

Gray Eagle's head had been lowered, so neither Powchutu nor Alisha saw that he watched the strange exchange between them. Why was Alisha not in her teepee asleep? What was she doing out here? Why did she want to speak with her friend in secret? Had she realized what was in the juice and faked drinking it? Had her display of affection and happiness been a trick? Did she know his secret now and wish to tell her friend of her discovery? Had he been the one tricked tonight instead of her?

Just what were those two up to? He had watched suspiciously until the darkness had engulfed them, then rose to follow. He moved around quickly and quietly until he caught sight of them as they entered a small teepee. Did they plan some lover's last meeting? He flamed in anger and jealousy. What was she trying to pull with this man? He silently and stealthily walked up to the rear of the teepee and alertly listened.

"What is wrong, Alisha? What are you doing awake here? Wanmdi Hota said he gave you a sleeping potion to help you relax and sleep tonight. You should have slept until morning."

Powchutu watched her ashen face as he bombarded her with questions. What was the matter with her? He caught her full expression and panic. He asked, alarmed, "Alisha, what is it? You're as pale as snow. Tell me!"

She met his steady, worried gaze and said, "I was asleep, Powchutu. But something woke me.

I drank some of the juice, but it tasted bad so I poured it on the ground under the skin while Wanmdi Hota wasn't looking. I didn't know it was drugged then. Later, I didn't know if it was drugged or poisoned. I wouldn't put it past him to try to get rid of me for good this time! I wish now it had been poison or I had drunk it all. Then, I would have slept through this whole nightmare."

Powchutu grabbed her by the shoulders and shook her, saying, "Alisha, you don't know what you're saying. You know he wouldn't try to kill the daughter of Mahpiya Sapa. Never wish for a thing such as death!"

He was alarmed by her hysterical laughter at his second statement. Did she really believe Gray Eagle would kill her? Did she fear him that much? Gray Eagle was also asking himself those same two questions.

Powchutu stared at her in confusion and asked, "What are you saying? You aren't making sense. What nightmare?"

Her voice carried anguish and chagrin when she spoke. "This whole crazy, dangerous farce! Don't you see, Powchutu? It's all a joke on me! They lied . . . he lied . . . it serves me right for even believing such an idiotic thing could possibly be true! Once again, stupid, naive Alisha shows her ignorance of life and people! I would laugh if I didn't want to cry instead." She began to weep bitterly. He enfolded her in his strong, comforting embrace.

He spoke soothingly, "Don't cry, my love. It's

just the wanhu juice making you think and feel this way. It has your mind all mixed up. He wouldn't harm you. Of course, you're Shalee. The akito . . ."

She jerked backwards and interrupted him, "That's the trick, Powchutu! Matu put it there when I was unconscious after the icapsinte. I had a scar there in the shape of a half-moon. She must have seen it and altered it to look like Mahpiya Sapa's akito. But I don't know why she did it or who knows the truth about it. Suddenly, I remembered the accident I had as a child which made the scar."

Powchutu argued, "Alisha, she wouldn't do a thing like that. You're just overly tired, confused by the potion and all that's happened today. Your mind is playing tricks on you, that's all. Come, I'll take you back to your teepee."

She adamantly retorted, "Not my mind, Powchutu, but Matu's hand! I am not confused or crazy. Let me tell you everything and then you'll see I'm right. God help me, for I am right . . ."

She nervously paced around as she related everything she had found. She left no thought or feeling covered in her recounting. When she had finished, she asked him, "Don't you see now, Powchutu? That was why I always felt fear and danger around her. Those were the memories which kept nagging at my mind, but I couldn't, or wouldn't, recall. I tried to tell you and the chief I was not and could not possibly be this Shalee. Why did you force me to accept this lie? Now I am trapped by it, and by Gray Eagle. I will never know when he might spring his trap and let it crush me . . ."

Powchutu fearfully studied the items in his hand and reasoned, "You are right about it being against their laws for anyone to have these things or use them except the ceremonial chief. I don't know how Matu came upon them, but I believe all you said. We must find the reason for the treachery from her. These things are sacred and should not be here. I think perhaps she is the only one who knows of this."

Alisha lifted terrified eyes to his and asked, "But what if Gray Eagle has learned of this trickery? What if he thinks I am a part of it? He might only be waiting until the best moment to pounce upon me with his discovery. They'll kill me, Powchutu! My only protection and security here was being this girl Shalee, and when he shatters that illusion tomorrow . . ." She trembled in uncontrollable terror and nearly fainted.

He grabbed her and said, "You better sit down. You look as if you're about to faint. I'll get some water and you can drink it and splash some on your face."

As he was giving her the water, he asked, "But what if he doesn't know anything? What if only Matu knows? I can't imagine her motive, but I believe she did this in secrecy."

"But if she did it for revenge against this Jenny and blurts it out at the ceremony

345

tomorrow night, the results will be the same, my torture and death! Gray Eagle will be consumed with rage that he had challenged for a white girl and then was about to marry her. Can you think of anything worse for a warrior like him to be shown this publicly? That honor you spoke of so often would take its worst beating and he would hold me, me, Powchutu, responsible for it! I am surely doomed. There is no way out of this charade. Matu has always hated me. This won't be the first time she's arranged for me to suffer because of her tricks. Could she really hate me enough to put her own life in danger this way?"

Recalling the event of a few days ago and this very afternoon, she answered her own question, "Yes, she would. Chela hated me enough to want my death at the risk of her own. Just as Gray Eagle risked his life this very afternoon to get me back in his power for further revenge. Why do they all hate me so much, Powchutu? What did I ever do to them? Is it me or what I am that instills in them this great hatred for me and desire to hurt me?" She began to cry again.

At that moment, the flap was lifted and Matu came in. Her eyes quickly took in the weeping girl, her angry friend, and what he held in his open hand. She hastily tried to flee, but Powchutu grabbed her by her arm and pulled her back inside.

He nearly shouted at her, "Why, Matu? Why?"

She turned her nose up at him in contempt

and silence. He shook her roughly and demanded, "Why did you do this to her? What has she ever done to you?"

Still, Matu only stared at him coldly and belligerently in stubborn silence. Again, he asked, "Who knows about this? Does Wanmdi Hota or Mahpiya Sapa?"

The last name brought a reaction from her and she glared at him. She had thought no one would ever find out what she had done. Dare she trust these wasichus with the truth?

Alisha stood up and stepped before her. She gazed into the face of the old woman and pleaded, "Why, Matu? They will surely kill me tomorrow. Does Wanmdi Hota know about this? Is he a part of it?" Powchutu translated for both of the women as they spoke.

Matu replied to her, "Matu wanted to come home. Matu gone too long. Matu see scar after beating by Wanmdi Hota. It sign from Napi! Matu change scar to match Mahpiya Sapa's akito. Ska wincinyanna look like his old squaw. Mahpiya Sapa unhappy many winters. Matu unhappy many winters. You unhappy many moons. Matu see and fix, now all happy and Matu home again. You good winyan and suffer much at hands of Wanmdi Hota. Chela suffer, too. I fix! I put you with Mato Waditaka and Chela with Wanmdi Hota. But Wanmdi Hota still want you, not let Mato Waditaka keep you. No matter. Only Matu know of akito and truth. You stay cunwintke of Mahpiya Sapa and Matu stay here with Si-ha Sapa. I save you, now you save Matu? Tell no one! Then all stay happy and free. After akito fixed, you rescued by bluecoats. Matu must wait for your return from fort. All is good now. On new moon, you join with Wanmdi Hota. Matu see and know you love him. I home and no longer shamed. You safe and happy. It is done!''

Alisha stared dumbfounded as Powchutu related Matu's words. She asked, "Could she possibly be telling the whole truth, Powchutu? Did she do this for both of us? But if they find out, they will still kill me. She will probably only be punished, but I would be . . ." Sheer terror crossed her face as she finished, "I cannot even imagine what he would do to me."

Matu gently touched her arm and said, "No worry! Matu come home to die. Matu old. Will tell no one. You no tell no one and be Indian winyan. Matu be happy . . . Mahpiya Sapa be happy . . . You be happy with Wanmdi Hota . . ."

She made it all sound so easy, but it was not. Tears filled Alisha's eyes as she thanked Matu for what she was foolishly trying to do for all of them. "She doesn't realize I can never be happy with him for he'll never allow it. I can't tell anyone about this, Powchutu. She only wanted to come home and be with her people. I can't blame her for that. She did try to help me. If they do find out, I will take the entire blame. There is no need for both of us to suffer and die. I'll say I had it done at the fortress or something. Tell her to deny any knowledge of it, other than being

348

the one to find it. I owe her that much."

Powchutu told Matu Alisha's last words. She asked, "You do this for Matu?" She gazed at Alisha in astonishment and smiled. "I right! You good winyan. Napi will guard life of ska wincinyanna with pi-zi istas and Indian heart."

Powchutu warned Alisha, "No one must ever learn of this. Trust no one with this secret, Alisha, no one!"

Alisha looked up at him with wretched eyes and asked, "How will I ever hide it from him, Powchutu? He reads me like an open book. Besides, I've never been any good at lying or concealing things. At least that's what my mother used to tell me all the time. My mother would call me 'Mirror Eyes' whenever I was upset."

Powchutu advised, "Return to Mahpiya Sapa's teepee and act as if nothing is wrong. We will talk tomorrow. It will be a long, trying day for you. You must get some sleep."

"Sleep!" she retorted. "How can I possibly sleep when my whole world is falling apart and I could be dead tomorrow?" With these words, she ran crying from Matu's teepee. She moved quickly through the darkness to her teepee and threw herself down upon the mat and sobbed.

Powchutu remained behind for a short time to be sure everything was settled with Matu. He had to make sure she held no hate or vengeance in her heart for Alisha. He must be absolutely sure this old woman offered no threats to his beloved.

Alisha was startled when Wanmdi Hota gently seized her by her arms and pulled her up to face him. Tears were streaming down her ashen face and brightly flushed cheeks. Her wide, sad eyes spoke of total defeat.

She quietly said to him in a small voice filled with anguish, "As always, Wanmdi Hota, you are the victor. There is no fight left in me. Do as you will with me. It matters not anymore."

He knew her will and spirit were at last broken, but somehow it did not please him as he had thought it would. . . . To confront Alisha when he already knew the truth would only complicate matters now. Again, deadly silence was a necessity!

Powchutu entered. He had come to be sure she had reached her teepee and was all right. He should have been suspicious at why Gray Eagle did not question Powchutu's being in Alisha's teepee.

Gray Eagle looked at him and said, "Tell her she must not fear me so. I would not harm the daughter of Mahpiya Sapa." He had intended for his words to make her think her secret was safe and still hidden. But it had the opposite effect on her and she stonily glared at him.

Her thoughts screamed, does he know? Does he suspect? Did his words sound ominous? Surely not. My imagination is only playing wicked tricks on me. He couldn't know, could he?

He realized the devastating effect his words had taken. He had not relieved her fears, he had only heightened them. He quietly said, "Tell Shalee to get some sleep. Tomorrow will be a busy day. She is very upset tonight. I am surprised the wanhu juice did not help her relax and sleep. Ask her if she would like for you to bring her some more?" To anyone listening, his words and tones sounded full of concern and tenderness.

Powchutu related his query. She looked at him and nodded yes. He asked Powchutu to go to the pezuta teepee for it. While he was gone, she tried to avoid meeting Gray Eagle's keen, searching eyes. He stood up and walked to the peg to retrieve the wanapin she had placed there earlier. He put it back around his neck, until she decided she was ready to accept it again.

He came back to where she was sitting and sat down before her. She nervously toyed with the necklace and wristlets. She fingered the small teeth on the necklace and traced the designs on the wristlets. He put his hand out and caressed her long, silky hair and ivory cheek.

He was thinking of how very beautiful and innocent she had looked tonight, but also how very vulnerable and frightened. She tried to move away from his touch, so he pulled his hand away and let it rest in his lap.

Powchutu returned with the wanhu juice and handed it to Gray Eagle. He passed it to Alisha with these words, "Tell her to drink it all this time, not empty it under the mat. Tell her I knew she would need something to help her relax and sleep this night. This has been a hard day for her as well as others." His slightly mocking tone had gone serious at his last statement. The devilish twinkle in his ebony eyes had softened to tenderness. She was terribly confused by this.

When Powchutu related his words, she flamed red and shot him a look of surprise. "Does nothing escape your keen eyes?" She took the juice and drank all of it as Powchutu looked on.

"Very little happens around me that I do not see or learn, Shalee. So do not ever try to deceive me, Cinstinna, for your eyes always reveal the truth . . ."

She blanched white at those words. She stared at him, trying to decide if he was trying to tell her something more than a future warning. What was there about this man that totally unnerved and bewitched her? Her weary brain cried and begged, leave me alone . . . let me rest . . . I'm tired . . . no more reasoning . . . enough for one day. . . .

Alisha failed to realize Gray Eagle had answered her last question without Powchutu translating it to him first. He didn't even realize he had done it, but Powchutu did. He smiled sardonically and patted the little pouch at his wanapin.

She finished the juice with a wrinkled nose and handed the holder back to Powchutu. Gray Eagle turned to him and told him to leave them now so she could sleep. Powchutu reluctantly nodded, wishing he had warned Alisha to remain silent around him for she might inadvertently tell something she should not. He quickly realized from her actions that she would soon be asleep, so he smiled and left. He would warn her later.

Gray Eagle had seen his worried expression and knew its meaning. For once, he could not fault Powchutu's deceptive actions, for he also knew the truth of the akito could cause Alisha certain death. *After the joining, I will tell him I have known the truth all along and the secret will remain with only the three of us. Matu must sleep the sleep of the spirits with the help of the May Apple, for he did not trust her future help or silence.* He would tell Hehoke Sapa to handle this for him after the ceremony tomorrow night. *By the time of the joining, her secret would be safe forever.*

He had pushed her down to the mat and covered her with a buffalo skin as he was thinking and planning. He tenderly pushed some loose hair out of her face and eyes and stroked it lovingly. He lay down beside her and propped up on one elbow, gazing down into her face. He caressed her cheek as he surveyed the delicate features of her face.

Her lids began to droop and close. He leaned down and kissed her. She automatically returned his kiss and snuggled closer to him. She drifted off to sleep while he was kissing her.

He smiled and brushed another light kiss upon her slightly-parted lips and whispered against them, "Trust me, Lese. I will never let

353

anyone or anything ever harm you again, including Wanmdi Hota. I will take care of everything from now on. Do not worry, Cinstinna." He cradled her in his protective embrace and he; too, slept.

Alisha was awakened to the cheerful, melodious singing and trilling of meadowlarks and warblers. She lay there for a long time listening to their twittering and chirping to the feeling of freedom and happiness. She thought how wonderful it would be to be a little white bird and be able to fly anywhere she wished in freedom and sing until her very heart burst with joy.

She yawned and stretched like a feline after a long nap, then sat up. Matu entered as she was waking up. She came over to her and smiled as she gave her the fruit and aguyapi. She returned the smile from Matu and thanked her. Why was it she still felt a slight nagging of suspicion where Matu was concerned? Could she trust this old woman to keep her silence forever? Please, Matu, her heart pleaded.

Matu was scurrying around like a mouse getting things ready for Alisha to get dressed later. Alisha daydreamed as she ate. In all her wildest thoughts, she would never have imagined she would be marrying an Indian, and Wanmdi Hota, at that.

My wedding day. . . . Alisha gazed around the teepee and thought, not exactly a cathedral but does that really matter? She would not have a man of her religion performing the rites, but still she would be married to him in the eyes of God and in his custom. She was happy she would no longer be living in sin.

She smiled, thinking how handsome he would look dressed for dinner in her native attire. How very different this wedding would be from what she had dreamed as a younger girl. She recalled the many glamorous, beautiful weddings she had attended back home. She recalled all her grandiose dreams of her own wedding day . . . the tall, white cake with tiers and tiers of icing and flowers, with wedding bells atop . . . hundreds of fragrant orange blossoms and lilies-of-the-valley all around . . . music filling the air from harps, violins and the pianoforte . . . the most handsome man in the world waiting for her at the end of that long, white, satin-carpeted aisle . . . and she, waltzing down to meet him in her gown of white chantilly lace and seed pearls.

White . . . color of purity and innocence, two things lost to her forever. Today, she would have none of those dreams.

No, not really. She would have lots of guests, some very important ones, too. Wasn't a chief the same as a king in her country? She suppressed a laugh as she thought, that makes me a princess and this a royal affair. Her father . . . he would never see his little Lese wed, nor thankfully know the circumstances surrounding her life here in the New Land.

Oh Papa, how glad I am you are not here to witness my defeat. Nor you, Mama. All your beautiful plans and talks that we shared so long ago about this very special day in a girl's life. How very sad the killing of childish dreams and illusions, to have them torn down and trampled into the blood-soaked earth. Why do I not feel the joy and happiness this special day should bring? Was that also left behind with all my yesterdays?

Matu touched her arm. Alisha started from her melancholy and looked up. Matu held out the white elkskin dress to her, saying, "Mato Waditaka . . ."

She realized Matu meant it was a gift to her from him. She would have been wearing this very dress to join him tonight if things had turned out differently yesterday. She must send Powchutu to thank him with all her heart. This gift, a white wedding dress, would soothe some of the pain in her heart this day.

She held it up and examined it. It was trimmed with small, round, gold-colored beads. The skin was as soft as velvet and as white as the new-fallen snows. It had a fringed border at the hemline and the sleeveless armholes were also fringed with long, flowing strips from the same skin. She looked at the quilled white moccasins to match, too excited to even try them on.

She looked at Matu in astonishment and exclaimed, "They're beautiful! I love them. Thank you, Matu." Impulsively, she hugged the old woman who flushed in embarrassment at the girl's reaction. She gazed into the radiant face before her and smiled before leaving.

Alisha lovingly stroked the softness of the dress, then hugged it to her breasts. "I will have my white wedding dress after all. I'll never be able to thank Mato Waditaka enough."

She fingered the intricately quilled moccasins and the beaded headband with the two feathers attached, one red and gray and the other a fluffy white. "Oh Matu, you have made my heart leap with joy. They're so beautiful. A wedding dress . . . a white wedding dress . . ." She hugged them to her heart once more.

Suddenly feeling eyes upon her back, she quickly turned to find Wanmdi Hota standing just inside the flap with a very strange expression on his face. She looked embarrassed he had seen her silly display of happiness over the dress.

He walked over to where she stood and took the dress from her hands to examine it. He looked at the moccasins and headband with a lot of interest. He held up the dress before her, studying the fragile, delicate picture she would make in it.

She was surprised when he smiled and nodded his approval and returned the items to her. She refused to meet his steady gaze as she took them back. He realized he had not even thought of bringing her anything to wear on this special day. He had been so consumed with winning her from his rival. He was very pleased she had such a beautiful dress to wear tonight. He must find Mato Waditaka and thank him for both of them.

He watched her as she carefully folded the new garment and put all the items in a neat stack on her mat. She nibbled on the fruit, berries and aguyapi as she went about the storage area collecting the things she would need for her bathing and dressing. She put the remains of her breakfast near the fire for Matu to remove later. She finally had everything gathered for her bath, and piled her clothes neatly on her mat.

She had managed to avoid eye and body contact with Wanmdi Hota so far this morning. But now, she glanced over at him to see what he was doing. He seemed contented just to sit on the end of her mat and watch her every move with an odd, curious expression on his face. What was that glint in his eyes—victory, possessiveness, or perhaps a mocking sneer?

She glared at him in bewilderment and asked, "Is something wrong? Did you wish something from me?" She waited . . . no change or answer. "One day you'll have to teach me your tongue so we can talk to each other, unless you still prefer we don't communicate in any way except on your o-winza!" She hastily pinkened as she realized what she had said. She immediately sighed to herself, "At least you don't know my language."

He ignored her rumblings as if she had not even spoken, but secretly smiled to himself in amusement and agreement. He leaned over and picked up her new headband and touched the two little feathers attached. He wondered if she knew the meaning behind the two feathers and surmised she did not. He would tell her later.

He fingered the red and gray queque, the symbol of her father and Mato Waditaka; then the fluffy, white one, symbol of a daughter to a chief. He grinned mischievously as he blew on the two little feathers, making them tremble in the wind of his breath.

She stared at the quivering feathers as they trembled in the breeze he had created, then her eyes were drawn to the crooked, half-smile playing upon his lips.

He removed the two little feathers from the headband and lay them down on her new dress. She stared at him in horror. He knows! He's telling me he knows! Somehow, some way, he's found out and he's taunting me! He said nothing escapes his eye and now this little display of teasing. As surely as the sky is blue today, he knows and is just waiting to . . .

She halted in mid-thought as she watched his actions. He had taken a yellow feather from his own hair and was placing it in her headband. When he had secured it into the band, he looked up at her with his smoldering, ebony eyes which bore right into her very soul and mind. She stared at the headband, then at him in puzzlement and fear.

He rose and came to her. He placed the headband around her forehead with a mocking grin on his lips and murmured, "Ni-ye mitawa, Cinstinna." Still, she gazed at him in confusion. He spoke possessively, "Shalee,

Wanmdi Hota's."

Her eyes widened in understanding. She tore the headband from her forehead and jerked the yellow feather from it, angrily throwing it to the ground. She picked up the other two, original queques and replaced them as before. That old power play again!

She met his amused look with rebellion and challenge. "Shalee is Shalee's! Shalee is Mahpiya Sapa's! Shalee hiya Wanmdi Hota's yet!"

She put the headband back around her forehead and her gaze met his, daring him to deny it. Her heart pounded in rising terror as he just stood there looking her over, grinning triumphantly. She turned her back on him and that damned probing stare of his. What now?

She was abruptly whirled around and held securely in his strong grip. She kept her eyelids lowered and would not look at him. Deep, rich, rumbling laughter came from his chest as he mocked, "Shalee ye Mahpiya Sapa cunwintke. Shalee Wanmdi Hota winyan!"

Her eyes flew up to meet his and stare into their pitch black, bottomless depths. Without any warning, his mouth covered hers in a fiery, demanding kiss which nearly took her breath away. It ended as quickly as it had begun. She swayed against him in betraying weakness.

He gazed deep into her bewildered, emerald eyes and repeated, "Ni-ye mitawa . . . mitawa!" He flashed her a full smile which caused her heart to flutter madly.

Time passed. He appeared to be waiting for

her to say or do something, but what? He covered her mouth with another kiss which brought trembling to her knees. She burned with its heat. He leaned back and repeated his words, "Shalee Wanmdi Hota winyan!" Again, he waited . . .

He scooped up the yellow queque she had thrown to the ground and placed it inside her headband, this time, with the others. His flaming eyes engulfed her again as he spoke slowly, "Shalee Mahpiya Sapa cunwintke. Shalee Wanmdi Hota winyan!" Again, the hesitation . . .

Her hand went up to touch the three feathers and think upon his words and actions. Her face brightened and a smile touched her eyes and lips. Did he mean she was both the chief's daughter and his woman? Was he only trying to tell her she was both, or could be both? Did this mean he did not know, or that if he did, it didn't matter? No matter, she would concede to the point he was striving for—she belonged to him for as long as he wished it so. She felt great relief that he had not pressed the removal of the other two feathers.

She met his waiting gaze and spoke softly, "If I understand what it is you're trying to force me to say, then I will agree. Alisha belongs to Wanmdi Hota."

He quipped back, "Alisha? Hiya. Shalee Wanmdi Hota's, hiya Alisha." He kissed her fiercely, then abruptly released her. She nearly fell backwards with her sudden, unexpected release, and would have if he had not caught and held her. He was grinning devilishly as he steadied her on her feet. Then he turned and left.

She stared after him in soul-shaking terror. He had just told her he would not accept her as Alisha, only Shalee. Hadn't he taken the feathers from the headband to tell her she had no right to wear them? Hadn't he forced her to admit she was his, and to lie about who she was? Hadn't he laughed and mocked at her proclaiming to be Shalee? He had forced her to commit herself to this deceit. She was no longer an innocent party to this farce. He had cleverly trapped her.

But what were those other words he had spoken to her and why had he kissed her like that? In fact, what was that whole bewildering scene all about? What was he really trying to say? He forced me to admit I was his, and when I did, he teased and laughed at me. Why? I must find Powchutu and discuss this with him. I am more confused now than ever.

What Alisha had failed to grasp was that Gray Eagle was trying to tell her that he would let everyone believe she was Shalee. He was telling her he wanted her and would accept her no matter who or what she was. He was trying to tell her she must think of herself as Shalee so he could join with her in the eyes of his people. He was also telling her she must be Shalee to stay alive.

His smile had been one of happiness on this, their joining day. He had beamed with love and

362

possessiveness for her. He was proud of her beauty. He was overjoyed at this turn of events which had enabled him to claim her as his mate. Couldn't she read these things in his face and in his touch? Couldn't she hear the love and pride in his voice? Surely she could feel his desire for her coursing through his body. But he had also wanted her to know she had no secrets from him and never would. He wanted her to see she was his and he would take care of her and everything. Didn't she know the power he carried? Didn't she see how relaxed and happy he was about their coming joining? Didn't he just show her how much he loved and wanted her? Didn't he try to show her everything was all right now and for her to stop her worrying?

She frantically thought, I must find Powchutu! He will know what all this means. He will help me. She washed her face and adjusted her rumpled dress and tousled hair. She walked to the flap and peered out. She quickly located Powchutu at the same campfire he had been sitting at last night.

She hastily walked over to him. Disregarding the other two braves, she said, "I must speak with you, now! Come to my father's teepee." The panic and agitation in her voice warned him something had happened inside with Wanmdi Hota just now. Had she told him anything? He quickly followed her back to her teepee and they went inside.

As soon as they were inside, she began to speak rapidly. "He knows, Powchutu! I don't know how, but I'm sure he knows! The way he looks at me, the things he does and says. He's trying to tell me he knows! What's his game, Powchutu? What will he do about it? My head is spinning!"

Powchutu tried to calm her down. "He doesn't know anything, Alisha, not yet. But he will if you continue to act so suspiciously. There is no way he could possibly know. You must get hold of yourself or he will surely guess. I also must warn you to keep silent around him and all the others. We can never be sure of how much they understand. We must not speak of these things around anyone. Wanmdi Hota is very cunning and smart. I fear he could guess the meanings of our talks. You must never, never speak aloud before him. Do you understand me?"

His tone was a little frightening to her. If Wanmdi Hota knew any of her tongue, she would have guessed it by now, for he would surely have reacted to some of her words by now. Still, if he could guess from her tone or expression, then she had better do as her friend suggested.

She argued with him, "I tell you, Powchutu, he does know something. How do you expect me to act calmly when he looks at me like he does and acts in that strange way? It's as if he's trying to warn me or frighten me. Maybe he's known all along and is just giving me time to relax and gain confidence here, then at the right moment, he'll bring it all to light. Oh Powchutu, I'm so frightened. I don't know which way to turn. Just as I begin to think things might work out, everything turns around in another direction."

"If he had known all along as you just suggested, then he would have told them Matu changed the akito. He would not have turned his valuable slave over to them. He could have avoided the challenge which could have cost his life. Surely you do not believe for one minute he would fight a challenge to win the hand of a white girl! No, Alisha. If he had known, there would have been no challenge. He could not have learned about it here either. Only the three of us know this secret, and we didn't until last night. No, he could not have learned of it," Powchutu reasoned.

"Powchutu, listen to me," she nearly shouted at him for his full attention. "He knows! I don't understand why he says nothing yet, but he will soon. Perhaps there is some reason why he fought the challenge. He probably never imagined he could lose it. He will never go through with the joining, knowing who I really am. Can you even imagine how he feels knowing he could have died for a white girl's possession, or that he was almost tricked into marrying her? But if you're somehow right and he doesn't know yet of this deception, think what will happen when he does learn of it and we are already joined. His fury will be as black as the night and his vengeance as red as my blood. Besides, it is wrong to trick him this way. How can I lie and deceive the man I love this way?"

"You will do it to stay alive! Perhaps that is his reason for keeping silent, to spare your life and have you back. He has done this twice before. You will do this because it might be the only way you will ever have him, though I'll never understand how you could love a man like him. One day he will strike out at you in hatred and revenge and surely destroy you!"

She paled as she looked at him, comprehending his meaning. "I remember something my father once told me, Powchutu. He said hate was the sister to love. One spoke with a kiss and the other with a knife. Where one gives life and happiness, the other gives death and sadness. He said oftentimes you could not tell where one left off and the other began. Sometimes they are confusing to tell apart, for many acts of hate and revenge are done in the name of love. He told me each one possesses the power to destroy the other, and the one who feels it. Within each person there lives both love and hate, and it only depends on which of the two is the stronger. If, as you say, his hate is his stronger power, then you are right and one day he will destroy me. But by the same token, if my love for him is the stronger power of the two, then I will survive."

Powchutu harshly asked, trying to vanquish her illusions, "But what will be the prize, Alisha, and how cold and empty your survival? All you will have will be a man who hates you and who will always see you as Alisha, his ska kaskapi."

Alisha glared at him and said, "That's cruel, Powchutu! You don't need to remind me of his feelings for me. He has made me well aware of them many times. I have no illusions about how he feels about me. If I did, then I would not fear his discovery of this deceit. If I thought he cared at all for me, I would go to him with the truth. If he does not know as yet, then it will only be a matter of time before he does. As you so aptly described him before, he is as cunning as the fox."

She looked up at him and said, "The trap is set and I draw closer to it each minute. He is the hunter and love his bait. The only question is, when will he spring the trap and crush me in its iron vise? Is there no path I can take to avoid his snare, Powchutu?"

"If you're right, we'll have to find some way for you to flee him and this danger. We cannot risk his telling the others tonight or his learning of it later. Let me think for a time . . ."

He restlessly paced around, considering plans in his mind. Just as he would think he had found the perfect escape, he would see a deadly flaw in it. How could she possibly escape unnoticed before the ceremony? I am sure he does not know yet, but I must get her away before she unknowingly tells him.

A bright, thoughtful look touched his face and he grinned mischievously. He nodded to himself several times, then laughed out loud. The perfect escape plus revenge, too! He fondled the little pezuta wopahte at his neck and thought wickedly, I will pluck his little white bird right from his o-winza! He will not lose a promised one, he will lose his wife! He will have her for a short moment, only to lose her forever. Yes . . .

Now, all he had to do was convince Alisha this was the best and only way to pull this off and for them to get away. If things went as he planned, he could get her away from him. She would then belong to only him. He thought, I will find some way to make her turn to me and come with me. He smiled at the simplicity of it all. The key to his success was to work on her fear of him and his hate for her. Make her believe he truly hates her and will destroy her with his revenge. She trusts me and will believe my words, for she has no reason to doubt me or my motives. When I finish, there will be nothing he can say or do to change her mind about leaving him for good!

At last he spoke, "I know what must be done, Alisha. You must do all I say without hesitation. Do you trust me enough to do as I ask? Will you agree?"

She nodded yes and he continued, "I know the only way you can be safe is to get you as far away from here and him as possible. I am sure he does not really know anything yet. He might be suspicious, but if we are careful, he will not guess. We must get you away before he learns. He will wait until he gets you back to his village to storm you with questions about your behavior. Then, when he forces the truth from you, he will kill you in some accidental way and bury you as Shalee. No one will ever know the truth then. I am sure he will find some way to save his face and honor in this game. I am also sure he will not expose you tonight, even if by some freak chance he knows or learns. You will be safe until the time to leave here and return to his camp. You must act normal today and go through with the ceremony tonight. We must let no one suspect anything is wrong!"

Alisha asked, "You mean I am to go along with this joining?"

Powchutu nodded yes and continued, "We can make no moves to flee before then. They would be on our trail in minutes and the trick would be out in the open for all to see. The time for escape is after the ceremony tonight. No one will be watching you so closely then. We'll have the cover of night and the time we need until they discover we are gone in the morning. They will never overtake us then."

She said in confusion and alarm, "But I will be his wife after the joining! How could I possibly get away from him on our joining night? I will have to go to his mat and he sleeps as light as a feather. There's no way I could leave him then." Powchutu missed her full meaning, for she had also meant that once he touched her and began to make love to her, she would have thoughts of nothing else but him. She would never be able to leave him then, for she would not have the willpower to leave his arms on their wedding night, hate or no hate . . .

She asked questions to tear her thoughts from him and tonight. "How can we pull off this escape tonight without discovery? Where could we run that he would not follow us, find us, and kill us? There is no place far enough to run, and we could not flee fast enough to get beyond his fury and revenge when he discovers our plot. I cannot ask you to do this for me. It is much too dangerous and deadly. With a little help and planning from you, I could make it alone. If you tell me where I can locate some of my people and get a horse and supplies, this time I could make it. There is far more at stake now than before when I tried."

"No! I cannot let you go alone. It is too dangerous for you out there. There are wild animals and other Indian tribes, not to mention other white men who wouldn't think twice about capturing you just as he did. I must go with you to protect you and help you. Remember . . . we're to be a family."

She smiled at his reminder of her words of another day and for his protective nature and loving feelings for her.

"I have a plan that will work. Listen to me closely. Tonight after the ceremony, I will bring you and Wanmdi Hota a drink to toast your joining as is the wasichu custom after joinings. Be sure to take the one I hand to you and drink it willingly. I will put a sleeping potion in his. He will sleep all night, giving us the time and secrecy we need to get away. I will prepare the supplies today and hide them near the rocks by the falls. After you enter the teepee with him, I will get the horses and bring them to the falls and wait for you to come to me. Before the sun is high in the morning sky, we will be far away and out of his reach."

He continued on as she did not stop him for questions or comments. "He will not be able to track us for I shall cover our trail carefully. We will have to ride hard and fast at first to put many miles between us and this camp. We will ride day and night with little rest or sleep. I will see we carry much food and water to avoid stops for them. I have kodas in other villages to the east. When we reach their camp, we will stop and rest before going on to this place you have spoken of to me at the fort. By the time Wanmdi Hota awakens, it will be too late for him to catch us or find us. He will never hurt or use either of us again, Alisha. This I swear to you. When we reach safety, I will take care of you and let no harm come to you."

She paced around for a time, thinking on his plan and words. "I agree and understand all you say, my friend. If he knows anything, it would only make sense for him to wait until he could handle the problem alone and in secret. If he does not betray me at the joining, or if Matu doesn't do it for him, then I will do as you say. From past experiences, I can only think and believe he will do the worst to me. I have no choice but to try to flee once more. But God help me if he catches me this time . . ." She did not dare to tell Powchutu how hard it would be to leave him forever.

"The only thing he could possibly do to me that he hasn't done already is kill me. And if he chooses my death, then it will be over. Oh, Powchutu, if only I weren't such a coward! Sometimes I fear his love more than his hate. Are you sure we could not wait until tomorrow and do this?" She wanted this one last night of love with him to remember for the rest of her life.

Knowing the reason for her question, he coldly said, "No, Alisha. It must be tonight. You must be brave and strong. The toast will be the only way to slip him the potion. In the excitement of this night, he will not suspect or refuse it. Later . . ." He shook his head.

He didn't have to finish, she knew his meaning. He needed to give her some courage and strength. "To fear torture and death is not being a coward, Alisha. He lied to me and tricked me into coming here to help him get at you. I wish I had not agreed. He led me to believe he did not hate you and would not harm you again. They were all lies! He waits like a vulture for its helpless prey to die. Your words at the fort were true. He hates you and will continue to make you suffer at his hands. I fear this time he demands your life and I cannot allow it. He hates all wasichus. He will know you are one. He will find some way to get rid of you for good and have this thing ended. His pride will demand it!"

He thought malevolently, I will place such

hate and fear in your heart and mind for him, my love, you won't look back or change your mind. This is the chance I have dreamed of and waited for. In the end, Wanmdi Hota, it will be Powchutu who has your Cinstinna. It will be Powchutu who takes her from you. And if you try to come after her, I will kill you! If necessary, I will kill her before I let her return to your hate. Alisha and I will live together, or we will die together . . .

Alisha was speaking to him and he stopped his thoughts to listen. "Powchutu, we must make one change in the plan. I must leave here first and alone. When he sees you still here, he will think you know nothing of my escape and you will be safe. You will prepare things for me as you said and leave them by the falls. Fix a map for me to follow, marking where to stop and wait for you. I will follow the river for a long way and hide my tracks. You can be sure he does not come in the right direction. You could make a phony trail to confuse him. When he has left to look for me in the wrong direction, then you can sneak off to join me at the appointed place.

"No, better still, you remain here for a short time. I will locate some of my people and escape unnoticed with them. You will join me back East later. As white, I can best flee in the company of other whites and you can travel through Indian territory dressed as an Indian. I will not make the same mistakes with my people as I did before. Now that I know of their feelings about ex-captives, I will find some story to tell them about my family being killed and my being the lone survivor. Or, I can say we were taken prisoner, but I luckily escaped before I was ravished. That should satisfy their curiosity and hate. If all else fails, I could latch on to some available young fellow to help me . . ." She laughed bitterly, thinking of Horace.

Powchutu shook his head vigorously. "No! I cannot let you go alone."

Stubbornly and rebelliously she stated, "Yes! It must be this way. I will not risk the life of my only friend and family. I go alone or not at all!"

Still, he argued, "We leave tonight and together! Families stick together and help each other! I have told you he cannot possibly catch us."

"He could! There could be an accident or one of the horses could go lame or die. We couldn't get away riding double. I could not live with your death on my head if if came to that. Do not ask me to risk your life because of your love and concern for me. My life and freedom in exchange for yours is not a fair exchange. You can pass for Indian when necessary and white when necessary. I can only pass for white. My chance for escape lies in finding and joining one of their wagon trains. I will draw you a map where to find me back East. You speak our tongue and will have no trouble finding your way. It must be this way."

Alisha looked at him, full of determination

374

and confidence at her decision. Powchutu fussed and argued, but she refused to budge or be swayed. She stood hard and fast and would not be persuaded to change her mind. Seeing he would have to pretend to agree, he said, "All right! We do it your way. If you follow the map carefully, it will lead you to a trail the white settlers use. Ride along the treeline at night until you spot some wagons, but stay well hidden in the daylight. I will follow after you in a few moons to be sure you made contact with some other whites. If you are still alone, then I will take you the rest of the way back East. If you are gone by then, I will travel a different path and meet you where you have said."

She threw her arms around his neck and said, "Agreed. I must get things prepared to leave and for the ceremony tonight. When I go to bathe, I will hide some clothes near the falls until tonight. You get the things and the horse I'll need. When Wanmdi Hota falls asleep, I will come to the falls to meet you. This time you might have saved my life, my friend. Until later tonight . . ." She smiled.

She left to find Matu. Powchutu remained behind for a few moments doing some last minute planning of his own. He unconsciously muttered to himself, "I cannot let you go alone, my love. It will not be wise or safe. I will allow you to think you go alone, but I will be close behind. I will cover both our trails. This time, he will not ever find you or bring you back. I have sworn to love and protect you always. I will kill him if he follows us. Within two days, you will be out of his reach and life forever, and into mine . . . He will take no more revenge out on your back. I hope this loss of you brings him much suffering and shame."

Gray Eagle stepped from behind the teepee with narrowed, cold eyes as he watched Powchutu walk away. For all his daring and courage, Powchutu would have trembled if he had seen the glint in those obsidian eyes.

So, you will try to steal my Cinstinna from me. . . . There will be many surprises in store for both of you this night, my koda! This will be a night long remembered by both you and Alisha!

He turned and walked away from Mahpiya Sapa's teepee in search of White Arrow to make some plans of his own—very different from those just overheard . . .

Chapter Eight

Alisha returned later to her teepee with the clothes Matu had taken and washed for her in a gesture of truce. She carefully tied them, a few personal items, and possessions up into a small tight bundle. As she was about to leave for the cave to start preparations for tonight and to hide this bundle for her escape, she heard a thunderous uproar and loud commotion coming from outside. The pawing and pounding of horses' hooves; snorting and wheezing from exhausted animals; loud, vociferous yells; and shouts of surprise and excitement filled her ears. What in the world is going on? she wondered as she promptly ran over to the flap to curiously peer outside.

She instantly recognized two of the braves as being from Wanmdi Hota's camp, friends of his. But, there were four men dismounting the lathered, winded horses. From the looks of both men and beasts, they had travelled hard and fast to get here. The riders were speaking and laughing with a few Si-ha Sapa warriors who had walked over to join them. She watched as Wanmdi Hota seemed to come from nowhere and hastily strode forward to join the boisterous group. He had a wide grin on his face as he embraced them all in turn with a warm, friendly bear-hug. She noted he joked and quipped with an older man in particular. He turned to another man and seemed to be discussing something serious with him. He nodded several times in understanding or agreement.

She studied him first. He was attired in a strange garb of deerskin clothes, animal hides, and feathers. On his head, he wore an elaborate headdress of a portion of a wapiti's head, antlers still intact. He held a long, slender staff in his right hand with a shaker attached to the top end and feathers up and down the length of the shaft. His stoical face was painted in a strange pattern of red and white paints. He was most impressive and solemn. She surmised he was the Oglala Shaman or medicine chief.

Her scrutiny shifted to the other man. It was this man who commanded the most attention and respect from the people surrounding him, including Wanmdi Hota. That noble, dignified bearing which suggested authority and pride emanated from him like an aura. She studied his features—the flashing, ebony eyes; the lean, muscular body still evident at his age; those bold, chiseled lines of his face; the thin, but shapely mouth; and his deep, rich voice. All these things told her he was someone very important and had been very handsome in his youthful days, for he still had a look that could stir the heart of an older woman.

Gray Eagle had made his way to this man after speaking with the Shaman. They had embraced lovingly several times, slapping each other on the back affectionately. She observed the expressions which passed between them. They smiled, talked, laughed and joked easily with each other. His voice carried a loving, respectful tone as he spoke with the older man.

Alisha wondered who he was. They evidently knew each other well and were very fond of the other one. She could clearly tell he was a chief from some tribe by his dress and carriage. Perhaps he had been invited as a guest for the joining ceremony tonight.

Alisha noted the long, fringed, buckskin leggins; the high-topped moccasins; the elaborate, beautiful jewelry and breastplate; the highly-decorated, etched armbands; and the full, flowing, yellow-feathered, chief's bonnet. Yellow! Of course . . . his father!

I should have immediately recognized the resemblance, she thought. I didn't even think about his coming to our joining. At last I will meet the great Chief Suntakca Ki-in-yangki-yapi. Now, I shall see where Wanmdi Hota gets his hatred and other qualities from, or if they are his very own. . . .

Sensing probing eyes on his back and a nearby presence, Running Wolf turned to her. Those familiar, ebony eyes bored into hers just as Wanmdi Hota's had done many times when he was scrutinizing her. All she could do was return the bold stare, unable to lower the half-opened flap because of the power of their gaze.

His deep, bass voice sounded like a thunderclap as he called to her to come to him. Unable to resist his command, she quickly and obediently came forward to stand before him, eyes lowered and face roseate. She quivered beneath his steady, searching gaze, but stood proud and erect.

"Shalee, wayaketo!" he ordered in a firm, but gentle, tone. She instantly looked up at him as he continued his study of her features with nerve-wracking intensity.

He turned to his son and joked, "So, this is the winyan who has captured your heart and clipped the great eagle's wings. She is indeed very beautiful. But, she is much more. This, I can see in her face and eyes."

Gray Eagle could not suppress a laugh and broad, pleased smile. His eyes glittered with love and respect for his father and his intuition. He glanced at Alisha to find her watching him closely and curiously. She had seen his warm expression and the intense emotions behind it.

So, she realized, he is capable of deep love and emotion. He is not totally coldblooded and unfeeling. His cool, reserved mask slipped back into place. She watched it go almost as if it had never been there a moment before. Just as I thought, this love and warmth exists only for his father and no one else. Her eyes lost some of their sparkle. Still, she continued to stare at him as he talked with his father. His tone of voice and his expression enchanted her.

Gray Eagle spoke with self-confidence and ease with Running Wolf. "She has been as elusive as an eagle, my father, but now she is mine. The matter has been settled between Mahpiya Sapa and me. We are to be joined this new moon. I have told Mahpiya Sapa we will give his son Mato Waditaka Chela's hand to replace his loss of Shalee. This will twice join our tribes in friendship. I ask you, my father, to command this. There will be no peace for me and Shalee in our camp with Chela there.''

Alisha perked up at the sound of her name so closely connected with Chela's. He must have told him I was to join with Mato Waditaka until Wanmdi Hota came and prevented it. He must be telling him he will also marry Chela when we return to their camp. He already plans to replace me with her and we're not even joined yet! Damn you, Wanmdi Hota! You'll never make me one of your concubines! I'll not remain here to be degraded like that! Neither man saw the look of heated rage and fierce determination which sparkled in those jade eyes for a brief moment before she struggled to conceal it.

The chief smiled and replied, ''It is good, my son. I would not want there to be enmity and war between the Oglalas and Si-ha Sapas. I am happy and relieved at this news. It seems I have arrived just in time.'' He grinned and laughed openly and honestly. His charisma and warm magnetism reached out to Alisha and she found herself smiling at him even though she could not understand his words. His manner brought awe and respect to her eyes and face. She could easily understand why Wanmdi Hota loved and respected him so much. She sadly realized he would not be her father-in-law for very long and she would never have the chance to know him better.

Running Wolf had been secretly observing Alisha as she in turn had been openly observing them. He was perplexed and slightly concerned by the emotions he read in her face. All is not well and happy in the eagle's domain . . .

He noted to his son, "She is much afraid of you and does not completely trust you, my son. This, I can see in her eyes, among other disturbing things . . . I would watch over this little bird carefully, my son, for she has flight on her mind. I also see much hurt and suffering in those eyes. It is not wise to let fear and mistrust fester and grow when there has been so much dishonor and suffering to cause them. You must deal with these feelings she carries in her heart against you, or they will lead to much trouble and sadness later. But I also see much love written there. This is good, for it will make it easier for the other feelings to vanish." He laughed mockingly and added, "She will be far easier to tame than Chela!"

Gray Eagle laughed and quickly added, "Perhaps it is you, O Great Chief, who frightens my little bird. We will speak of these things later when you have rested and are alone. I must tell you of many things which are in my heart and of all that has happened since I found and took her for my own. Then you will know and understand the reasons for her fears and doubts.''

As other men came forward to speak with Running Wolf, Gray Eagle watched Alisha as she sedately slipped from the group and returned to her teepee. Gray Eagle's gaze roved to the eyes of his father, who was grinning knowingly as he noted the look on his son's face as he watched her departure.

He spoke alertly, "My son, you look as if you see some secret in the undoing. I say there is a cunning fox loose here." Their eyes locked as they laughed.

Shortly, they all came to the teepee of Mahpiya Sapa to eat and rest for a time. The men sat around on the buffalo skins as they ate, talked and smoked. It had not been long since she had eaten and was not hungry. She made a point to sit as far from Gray Eagle as possible. She sat very near to Black Cloud, just like a loving daughter.

Every so often, her father would turn to her and gaze into her lovely face and smile proudly and tenderly. The old man's happiness reached out to her and she could not resist returning each smile.

Once, as he was speaking with Running Wolf, he touched her cheek in tenderness and said, "At last I have found the sunlight of my old heart. I thank Napi for returning her to me, if only to be taken away so soon by your eager son.''

Alisha took the wrinkled hand in hers and squeezed it affectionately and smiled as tears sparkled in her eyes. For a time, she was almost sorry she was not his Shalee and could not remain here as his beloved daughter.

For some reason, her attention was drawn to Gray Eagle. He was grinning like the Cheshire cat, a secret, mocking smile lighting his jet eyes.

In anger and fear, she lowered her eyes and hands to her lap and inwardly fumed, damn him! What right does he have to mock my emotions and actions? He is surely enjoying this little game of secrets and taunts. Well, soon he will be the one left holding the bag! For once, I will be the victor in our battles! She could not suppress a spiteful, smug grin to herself, which he saw and recognized.

She must find some opportunity to speak with Powchutu and be certain all was set for tonight. If anything went wrong now . . .

She stood up and walked outside to get some fresh air and to get out of sight of that constant, mocking stare. How she would dearly love to slap it right off his handsome face! She laughed, then paled, imagining his expression and reaction if she had dared to do it.

In this last battle, my love, it will be Alisha who is the champion. No more will you taunt and torture me with your love and kisses or your cold, cruel withdrawals. No more will you use me like some slave or trollop. At last, I will be free to be myself once more, to know happiness and joy in my heart and life, to not feel shame and torment by your actions.

Free, she thought. Tonight, I will be free . . .

She walked along the river bank to a rocky, shallow spot. Removing her moccasins and holding them in her hand, she waded in the stream as she had done so often as a child. She giggled as the water splashed and tickled her feet and ankles. She nudged smooth, round pebbles with her toes and made little whirlpools with a pointed toe. She threw back her head and filled her lungs with fresh air. She let her face soak up the warm sunlight. Her heart had not been this relaxed and light in days. With the final decision made to leave him forever, a great weight had been lifted from her spirits. It was done, and there was no turning back now . . .

She crossed the stream and began to wander through the meadow, picking colorful, fragrant wildflowers. She danced along to a lilting waltz heard only inside her head. Soon, she sat down, weaving the flowers into a coronet for her hair. She playfully mused, all princesses should have a coronet to wear on their wedding day. She found herself humming a love ballad she used to sing and play for her father. She began to sing the words to it in a silvery voice which rivalled the angels:

I drink from your love as flowers from the
   rain;
I touch you like the sun upon the lane;
I kiss you as the sun would kiss the dew;
I am filled with love for only you . . .

Alisha had lowered her head as she worked on the coronet. Then she lifted the fragile ring to her nose to smell its intoxicating aroma. Legs stepped before her eyes and she raised her head to see who it was. The bright sunlight was at his back and she could not make out his features. Her small hand went up to her eyes to shield them from the harsh, brilliant light and to make out the face before her. She should have guessed. Wanmdi Hota had come to check on his missing bride!

He held out his hand to her and said, "Ku-wa, Lese."

Without a thought to resistance, she took it and he helped her up. To her surprise, he went down on one knee and began to place her moccasins back on her feet. When he lifted her petite foot by her slender ankle to pull the slipper on, she had to place her hands upon his bare shoulders to steady her balance. How good it felt to touch him and share a moment of kindness.

Before he could rise after he had finished, she impishly placed the floral coronet on his head and said, "For your kind help, Sir, I crown you, Ruler of My Heart."

He stared at her with narrowed eyes, trying to decide if she were serious or if she mocked him. Seeing his chilling expression, she reached up and tore the flowers from his head. She threw them to the ground and angrily and spitefully crushed them beneath her feet. "That was a stupid, silly thing to do anyway! What would you know about kings or hearts or even love?" She fought to hold back the tears which glistened on her thick black lashes.

He reached for her hand to take her back to camp, but she angrily jerked it away and hurried on ahead of him. Within a couple of long, easy strides he overtook her and swung her around to face him. She refused to look at him. He seized her trembling chin in his hand and forced it up, making her meet his gaze.

He bitterly thought, once more I have hurt you, Cinstinna, without meaning to. He gently wiped away her tears with his fingertips and caressed her cheek.

She glared at him in confusion and asked, "How can you be so cold and cruel one minute, then so tender and warm the next? I shall never understand you, Wanmdi Hota, for it is too late to try."

He bent forward and brushed a light kiss across her cheek. It caused her knees to weaken and a quickening in the depth of her loins. How could his touch have such a devastating effect on her? She stared up into his face longingly, knowing she would never feel his love again. The pain which ripped through her surfaced in those somber, green eyes. He flinched at what he was being forced to put her through. But it will not be for much longer, Cinstinna.

This was the moment to tell him good-bye. Her two hands went up to his face and caressed his cheeks, then went around the back of his neck to pull his head forward. She slowly went up on her tiptoes and pressed close to him, hesitating to see if he would push her away at the last moment. He did not and their lips fused in a searing kiss. His arms instantly went around her and crushed her to him, each putting their all into their kiss. The sky could have fallen and they would not have known it.

Alisha weakly pulled away when the kiss was over. She gazed into his smoldering eyes and whispered, "You will never know how very much I love you." She smiled faintly as she added, "At least you did want me as a woman."

He took her hand and led the way back to the village. He left her at the entrance to her teepee and walked away. She stood watching him until he had disappeared into another teepee not far away. He could feel the heat from her gaze piercing him like a hot knife. She turned and went inside her teepee to find Powchutu waiting for her.

He told her it was time for her to prepare for the coming ceremony. She hardly heard a word he was saying, for her mind was still back in the meadow.

Powchutu's stern voice fought for her full attention, "Alisha! You're not listening!"

She whirled around to face him, noting the frantic, worried look on his face. "What is wrong, Powchutu? Is there some problem about the plans? Why are you so upset?"

Should he tell her about the talk he had recently had with Gray Eagle? Would it only add to her fretting and fear? Seeing his hesitation and unwillingness to go on, she asked, "What did he say to you? I would guess he has told you something which has panicked you."

He looked at her with guilt and amazement. "So, I'm right! What was it? Tell me this instant!" she demanded.

"I fear you might be right, Alisha. He certainly knows a lot more than I thought or realized. Like you said before, it's not so much what he says, but how he says it and how he looks. Those expressions and hints have me plenty worried. He came to me to ask where you had gone. I told him out for a walk. He lifted his eyebrows in mockery and said, 'Yes, she would never be so foolish as to try to escape from me again.' He muttered something about 'old scars and hurts would heal with time and many things could be forgotten.'"

"Perhaps you misunderstood his meaning, Powchutu. He could have been referring to my back and treatment."

He quickly disputed her reasoning. "But then, he began to talk about Matu and of how happy she was to be home. He commented on how lucky she was to have seen and recognized the akito. But his last words were the most alarming, Alisha. He said he had been deceived many times before, but would never accept lies or deceit from anyone again, especially someone as close to him as his wife!"

Her face went ghostly white and she swayed at the impact of the apparent meaning of his words. Powchutu caught her and steadied her.

"Alisha, are you all right? You're as white as the clouds. Surely this comes as no surprise. Isn't this what you already believed?"

"To assume something is real or true is one thing, but to know for certain it is, that is something entirely different. I had hoped I was wrong. I had hoped I could get away before he learned of it."

Recalling the scene from the meadow, she asked, "How can he even stand to touch me or look at me now? How will he ever force himself to join with me tonight knowing I am wasichu and I am living a lie? How can I possibly face him and go through with this farce now?"

"You will because you must! He will do nothing here. He will surely wait to return to his village. We will go on with our plans as before. He will know why you have fled him and perhaps he will not come after you. Perhaps he will be satisfied to pretend you ran from him in fear, became lost, and were killed by some wild animal. Perhaps he will allow you to go unharmed, but never stay here alive. He will look at you and touch you tonight as wasichu, just as he has done all the other times knowing what you are. He will join with you because he will know he must to save face! He knows you would not dare deny you are Shalee, so his honor will be safe. You seem to forget who is in the wrong here, Alisha. You forget who is good and who is evil."

She pondered on his words for a time, suddenly recalling what he had said before.

"He's been deceived! Surely he jests! I have never deceived him until now, and his hatred and brutality force me to do it this time. He is the liar, the trickster, and betrayer at every turn. Not I! He dares to hold me to blame for his cruelty and treachery, for Matu's . . . oh-h-h . . . he's mad! Never again, Powchutu!"

She looked at him and asked, "Could you guess what he is up to, or what he might do . . . other than what you have assumed?"

"No . . ." he answered doubtfully. "He said he was going out to find you so you could prepare for the joining tonight, then he left."

Panic seized her for a moment. Prepare for tonight . . . she nearly screamed at him, "He'll blurt it out at the ceremony tonight, Powchutu, before I have the chance to flee! They'll torture me and kill me! I know they will!"

Powchutu grabbed her by the shoulders and shook her fiercely. "Quiet! Alisha. They'll hear you and come to see what is wrong. Don't be afraid. I won't let them hurt you. If it comes to that, I'll tell them you knew nothing of the akito or how it got there before I told you yesterday. All they'll do is turn you back over to Wanmdi Hota as his captive again."

"They won't believe us, Powchutu," she cried out in terror.

"Yes, they will, for I have always spoken the truth to them. They will trust my words. As I told you, he'll wait until he gets you alone to kill or punish you. He will go through with this ceremony to save face. He would never wish it

391

known you had tricked him. Think of the dishonor and humiliation of allowing a mere white girl and slave to deceive the mighty warrior Wanmdi Hota! No, he would not risk such a disgrace."

"You truly think he will go along with this joining to save his face and his honor, then kill me in secret later? But why would he want to kill me later? He would have his slave and there is no way I could harm or dishonor him."

In deliberate callousness for fear of losing her, Powchutu answered, "Yes, because he hates you and you have dared to trick him. He has tired of using you and trying to make you an obedient slave. He wishes to be done with you, and this is the best way to save his pride and have his revenge."

Alisha stared at him in total bereavement. She was dazed and besieged by doubts and fears. Heartbroken, she sadly asked, "He could hate me that much, Powchutu?"

Powchutu had already thrust the knife in. Now, he brutally twisted it to kill any remaining love and trust she might feel for Gray Eagle. "Yes . . ." was all he answered.

She slowly sank to the ground and wept. Powchutu watched her for a few tormenting minutes, then murmured in Oglala, "I am truly sorry for this pain to your heart, my love. But it must be done to free you of Gray Eagle and the desire to stay. I fear the power his love has over you." He turned and left.

Gray Eagle clenched his fists in rage and fury.

He had immediately come to Alisha's teepee after she disappeared inside, knowing Powchutu was waiting for her. How dare he do this cruel thing to you, Cinstinna! he raged. He will pay dearly for this suffering to you! He will not be the one who follows you tonight. It is past the time for our talk! It has been too long in coming. I have allowed too many things to prevent it. But you must be away from here and any interference from anyone. You will be allowed to escape, but not to this East you speak of to Powchutu. We will meet in the far hills for this talk. You will learn of the secrets of my heart and life, as I have yours. He turned to go and talk with his father.

Alisha finally stopped sobbing when all the tears and intense emotions were spent. She was mentally and physically exhausted. I must get ready for this joining of hate with love. I must pull myself together. I will not let him see the pain and hurt I feel at this final betrayal. She sadly prayed, give me the strength and courage to face him this one last time . . .

She gathered her things and walked to the cave in an trance-like state. She knelt by the pool and lightly flicked the water with her fingertips. Will it never be over? Will my heart ever feel joy again? I sometimes feel as if he has plunged a hot knife into my heart. It bleeds for his cruel love. Why did I ever fall in love with a man like him?

"Oh Wanmdi Hota, why? If only I knew why . . ." she murmured in total despair.

He winced at the sadness and anguish in her tone. It ripped into his heart to hear and see her suffering so much. He was very worried about her state of fear, but hearing her now, he was more concerned about her despair. Soon you will know and understand everything, Cinstinna. He fought the intense urge to go in to her and confess all, but was certain she was not ready to believe and accept his words. It was most important to go through with the joining before he confronted her with the full truth. There was no guessing what her immediate reaction would be to his confession. He had come too close to truly having her to risk trouble now. The truth will be hard for her to accept after the damage Powchutu and my silence have done. She could expose this whole thing in a fit of anger and hurt. I dare not risk her life, or the life we can now have together.

Woefully, he returned to the teepee where his father rested and waited for him. He cursed what his silence was costing them both.

She undressed and slipped into the water. She scrubbed her hair and body roughly, as if she could remove the love it felt for him even now. "If only his love was as easy to wash away as dirt . . ." she sighed softly. She softened the strokes and languished in the cool, refreshing water. When she finished, she squeezed her hair dry and towelled off her body with a blanket. She put on the deerskin garment and went outside to sit upon the rocks to let the sun dry her hair. She refused to allow her mind to dwell on anything other than the beauty of the flower-filled meadow and the green hills not far away.

When her hair was dry, she brushed it until it was shining and lay slightly curling at her breasts. She went back into the cave to gather her things and returned to her teepee. She laced the flap tightly to dress and be alone.

Gray Eagle had bathed in the stream not far away and was now in the visitors' teepee, also preparing for the coming event. He talked with his father, telling him of the events which had taken place while he had been away. He told him about his capture and of meeting this girl at the white fortress. He told him about how she had tried to help him and, in spite of himself, he had found himself wanting her. He told of the raid on their fortress later and of her capture. He spoke of her defiance and rebellion and of her attempt to escape. He spoke sadly and contritely of her beating and rescue by the cavalry. "I would never have forgiven myself if I had killed her, or ever been happy if I had not been able to get her back safely."

He told him of her acceptance and submission after the destruction of the fort. "But our truce was too short. Mahpiya Sapa came for her the very next day and took her away from me. She was hurt and confused. Until yesterday, she believed I had sold her for a slave. She was told then who she really is and why she was brought here."

He spoke of the challenge and the agreement to give Chela to Mato Waditaka in Shalee's place. "She does not know I speak the wasichu tongue. The time for truth has not been right to tell her, or at least it seemed so. I had to wait until she accepted me and my ways before I went to her with open heart and truth. I was confused and alarmed to learn I loved and wanted a white girl over one of my own kind. It angered me to feel fear. And I feared the things this girl made me feel and think. I feared how much I wanted and needed her. I feared the happiness and light she brought to my heart and teepee. I feared keeping her, but more so losing her. But the Great Spirit has seen it in his way to give her to me for all time."

Running Wolf listened to his son and replied, "I see this girl is very important to you, my son. It is good she is the daughter of Mahpiya Sapa and you two can be joined. She will truly belong to you now. She will come to understand and accept the things you did to her if she loves you as I believe she does."

Gray Eagle did not look at his father as he spoke again. "Even if she were not Mahpiya Sapa's daughter, I would still take her. I have wanted and desired no other woman as I do her. She is like the very air I breathe. She is a part of me and I cannot lose her ever again."

In time when his father had come to know and love her as a daughter, he would tell him the truth. Hopefully he would accept it. He continued, "After the ceremony tonight, I will secretly take her away. We must be alone to talk of these things. I will return to our village in a few moons. You will tell the others we have gone and not to worry."

"Yes, to have this time alone would be wise, my son. These things will be hard for her to hear and believe. You will have to convince her of your love. Go to her with love and kindness, my son, and she will know the truth. May the Great Spirit watch over and protect both of you in this time of healing and learning. I will await your return in our village."

Alisha pulled on the white joining dress and moccasins. She left her hair hanging in tresses around her shoulders and tied the white pahin iyokaska with the two queques around her forehead. She carefully checked her appearance in the mirror. She wanted him to remember her at her very best, that is, if he ever thought of her again. Yes, she was pleased with how she looked, and should have been, for she had never looked lovelier or more desirable. She went to the flap and unlaced it, but left it closed for privacy.

Sometime later, Black Cloud and Powchutu entered and told her it was almost time for the ceremony. Powchutu couldn't take his eyes off Alisha. Never had she looked so beautiful and fragile. Black Cloud smiled and beamed with pride.

Powchutu explained what would take place at the joining. He would be nearby to tell her what she needed to do or say. This was a special ceremony and would be different from the one she had viewed. The joining of a chief's son to another chief's daughter was a rare event.

When the kettle drums began with a low, rhythmic beat, Powchutu took her hand in his and said, "Do not worry, Alisha, it will soon be over. We must be careful how we act and we must not speak again. It would not do for anyone to guess our words or plans now. I will meet you by the falls after he is asleep. It is time and we must go. Remember, soon he can hurt you no more. Act naturally and speak to no one."

Why did Powchutu think it necessary to keep warning her about silence? She wasn't a child! She understood the importance of secrecy.

Black Cloud lifted the flap and they walked out into the coming twilight. Gray Eagle watched her slow approach as he devoured her with his eyes. She looked stunning, yet vulnerable. Many of the other braves commented on how lucky he was. How could Mato Waditaka have taken the loss of such a rare, delicate beauty? But even his eyes glinted with regret and jealousy. White or not, she was the most beautiful woman he had ever seen. He could still feel the touch of her lips. Chela had never stood a chance with Wanmdi Hota after he had seen Shalee, especially after he had taken her the first time.

Alisha was astonished by the looks of awe and envy on the faces around her. How ironic! They think they are seeing an Indian princess, when in truth, I am their enemy! she thought. How foolish and tragic that being a wasichu makes such a deadly difference. The only two faces in the crowd to draw a dazzling smile from her belonged to Wanhinkpe Ska and Mato Waditaka. Mentally she thought, good-bye, my kodas . . .

Her eyes touched Gray Eagle's as he stood in the center of the group. His appearance reflected pride and majesty. He looked magnificent and impressive, but also imposing and haughty. She was powerless to look away. His arrogant, confident expression and smug smile were very familiar, but not the look in those obsidian eyes.

He could not hide the lust in his gaze for her and did not even try to. His eyes sparkled with deviltry and taunting, but also something else. His, too, revealed a fierce pride and appreciation for her beauty. That look of his caused shivers to chase up and down her spine. He had a way of unsettling her with just that particular look and he knew it.

Gray Eagle was dressed in thick, rich buckskin breeches and moccasins. He was wearing a headband with only three of his many yellow feathers attached, and etched rawhide wristlets and armbands. He was wearing the white eagle wanapin around his neck. She quickly tore her eyes from the eagle and her mind from the meaning of it. Secured around his neck and flowing full to the ground, he wore a beautiful, colorful, feathered cape. It had no doubt been made for Mato Waditaka, but she guessed he had also won the right to wear it tonight.

It seemed to take forever to cross the short distance between her teepee and where he stood waiting for her. Powchutu and Alisha halted before Gray Eagle. He had never looked so handsome and virile. Her treacherous body trembled with renewed longings for him. Her heart began to ache knowing she would never see him again after tonight; nor feel his hot, fiery kisses and gentle caresses; nor hear his husky, rich voice; nor be near him. It was almost as if he wished her to remember him at his finest.

Black Cloud and Running Wolf were in the full ceremonial dress befitting chiefs. The Pezuta Wapiye Wicasta Itancan and the Tokenpi-i-ceyapi Itancan came forward to begin the hinaton.

The Shaman danced and chanted around them, invoking the protection and approval of the Great Spirit for this joining. He sang,

Daughter of Mahpiya Sapa,
Son of Suntakca Ki-in-yangki-yapi,
Come before you, Oh Great Spirit, Wakan-
    tanka, Napi,
And before the Oglala and Si-ha Sapa.
Daughter of Mahpiya Sapa,
Son of Suntakca Ki-in-yangki-yapi,
Come to hinaton, forever to be one . . .
Come to join spirits for their Canhdeska
    Wakan.
Daughter of Mahpiya Sapa,

Son of Suntakca Ki-in-yangki-yapi,
Forever to be one, forever to hinaton . . .
Forever see and know who watches them
   this hunwi.
Wakantanka, behold, Shalee and Wanmdi
   Hota hinaton.

When he finished his part in the ceremony, the ceremonial chief came forward and began his part. He chanted in a melodious voice as Gray Eagle pulled her to his chest. They faced each other. Gray Eagle kept his hold on Alisha's upper arms to steady her trembling. She made the mistake of meeting his gaze, and now she could not break the hold he enforced on her. Her eyes never left his for the remainder of the ceremony.

She would have flamed a bright red if she had realized the open, bold look of love and passion written on her face. Sha, Lese, ni-ye mitawa . . . Your love grows with each new sun. You cannot hide these feelings from me, nor drive them from your heart.

His look was most disarming with its expression of total fulfillment, combined with that glint of satisfaction and tenderness in his eyes. All thoughts of hate, anger and escape were temporarily forgotten. Lost in the depths of those jet eyes, she thought, he is indeed the most handsome man in the whole world. Oh Wanmdi Hota, if only I had truly been born Indian, or you white . . .

He watched her eyes caress him. He was hard pressed to keep his body and emotions under rigid control standing so close to her. Her two small hands which rested on his bare chest were no longer cold, but warm and trembling.

He released his hold on her arms and lifted the edges of the feathered cape and pulled her within its circle into his arms. As he held the cape around her, his hand caressed the nape of her neck softly. He gazed deeply into her eyes as he clearly spoke his words of hinaton.

The warmth of his breath against her face, and the contact with his body sent her senses spinning. His touch was like fire to her skin, and she was consumed with hunger for him. She felt his being with every single nerve in her body. Desire ran free throughout her like molten lava after a violent eruption of a volcano. She was lost to the reality of everything but him. He could have seduced her right then and there and she would have offered no resistance.

She was rudely returned to reality by Pow-chutu's voice and light tap on her shoulder from behind. Embarrassed and bewildered by her display of weakness for Gray Eagle and revealing his power over her, she lowered her gaze.

Powchutu slowly told her the words to say and she began to falteringly repeat them. But as she did, Gray Eagle's fingers went under her chin and forced her to look into his eyes while she repeated the joining words. To gaze into those black depths and not forget what to repeat to him was one of the hardest things she had ever done in her life.

Powchutu had previously explained the full meaning of the words to her. She did not know the order of the vows, but knew she was promising to love him always and never forsake him for another, to obey him in all things, to be his helper, to bear his children, and to place him above all others, including herself. In simple terms, she pledged him her very life and heart, in life and death.

Alisha somehow managed to finish the words and Powchutu returned to his former place and did not hear her one last vow, spoken to him in English, "I shall love you forever and I pray you will accept and forgive what I must do for both of us."

His hand reached up and gently touched the lips which had promised him his one dream of happiness—her love. To his surprise, she kissed his fingertips lightly. He smiled.

He released her from his embrace under the folds of the cape and they turned to face the ceremonial chief. He held up a circular necklace with two ties and chanted prayerfully. She watched curiously as he separated the circle into two, single half-circles, placing one around her neck and the other one around his. This wanapin was to signify that apart they were only half spirits, but joined together, their spirits made the circle complete and unending.

She lifted hers and gazed at it, then at his. She softly whispered, "How very romantic and beautiful. Forever one together and yet apart . . ."

The sudden whoops and yells alerted Alisha to the fact she was wed. She remained where she was, not knowing what else to do. Wanmdi Hota took her by the elbow and led her to a buffalo skin by the fire and seated her there. Then, the feasting and merriment began.

She was hardly aware of the food she ate, the dancing she watched, or the chanting she heard. It was evident the joining of a chief's son with a chief's daughter was a joyous occasion, as Powchutu had told her. The celebration went on and on. She sat in a near daze, watching her husband most of the time. There were many lively dances done in very colorful costumes and garbs.

She began to listen to the haunting music and watch the steps in great fascination. When it was over, she turned to find Gray Eagle gone from her side. She searched the sea of faces until she found him standing by her teepee talking with White Arrow. He glanced her way and found her watching him. He possessively captured her gaze and held it until he was back at her side.

He pulled her to her feet and began to lead her to her teepee. Black Cloud jokingly commented that he himself would sleep elsewhere tonight. At the entrance to the teepee, Powchutu stopped them and handed them a cup of fruit juice. He said it was the custom of the wasichu to drink a toast to each other on their joining night.

They both took the cups offered and touched them lightly together as Powchutu had instructed him, but she could not meet his gaze. White Arrow approached and pointed to a beautiful, mottled horse which was being given to Alisha as a gift.

She stared at it and smiled. "Thank him for me, Powchutu. Good-bye, my koda." She kissed him on the cheek and embraced him tightly. "I shall never forget you and your kindness."

Powchutu told her to drink the toast and seal the joining. She did so as Powchutu watched Gray Eagle's cup leaving his lips. As they handed the two cups back to Powchutu, a secret look passed between him and Alisha. Neither had noticed the cup Gray Eagle had lifted to his lips was empty . . .

Gray Eagle took her hand and led her inside. He turned and laced the flap tightly. He moved to a side brace pole and began to undress. She remained glued to the spot where she was standing. She realized she had forgotten to ask Powchutu how long it would take for the potion to work. Until it did, she would have to go along with any intentions he had to avoid suspicion. She felt like a trapped animal.

He removed the cape, breeches and headdress and hung them on a peg. He then removed his moccasins and sat them at the base of the pole. He walked over to the mat dressed only in his breechcloth which all too clearly revealed his intentions! Her eyes darted about in panic and her face reddened.

Gray Eagle lay down and called for Alisha to come to him. She laughed at herself for feeling like a silly virgin on her wedding night. They had made love many times before, but somehow this time seemed different . . . they had just been wed!

She slowly turned as red as a beet from her chest up, partly due to embarrassment and partly to rising passions. He called to her again and she slowly came to him and knelt before him. He saw the fear and uncertainty toward what he would do to her and how he would treat her knowing what they both did about the akito and this sham.

She quietly spoke, "Why did you really marry me tonight, Wanmdi Hota? If I didn't know any better, I would swear you do not hate me and that you do want me. I wonder what tonight would be like if I had truly been born Indian or you white. This parting would be so very easy if I had not been foolish enough to fall in love with you. What will you do tomorrow when you find me gone? Will you allow me to go in peace, or will you track me down and kill me? All I said tonight was the truth, except not to forsake you, for I must. If I thought for the slightest minute I could change your heart about me, I would never leave you . . ."

His lids drooped slightly, then came back to full alert. She noted the action. He pulled her down on top of him, then rolled her to her back on the other side of him. He lay half on her body, allowing for almost no movement from her. His hand brushed some strands of hair from her face and stroked it tenderly. He unlaced the ties at her throat and pushed the neckline of her dress open. He shifted to hold her face between his two hands and brought his mouth down on hers in a demanding, hungry kiss.

He spread kisses over her mouth, first taking it lightly, then passionately. His lips roamed her eyes, ears, face and throat, leaving a trail of searing fire behind. His hands moved along her shoulders and arms, caressing her soft skin lightly. Soon, his kisses deepened in desire and increased in passion. His mouth hungrily claimed hers time and time again.

Alisha desperately fought the flames which threatened to engulf and consume her. His hands at her breasts were teasing and tantalizing her right through her dress. She could feel them swell and harden with desire.

His hand slid down her stomach, causing ripples throughout her entire body. His deft hands slowly pushed her dress up to her waist, and in a few moves had it over her head and arms and lying on the ground beside him.

Unhindered by her dress now, his hands freely roamed her tense body at will, touching here and caressing there. She pleaded with him to stop this wild assault on her senses, but he just covered her mouth with his in another fiery kiss. His hand fondled her breast, kneading the nipple lightly, then made its way down her stomach to her breechcloth. He easily untied it and removed it with one hand and began to touch and caress her there. She inhaled sharply at this new sensation of delightful torment. She arched her body in desire and moaned against Gray Eagle.

Alisha was imprisoned beneath his body and strength. He touched and caressed her in ways he had never done before. Her mind was intoxicated by his kiss and his touch. She burned with longing. She clung to him frantically and wildly. She began to respond heatedly to the exquisite delights which filled her. She was breathless and quivering from the scintillating pleasures he was bringing to her.

She returned every kiss with fierce abandonment. He was awakening emotions and hungers which had lain asleep for days, and new hungers she had never felt before. She begged for more and more from him with her hands and her lips. Her responses spoke loud and clear to him, and he smiled in satisfaction.

He cut a blazing trail of kisses down her neck to her breasts. His lips teased and kissed each one until she begged for him to come to her quickly and end this terrible hunger and craving deep within her. Her mind urged for the total union of their bodies and desires. Her body cried out for release and fulfillment. She felt she must have him this one last time.

She moaned and thrashed upon the mat, begging and pleading, "Love me, Wanmdi Hota, one last time . . . take me now . . . love me like there will be no parting . . . I need you . . . don't push me away from you tonight . . . I want you . . . please . . ."

Gray Eagle abruptly collapsed limply across her body. Dazed for a minute with the sudden stopping of his touch and kiss, she queried, "Wanmdi Hota?"

Nothing . . .

She shook him and called to him again, thinking he was only teasing or torturing her again, "Wanmdi Hota?"

Nothing . . .

The truth dawned on her. "No-o-o . . ." She moaned and cried in anguish. "Not now . . . not again. I cannot bear it!" But this time, the rejection was of her own doing.

The fires and yearnings raged within her blood and body. She panted breathlessly and cried in agony and frustration. She actually felt pain in her womanhood and breasts. She writhed in unrequited passion. Her body ached for his kiss, touch, and union. She felt as if every nerve in her body and mind would snap with tautness and tension. This agony of being so sexually excited and driven to the point of no return, then thwarted and frustrated was almost too great to bear. She did not possess the knowledge to control or subdue what she was experiencing.

She frantically shook him again, crying, "Wake up! Wake up, Wanmdi Hota! You can't do this to me again! You owe me this night! Please don't pass out yet! Oh why did I ever agree to give you that potion anyway? Tonight of all nights! Why did I agree to be a part of this

409

farce? The only thing I ever wanted was you, and for you to want me in return." She wept bitterly for what she was being denied this last time.

She angrily began to slap him on his chest, then halted and threw herself upon his body and sobbed for a long time. She hugged him to her, gently caressing his face and chest. It took all his willpower and determination to force his manhood to go limp during her embrace. He fought to stifle his sexual stirrings.

She must stay because she wants to, not because I force her to with love and passion, he thought. He fiercely struggled to quell a new stirring of passion in his loins. You must be free to decide for yourself, Cinstinna.

Finally managing to bring her sobs and quiverings under some type of control, she eased off the mat and stood painfully looking down at him. She gazed at the handsome face in the moonlight, memorizing each detail of his feature.

She knelt and ran her fingertips across his lips, then bent to place a kiss there. Her quivering hand touched his cheek; ran across the proud nose; the high forehead; the square, arrogant jawline, tracing his length; and caressing his chin with the back of her hand. Her touch was as light as a feather, but as cold as ice.

Tears ran down her cheeks and dropped onto his chest like molten beads. She reluctantly removed her joining wanapin and placed it around his neck. She secured the two half-circles together to form the one never-ending circle of love. "Forever one together now, for we shall always be apart . . ."

She removed the little white eagle from his neck and whispered, "Forgive my stealing this, Wanmdi Hota, but it is far too precious to leave behind again. It will always remind me of an all too brief, but beautiful, love we shared . . ."

The tightness in her chest was so great she could hardly breathe. She touched the wanapin and said, "May you protect me from his wrath, little eagle of love, if he comes after me."

She rose and slowly redressed in the white joining dress, unaware of his longing gaze upon her slim, nude body. She walked to the flap, but hesitated before she unlaced it.

He watched her indecision. She turned and came back to kneel beside him. If she had laid back down beside him on the mat, he knew he would turn to her and make love to her. He would tell her he loved her in her own tongue. In fact, if she hesitated much longer, he would never let her leave.

Her hand went out to caress his chest, smooth and supple, yet hard and powerful. "How can I possibly give you up? But I'm not really giving you up, for I have never truly had you. It rends my heart to know I shall never see you again. I had never known love before you came into my life. Why couldn't you have loved me, Wanmdi Hota? If only I dared to stay and see if . . . but I can't, for you already know the truth. Besides, you showed me yesterday you no longer wanted me. You would probably have done the same thing tonight if you hadn't been drugged, wouldn't you? I shall leave with the memory of those two golden days of love we shared. At least you gave me that much of yourself. If the plan were not already in motion, I would go to them with the truth and let my death be on their heads, not yours, my love. We simply met in the wrong time and place. There can be no more dreaming or looking back now for me. I shall carry this love for you in my heart forever and a day."

She placed one last kiss upon his unresponding lips as her tears fell to his face and chest. She quickly rose and left without looking back.

She carefully slipped from the teepee and made her way quietly through the village where she had spent a few happy days as Shalee, Indian princess. Recognizing her scent, the animals did not warn of her passing. She walked along the river path to the bushes near the falls to retrieve her bundle. She made her way behind the rocks to where a horse awaited her.

It was the one White Arrow had given her earlier this evening. Powchutu had dared to steal that horse! she thought, amazed at his daring, then corrected herself, but he is mine! She glanced around for a sign of her friend.

She paced nervously for a time, thinking he must have forgotten something and had gone back to get it. Time passed on and she began to get edgy and tense. She walked over to her horse to pat his nose fondly and lovingly. Her eyes saw something on his back. She walked to his side and took it down. It was a light-colored piece of skin with a map traced upon it in charcoal. She looked at it and studied the markings. It seemed clear enough for her to follow. She noticed the horse had a sleeping skin and blanket rolled and secured to his back. She looked at the strange, light saddle-like rig on his back. There was a type of horn she could hang her bundle on. She nervously looked around once more, but still no Powchutu.

A thought struck her mind, perhaps he could not bear to say good-bye. No matter, I can wait no longer. He has prepared all I need and I cannot risk further delay. He could be out setting a false trail right now for me. Perhaps he didn't know how long the potion would take to work. Still, I dare not wait longer.

She mounted quickly and easily with natural agility and skill. She looked back at the sleepy, peaceful village and whispered, "Good-bye, my love . . ."

Her heart and spirit were heavy as she walked the horse along until she was far enough away to put him into a steady gallop. Gray Eagle stayed just far enough behind her to avoid her sight and hearing. Occasionally, she would slow and stop to check the map and landmarks, then hurriedly press on.

At this same time back in the Si-ha Sapa camp, Powchutu was desperately arguing with White Arrow. He was sitting in a teepee with his hands and feet bound securely. He had not been the one to follow her. Gray Eagle was at this very moment stalking Alisha like a deer!

So, he had known, and he had guessed their plans! How much had Alisha inadvertently spilled to him? She'll be completely at his mercy, he worried. Would he capture her and bring her back, and kill us together? Or will he return alone to kill me? We played right into his hands once more. In hindsight, he thought, perhaps I should have spoken the truth to Mahpiya Sapa and Mato Waditaka and pleaded innocence and mercy. What man could have dared to punish a beautiful creature like they saw tonight?

He asked White Arrow, "How can you, who calls himself her koda, go along with her murder? You betray her love and trust as he does. Even more so, for she knows he is her enemy, but she believes you her koda!"

White Arrow turned and glared at him. "What do you mean, her murder? How do I betray her?"

"Do not play games with me, Wanhinkpe Ska! You know he will kill her when he catches up to her out there, or when he allows her to get far enough away to do it in secret."

He laughed and scoffed at such foolish words. "Perhaps he will punish her, but kill her? Never!" Noting Powchutu's serious expression and tone, he inquired, "Why did she do this? Why would you agree to help her? Did you not know how angry it would make him? Their joining day of all days! Why?"

Powchutu studied his face for a time, then asked incredulously, "He did not tell you why she runs away? He did not explain what has happened? How did he learn of the plans for her escape? What did he say to you before he left to go after her tonight?"

White Arrow felt compelled to answer him and to learn the meaning of his confusing words. "He said he had overheard you two talking in Matu and Mahpiya Sapa's teepee."

Powchutu gasped in shock and torment, "You mean he did not know until then? It is all my fault. He knows everything now. He will surely kill her to save face and for revenge. That is why he did nothing before, he did not know the truth. It is as I thought, he went along with the joining to keep the truth hidden." Powchutu moaned in despair at his part in all of this. He was so angry and hurt that he failed to realize if his words were true, Wanmdi Hota had really come to reclaim her, even challenge for her return. Powchutu was forced to see how much Gray Eagle wanted Alisha back.

White Arrow drew him from his thoughts before he had a chance to reason it all out. "Knows what? What truth? Why do you say he will kill her to save face? She is his mate and no one knows of her attempt to escape. Your words do not make sense to me. He has no honor to protect."

"I dare not tell you the truth if you do not already know. There is another who could suffer if I speak. But I swear to you, Wanhinkpe Ska, he will find her and kill her! No doubt, he will make it look like an accident . . ."

Anger and alarm flickered in White Arrow's eyes. "You will not speak of Wanmdi Hota in this way! He would not kill Shalee. This I know! He has longed and waited to have her back with him for many moons."

"That was before he knew . . ." Powchutu eyed him carefully, then asked, "Are you truly a koda to her? Would you go against him to save her life?"

It was White Arrow's turn to eye Powchutu suspiciously. "She is truly my koda. But I would not have to stop him from killing her, for he would not."

"Even if he must kill her to save his honor? He thinks he has been tricked by her. These words must remain between us, or it could cost her life . . . if he does not take it this day. Matu changed a scar on Alisha to match the akito of Mahpiya Sapa. Then, she came to him with the story the white girl held captive by Wanmdi Hota was his lost daughter. Alisha is not Shalee. This is what Matu told us in her teepee. This is what he overheard. Wanmdi Hota has challenged for and joined a ska wincinyanna! Alisha is not half Si-ha Sapa. She is all wasichu! This is the truth he knows now. You have been his koda for many winters and you know him well. What do you think he will do to her for her part in this deceit? She let him join her knowing she was not Shalee, but his white slave. Do you think he would have fought for and joined a ska kaskapi? The mighty warrior Wanmdi Hota, feared and honored by all, even his enemies?" He laughed bitterly.

White Arrow shifted restlessly, but argued, "But he did fight for her and join her! He will surely keep this secret, so he can have her as his mate and protect his honor."

"No! He challenged before he knew she was only Alisha. He fought for Shalee! She is not Shalee! He only joined with Alisha knowing she was wasichu to save face. He has gone after her to kill her. That way, no one can ever find out the great Wanmdi Hota has been tricked by a mere white girl and he is joined to her!"

Powchutu went on angrily, "He kept the secret until she left and he could go after her and kill her in the desert. Do you think he would ever want the others to know of how he was fooled? The only way to insure silence is to kill her. No one would ever know then she was not Shalee. They will mourn the life and death of Mahpiya Sapa's Shalee and Wanmdi Hota's winyan, not Alisha's."

White Arrow glared at him, shaking his head in disbelief and disagreement. Powchutu quickly added, "That is why he did not tell you the truth. He feared you would not agree to her death, as the only solution, and would not cover for it. How will he explain this deed when he returns alone I wonder? He assumes neither Matu, nor I, will speak out against him or this deed for fear of torture or death for our part in it.

Or has he left orders for our deaths, too? You must let me go free to go after him, to stop him."

"I cannot, Powchutu, for I promised him I would hold you here and not allow you to follow them. There are reasons for what he does, and he will tell me when he returns. He would not lie to me. He goes after her to tell her the truth of his love for her. He will not hurt her. He will bring her back home with him, you'll see. . . ." He finished in trust and confidence, trying to forget the fact Wanmdi Hota had ordered Matu's death for some strange reason, and Powchutu's capture and return to the Oglala camp.

Powchutu gnawed at some of his trust and confidence with his next questions. "If he loves her as you say, then why did he push her away when she reached out to him in submission after the challenge? Why has he threatened and taunted her at every turn for the past two days? Is this his way of showing love and acceptance, or joy for their joining?"

His tone was filled with sarcasm and bitterness. "He has even made hints of danger and death to me, her koda. She is terrified of him and he has done nothing to ease this fear and doubt. This shows his love for her?"

White Arrow said, "He told me to tell everyone he has taken her away so they could be alone to talk and become kodas. I do not know of these things you speak of to me, but I trust him. Tomorrow, we will go to our village. If they do not return within two moons, we will go to look for them." He silently wondered if these things were what Wanmdi Hota had said he needed to tell him about when he returned to their camp. But why did he not speak of these things before he left? If this man's words were true, why has he been so cold and cruel to her since the challenge? I do not understand . . .

White Arrow thought suspiciously and in alarm, why had Wanmdi Hota said, "When I return," instead of "When we return"? Surely he would not . . . many times before he has hurt her and I have tried to prevent it. He knows of my true feelings for her. Does he still see her as his ska kaskapi, or as his mate now? He joined Shalee . . . but she is not Shalee! She is Alisha. White Arrow could not help but tremble in fear and doubt.

Powchutu hung his head sadly. "It will be too late in two moons, Wanhinkpe Ska, for she will be dead. She will be buried out there somewhere, and only Wanmdi Hota will know the place."

White Arrow realized he must trust his friend and his gut instincts which told him Wanmdi Hota loved Alisha, whether she was Shalee or not. No, he would not harm her.

The night slowly and painfully crawled by with both men sitting near the fire, unable to sleep or rest.

Much later, White Arrow began to talk again. "Did you encourage this new defiance to Wanmdi Hota? Did you suggest she run away tonight? Did you plan and prepare things

419

for her?''

Powchutu could only sadly nod yes to all his questions. White Arrow went on, "I have given this much thought. I am certain he knew who she really is and did not reveal it because he wanted her as his mate, and this was the only way he could ever truly have her. He also knew they would kill her for this trick, innocent or guilty. I am sure he remained silent to save her and to have her. She would no longer be his slave, but his mate to live openly with honor. He said before he left it was past time for her to know the truth of his love for her. He said he would tell her everything. You have already guessed he can speak her tongue, and yet, you did not tell her. He will tell her all these things when they stop for the night. He will let her remain Shalee so they can be together. I have seen them together many times, Powchutu, and I know they love each other. Your hate, jealousy, and love have blinded you to these facts. He will not harm her. This, I swear. He will only love and protect her."

Powchutu sadly disagreed. "He would do this secretly for Alisha, or openly for Shalee, but never openly for Alisha. Can't you see and know the difference, my koda? He has done many terrible things to her before. This time, the deed and the danger to his honor is far worse in his and your peoples' eyes than ever before. Being Shalee will not deter his punishment, for she is not Shalee. Can you be so sure he loves her, and if he does, will not harm her?"

"I have known him since childhood and we are as brothers. He has told me of his love for her, and I have seen it. Who she truly is will not matter to him, only to others."

Powchutu asked pointedly, "Did it not matter before that she is white and his enemy? Were those not the very reasons for all her torment and treatment? No, Wanhinkpe Ska, it did not matter before that he loved her, for he still hurt her. It will not matter this time either. You are the one blinded by your love for him, and her, for you see this as you wish it to be, not as it truly is."

White Arrow pondered to himself for a time, realizing even if the scout was correct, there was nothing he could do to help her or to save her this time. Could a man go against his best friend and brother even to save another's life which was so precious to him? If Wanmdi Hota truly believed he must be free of her love and this was the only way out for him, then he must allow him to make that decision, right or wrong. For he would never do such a drastic thing unless he saw it as the best and only path to take.

But could his koda live with that decision and deed once made and done? Does he seek to stop the changes she brings to his heart and mind, to his very life and existence? He has never known a winyan like her, nor ever even loved one. Could it be he does not know how to deal with the things she makes him feel for her? Do these things frighten the great warrior? He has been trained as a warrior and an Oglala, and Alisha and her love bring threats and changes to both. Does he seek to stop her spell over him, and his love for her? I pray not, for their love is stronger than death itself. I pray he does not realize this when it is too late.

Powchutu was also thinking and praying. He hoped he was wrong about this situation and Wanhinkpe Ska was right. If only Wanmdi Hota had told both of them the truth before he had left tonight. Powchutu prayed the light of love he thought he had read in Gray Eagle's eyes that day at the fort and that morning at Grota's camp was real and strong. It could be true this gives him a way to have her openly. Was it possible he would find her and somehow tell her this? But I can find no trust in my mind for him, nor the power in my heart to give her up to him. Someday, it will be different . . .

Powchutu met White Arrow's gaze and murmured, "I pray you are right, my koda, for if you are not, it will be too late for Alisha in two moons and she will be lost to us forever. Her blood will be upon our hands for allowing it."

Alisha rode beside the river bank for hours until she came to the tall tree which was bent like a crooked, old man. She looked at the map in the waning moonlight. The map indicated she should enter the stream here and ride until she came to a stand of three large trees on the left bank. She did as it implied.

When she finally came to those trees, she left the stream and headed for the tallest peak in the far range of mountains. They looked so very far away. She was so tired and sleepy and ached in every muscle of her body.

Dried sagebrushes pulled at the saddle blanket and nipped at her bare legs. She listened to the coyotes off in the distance, and to the cries of the night birds and nocturnal creatures. The sky above was clear and bright. It was filled with millions of blinking stars. They looked like diamonds scattered across a piece of black velvet with candlelight shimmering on them. The full, platinum moon gave her plenty of light to travel by.

She was fully aware of the vast emptiness and loneliness of the open plains. The solitude and eerie shadows cast by the moonlight made her tense with fear. She wished now she had let Powchutu come along. She thought about the plans to meet in a few days, but until then . . .

She would occasionally stop riding and walk for a time, allowing her horse to relax and rest. She would hold water in her two, cupped hands for him to drink, then stroke his nose and neck softly while speaking to him in a gentle tone. He would soon be accustomed to her voice and touch, and would obey her every command quickly and confidently.

Her father had taught her a great deal about horses and their treatment. He had told her many times about how important it was to constantly touch and speak with them. This developed a closeness which inspired trust and dependability in the animal toward his master. She would rub his forelegs each time they halted to rest. Gray Eagle watched this love, care and gentleness she gave to Wildfire. He was pleased and touched by it.

Then she would mount up and ride on for what seemed like many more hours, until she came to the large group of boulders marked on the little map. She halted to check the map to be sure she was right. She got down and studied the little map, trying to judge the distance to those bluffs marked on it.

She tied Wildfire's reins to a sagebrush and gazed at the rugged terrain before her. She had failed to realize she was heading west, not east, as she should have been if the map had been drawn by Powchutu.

Each time she studied the map and the landscape, he feared she would catch this clue and realize it was she who had been tricked, not he. Such blind faith and trust in an unworthy koda, he thought . . .

She guessed the distance to the odd-shaped, high bluff marked on her map. Her finger traced over the large, dark X drawn there and sighed heavily. The mountains looked almost close enough to reach out and touch, but then so far, she felt she would never make it there.

Distance and timing were so deceiving on the plains and prairies, for what appeared a short distance, could go on and on for miles and miles, hours and hours. Knowing this from her trip out here, she tried to decide if she should push on immediately or rest for a while here. They had travelled for hours and Wanmdi Hota would be unconscious until morning. What harm could it do to rest there for a short time? No one would know of her escape until morning when he told them. That is, if he tells them before he comes after me . . . surely there was enough time for a brief rest.

She strolled around for a little while, trying to relax and limber up strained, taut muscles. She was so weary and sleepy. She should have taken a nap this afternoon. She walked back to her horse and spoke softly to him as she took a blanket from his back to ward off the slight chill of the night.

"We'll rest here for a little while, Wildfire, then push on to the mountains. You eat and rest, my beauty. I'm sure you're just as tired and sleepy as I am. Guard us well."

She sat down on the ground beside the rocks which had been marked on her map and leaned back against one to rest her weary head, eyes and body. Soon, without realizing what was happening, she closed her eyes and was fast asleep.

Gray Eagle patted Wildfire's nose and stroked his alert ears. Alisha should have known from the strange, splotched markings he was Chula's son. The gift had been from Gray Eagle, not White Arrow. He came to stand in front of her and gaze down into her sleeping face. Istimna, Cinstinna. I will watch over you, he thought protectively. He took his blanket and sat down upon it not far from hers.

He shortly arose to go for a sleeping skin to place on the ground beside her. She was slowly sinking to the earth as she fully relaxed in peaceful slumber. She was soon to the ground and snuggled into the warmth and softness of his sleeping skin. He smiled to himself and vowed, this will be your last night to be cold and alone, Cinstinna. From now on, you will sleep warm and safe in my arms.

Fingers of warm sunlight danced and played across her face and eyes, bringing her to alertness. She sat up, yawning and stretching. She opened her eyes very slowly, then instantly froze. Her heart caught in her throat.

Directly in front of her, about three feet away, sat Wanmdi Hota chewing nonchalantly on a dried twig. He was resting in a squatting position, sitting on his haunches. He was leisurely gazing at her, or should she say smiling at her like the cat who had eaten the canary!

Her eyes darted back and forth until she knew there was no path or hope of escape. She was trapped! There was no place to run or hide. Their roles were cast and this drama must be played out, no matter the climax.

She returned his bold stare for a long time, just waiting . . . "I guess it's your move first, Wanmdi Hota. What will it be this time—slow torture or quick death?" She watched him closely for a clue.

He seemed to ignore her words and continued to study the girl he had joined last night. He was trying to find the words to begin to tell her all the things it was past time for her to know. He noted the rising panic in her eyes at his silence.

She thought wildly, so he had known every-thing, even about her plan to escape. Had he cunningly pulled her same trick and disposed of the potion? She paled, then reddened. That meant he had been awake the whole time last night! He had let her make a complete fool of herself while he pretended to have passed out! Shame and anger flooded her at the same time. He must have been trailing her all night. Powchutu should have . . . Powchutu! Wanmdi Hota must have known about his part in all of this and had waited to trick them. She had innocently played right into his scheme to get her alone!

She frantically asked, "What have you done with Powchutu? Did you kill him? He was only trying to . . ." She lowered her head and began to cry, certain of his fate at Wanmdi Hota's hands.

"It's all my fault. I should never have agreed to this plot. I should have remained there and taken any punishment you dealt out."

He spoke slow and even, "He is safe for now. I will deal with him later."

She shouted at him, "You knew! You knew all along and only waited to trick me! Well, what are you waiting for? Kill me and get it over with! That's why you followed me, isn't it?"

He grinned mischievously and mocked, "Why should I kill my wife?"

She automatically retorted, "Because you're cruel and brutal! Because you . . ."

Her mouth fell open and her eyes widened in disbelief and shock. She stared at him in complete astonishment. "You're speaking English . . ." She glared at him dumbfoundedly, then screamed angrily, "You're speaking English!"

Chapter Nine

Gray Eagle answered her easily and matter-of-factly, "Yes, I can speak the wasichu tongue."

In bone-chilling horror, she realized how very well and easily he did so. She accused, "You could all along . . . this whole time I've been with you and known you . . . every, single word I've ever said, you've heard and understood . . . all this time and never a word from you . . ."

Her hand flew to her mouth in shock, as if this action could recall all the words she had ever uttered in his presence. Full comprehension set in. Every, single word, every time and place, he had heard and known all.

It all flashed vividly and quickly before her mind. That night in the smokehouse . . . during those long, terrifying hours of the torture of her people and herself . . . all those nights in his teepee . . . the teepee Sa . . . her escape . . . his recapture of her . . . her icapsinte . . . the begging and pleading . . . the love and hate . . . the passion . . . Chela's icapsinte . . . her selling to Mato Waditaka . . . the challenge . . . the cave . . . the wedding . . . last night . . . most of all, last night!

Memories of many words and times of love, hate, happiness and suffering flooded her mind.

He had heard them all, understood them, and kept his silence! Her face would flame red, then pale as white as snow. Her eyes would flash hate, anger, revenge and betrayal with each new thought and memory. Her silence seemed endless as he waited . . .

He was giving her the time to get over the initial shock of this discovery, and time to work out some of her deepest resentment. It would be easier to deal with them if she let go and let it storm out. It must spill forth and not be allowed to stay inside where it would fester and grow into real hate and bitterness.

She suddenly screamed at him, "Why? How could even you do such a cruel thing to me? All along you've heard and known the Hell I was going through, and you said nothing? Nothing! You kept your mouth shut and let me suffer like that in silence! Only a few words and you denied me even that much? How you must hate me to have done such an evil thing. You've never said a word, nothing . . . not even a hint . . ."

Tears of anguish and betrayal clouded her vision. She whispered, "Why now? Is it because I'm going to die and it doesn't matter if I know now? I'll not be able to spill your evil secret, just like Ben? Did you save this for your best and final torture?"

She glared at him, but he remained silent again, for now. He was hoping for her to rid herself of some of the hate and hurt she was feeling before he attempted to tell her everything. He must wait until she settled down and was ready to listen, really listen, with her heart.

"How could you treat me like this? To use me so coldly and never say anything! Why aren't you laughing at my stupidity? Why don't you taunt me for being so dumb and naive? All those times I thought you had some magic power and could read my very thoughts . . ." She laughed almost hysterically. "But you didn't have to read my mind, did you? Little Lese told you everything you ever wanted or needed to know. The times I bared my very heart and soul to you!" she exclaimed bitterly.

Tears flowed freely down her flushed cheeks, emotions constricted her throat as she lashed out at him in fierce anger and anguish, "You betrayer! You liar! You . . . you . . . I hate you . . . I hate you!" She lunged at him, clawing, slapping, kicking and screaming.

He seized her flaying hands and wrestled her struggling body to the ground and pinned her beneath him. She continued to struggle until she was panting breathlessly. She yelled insults and threats at him. It had not taken long for his brute strength to overpower her and imprison her. Still, he did not speak, but only stared at her, grinning.

Her chest heaved in a fight for air from her heated exertions. Anger and frustration were evident in her flushed face and bright, emerald eyes. She shrieked at him, "If you don't kill me this time, I will run away again! Every time you find me and bring me back I'll fight you all the way. I'll keep on trying until either I succeed or die from one of your icapsintes. Perhaps that's the only way I'll ever be free of you. I'll defy and rebel and run away every chance I get! I'll force you to keep on punishing me until one day you'll go too far and kill me. I'll never forgive you for this. Never!''

She appeared to have exerted most of her energy and talked most of her feelings out loud. He threw back his head and laughed in her face! What a tantrum! Anger and hate glittered in those bright eyes of hers as he had hoped his laughter would accomplish. He needed to get her mind off of hurt and betrayal. Anger and fire would help him dispel her mistrust in him and hopefully bring acceptance of his words.

He calmly spoke to her, ''No, Cinstinna. You'll never trick or force me into the icapsinte again. That was a very bad, almost deadly, mistake on my part. I almost lost you the last time. Never again! Hear me well, Lese, you are mine. I will never allow you to leave me, nor will I allow you to force me to hurt or kill you. Ni-ye mitawa! That means, 'you are mine.'''

She recalled hearing that phrase before, but when? She comprehended her total helplessness and relaxed under his grip and power. His words were strange and confusing. He was supposed to be taunting, threatening and laughing. He should be trying to hurt and punish her, even killing her, but he did none of those things. What was this new game he played?

''Why, Wanmdi Hota? Why do you wish to

torment me so? Why do you hate me so much?"
New tears now flowed from the corners of her
eyes and down into her hair. She had ceased all
struggles and lay submissively beneath him.

He gazed deeply into her eyes and answered,
"You bring much of the hurt and suffering on
yourself, Lese. You have known and learned
what is expected of you, but you continue to
resist and fight doing it. You defy me at every
turn. You rebel and disobey. You interfere with
my leadership and authority before my people.
You try to shame and dishonor me with your
actions and words. You gave me no choice but
to try to subdue and cower you with fear and
power. Didn't you see I gave no punishment or
shame when you behaved as you should?
Couldn't you see and feel my tenderness to you
when you allowed me to show it? You knew I
could not take you openly and love you before
the eyes of my people. Yet, you tried to force me
to choose your side or theirs many times. You
forced me to either cower or strike out at you,
and I could not cower before you. Didn't you see
we had to live two lives, one in my teepee, and
one in the eyes of my people? In your heart you
knew this, but refused to accept and do it. You
demanded what I could not give to you. You
demanded my honor for your love."

He carefully observed her expressions as he
spoke to her. "You must learn to bend your will
to mine. I am your mate, and a warrior. I am the
chief's son and the next Oglala chief. I can show
no weakness. You must do all I command, with

respect and honor to me. As for hating you, I do not and never have. I have loved you and wanted you since that first day I was brought into your fortress and saw you. I desired you, and I took you! Many times I have tested your courage, wisdom, and strength. I have also allowed my heart and feelings to test your love and the right to belong to me. You ran from me last night for the same reason you ran away before. You ran from fear, mistrust, and your love for me. Was it so degrading and terrible to fall in love with an Indian, an enemy?"

He challenged her to answer him. She was staring at him with suspicion and disbelief in her eyes.

She instantly retaliated with, "Is it so degrading and terrible to fall in love with a wasichu, a ska wincinyanna? Must I accept and love you, and expect no love and acceptance in return?" Their eyes fused in challenge to her words. She was totally bewildered by his words and feared to glean the truth from them.

He laughed and quipped, "Only when that ska wincinyanna refuses to be tamed ‚and respectful!"

She retorted, "Those were not the only reasons I . . ." She stopped immediately as he lifted his eyebrows in interest. Was he trying to trick her in some new way? He noted the new flicker of suspicion and doubt.

He continued for her, "And what is the other reason you ran from me?" He wanted her to come to him with the truth, with complete faith and trust, but he saw her hurt was still too fresh in her mind and heart at this moment.

"What do you plan to do with me this time? Does this new defiance rate ten lashes with the whip?" she asked very sarcastically. "Or does it rate another visit to the teepee sa? Who will it be this time, Wanhinkpe Ska again or another friend?"

His eyes darkened and narrowed in anger. "You are not a fool, Lese, so don't talk like one! You know why I took you there before, and you also know nothing happened to you. I will never allow any man to take you that way, not Wanhinkpe Ska, nor Powchutu, nor Mato Waditaka. No one, ever! I was only trying to quell your defiance and force you to cling only to me for love and protection. I also wanted to instill such fear in your heart for my anger that it would force you to never defy me again before my people. Did you think I could allow you to force the council to demand your life and blood in payment for your dishonor to me, their leader? I wanted you to see and know you needed and loved only me. The icapsinte is the law of our tribe. I was powerless to stop it and furious at you for bringing it upon yourself. I foolishly believed I could control the whip and did the punishment myself instead of the ceremonial chief as is the custom. But I found the whip had a mind of its own and would not be controlled. Our law says five lashes, and it would have shown weakness to have given less. I felt each one of those lashes myself, as if it were me taking the beating instead of you. You do not know how I panicked and suffered when I thought I had killed you. You do not know how deeply and cruelly your last words and looks cut into my heart. You do not know how I prayed all night at your side, begging the Great Spirit to spare your life and return your spirit to me. You do not know of the pride and love I felt watching your great courage at the post. I was greatly honored by it in the eyes of my people. They still speak of the grass-eyed, white girl with the heart of the bear. You showed more courage and bravery than most men do at the stake. My people respect and honor you for this, and for the kindness and friendship you have shown to us. They know what you did for me at your fortress, even when we were still enemies. You were working your way into their hearts. This was what I worked and waited for. When this happened, then I would have been freed to accept you openly as my woman, but I would never have been able to join with you.

"They expect and demand much from their leader, as they should. Wanhinkpe Ska does not feel this demand for extra strength, greater honor and wisdom which I must have and show as their leader. I am sorry I took his friendship from you. I feared you were turning to him more and more, and I could not permit this. His willing acceptance made my seemingly cold rejection harder and crueler for you to bear and understand. I will no longer deny you his friendship.

"I am also shamed for the destruction of your locket. I reacted in jealousy and anger. I thought the man to be a wasichu you had loved and lost. I could not bear the look of love I read in your eyes for him. When I heard your words of pain, it was too late to save it.

"The day you ran away from me, I was blinded and filled with rage at your dishonor of my trust in you. I came back that day to tell you all that was within my heart for you. Our hearts and loves had touched and joined that night before and I believed you were ready to hear and learn all these things. My anger at your betrayal was so great I could not think. After the icapsinte, I swore to reveal the truth to you as soon as you woke up, but the bluecoats came and took you away before I could tell you. When I bluffed your release at their fort, I knew and felt your hurt and shame that day, but I could not risk their hatred for my turning on you. For your safety and my honor, I had to treat you coldly and cruelly before them all.

"I felt and saw you reach out to me on the way back to my village. I thought in a few days you would relax and accept my taking you again. After Chela's attempt to kill you, I came to you to tell you all that night, but you had cried yourself to sleep. I was angered at my near loss of you and for your renewal of defiance and dishonor to me again so soon after our truce. I was waiting for you to awaken the next morning so I could come to you with open heart, but again, it was not to be. Mahpiya Sapa came to take you from me. If I had tried to explain things to you that day, you would have been too hurt to listen and believe me, and the truth could have cost your life. I had to remain silent until I could find some way to help you without it being dangerous to you. At that time, I also did not know the full truth of your part, if any, in the deception. I knew if I allowed you to be accepted as this Shalee, then I could join with you."

Alisha did not fully grasp what he was telling her here, for he was saying he knew at that time she was not Shalee.

"You tried in every way to kill the love you felt for me. I could not tell you of the things I felt for you until I was sure you loved me completely and would come to me willingly and trustingly. That day we left the fort, I thought you had done this, for I only saw love and trust in your eyes for that day and the next.

"You must see and fully understand my position as the leader of my people. I could not allow even the woman I loved and wanted to shame me before them. I could not help you find this love, acceptance and trust in me. It had to come from you willingly and openly.

"I wanted you to love me and desire me as a man, not as your owner and master."

Alisha spoke up here, "Are you trying to tell me that all that cruelty and torture were lessons in obedience and love? You beat me and shamed me to make this learning and accepting easier for me? You have the nerve to say all my suffering was my fault? I can't believe I hear you correctly! My fault!" She glared at him in astonishment and spat at him, "All it would have taken to have won this love, trust, and acceptance you say you wanted from me and worked so hard to get was just a little kindness and love from you. All it would have taken would have been just a few words of teaching and gentleness to let me know you cared at all, or how to behave correctly."

He lightly taunted, "Do you mean to tell me if you had known I could speak your tongue, you would have submissively accepted the deaths of those men and your place as my kaskapi? You would not have begged and pleaded for their release even more so with words? If you had known I heard and understood, but would not listen or change my mind, you would have done nothing, but quietly accept what you could not change?"

She realized the point he was making and did not answer. He went on, "I believe you would have rebelled even more with words, insults and screams. Do you know what I would have been forced to do to you for that? Do you think for a moment my people would have stood by watching a white captive taunt and defy their leader? Which was more important, your life or my silence?

"Besides, you would never have spoken so freely before me if you had known I heard you. How would I have known the feelings in your heart for me? How would I have known you and your ways? Would you have heard me say 'I love you' with one breath, then 'You must go to Mato Waditaka' with the next, and have trusted me? What would your heart have felt then; if not the final betrayal?

"Do you forget we met as enemies? Did I not have to learn to trust in you also? I have known no woman, such as you before. At first, I believed I only desired you as a woman, but I came to know I loved and wanted you for yourself, enemy or not. Can you not think what I felt wanting you and loving you, but knowing I could never really have you completely? Do you know I could have been forced to give you up when I joined Chela, just in order to keep peace? Can't you see, with you as Shalee, I was freed to love and take you openly?

"When I first saw you at your fortress, I thought you mad. I slowly came to see your love and kindness were real. Still, I could not bring myself to allow a white woman to help me. Can you not imagine what it would be like to be a warrior who had been foolish enough to be captured by his enemies, then treated as I was? Do you know how I felt to be whipped for no reason, to be openly taunted and called such vile names, to be bound helplessly like some rabbit, to be so shamed and dishonored? I was filled

440

with rage and bitterness, shame and vengeance. I struck out at you because you were one of them, and you were vulnerable. I saw you were special to the men there. I was going to use you to taunt them with. I was going to punish you for the feelings you stirred in me against my will. I needed to force you to hate me, for I could resist a cold, hating woman far easier than a warm, loving one. But I was defeated, for you came to love and want me as I did you. You made resisting you painfully impossible. It was a good thing you never realized the power your love carried. Even though I tell you this now, do not ever try to use this truth against me, Alisha. The only thing which has changed, is you are now my mate, but you are still mine and under my power.

"When I attacked you in the smokehouse, I wanted to see how deep your feelings were. I wanted to see how much you were willing to suffer for my protection, to see if it went so far as to save my life. Your courage was even greater than I had thought. I hurt you greatly that night, not only your hand, but your heart. This I saw in your eyes and heard in your voice. That was the very moment I knew I must have you. I knew where you would hide during an attack and that you would be safe. I overheard your uncle and the big man called Ben speaking of this hiding place. I knew I would be back for you."

Alisha was beginning to understand Wanmdi

Hota, but she still could not accept the truth of his words. "But I don't understand why you took those men back to your camp to torture them. Why didn't you just kill them all at the fortress? You forced me to watch all that brutality, then expected me to turn to you in love? How could you think I could come to you willingly after I had endured such things? Didn't you stop to think I would believe I was also there for your revenge? It seemed you took only those who were connected with your treatment at our fortress," she said in puzzlement.

"You were there because I wanted you. The gold sash said you were mine. But at that time, you were only a white slave who was both beautiful and desirable to me, or so I thought! The others were there for punishment. Not only for what they did to me, but for what they did to Chenuhula and Okiliea."

He saw her bewildered look and explained, "Chenuhula was an Oglala brave and Okiliea was his younger sister. They had gone to the forest beyond your fortress to gather plants for medicines. On their return trip, those three men attacked them, killing Chenuhula and raping Okiliea brutally many times. She later managed to get close enough to our village for one of our people to find her. She told us of the three men who did this thing to her and her brother before she died from her injuries. We found where your people tried to hide his body and brought it home for burial.''

"But how could they do such a terrible thing and to a stranger? To kill for no reason, to hurt the girl so badly she died?'' Alisha was feeling the pain and shame the Indian girl must have felt for she had endured a similar incident. She glared at him and angrily accused, "But you did the same evil thing! You raped me!''

"But I took you with love and gentleness! They took her with hate and brutality. There is a big difference!''

He watched to see if she disagreed with him. She stared at him for a time, but did not argue his point. "They killed Chenuhula because he was Indian. Okiliea was only thirteen winters old,'' he added bitterly.

Alisha gasped, "Thirteen! That's only a child! How could they do such a vile thing? I saw how cruel they were to you, but to such a young, innocent girl . . . Jed, Horace, and Ben? Ben . . .'' She had been right before when she said she did not know or belong with those people. Her eyes nervously darted about as she was trying to accept this new, disturbing discovery. Then her eyes met his gaze.

"Powchutu told me at the fort why the others had been killed. That was also for punishment. If you had told me the truth at that time, would I have believed or listened or trusted you? I honestly don't know, Wanmdi Hota. Who can truly say what they would have done or said at another time?''

He happily realized she was listening and trying to understand what he was saying to her. She does not close her heart and mind to me yet, he thought. Already she accepts my words, even those that contradict hers. This is very hard for her to hear. She was no longer screaming at him. She had stopped her crying. She was truly listening and trying to find the truth. More than that, she had not called him a liar and her eyes said she trusted what he had just said. If only he could help her to trust him completely and believe all his words.

"Powchutu has filled your head and heart with many lies and fears, Lese. He wishes to destroy your love for me. He wishes you to turn to him, for he loves you and will do anything to have you."

She met his gaze with surprise. "Powchutu loves me? But we are only good friends! You sound as if you mean he loves me as a man loves a woman. I don't understand what you mean. He only loves me like a sister. He only seeks to help and protect me. Why would you think otherwise?"

"He was not helping you flee for your life or from my hate. He was trying to help you escape from me so he could follow you and force you to turn to him. I had Wanhinkpe Ska stop him and hold him there. He knows I speak your tongue, but did not tell you. This is why he always spoke the truth before me, but lied to you in secret, telling you I hated you and would kill you. I had

444

told him I loved you and would not harm you again. I brought him here to speak with you, to tell you what had truly happened to you that morning in my camp, and to ask you to join with me, but he would not. He knows the words of Wanmdi Hota are true, but denies them.''

Stunned by this confusing revelation and recalling Powchutu's numerous, strange words of warning about silence to her, she asked, ''You mean he knew and did not tell me these things? He tricked me and lied to me? He is the one person I felt I could truly and completely trust, even with my life.'' He saw her eyes fill with pain at this knowledge, but again, she believed Gray Eagle.

''Not at first, Lese. He spoke the truth to you at the fort. But he loved you even then, for I saw it in his eyes when he begged for your life and safety. He offered his life in exchange for yours. He even challenged me if I dared to hurt you again! He did not know of my secret until I went to him for help. Then, he only suspected it. He was certain when he saw my face when you spoke at the challenge. I realized he had guessed the truth, but I knew he would not tell you. Partly because he knew how it would hurt you to learn I had always heard your words of love and pleas for mercy and had said nothing. He was very angry and spiteful and felt I had tricked both of you. But what he said and did at the Si-ha Sapa camp was done and said in hate of me, and in love of you. He also knew if he told you the truth, you would immediately come to me to see for yourself. If you had come to me, I would have confessed the truth then, and he did not wish for you to learn of my love for you. He wanted you to go on believing I hated and rejected you. He knew I would love and keep you always, now that we are joined.''

She looked up at him in doubt and asked, ''Would you still love and want me and keep me as your wife if I were . . . only Lese, the white girl you captured and not this . . . Shalee, Mahpiya Sapa's daughter?''

He calmly asked, ''Are you only Alisha, my little white slave?''

She smiled for a minute, staring at the mocking grin on his handsome face. She tartly replied, ''Yes!'' Get it in the open, Lese, and deal with the consequences now, she thought. Besides, he already knows the truth.

He seriously asked, ''Does Lese love Wanmdi Hota as much as Shalee would have?'' He nearly caught her off guard.

''I cannot speak for this Shalee, but Lese . . .'' She halted and spoke angrily, ''You mock me, Wanmdi Hota! What difference would either answer make? Besides, you already know the answer, since you know my tongue so well. You must be acutely aware of my love for you, for I have spoken of my feelings for you many times.''

He nodded and said, ''I only wished to hear you say it again.'' He repeated her words at the joining, "'Forever one together and yet apart.' You said you would love me forever. Did you not mean this?"

She stared into his ebony eyes with the dancing lights, trying to read the truth there. How could he have always heard all her words and never have responded to them before?

"If you really loved and wanted me, then why did you push me away in the cave, and why didn't you take me last night?" She asked these two questions, recalling the shame and agony he had put her through both times.

"I had only meant to hold and kiss you in the cave, and to let you draw comfort from my arms, and to drive away some of your fears and doubts. I did not expect your heated response so soon. I, too, was lost in the passion of our love. When Wanhinkpe Ska came to get us, I knew I had let things go too far. I knew it was not the place or time for our next joining of love. You cried out to me for help, and I gave it in the only way open to me. Last night, I was trying to make you want to stay with me. I wanted you to see and feel how much we loved and wanted each other. I knew if I took you, then I would not be able to let you go. Then, you would never believe you had stayed because you wanted to. You would think I had tricked you in a moment of weakness for me. Did you not feel how much I wanted you both times? If you had come back to our mat and stayed that last time you kissed me and hesitated, I would have taken you then and loved you. I would have told you the truth at that time. Do you know how much it took not to force you to stay with me, not to make love to you? Never have I done anything harder in my life than to remain still while you cried and told me how much you loved me. I thought it best to let you go, then follow, so we could be alone and far away for this talk. I did not know how you would react, or what you would do. There is nothing here to interrupt us."

For some reason, Ben's face and cruel death flashed before her and she said, "Ben knew and was about to tell me the day you killed him. He was trying to say, 'the brave can . . . speak.' For that you killed him?"

He quickly answered, "Yes! He was going to tell you and it was not time for you to know this yet, and not from him. He would have died that day anyway. He only made it happen sooner and quicker." He released his hold on her and let her sit up, confident she would not try to flee or fight him.

"Poor Ben . . ." she sighed sadly.

But he retorted, "Poor Okiliea . . ." She glared at him for a moment in bereavement for her friend, then lowered her eyes in understanding.

Remembering what she had said to him only moments before, she reminded him, "I told you I am not Shalee. It was all a trick. I am only Alisha and I am white, Wanmdi Hota, all white . . ."

She waited tensely for his reaction. . . . He smiled at her and said, "I know this. I knew it even before I heard the talk in Matu's teepee. I knew this the day they came and took you away."

In total confusion she asked, "Then why did you let them take me? If you loved me and knew the truth, then why did you not speak up? You knew what I felt! Why the challenge? You could have been killed for a white kaskapi."

"I have seen you naked many times. I know every mark upon your body." Her face modestly flamed at his words. He continued, "I knew the scar was only a half-moon. I could not guess how it had come to be an akito, nor who had done it. I did not know at that time if you knew about it, or had anything to do with the change. I was confused, angry and upset, and could not think right. When Matu said she had seen it before your rescue by the bluecoats, I knew it had not been done at the fort. I could only guess Matu was in on it. I learned the full truth at the same time you did. If I had told Mahpiya Sapa the half-truth at my camp that morning, he would have demanded your death for this trick. I had no choice but to remain in silence. I also knew if they accepted you as his Shalee, we would be joined and I could have you openly in honor as my mate. The only thing I had not counted on was Mato Waditaka. If necessary, I would have killed him before I would have allowed him to take you."

"Are you telling me you will keep this a secret? You will allow me to pretend to be this Shalee to all the others?" She could hardly believe her ears! Did she hear his words correctly? She eyed him curiously and replied, "I don't believe you, Wanmdi Hota. This must be a trick, a new taunt. What is your game this time? Surely you can't expect me to accept that you have loved me all this time? What kind of lover humiliates and tortures and hurts the one he claims to love? I can never forgive or forget the things you have done to me. Especially when you could have told me why, but did not. If you truly loved me, you would not have let me suffer like that for so many weeks. You would not have done those terrible things to me."

He confidently stated, "In time, Lese, you will be forced to trust and accept me. But until then, if you make it necessary, you will live with me as my kaskapi and wayakayuha. I'll keep you under guard during the day and bound to me at night. The choice is yours—winyan and wayakayuha! Knowing your words, I have also heard your words of hatred and spite to me. I had to wait until I was sure of your love, and now I am. Do not fight what we both want, to be together in love."

She thought and studied on all he had just told her and was even more bewildered and confused. She queried, "Why should I believe you or trust you?"

He calmly answered, "Because you love me

450

and want me. Also, you need me as much as I need you. It is right we should be joined, no matter our differences in colors and peoples. Our spirits and hearts are already joined. Why shouldn't our lives be joined also? Do you know how I felt each time you reached out to others and not to me? Do you know how it cut my heart to hear your cries and to be unable to help you and comfort you? I am an Oglala warrior, my people's next chief, Lese! It has been hard for me to deal with the things I felt, and still feel, for you, my wasichu enemy. Many times my heart and mind have battled against all I have ever known and learned since boyhood. A warrior should never feel fear, Lese, but I feared the things you brought into my life.''

Alisha pondered on all the things Powchutu had told her about warriors and their society. She recalled his words about the great importance of honor and pride. She also recalled what he had told her about the mighty warrior Wanmdi Hota himself. Was he not telling her many of the same things she had learned for herself?

Still, this sudden, drastic about-face was difficult to accept so quickly and completely. She gazed into his eyes, longing to believe every word he said and to trust him completely. But, did she dare? What if this was all some cruel joke? Was he speaking the truth? Could he really have loved her all this time and still remained silent? Could he have put her through so much heartache and never tried to comfort her? Could his pride and honor before his people be that important to him? Did the sham of her being Shalee free him to love her openly as he had said? Had her heart guessed right on the way back from the fort when she believed he had reached out to her in love? Could she take the chance he spoke the truth, that this was not a new torture? Her mind reeled in confusion and doubt.

She quietly spoke, "I can't afford to believe you, Wanmdi Hota. You have given me no reasons to trust you. A few words cannot erase the actions and sufferings of many, many days. I dare not hope for what you say to be true, for I could not endure it if you were lying. I must not love you. I must forget you. If you love me as you say you do, then let me go. We cannot find love and happiness together for your people would not permit it. Then one day you would turn on me again. You would tire of me, for you will always think of me as white and beneath the love of a great Oglala warrior, especially a chief. You would take another from among your own kind. Then what would I have? I would have no one, and I would only be Wanmdi Hota's ex-squaw. No! That is not enough for me." Her eyes were filled with anguish as they begged for him to prove her wrong.

"It is too late for that now, Lese. Your love runs deep and strong. Your heart belongs to me—and your life does as well. I have tried to tell you and show you how I feel about you, but you are too frightened to see and hear the truth. You must believe me, for I do not taunt you. There is much for you to forgive, but you love me and you can do it. I cannot let you go for you are the very air I breathe. You are as much a part of me as my own body. I cannot free you, for I love you too much to let you go. Many times before I have thought this and now I will say it to you, I will have your love, or I will have your hate, but I will have you! You were sent to me by the Great Spirit to fill my life. You are mine! I will never tire of you and I will always keep you with me. This, I swear to you! My people will permit it if you will remain Shalee in their sight. I do not like it to be this way, but if we are to have each other openly, then it must be. Can you not understand this and accept it for me, for us? You must take this chance. Give me time to earn your trust, this is all I ask. Do not close your heart to me. Forgive what I have done and give me this time." He let the cool, facial mask lower completely to allow her to read his very soul.

She stared into the brave's eyes filled with love and desire, and pleaded, "Please don't be lying to me, Wanmdi Hota, for I can stand no more hating and suffering. I cannot live this way any longer. Love me, or free me! If you can love as deeply as you can hate, then I will have enough to last a lifetime. Are you sure you do not still

453

hate me and see me as white?"

"I love you more than my own life. I would have died in the challenge before I would have given you up forever to another. I do not see you as wasichu or Si-ha Sapa. I see you as Alisha, the woman I love. I would have let you and the others go on believing you are Shalee. I do not wish to see you hurt in any way. The morning of the challenge when you came to me, I could not tell you the truth, or that I loved you and I was doing this to get you back for myself. If I was to be the one to die, I thought it best you remember me in hate and anger to help you get over my death and forget me. It would have been cruel to tell you I love you, then die and leave you forever. But, I could not bear not to try to ease some of your fears and hurts. Why did you think I rescued you from the fort, then came to challenge for you, if I did not love you?"

Alisha replied, "I believed you did everything for your honor and pride. Would you have let me go on for the rest of my life loving you and believing you hated me? It would not have been crueler to hear the truth! It would have given my life and your death some meaning! Don't you know how very important and precious those few words would have been if I had lost you to death? The loss of you would have been terrible to bear, but never having known of your love would have been far worse." Tears filled her eyes, spilled over her lids and down her cheeks.

"I am sorry, Lese. I did not think of it that

way. This is hard for me to say, for Wanmdi Hota asks forgiveness from no one, nor does he say the words of apology lightly. There are many times I have been wrong. I ask your forgiveness and I tell you I am sorry for all I have done. But, all I did, I did because I loved you and wanted you.''

She lifted her tear-filled eyes to his and saw he spoke the truth. He was not a man to say such things and not mean them. She asked, "What about Chela? When will you have to join with her? How soon do I have to share you with someone who wishes me dead? Will I also have to share you with others?''

He laughed and said, "No, jealous wife. I know of the wasichu way, to have only one mate. Chela is to join with Mato Waditaka. I do not want her near us. I told them I neither wanted nor needed any other wife but you. You will share me with no one, Cinstinna. I love only you, Lese.''

She could not suppress the look of delight and relief in her face and eyes. He was lost in the warmth of her smile for a time. They talked on and on for a long time . . . She questioned and he answered . . . she argued and he rebuffed . . . on and on the words and feelings spilled forth until all had been said, forgiven and accepted by both of them.

Gray Eagle stood up and walked around, loosening up his muscles tired from his fear of rejection. Alisha sat thinking on all he had said to her. He gave her all the time she needed to settle these thoughts. He rubbed Wildfire's nose and spoke softly to him. Wildfire nestled his nose in Wanmdi Hota's hand and neighed in answer.

He felt her gaze following him. He had always been aware of her feelings about his looks, for she had been unable to hide her attraction to him. He was glad she was pleased and attracted to him. I must use this desire to help break that final resistance, he thought. He came and stood before her. She looked upon his muscular, lean body; that handsome face; the flashing, ebony eyes, and that beguiling, devilish smile.

Her breath caught in her throat and passion leaped into her eyes. Why did he always have this effect on her? How could she resist and turn her heart from him? Did he not offer her what she had longed for? Could she refuse to give him a chance? No . . .

Alisha held her hand up to him and he took it. She pulled him down to sit beside her. She cautiously asked, "If I say I will give you the chance to teach me trust and love, what would you say?".

He smiled warmly at her and said, "You must promise to accept all you said as truth and law at the joining ceremony last night. You must willingly give me your heart and life."

She looked at him confusedly and replied, "But you ask for what you already possess."

But he asked again, "Do you promise all of this to me willingly?"

She was not sure if she understood his full meaning, but she replied, "I do, Wanmdi Hota."

He could not stop the sigh of relief from escaping his throat, nor the look of triumph in his eyes. He was amused when she mockingly asked, "And do you promise these things to me willingly and truthfully?"

He grinned and replied, "I did and have since the day in the smokehouse when I branded you mine with my teeth. I will love you always. I will never forsake you in life or death. I will always protect you, even with my life. I will rule you justly. I will provide for you and with the help of the Great Spirit, I give you children."

Alisha watched him as he spoke the joining words in English so she could hear and know their meaning from him. She could not suppress a giggle at the way he had looked and sounded as he spoke those words. Her eyes danced with laughter and happiness.

His face went solemn as he said, "It is good to hear your laughter again, Cinstinna. It is good to see the smile and light return to your eyes. There have been too many tears and too much sadness. It is time for smiles and joy. We have found our time and place for love. It is here and now."

His words were like music to her heart and it jumped with joy. She threw herself into his arms and hugged him tightly and possessively. He looked into her face and eyes and said huskily, "Waste cedake . . . I love you, Lese."

His mouth closed over hers in a tender kiss of love as they slowly sank to the ground, oblivious to all but each other and their need for each other. She had not known love could be so much more than she had already known with him. But somehow, it was deeper, richer and fuller when it was shared and returned.

They lay there in the warm sunlight, kissing deeply and hungrily.

They lay entwined in the arms of love. His kisses burned like the desert sun across her face and throat. He whispered soft words of love and endearment to her, sparking her response to him. Her blood raced wildly through her veins. It pounded instinctively in demand for fulfillment.

Her hands caressed his hard back with light, tender touches and then hard, passionate caresses. She pulled him even closer and tighter to her, inspiring him to bolder moves. He nibbled at her lips and ears with light bites and kisses. He moved away for a moment to remove her dress and his clothing. For the first time, she felt no embarrassment or shyness at the sight of their naked bodies in the bold daylight.

He came back to her and began to fondle and touch her in the new and daring ways he had done last night. He explored every inch and recess of her mouth and body, as she did his. He teased and tantalized her again and again with lips and hands. She moaned in desire and pleasure and begged for even more. He was sending fires leaping and raging through her. There was no holding back in any way with either of them.

Her head rolled from side to side as he nibbled and caressed her breasts which were swollen with hunger and passion. She found the intoxicating thrill and joy of touching him and bringing him the same joys he gave to her. Boldly and heatedly she gave and took with a new hunger and desire.

When he finally entered her, she took him with a desire unmatched by any woman he had ever known. She demanded and took all he would give to her, bringing him intense pleasure. Never had he known love like this before. He could not touch her enough. He could not kiss her enough. With each move and stroke, his body craved more of her. She was around him and within him. She was a part of him and he would never let her go. This was the woman he had waited for, had yearned for and had hoped for, for twenty-five winters.

They would never know parting or sadness again after this day. He was making her his for all time. She arched to meet every thrust he gave and begged for more. He gently coached her in the things she did not know. Soon, their bodies worked in perfect unison. They were entwined in total commitment and consummation of love and desire.

Higher and higher they climbed on the spiral of love and passion. They reached new heights of joy and pleasure. She clung to him taking and giving all the love she had felt for him for a long time. They touched, kissed, caressed and mingled the long months of heartache and suffering with their love and happiness.

When they could no longer suppress or restrain themselves, they exploded into total bliss. They shook with the power and depth of this, their first real union of heart and body.

This was what each had waited and longed for since that day in June when they first looked into each other's eyes as enemies. It had been inevitable for them to be together and complete. Their destinies were matched just like their joining necklace—forever one together and never apart . . .

They lay locked together for a long time afterwards, savoring the sweetness and bliss of this union. Later, there would be time to mend the wounds and hurts. With her acceptance of his love came the acceptance of his ways and people. With it, she gave him her love and forgiveness for all he had done to her in the name of love.

There would be many things to be learned and accepted by both of them. But with a strong love like theirs, they would find a way to work everything out. With all the whites purged from their lands, there would be no more raids and tortures. Perhaps in time with the next coming of the white man, for surely more would come one day, there could be peace and understanding. But Gray Eagle secretly hoped and prayed that day would be very long in coming, for the wasichu would not accept him and his people as his beloved Lese had done. Until then, their love and their lives together would be all they needed or wanted.

He joked that if they lay there much longer, Lese's fair skin would be the color of his people's—but with a lot of pain. They both laughed at this. It felt good to laugh and be happy together for a change. This will be our new way of life, he thought. Life is meant to be shared with the one you love.

She hugged him tightly and kissed him boldly, saying, "You will never know how much I truly love you."

He smiled and replied, "Yes, I will. For I also love you that much." Their eyes met and locked in love and understanding, her heart fluttering at the look written in his. It was the look she had prayed she would see someday, and now she did.

Looking into the beautiful serene face of his wife, he said, "I should not have waited so long to see and feel this love between us. My pride and honor dulls in the face of such love and beauty. Come, Cinstinna. Let us go home . . ."

He stood up and pulled her up to him. They retrieved their clothing and redressed. She smiled as tears of joy threatened to spill, and repeated the words of her future, "Home . . . yes, my love, let's go home."

She helped him gather the skins and blankets from last night and he placed them on the horses. She picked up his bow and quiver of arrows from where he had placed them last night. Turning happily to him, she mischievously said, "Your arrows, Cupid . . ." and smiled secretly to herself.